DEAD MEN'S BONES

Also by Mary Clayton

Pearls Before Swine

DEAD MEN'S BONES

Mary Clayton

HEADLINE

First published in Great Britain in 1996 by
HEADLINE BOOK PUBLISHING

10 9 8 7 6 5 4 3 2 1

British Library Cataloguing in Publication Data

Clayton, Mary
Dead Men's Bones
I. Title
823.914 [F]

ISBN 0-7472-1373-9

Typeset by
CBS, Felixstowe, Suffolk

Printed and bound in Great Britain by
Mackays of Chatham PLC, Chatham, Kent

HEADLINE BOOK PUBLISHING
A division of Hodder Headline PLC
338 Euston Road
London NW1 3BH

For my grandchildren
Mary, David and Gracie Lide
and
David Austell Whitcomb
With much love

ACKNOWLEDGEMENTS

I should like to thank my editor, Cate Paterson, and my agent, Arnold Goodman, for all their advice and suggestions. My thanks too, to Nellie and Deborah, for reading the manuscript and offering such useful criticisms; to Tony for retrieving a chapter from the depths of the computer, and to Ron, among many other things for showing me the 'real' Cornwall.

Chapter 1

It began on Mrs Sparks' washing day. Or rather with what happened to Mrs Sparks that Monday morning while her washing was spinning round and round in the machine recently installed in her house.

Like her, the house was old, an uneasy mix of old and young. With its grey granite walls, now painted a Mediterranean pink, its small windows, enlarged and double-glazed, its sea view, obscured by a hedge of newly planted leylandii, it sat uneasily near the cliffs within the outer limits of St Breddaford parish in Cornwall, not far from the village of the same name.

Mrs Sparks was a relative newcomer to the area, a widow who had arrived unheralded years before, and although she was a familiar sight in the village no one really claimed to know her well. For one thing her new abode was isolated. It was what was called a 'small-holding', cut out of the two acres of rough land that had once been large enough to keep a cow or two and pigs, now let run wild. A strange choice, people whispered afterwards, for a widow so gregarious, but there's no accounting for taste. Mrs Sparks, albeit gregarious, was reserved, at least about her own background. No one, for example, knew where she hailed from, although she was undoubtedly Cornish, her country accent always showing when she forgot to mute it.

However on one point all were agreed: she never tired of boasting about her new home, especially the new 'conveniences' as she called them, paid for, as she was quick to add, by her daughter and rich son-in-law. 'Real good to me,' she used to say, with a glint of triumph that others weren't so fortunate.

She herself was one of those women who keep age at bay with girlish hairstyles and garish clothes. She liked good food and wine, lavished attention on herself, never gave to charity and turned her nose up at village matters – in short was the sort of woman the denizens of St Breddaford detested and envied. 'Needs taking down a peg,' they said.

So on a Monday that couldn't have been finer if it tried, the sky the fragile colour of a robin's egg and the sea a brilliant blue, with the June sun overhead and the garden a blaze of flowers – to say nothing of electric washer and dryer whirring in their plastic-roofed addition – their prediction came to pass.

Mrs Sparks was strolling through her garden, smoking the first fag of the morning. 'Can't do without,' she said. She was just moving away from the leylandii (she'd been fingering them to judge if they were living up to their promise of rapid growth) when the rough grass where she was standing subsided. Subsided, caved in, collapsed – all of an instant, without warning, with a rumble like the distant sound of thunder.

The pit made a circle in the grass, thirty feet round, sliced out as neatly as if with a biscuit cutter, sloping inwards at the bottom, some twenty feet below the surface. An old mine shaft, the rescuers said when later, much later, they found her. The cliffs round here were riddled with disused mine workings. And the mines themselves dated far beyond living memory, perhaps back to the age of the Phoenicians, who came to Cornwall for tin when Rome was still a hamlet.

It was the postman who saw the hole first, who ran to peer down into its depths. And saw, half buried under the subsequent fall of earth, the crumpled figure, its pink-trousered legs covered with debris, its golden wig knocked askew. Not daring to climb down himself, he rushed for help, but the door was locked. It seemed that Mrs Sparks, ever fearful of burglary, never even went into the garden without shutting everything up. Hoping one of her rich relatives was inside (there'd been talk of a posh car parked in the driveway), he shouted and banged. No one answered; no one stirred; all he could hear was the hum of labouring machinery.

There were no near neighbours; time passed before he could reach a telephone; more time elapsed before the ambulance and fire brigade arrived and someone was able to climb down to retrieve the victim.

By now the pit was crumbling at the edges, smelling of raw earth and grass and some strange odour that could have been methane but wasn't. At the bottom, when gingerly a fireman reached it, he found Mrs Sparks, semi-conscious and, except for a few bruises, seemingly unhurt – a miracle, everyone agreed as she was lifted out, a woman her age to survive the shock, let alone the fall.

But when she had been loaded onto a waiting stretcher and rushed to the nearest hospital, when in a sudden fit of thrift (or curiosity) someone else climbed back down to retrieve the wig, it wasn't the miracle of Mrs Sparks' survival that ran round the village. It was what came out of the pit entangled in the hair.

Chapter 2

Early the same morning, even before Mrs Sparks had fallen down the mine shaft, John Reynolds, ex-inspector of the Devon and Cornwall Constabulary, was climbing on the cliffs whose view was partially obscured by the leylandii trees. He was a tall, energetic man, with close-cut greying hair and hazel eyes, looking closer to forty than his real age of fifty-five, and like Mrs Sparks he was a relative newcomer to the district. Actually he lived in St Breddaford itself, in Old Forge Cottage, close to the centre of the village. Unlike Mrs Sparks, he was accepted by his neighbours with good-humoured tolerance, albeit he was a divorced man, a former police officer, and, since his early retirement, a well-known writer of detective stories – three eccentricities that could have been viewed with suspicion.

Reynolds loved these early morning expeditions, especially since, like Mrs Sparks, he was taking time off while something did his work for him. In his case, the work was the latest chapter of his new book, left behind for his secretary to type (he could afford a secretary these days), the book itself part of a series that had brought him more acclaim (and certainly more money) than his previous profession. And to some extent he'd convinced himself he was working as he 'played', since these expeditions often gave him ideas for new plots, and if he was wasting time, as he sometimes guiltily felt, it was mainly on account of that secretary – as he'd left the house Miss Tenery's reproachful look had reminded him of a spaniel abandoned by its master.

His original plan to leave his car at a well-known beach resort and then, by way of climbing down the cliffs, to work round the headland to a small cove on the eastern side, famous for its colonies of guillemots, had changed at the last moment. Tempted by a glimpse of a flock of unknown birds, floating just beyond an outer reef, he had decided instead to clamber out to them.

The tide had gone far out today, farther than usual, and when he reached the base of the reef he saw that it was just on the turn. In front of him lay the open sea and, when he looked round to measure the distance he'd come, suddenly the shore seemed a long way off. Beating down the instinct to make a hasty retreat, he drew out his binoculars.

The birds were still there, on the seaward side of the reef. They bobbed up and down, drifting with the bubbles that marked the line of the current, then, without warning, taking flight, sweeping away before he could properly identify them, leaving him with the daunting prospect of getting back to dry land before the tide caught up with him.

Now, he was on his way back up the cliff again. After an exhausting scramble up a line of shale and rock where he'd had to use hands as well as feet, sometimes swinging himself from ledge to ledge, like a dancer on air, he had stopped to catch his breath beside a gorse bush bursting into triumphant flower.

Beneath him the sea lay tranquil, a sleeping beast, only the edges of the outermost reef tinged white from the usual Atlantic swell. He again drew out his binoculars, for the first time surprised by the clarity of the water. From this height he could look down to the sandy bottom of the sea, where purple patches of weed swayed like underwater forests and only dark outlines suggested the pinnacles and depths that he'd climbed or waded through.

The birds were back, scattered like white confetti on a brilliant blue. As he studied them he was struck again by the brightness of their plumage, as if they were lit from beneath by some fluorescence.

He shrugged. All in all a waste of effort, he thought, a lost opportunity. And yet, he reconsidered, perhaps not. Surely there was material here for a next chapter. His hero could escape down the cliffs, be trapped by the tide and have to swim . . . He grinned. Rather you than me, chum, he thought, as he prepared to climb on, my being a non-swimmer, a real landlubber, doesn't matter, at least on paper.

He was still quite alone. Only once as he turned round did he catch a flash of light inland, the twinkle of sun on glass, a car window, he supposed, or perhaps a window in a house he'd not noticed before. Only once did a rustle in the heather suggest that some small creature had scuttled away at his approach, and when a fulmar petrel floated by on slack wings he suspected he regarded it as much an intruder as it presumably regarded him.

When he reached the top of the cliff he glanced at his watch and was pleased how quickly he'd made the ascent. If he kept up this speed he'd have time to cut across the headland after all and get down to the cove by the inland route he'd intended to use on his way back.

Heaving himself over a high stone stile that led to the original farm lane he strode along, between hedges that blocked the sea and soon twisted inland away from the coast. Gradually even the sound of the waves faded. The hedges were typical old north Cornish – made from slate, set in a herringbone pattern, topped with bushes to form a shelter from the prevailing winds. As for the path itself, reduced now to a single tractor width with no passing places, it seemed to sink lower as the hedges rose higher.

The air was cooler here, and he was glad of the shade. It's like walking through a tunnel, he thought, looking up at the overhead arch of thorns. The verges were thick with ferns, and brambles and grass covered the centre – not used much, he thought, although come harvest time it'll be busy. And, as if to echo his thought, away in the distance now and again he caught the sleepy drone of a tractor in some field on the landward side.

He paused. Here's peace, he reflected. After all the fret of official life and the sharp pain of domestic betrayal I've come through to peace on the other side . . .

It was then that he heard the car. Perhaps at first he didn't hear it consciously, the twists in the lane and the deep hedges cut off all but the loudest sounds. But when it came again some sixth sense brought him sharply round. All he had time to think was, silly fool, he's driving too fast, before he realized it was upon him and he was trapped.

Instinct again, self-preservation, made him leap for the side of the hedge, flattening himself against the wall and thrusting face and body into the sharp stones and thorns. He scarcely noticed them, felt the rush of air and scrape of hot metal, felt the sharp blow upon his left shoulder as something caught.

It hit with sufficient force to knock him to the ground. For a moment he lay stunned. It could only have been a moment or two but it seemed longer before he struggled to sit up, his face streaked with blood, his hands gashed, his clothes torn. It was only when he tried to move his left shoulder that a sharp pain cut through the numbness, so sharp he bit his lip. My God he thought, I could have been killed. And whether from shock or from the sudden contrast – in the midst of life, death – he found his legs were shaking as he hauled himself to his feet.

He gazed down the path but the view ahead was obscured by another bend. There was no sign or sound of the car. It must have cut its engine and stopped. He'd only had a fleeting glimpse of it, not enough to identify it by make or size, but it was powerful, and fast. And he'd only a momentary impression of its driver – a face split by what he thought was a grin. Some silly idiot, he thought, some fool kid, joy-riding. He was about to start forward to give the driver a piece of his mind when something held him back.

Now, as he listened, he heard the car start up again and begin to reverse towards him, slower, as if looking for him.

'Looking for him'. The phrase jumped out at him with the force of a second blow.

Although there was no sense to it – why would a car or its driver be 'looking for him'? – although there was nowhere to escape, no widening place, no gap in the hedge, he forced himself to run back the way he'd come, making his knees bend and his legs work, grasping his left arm against his chest to stop the pain.

The effort made him sick. He heard himself wheeze like an old man. Yet he resisted the temptation to stop and turn when the car came round the corner, forced himself on. He didn't have to turn. He could tell by the car's engine it had come out on the straight. He must be in plain sight – yet it was accelerating towards him.

Afterwards he couldn't be sure – thought that perhaps he exaggerated what might have been a natural impulse on the driver's part to catch up with him to see what damage had been caused. He himself didn't panic easily and if he'd the use of both arms, if he hadn't been so shocked, he might have stood his ground. At the time he didn't, because he wasn't sure. And between not being sure and survival is usually only a hair's breadth; he'd learned that a hard way, in a war.

He did remember thinking that he had just a few more strides left in him before impact, and that this time there would be no error, no miscalculation. Damn it, he remembered thinking, I won't go out like this.

It was anger that gave him new impetus. He swore now as he ran, willing himself on. Another curve, and then several in quick succession, made the car slow down again and gave him a few seconds' grace. He heard the wheels spin on the damp grass and the snarl of the engine as its driver tried to bring it round and hold it on line. That moment's delay gave him the chance he needed, a gap in the bushes overhead, on the inside of the bend. He leapt for the gap as he saw it, swinging himself up the hedge with his good arm. For a moment he swung back and forth, like some damn monkey on a stick he thought, his feet actually brushing the side of the car as it rushed past. Then it was gone. With one last tremendous heave he broke through the bushes to the other side.

He fell heavily, landing on his injured shoulder in what felt and smelled like hay. There were swathes of grass all about him, the air smelled of flowers, and from his high seat, like some toothless god, a bemused farmer looked down as he brought his tractor to a grinding halt. Farther off in the lane, the car's engine faltered for a moment, then continued. And darkness collapsed as if the sun had been shuttered out.

Chapter 3

He was struggling in the sea, unable to breathe. His father was leaning dispassionately over the side of the boat, his other son beside him. He could see his elder brother's grinning face.

'Swim, damn you,' his father said. And he was thrashing with a five-year-old's arms, the green water pouring down his throat, the green weed coiling round his legs, the green depths treacle-thick and the sun glinting in his eyes.

He surfaced from the memory, or the nightmare of it, for a moment disoriented. He blinked against the light, gradually locating its source, a window, set central in a white wall. In fact he was surrounded by white, not green – white ceiling, doors, bed covers – hospital white. He squinted, trying to gauge the time, well past midday by now he guessed, the heat filtered out but still quivering there behind the gauze curtains.

A figure surfaced from this blur, a solid blue, comfortingly familiar. 'Here's a fine to-do,' a well-known voice said. 'What's come over St Breddaford? Two in as many hours.'

Reynolds turned his head, shifted his left shoulder, which was strapped into a sling. It hurt like hell. And why not, he thought, remembering now the reason for this trip to hospital and the subsequent anaesthetic. His head ached and when he ran a hand over his face it felt as if he'd shaved with a saw, the cuts and bruises ragged raw.

'What are you doing here?' he said, squinting again into the light, against which Derrymore, the young village policeman, had apparently just seated himself.

Derrymore was looking harassed, his round, good-natured face set in a frown. On hearing Reynolds, he sighed as if relieved, and settled his considerable wrestler's bulk in the chair. He always sat like that, Reynolds thought, amused – back straight, helmet on his knee like a teacup, feet close together as if on parade, ready to jump to attention.

'Two freak accidents in one day,' Derrymore repeated lugubriously. 'So, to save time, I thought I'd pop in on you first to see how you were doing. And bring you this.'

He tapped a brown suitcase with his foot. Mine, I suppose, Reynolds thought, squinting again. Packed by someone, probably my too-efficient secretary. (And won't there be a rumpus about that when I see her next, he thought, won't she be in a right old dither. 'I'm here to type, Mr Reynolds,' he could hear Miss Tenery's accusing voice, 'not to play at nursemaid.')

'Your clothes were in some mess,' Derrymore added when Reynolds made no comment or gave no explanation. He studied Reynolds with the careful ease of an old friend who knows when not to overstep the bounds of professional comradeship. 'Always thought clambering on the cliffs was risky,' he added, 'but falling over hedges into farmers' fields . . .'

He paused expectantly. About to set the facts straight, Reynolds hesitated. To say a car had deliberately attempted to run him down, not once but twice, when he had no proof,

14

seemed exaggerated. He'd had time to think about it since, drifting in and out of consciousness on the way to hospital and after the fixing of his shoulder, and now common sense told him to keep quiet.

The farmer seemed to have seen nothing, hadn't mentioned hearing a car – but then he probably wouldn't, perched on a tractor whose own engine rattled like a tin can. And in the Emergency Room Reynolds had let Farmer Meneer do the explaining, which he'd done with vigour – how he was minding his own business, when wham, Reynolds had crashed through the hedge almost under his wheels, although why a middle-aged man should want to scramble through a blackthorn hedge— 'Sheer lunacy,' Farmer Meneer grumbled. Elaborating on the accident to the fascinated nurses he had become more expansive. 'Silly bugger' – this the least of his expletives – 'when I got to him I thought he were dead.'

Well, thought Reynolds now, easing himself up in his hospital bed, if Farmer Meneer hadn't been around I might be. Dead that is. The impression he'd had was still very vivid – that getting through the hedge was only a temporary respite; that whoever was 'after him' would have continued the pursuit, on foot if need be. But why? There was no answer to that question yet – although memory of the jeering smile still lingered, presenting him with its challenge.

Not willing to dwell on the incident, he changed the subject and asked, 'Who's the other casualty?' And listened with an impassive face while Derrymore explained in great detail how Mrs Sparks, widowed, had fallen down the shaft of a mine that no one knew existed.

'I'm about to see her now,' Derrymore said. He picked up

his helmet and rammed it firmly on his head. 'Damned if I know what's what,' he said. 'Meneer says you scared him out of his wits, all over blood and your shoulder obviously dislocated. Never known such a to-do, he said, and him in the best hay mow in years. Mind you, he didn't waste time. After getting the missus to telephone on and wipe you down a bit, just shoved you in his own car and drove you here.'

He grinned. 'Careful with their cars, those farmer folk,' he said. 'Got to last for years.'

Reynolds eyed him. He knew the younger man well enough by now, having worked with him on other cases, to guess it wasn't Reynolds' 'accident' alone that made Derrymore worried, although no doubt he did feel genuine concern for his friend. He said quietly, 'What about Mrs Sparks?'

'Tough old bird,' Derrymore admitted. 'Sprightly, know what I mean. A fall like that might have finished off someone half her age, but she'll be right as rain. Just a few bruises and shock they say, but that's natural. In fact once the shock wears off I imagine she'll enjoy the publicity. No, it's what they found under her.'

And at Reynolds' questioning look, he sighed again, took off his helmet once more, and explained.

And when he'd finished explaining, and when Reynolds had deftly sorted out the details, 'So you see the predicament,' Derrymore concluded. 'And what am I to tell her?'

There was perhaps an unconscious added inquiry in his voice which made Reynolds make up his mind. His head still swam, but that was just the effect of the anaesthetic. He swung his legs cautiously over the bed and with his good arm gestured to

Derrymore. 'Throw me that case,' he said. 'Give me time to dress. I'll be with you in two ticks.'

At Derrymore's mutter of alarm, 'Come on, man, don't expect me to lie here like a bump on a log when there's game afoot.'

He grinned, although even turning the corners of his mouth made his face feel as if it were cracking apart. 'Feel like a trot round anyway,' he said. 'Besides, I'm not used to being babied. If you've no objection I'll wander along after you and look in at the celebrity.'

Giving up on remonstrations, Derrymore handed him the case and waited tactfully outside the room while Reynolds struggled one-handedly into his clothes. It was like Derrymore, Reynolds thought, not to offer help when he knew it would be construed as unnecessary interference. And if pride didn't make me so obstinate, Reynolds swore to himself as buttons and sleeves defeated him, I might have been glad of help at that. Giving up on the shirt he draped a jacket over the sling, although even that effort made him dizzy.

Shaking his head vigorously, he felt his way to the door and looked out at Derrymore. 'By God,' he confided, 'I'm trussed up like a turkey. But never fear, I'm too old a warhorse to resist temptation. Still, it's your prerogative, constable, you carry on. And if you've no objection I'll just sit in the back and listen.'

A phrase which by frequent repetition had acquired the ritual of formula. It was what Derrymore had wanted him to do in the first place, and what, under the circumstances, was all he could do, or had the right to do. Although curiosity is common to all men, he thought wryly, and I'm no better than the next. And at least it'll have the advantage of putting my own problem out of mind, for the present anyway.

He followed Derrymore cautiously on legs that at first felt like cotton wool, leaving him for a quick detour to the hospital shop. There he purchased as large a bunch of flowers as he could afford. 'Expensive camouflage,' he told himself ruefully as he looked at the meagre change from twenty pounds, 'but my way of warding off suspicion.' Although what he had to be suspicious of at the moment, he had no idea. Nor why that exact phrase had come into his head.

Mrs Sparks was holding court from her bed, her spare wig once more in place and gleaming from vigorous brushing. A nurse hovered near her and the other occupants of the ward, although presumably busy with their own visitors, were openly straining to hear every word. Mrs Sparks herself was decked out in what could only be termed a 'flimsy garment', from which her skinny arms protruded. There was a great flashing of gold as she waved her hands about – gold bracelets, gold watch, gold rings – but except for a bruise down one side of her face, carefully hidden under powder, and a certain reluctance to shift her position, she showed no outward injury.

She lay propped up on pillows like a dowager duchess. Or some seventeenth-century French princess, Reynolds thought, as he eased the door open. Although that might be the effect of the wig. He eyed it dubiously. It, or one like it, was, after all, a prime piece of evidence.

'And you had no idea, no warning?'

Derrymore, punctiliously correct, was standing stiffly some distance from the bed, his uniform with its array of buttons

18

adding to the impression of an armed retainer.

'Not a thing.' Mrs Sparks had obviously rehearsed this part before, she spoke with relish. Her voice had a strange affected twang to it, which attempted coquetry made tinny. 'Not a thing,' she repeated. 'One moment there I was, walking along, enjoying the sun. Then all went black.'

She crooked her finger confidentially to beckon Derrymore closer. 'I love my house. It's a shock to learn there's a great pit beneath it. Gives me the willies.' She shuddered dramatically, the bones of her shoulders sticking out under the pink satin.

'A man comes in twice a week,' she went on, 'does all the heavy work. You'd think he'd have noticed something wrong. My daughter recommended him. She's very helpful like that. Why, she actually pays his wages. Mind you, he's not much good at digging, I've found that out.'

As she had been talking and Derrymore had studiously been taking notes (he was asking now the name of the gardener – Blewett, Mr Blewett) Reynolds himself had focused on another figure sitting by the bed.

It was a young woman – the aforementioned daughter, he presumed. Her back was to him so he couldn't see her face, but now she turned and said quietly, 'We can sort all that out later, mother. You need to rest. You said yourself Tom Blewett was pretty good.'

The face was one Reynolds was to remember, thin, pale, the eyes large and prominent above high cheekbones, their colour blue-green like the sea. The hair was dark, untidy, sun-streaked; he had the impression of curls, which she tossed aside before turning her back again. Nothing in common with

19

her mother, Reynolds thought, not her mother's daughter. Then presumably like her father. It was an interesting thought.

'There,' said the mother, reverting suddenly to more normal speech. 'Madam doesn't like to hear me talk of getting help, does she. And never takes my side in anything. Blewett isn't the best gardener in the world but he's the best we could find, and if he was worth his salt he surely would have heard if the ground was hollow. Wouldn't it sound hollow, Inspector?' She turned back to Derrymore, her painted lips widening into what must have once been a flirtatious smile. 'Don't you think it would, well, rattle, if he dug into it properly?'

Derrymore was the last person to con with seduction, at least not from a seventy-plus old woman, and certainly never on duty. 'I don't know,' he said, politely, 'but we can make inquiries. Now, Mrs Sparks, you are sure you knew nothing of a mine when you bought the house, several years ago now, I think you said? There were no papers, no deeds showing it, you never had the ground surveyed . . .?'

Mrs Sparks grew impatient. Before he had finished she had twisted her head round and, catching sight of Reynolds, beckoned him forward with a gesture that could only be called imperious. 'Another visitor,' she simpered. 'My, how kind, Mr . . . Mr . . . And roses. Look, everyone, red roses, my favourites.'

She clutched the bouquet to her with the extravagance of an actress taking a curtain call. 'Such scent!' she said, closing her eyes as if in ecstasy. 'Heavenly.' Then, with the same abrupt transition to more normal speech, impatiently to her daughter, 'Oh, if you're going to sit and sulk, make yourself useful. Get a vase from somewhere and fill it. Fresh water, mind.'

There's gratitude, Reynolds thought, surprised at the change of tone. I thought all those lavish presents, those many benefices, came from the daughter and her husband. You'd think Mrs Sparks would show some appreciation, not talk to the daughter as if she were some kind of servant. But then, family ties always defied categorization. Take the use of that word 'mother' for example, surely it's not what daughters call their mothers if they're really close. And there's such a thing as buying affection, although it never works.

He watched the daughter as she rose obediently, took the flowers from her mother with what could only be called an air of resignation and went out of the room. Standing up, she was taller than Reynolds had thought, and older, yet her figure under the loose-fitting jumper was quick and lithe. She passed him without a word, but with a lift of her eyebrows that spoke volumes. Not as resigned as one might have thought, Reynolds surmised, there's a temper somewhere, held in control. He didn't know whether to be relieved or sorry.

Meanwhile Mrs Sparks herself had opened her eyes even wider and patted the vacated chair. 'And you a patient here yourself,' she said to Reynolds with a large and painted smile that could only be called grotesque. She pointed to the sling on his arm. 'Surely that makes us bedfellows of a kind.'

She waited with an actress's timing for the laugh that should have followed her remark, glancing at Reynolds sideways when it didn't, with eyes that once must have been as brilliant as her daughter's. A woman who's been attractive to men, Reynolds thought, who's revelled in men's attention. And who even in old age can't quite give up expecting it. Suddenly he felt sorry for her.

'I'm only masquerading,' he told her. 'Nothing wrong with me. I'm about to leave.'

The nurse, who all this while had continued to hover, made a murmur similar to Derrymore's, shaking her finger at him silently as if to say, 'That would be foolish.'

Reynolds shook his finger back at her. 'Can't waste beds,' he said. 'Not when there's real casualties needing them. I don't deserve a room here while I've my own house to go to.'

'You have a single room?' Mrs Sparks, perhaps not liking the attention drawn away from herself, broke in, sounding envious. 'My son-in-law and daughter will be interested to hear that. They'll never let me spend the night in a common ward.'

Her voice dropped. 'It was the only bed free, you see,' she whispered confidentially, 'or rather it's what they put me in when I was admitted, not knowing who I was of course, and me being in no fit state to argue. But they'll have to move me. Actually' – she drawled the word out as if dredging it up from some half-remembered elocution lesson – 'actually it's so very embarrassing to be here with all these other people. I'm a very private person, I'm used to privacy.'

But you don't mind a captive audience, Reynolds thought, you don't mind playing it for all it's worth. He suppressed a smile. Even in adversity some of us can't resist putting on airs, he thought, even at death's door we keep up pretences.

Derrymore was less indulgent. He'd had enough of play-acting. He closed his notebook with a snap, glanced at Reynolds and the nurse, and came closer to the bed. 'Now, Mrs Sparks,' he said again, 'I don't want you to be upset. Perhaps the nurse here can pull the curtains round the bed because I've something

22

to tell you, something' – he hesitated – 'not nice,' he said.

The nurse, probably previously alerted, was already pulling the curtains efficiently into place. They fell with a soft swishing sound, enveloping the bed and the men beside it. The nurse herself departed with one backward reproachful glance at her patients, including Reynolds in her displeasure, while Derrymore commenced the distasteful task of telling Mrs Sparks what had been found in her garden.

'Buried.' She almost screeched the word. 'You mean a body's buried where I fell in? 'Tain't possible.'

She turned so pale under the powder that even Reynolds was alarmed. He was about to ring for assistance when she controlled herself with a shudder that was real. 'A skeleton?' she said through bluish lips. 'Do you know whose 'tis?'

Before Derrymore could answer the curtain was dragged apart so violently the rings rattled. The daughter stood in the opening, her face as white as her mother's. She clutched the roses in the vase against her, the red in vivid and shocking contrast to her skin and hair. 'What's wrong?' she cried. 'Mother, are you all right?'

Then, seeing her mother in the same position as before, and obviously still breathing, she raised her voice accusingly. 'What are you doing to her?'

'Nothing madam.' Derrymore was soothing. 'I'm just explaining—'

'He's just explaining he found some bones in the mine shaft.' Mrs Sparks was recovering her natural vigour. 'Imagine, I fell on them. They must have been there for ages, perhaps some dead miner.'

Her daughter ignored her. 'What's it got to do with us?'

23

she asked, the anger still apparent. 'My mother's in no state to be questioned. You should be ashamed.'

Derrymore didn't flinch, nor blink as much as an eyelid. 'Yes, madam,' he said blandly, 'but the doctors have said she's well enough for me to see her, and it is a police matter. As for who the body is, well, we don't know that yet except it's male and has been there some time.'

Here he stopped and looked at his notes, then went on as if on another track, addressing Mrs Sparks specifically. 'I think you've been living on the property for nine or ten years?'

'Yes.' Mrs Sparks' reply was reluctant.

'And before that you lived where?'

'Padstow,' she said, 'but . . .'

'And your husband is dead? What was his name?'

For a moment she didn't answer. When she did, her reply was even more reluctant. 'Yes, I'm widowed,' she said, 'and his name was Richard.'

Derrymore ignored her hesitation, kept his questions brisk.

'Richard Sparks? No middle name? His initials then were just RS?'

At her nod, 'And he was accustomed to wearing a wedding ring?'

'Of course.' Here Mrs Sparks took a breath and positively bridled. As if a farmer had been asked if his bull had a ring through its nose, Reynolds thought, amused despite himself. 'He was a Christian man, my husband, very devoted, never smoked or drank, went to church every Sunday, called it a holy day. Why, when there was a saint's festival he wouldn't even work. So don't you go hinting otherwise.'

'And the ring?' Derrymore was patient, drew her back to

the topic under discussion. 'Could you describe it?'

'It was real gold,' she cried, aggrievedly. 'Thick, none of that cheap modern stuff.'

'No one's questioning your taste, Mrs Sparks,' Derrymore said soothingly, 'and certainly not your husband's religious feelings. Did the ring have your husband's initials on it?'

When again she cried, in the same almost triumphant voice, 'Yes, I had it engraved special, RS, like I told you. We was, were married in Lanlivery church, a double-ring ceremony, not usual in our day, and there's the register to prove it,' Derrymore closed his notebook with a decisive snap.

'Then I must inform you,' he said, sternly, 'after the remains were gathered up – naturally, they were disturbed by the cave-in – among the finger bones was a ring.'

He paused. Not for effect as Mrs Sparks would have done, but professionally, so he could gauge the result of his disclosure upon the two women. Well done, Reynolds thought, he's made good use of the situation. He too searched the faces for clues. But both women continued to stare at Derrymore as if bemused.

'A wide gold wedding ring,' the constable was continuing, 'with initials engraved upon it.'

When no one made any comment, 'RS,' he said.

Here Mrs Sparks was seized with a fit of coughing that shook her and the bed. She clasped the blankets to her chin and lay back, looking at them with soulful eyes. Already the mascara or whatever she had used to outline them was beginning to run and she suddenly looked her age.

Her daughter, still clutching the vase of flowers, rushed forward, pushing her way past Reynolds and leaning over the bed. 'There, there,' she said, 'it's all right. No need to be frightened.'

She turned on the two men. 'I told you she wasn't up to it,' she cried. 'This sort of grilling shouldn't be allowed.'

As if she had just then noticed Reynolds she pointed at him. 'And who's he?'

Feeling rather foolish, Reynolds started to explain, but Derrymore broke in. 'This is ex-Inspector John Reynolds,' he said firmly, 'here at my request. And I must ask you too, madam, if you can verify that your father, Richard Sparks, always wore a wedding ring.'

She muttered something he took for affirmation. 'Would it have had his initials on it?'

Again she said yes, and started to add something, but was interrupted by her mother, who by then had once more recovered.

'This is ridiculous,' Mrs Sparks cried, her voice, at first muffled through the bedding, gradually rising, so that, beyond the curtains, certainly the other ladies in the ward must have found their eavesdropping had finally paid off. 'The very idea is absurd. My husband died at sea.'

While her daughter, as if on cue, now echoed her. 'My father was a fisherman. He drowned in a storm, ask anyone. That's why mother left Padstow.'

Here Mrs Sparks turned on her daughter. 'No need to give all them details,' she snapped, as if having a fisherman for a husband or father was something to be ashamed of. Or to keep hidden, Reynolds thought, hidden rather than forgotten.

Derrymore continued to keep his attention fixed on the daughter. 'And would your father be presumed to have been wearing his ring on this last so-called fatal voyage?' he asked.

She ignored the inference. 'I imagine so,' she said slowly, as if trying to remember. 'Yes, he would. Why would he take it off?'

'But he did.' Mrs Sparks again broke in. 'He never wore it to sea. Superstitious like that, he was. Too precious to lose, he said. Not the cost, he meant, he—'

'And do you have it still?' Derrymore broke through the chattering.

'Yes.' Her voice had become tearful. 'It was all I had left to remember him by. I always keep it in a wooden box.'

Wiping her eyes, she turned to her daughter as if for confirmation. 'The inlaid jewelry box with the lock and key I keep in my bedroom.'

But the daughter didn't, or couldn't, answer. For at that moment of her mother's speaking she herself must have straightened up, or made a careless move, although she hadn't given the impression of being clumsy. Her feet caught in her bag, a large straw contraption that stood by the chair, and, as the contents spilled out in an untidy heap, the vase slipped through her fingers and crashed to the floor.

She stood as if frozen, her arms outspread, while the water flowed round her possessions and swept the roses into a steady stream under the bed. Even Derrymore was obliged to step out of its way. A good attention-getter, Reynolds thought, and an even better attention-shifter, away from matters that she doesn't want discussed. He said to her, his own voice suddenly hard, 'And have you seen it there yourself?'

The woman turned. She stared at him again. She opened her mouth to speak, but this time it was her mother who broke

27

in. 'What a mess,' the old woman wailed, 'you stupid girl. And all my lovely flowers ruined. I never even thanked you properly, Mr . . . Mr . . . Why, it's never Mr Reynolds, the writer! Mr Reynolds lives in St Breddaford,' she told her daughter, 'the well-known author. Fancy, a famous man like that coming to see little me.'

Her daughter said slowly, 'Does it matter? Plain Mr Reynolds, or ex-Inspector Reynolds, I still don't see why he's here. And if he's an ex-inspector he's even less right. So you clear off,' she said, the anger full force now, blazing. 'Stop badgering an old lady without cause.'

Reynolds and Derrymore exchanged glances. Then Derrymore said firmly, 'There's no need to get upset. But as I can see you are I'll come back later. This is just a routine call. No cause yet for alarm.'

'Yet.' She pounced on the word. 'What do you mean by yet?'

He didn't answer. Reynolds answered for him. 'In a case like this,' he said, 'there's bound to be more questions. It's normal, if foul play is suspected. So it would help if your father's ring could be found.'

He turned to leave and Derrymore followed him. Mrs Sparks' voice went with them, alternately berating her daughter for stupidity and apologizing for the dropped flowers – 'As if,' Derrymore said outside the ward, wiping his forehead, 'she's more upset by the loss of the damn roses than the prospect of a body turning up that may be her husband's. So what do you make of it, sir? Isn't it a rum go?'

'Rummer things happen.'

Reynolds was more abrupt than he meant. Suddenly he felt

drained. His shoulder was on fire and his whole body felt it had been pushed through a mangle. He wanted nothing more than to go home and lie down.

He tried to keep his voice steady. 'Tough luck, old son,' he said. 'Looks like another round of trouble ahead. Of course you'll know more when Forensic's been busy but I suspect . . .'

He fell silent. Derrymore had to ask, 'What?'

'I suspect,' Reynolds said, 'that both ladies are trying, each in her own way of course, to cover up. But what it is they're covering up, I've no idea . . .'

'Except a murder.' Derrymore sounded morose. 'Who would have ever thought it, looking at the pair of them.'

'Who indeed,' Reynolds said. But murder was at the back of his thoughts too, and it looked especially complicated.

Chapter 4

Leaving the hospital, or rather discharging himself from its tender care, took Reynolds more time than he'd anticipated, especially since he was still feeling so drained. Weakness was new to him. He hated it in anyone, most of all in himself; weakness had to be fought against and ground under. Which was probably why, he thought, as a young man he'd chosen soldiering, rigid self-discipline, that sort of thing.

Smiling half at himself he said to the staff sister, 'I'll be dreadful as a patient, so you'd better give in. Besides, your special arrival in the women's ward is after a spare bed, even if it's only in a recovery room.'

He meant it as a joke and was suitably chastened when she didn't smile back, merely retorted that all beds were at a premium these days and he was old enough to know better. When eventually he joined Derrymore in the younger man's car he was in sufficiently poor humour to complain, uncharacteristically, about its lack of springs.

'Time this wreck was replaced,' he growled, easing his aching body into the passenger seat. 'Or you took better care of it, like Farmer what's-his-face.'

'All HQ can afford at the moment, I'm afraid.' Derrymore

ground the gears in his usual vigorous fashion. 'But it does for the time being.'

He hazarded a glance at Reynolds, narrowly missing the gatepost as they left the hospital grounds. 'Where next?' he asked hopefully.

'Home for some kip.' Reynolds cut short the other's enthusiasm. He closed his eyes and let himself be bounced half way towards St Breddaford before he remembered his own car, left in a park which closed at dusk.

He sat up with a jerk. 'Damn,' he said, 'you'll have to drop me there instead.'

And as Derrymore began to protest, even offering to go later to pick the car up himself, 'Goddamn it, stop fussing. I can drive one-handed. I've done in my bloody shoulder, not my head.'

Crushed, Derrymore fell silent, pretending to occupy himself with reversing in the nearest gateway. Reynolds' conscience pricked. Derrymore had enough to handle without having to put up with a bad-tempered fellow feeling his age, who had caused enough trouble for one day. He forced himself to sit up straighter. 'You don't appreciate modern cars,' he said, only half joking. 'Automatic shift, automatic power steering, automatic everything except self-destruct. Get it in gear it'll drive itself, no problem.'

Derrymore's mouth twitched. He visibly relaxed and drove off in his usual erratic fashion while Reynolds continued in the same conciliatory tone, 'A real conundrum wouldn't you say? Any ideas?'

'Well.' Derrymore, offered an olive branch, seized it eagerly. 'Could all be coincidence,' he said. 'I mean, Mrs Sparks fell on top of the bones by accident; they've been there a long time, are the remains of some dead miner like she suggested.'

'She was quick on to that,' Reynolds admitted. 'But a dead man with initials the same as Richard Sparks – if the ring is taken as evidence, that is? Too much of a coincidence for me.'

He brooded for a moment, forcing himself to concentrate. 'Tell me about the cave-in?' he said. 'You must have seen the hole in its pristine state.'

'Not exactly,' Derrymore confessed. 'They'd got her out before I arrived; the ambulance was just starting off with her on board. As a matter of fact' – here he sounded somewhat aggrieved – 'they said it was slow, but I've never known it or the fire engine move so fast. In the meanwhile, plenty of people had already gathered round the site – would-be helpers, spectators, you name it, they'd trampled the edges down without a thought of danger. As for the pit itself, well, it wasn't so much deep as wide.'

He thought for a moment. 'Tell you what,' he said, 'its shape reminded me of a flying saucer.'

'And the skeleton?'

'I went down myself briefly but you could see better from the top. As I've said, earth was scattered everywhere, but it looked like the start of an archaeological dig. I wasn't able to find out if it was uncovered by the original fall, or if the firemen found it as they dug out Mrs Sparks. No one seems to remember.'

'What about the fellow who made the discovery?'

'His mates said all he could talk about was putting his hand on what he thought was hair and coming up with bone,'

33

Derrymore said, with a grin. 'But as far as I can tell he didn't actually move the bones, just discovered where they were at, if you get my meaning.'

'At least he had enough sense to hang on to the wig!' Reynolds' voice was dry. 'So after Mrs S. was removed, and the bones were found, what then?'

Again Derrymore thought for a moment. 'Everyone was milling about and talking, you know how it is,' he said. 'So I told them to keep back and wait until the Forensic people arrived. But no one touched anything after I got there, I'll swear to that.'

'Then the ring wasn't added afterwards,' Reynolds considered. 'What about before?'

Noting Derrymore's puzzled expression, he explained, 'I mean while she was still unconscious, before help arrived.'

Derrymore's expression brightened as he began to follow Reynolds' reasoning. 'Well, I gather she herself was certainly unconscious most of the time she was in the hole,' he said, 'although she'd come to before the ambulance left. Not alert enough to be moving round or meddling with bones or such, but certainly well aware of where she was and what she was saying. Apart from that there were only two periods – before the postman arrived and when he went off to get help – when she was left alone with no one else around.'

'No one else around?' Reynolds pounced on the words. 'How do we know that?' he asked.

'Well, I don't know, well . . .' Derrymore floundered until Reynolds came to the rescue.

'We can only presume,' Reynolds said, 'that during those two periods no one else went near the hole. No one else went down and saw the unconscious Mrs Sparks. No one else touched the bones.'

He smiled to take away the sting. 'It's an assumption that makes sense of course,' he said. 'We can't imagine someone finding her and not trying to help. But suppose someone did.'

'If so, we'd have to assume there was a motive.'

Derrymore sounded plaintive, as once more Reynolds' line of argument escaped him.

Reynolds nodded slowly. He too was trying to work out various patterns, none of which made sense. 'Pull up a tick,' he said. Then, as Derrymore nudged his way into a passing place, 'Let's start at the start, as one of my early mentors used to say.'

Thankful to rest his shoulder, he fought against another spasm. 'As I see it, at the moment we've three possible scenarios, each more improbable than the last. One, the skeleton was there by chance, possibly a long-dead miner, as Mrs S. suggested, killed in some mine accident, although the skeleton was fairly close to the surface not to have been found before. Or possibly it's some other murder victim, which is a new story altogether. Both ways, the find has nothing to do with the Sparks family – although, unfortunately for them, there's a ring with the same initials as Richard Sparks'. But, as I've already said, I think such a coincidence is improbable. Although I hope I'm wrong.'

He frowned, working out his next line of thought. 'The second scenario isn't pleasant. The body's still unknown, but someone's dropped a ring among the bones to make us think it's Mr Sparks.'

He paused again. 'The complications are enormous,' he said. 'Some unknown person would have had to see the ground collapse, would have had to see Mrs Sparks lying at the bottom – and would have had to see the skeleton. Immediately, without a moment to lose, he must now enter the house, find Mr Sparks' ring, then climb down into the pit and carefully place said ring among the finger bones. All without being seen himself. After which he makes good his escape before anyone else shows up. As you say, a lot of work for no apparent cause.'

The idea was so ludicrous he laughed and immediately wished he hadn't – the physical effort of laughter made his whole body throb. 'And pretty near damn impossible,' he added. 'To begin with, we don't even know if there is a ring or if it's kept where Mrs Sparks said it was. And how does he get into the house? Didn't the postman say Mrs Sparks always locked the door even when she went into the garden? I presume the house was still locked up when you arrived, no sign of a break-in?'

'Yes, to both questions.' Derrymore was positive. 'I went round the place myself with a fine-tooth comb. And the postman certainly couldn't get in to use the phone. In any case, the daughter seemed certain her father's wedding ring was with her father at the bottom of the ocean – which does make sense, even if Mrs S. insists he never wore it at sea. And to my mind you'd have to be stupid to invent a tale that someone's drowned in a storm in a fishing boat unless it really happened. For starters, it's too easy to prove or disprove; there'll be records and public inquests, inquiries and so on.'

He too laughed, then grew serious. 'The thing is, both were

36

pretty positive they were right, even if they contradicted each other.'

Once more they sat in silence, mulling over the contradictions. 'Mind you, we said we thought they were covering for each other,' after a while Derrymore continued. 'And Mrs S. didn't like the daughter talking about the father.'

'Right.' Reynolds was warming to his task now and beginning to enjoy the intricacies of detection – as much as one can enjoy oneself, he reminded himself sombrely, when dealing with murder. There must be other professions where working out the deviations of human nature doesn't always have such tragic connotations – perhaps that's why I've become a writer.

These thoughts passed through his mind even as he said, 'I assumed at first Mrs S. didn't want us to know her husband had only been a fisherman – she has her little pretensions, don't you agree? But suppose for a moment someone did plant Richard Sparks' ring (although for the life of me I can't think why) and she knows who it is? She wants to be sure no one else suspects and—'

'But what on earth would be her motive?' Derrymore, ever practical, harked back to his first observation. 'All I can say is that whoever the person was he'd have to be very familiar with the Sparks house. Familiar enough presumably to have a key. And to know where Mrs Sparks kept her husband's ring. Surely that means a member of the family.'

Reynolds tapped on the dashboard with his sound hand. 'Right again,' he said. 'Meanwhile the matriarch lies there, and no one knows if she's dead or dying. As I said, not a pretty picture.'

He looked at Derrymore. 'So that leaves only the third assumption,' he continued, 'equally unsatisfactory – that Mr Sparks, presumed drowned at sea, has somehow ended up in the garden of his widow's new house, with his wedding ring where it should be, on his finger. Which means his widow's tale of the jewelry box is a pack of lies, and Mr Sparks' body has found its way, probably by foul means, into a mine shaft that no one seems to have known about!'

He had all of Derrymore's attention now. 'But again, as you rightly say, you don't claim a man is drowned when he isn't. However, you could pretend.'

'You mean organize a disaster at sea to hide a murder?' Derrymore looked thoughtful. 'That'd take some doing, too,' he said. 'There'd not only be the actual killing itself but the transfer somehow of the body to a distant grave site, plus finding such a site. As well as the even more complicated arrangement of taking a boat out and sinking it in a storm, etc., a massive cover-up. Although I grant you it came as a surprise to hear anything about Mr Sparks at all. As far as I know Mrs S.'s never talked of her husband or her previous life. There's been all sorts of ructions in the village because she didn't.'

He glanced at Reynolds. 'I mean, people don't like being kept in the dark,' he explained somewhat defensively. Reynolds grinned. He knew what Derrymore meant. A close-knit community likes to know who a stranger is and where he comes from.

'Well,' he said again, 'I said it was impossible. Too many difficulties. And what about Mrs Sparks' age.'

He glanced at Derrymore. 'How long did she say she'd

been living near St Breddaford, ten years or so? Even ten years ago Mrs Sparks wouldn't have been young. She couldn't have managed on her own, without some accomplice. It'd take physical strength, if nothing else, to mastermind the type of murder we're contemplating.'

At his nod, Derrymore started up the car again. 'Of course there's that "rich relative" we've heard so much about,' he added, almost idly, as they now drove along. 'The daughter we've met would fit the description nicely. And although we've been mainly speaking of a "he" it could be a "she" just as easily.'

At this suggestion Derrymore braked hard. 'I don't know,' he said dubiously. He shook his head. 'I guess she's coming up to thirty or so now. Ten years ago she'd be, what, in her late teens. Doesn't seem right to me, a young girl like that being a killer. After all, we're talking about murder of a father.'

'So we're left with no leads at all.'

Deftly Reynolds demolished his own theories. 'Except of course there're traditional ways of identifying bodies. To say nothing of newer methods . . .'

'Right,' Derrymore interrupted. 'I've heard of tests, what do they call 'em?'

'DNA tests,' Reynolds said. 'Genetic codes. In time they'll revolutionize detection, especially once a DNA bank is established. If the Russian royals, or what was left of them, could be identified in that way you can bet your life "our" bones can be too, or at least we can determine if they're Richard Sparks' or not. All that's needed is samples from a relative to make a match. But until some identification is made, the future looks unpleasant for Mrs Sparks and her daughter.'

And how and why the body's there, he thought, we'll have to come to in time. I joke about being an old bloodhound but sometimes I wish my instincts were wrong. There's got to be something abnormal about a fellow who's attracted to murder like by a magnet.

'Head Office may not want to use these latest tests,' he went on, speaking now almost to himself. 'My guess, they'll stick to the slow, more traditional methods unless there's some pressing reason for hurry.'

Here another thought struck him. 'Head Office will have to be informed I suppose,' he said. 'There'll be no way out of it.' And he felt more depressed than ever.

'I know,' Derrymore said sympathetically. Both men were again silent. After all, Reynolds thought, we've tried to work with Head Office before and found them the devil of a headache. But perhaps it'll be easier this time.

'There's always hope,' he said. 'Cheer up old son, it can't be all bad.'

'Can't it?' Thought of Head Office had also spread a pall over Derrymore. 'Just you wait.'

He turned into the parking lot and drew up by Reynolds' car to let the other out. 'Now you be careful,' he said, his tone a comic mixture of the professional and the paternal. 'We don't want to be picking up more bones. That knock of yours was bad enough. And, come to that, your doctor pointed out you probably didn't get your busted shoulder just from crawling through a hedge.'

Another man would have made more of that, Reynolds

thought, would have grilled me while he had the chance. Suddenly he liked Derrymore for being so circumspect.

He didn't reply, just grinned, a grin which faded when Derrymore, having issued his warning, called over his shoulder, 'Just our luck. The first pretty girl to happen along in ages and she's married, has a witch of a mum and is a suspect in a murder case.'

Somehow this summing up of the daughter wasn't appealing. Derrymore's got a knack of stripping things down to the bare essentials, Reynolds thought, although you'd never even imagine he'd noticed the daughter's looks, the old son-of-a-gun.

He waited until Derrymore's car had rattled out of earshot. If he were going to drive himself he'd do it under his own steam, no hangers-on, thank you, no hovering do-gooders, however well-meaning. I'm an ungrateful sod too, he thought, as, trying to avoid jarring his shoulder, he started the car and then struggled to push the gear into drive with his right hand instead of the usual left. Funny thing, gratitude. Some people seem to find it impossible to say thank you gracefully, as if even the very act of thanks is humiliating. That gives me and Mrs Sparks something in common – a sobering thought.

Focusing on moral dilemmas got him out of the car park onto the road, where the driving was easier. He actually found pressing his shoulder back against the well-padded seat eased the pain. And it was true with these push-button cars one just had to steer and let the engine do all the work. Not that he'd really wanted an automatic car, manual control was much more his style, more macho. He made a grimace. So much for macho now, he thought.

It was when he came to the turn leading to Mrs Sparks' house that he let himself be tempted. He knew somewhere ahead was the lane to Meneer Farm and he was curious to have another look at it. But that would have to wait; now there were more pressing problems to be resolved.

Afterwards he tried to defend his actions, at least to himself, by saying that when murder was suspected even a private citizen, such as he now was, had the right to be involved. At the time he told himself that being an ex-inspector didn't make him privileged. I don't really hold with citizens' patrols and such, he thought, although they're all the rage these days. Most private citizens aren't compelled to intervene, aren't spurred on to take risks or break the law, or take the law into their own hands. Yet admitting all this didn't stop him from pulling into the nearest lay-by and setting out to have a look at Mrs Sparks' mine shaft for himself.

Chapter 5

Mrs Sparks' garden surprised him first by its size; it was part, he guessed, of a former field, or even of several small fields, now combined. Then too he had not expected so much to be left in its wild state; given what he'd heard of Mrs Sparks he'd thought she would have everything tamed into submission. In fact only a fraction round the house had been altered into an approximation of the requirements of a modern dwelling: a brick patio, a built-in barbecue, and a series of so-called flower beds, some sadly needing attention. Mr Blewett's been neglecting his duties, he thought.

The roadside boundary was marked by lines of spindly trees; he recognized the leylandii, which, as a gardener himself, he disliked and whose only virtue was their habit of vigorous growth – if the wind didn't stunt them first. He'd already noted with practised eye how they were starting to lean over, out of line.

The gate was open and the driveway, new, ugly, wound past a lawn which conversely was carefully clipped along the edges – to give a good first impression, he thought. That fitted with what he'd seen of Mrs Sparks.

The house itself seemed unoccupied, as he had expected.

There were no open windows on a day still as hot as you could want, and no parked car, or at least not one visible. He noticed at once the unhappy architectural blend of old and new – like a botched facelift, he thought – and again the image of Mrs Sparks herself immediately came to mind.

Unsure what excuses he could give if someone saw him, and resolved at all costs to avoid that possibility, he kept off the drive, using the older bushes that lined it as cover and walking on the grass to deaden his footsteps. It was as well he did. Where, on the far side, close to the leylandii hedge, a ragged circle of trampled earth resembled the flying saucer of Derrymore's apt description, a young man's head and shoulders were emerging from a hole marked by fluttering tapes.

The body that heaved itself out after was burly, dressed in the ubiquitous gear that everyone wore these days: thick navy jersey, washed-out jeans, canvas shoes. Fisherman's gear, Reynolds thought, fading into the shadows, or yachtsman's play clothes, suitable attire for a rich man who can afford to amuse himself with boats. So this must be the daughter's husband who is so generous to his mother-in-law. He immediately felt prejudiced.

The man made his way rapidly across the lawn, pushed at the front door and went inside, leaving it ajar. The son-in-law isn't as paranoid as Mrs Sparks, then, Reynolds thought, and presumably he has a key. Registering that fact and resigned to the lost chance of doing a bit of private sleuthing he was about to retrace his steps when he heard a cry.

The voice was a woman's, raised in anger or surprise. At first he couldn't tell which, but the shouts that followed were certainly masculine. As he watched he heard an inner door slam and a woman, the daughter – he recognized her by her clothes as well as her way of walking – came out onto the patio. She was carrying something under her arm, and was speaking over her shoulder, to her husband presumably, for he now followed.

He was angry. His dark face was flushed, making an unpleasant contrast to his black curly hair, and his voice carried. 'Damned if I will,' he cried. 'I'm out of it.' 'Out of what' Reynolds was thinking, but before he could come to any conclusion the husband seized the woman's arm. There was a clatter, a rattling sound, as a second time that afternoon Mrs Sparks' daughter dropped what she was carrying.

With a cry clearly of distress she bent to pick the fallen object up, but the man wrenched her back. 'Shut up and listen to me for once,' he shouted, 'stubborn bitch.' And hit her with his free hand.

The sight was more than Reynolds could stomach. His own brutal childhood evolved before his eyes. Without meaning to he broke from his hiding place and began to run, although he scarcely managed more than a few yards before he had to stop. Clutching his injured arm to his chest he shouted, 'Hey there,' in his loudest voice, well trained on the parade ground, and made his way more slowly towards the patio.

The pair had apparently been so engrossed in their own quarrel that they hadn't noticed him until he shouted. Now they both swivelled round, the man still grasping the woman, the woman holding her cheek, the spilled contents of the box glittering on the ground.

The man recovered first. 'Who the hell's that?' he snarled in his broad accent. Then, as Reynolds came up, 'Who the bloody hell are you? And what in bloody hell are you doing, crawling about in the bushes?'

He took a belligerent stride forward. In a voice still dulled by the force of the slap, the woman said, 'It's Inspector Reynolds, so watch yourself.'

She turned towards Reynolds. Her own face was pale except where her husband's fist had left a red streak and her eyes were watering – only from the unexpectedness of the blow, Reynolds thought. She wasn't a woman to cry easily, she had too much spunk.

He said in his most detached manner, calculated to restore the peace, 'Merely passing by. Thought I'd have a peek at the cause of all the trouble.'

The man was still staring at him, not so much in bemusement as dismay. But he had not lost his belligerence. Reynolds eyed him warily. He himself was as tall but the man was twice as wide, younger, and fit. And he looked angry enough to take a swing at anyone. But, to Reynolds' surprise, it was the woman who made the first attack. Stupid of me, he thought, should have remembered the old adage that whoever interferes in domestic quarrels gets the worst of both sides.

The woman's hair had come undone in the struggle; her face, which before had been so pale, now flamed red. 'Ex-Inspector Reynolds.' She emphasized the 'ex'. 'A so-called copper who's been badgering my mother at the hospital. I told him to clear off then, and if that's all the excuse he can drag up now he can clear off again. Peeping Toms, trespassers, sightseers, they make me sick.'

She flung off the insults easily – too easily, Reynolds thought, as if she expected to be insulted back.

'What's he done to his arm?' Her husband had concentrated his gaze on Reynolds' sling. She shrugged. 'God knows,' she said. 'Broken it, I believe. Should have been his nose the way he pokes it in.'

There was something about her voice that made Reynolds laugh despite the situation. '*Touché*,' he said. 'But before I go let me help you pick these up.'

During this brief exchange he had been working his way round carefully to get a look at what she'd dropped. The box itself had fallen on its side and opened; the contents, jewels he supposed they should be called, were scattered among the bricks. He tried to memorize them, remembering all the gold that had hung about Mrs Sparks' arms and hands.

'Well, you get on with it then. I'm off.' The man, either exasperated beyond control, or, Reynolds thought, equally possibly growing cautious, spun on his heel and tramped away. Curious, he watched the fellow crunch round the house, presumably to get his car. Not the sort of man he had expected, not the sort of husband the woman deserved.

The words sprang into his mind unexpectedly. He turned back to her but she was already on her knees scooping up the pieces as fast as she could. One or two eluded her and he squatted on his heels to point them out, although the effort to bend made him flinch. The box lay between them, its carved lid clearly visible.

She stood up, stuffing the jewelry back, ropes of pearls, bracelets, brooches, several rings, all twisted together, and snapped the lid shut. She stared down at Reynolds still squatting on his heels. 'You look as if you're stuck,' she said. Then, not unkindly, 'Well, I suppose one good turn deserves another.'

And she stretched out her hand to pull him up.

He rose unsteadily. If truth be told, he admitted to himself afterwards, he had overdone things. Just as he had overdone the gallantry bit. But it hadn't all been contrived: the contents of the box hadn't been his only preoccupation; he'd felt a genuine wish to talk to the woman on her own, get to know her a little, get beneath the guard. Although, annoyed with himself, again he admitted that catching her in the middle of a quarrel with her husband wasn't the ideal time and place.

He did not see but heard the car spin out onto the road. And she must have too, for she visibly relaxed. She must also have noticed what Reynolds' effort had cost him for she said, albeit somewhat reluctantly, 'You'd better come inside and sit down a moment. I'll make a cup of tea.'

Without waiting for an answer she led the way, telling him to go on into the living room while she continued towards the kitchen. She took the box with her. Biting down what he was about to say, under the circumstances unwarranted, something fatuous about tampering with evidence (which she probably was but which he had no right to mention), he allowed himself to accept her offer, glad for a moment's respite – but not so glad that he didn't make the most of the chance to look at his surroundings with a professional eye.

All was scrupulously neat and tidy as he might have guessed, not a speck of dust, the bunch of plastic lilies in a hideous stained-glass bowl set exactly central on the glass coffee table, the furniture carefully protected by embroidered linen arm and back coverings, the curtains, net, frilled, drawn close to keep out the sun, the old stone fireplace distorted by a gas fire, disproportionately large and, like the rest of the furnishings, glaringly out of place.

She came back into the room carrying a tray with two mugs on it. When she had given him one she sank back with a sigh of relief. 'What a day,' she said. Then, leaning forward, 'Don't take any notice of Mike. He's an idiot sometimes.'

That's a charitable way to dismiss what happened, Reynolds thought. He clasped the mug, feeling the heat of the liquid take effect. 'Quick-tempered,' she was saying, 'blows up like a storm. When it's all over, he forgets what he's said and done.'

She's covering well, Reynolds thought, there's loyalty. He couldn't resist a pang. It had been so long since he'd known any woman show loyalty, or even give it lip service, he'd come to doubt its very existence.

'But then,' she was continuing, 'I think you're not married. If you were you'd know how things are sometimes.'

Her eyes were large, almost colourless in the filtered light of the room. He couldn't see her face clearly, but the red mark was still visible. It would leave a bruise. He resisted the temptation to say, 'You're wrong. I know very well what an unhappy marriage is like, better than most.' That could wait. 'Tell me about yourself,' he said.

'I'd just come back to check everything was all right,' she said. For a while she sat silently, her eyes thoughtful, then stirred herself to add, as if in self-defence, 'Mother's particular. She frets if things aren't exactly so.'

'You have a key?'

'Why do you ask?'

Her sudden directness startled him. He hesitated. 'I'd heard the doors were locked so no one could get in.' The excuse sounded lame even to his own ears.

'Well, mother trusts me with a key at least,' she said, 'and if there's something to be done, she doesn't mind if I do it.'

He detected a touch of bitterness, quickly hidden. 'Mother says you write,' she went on, changing the subject with a deftness that he had to admire. 'A celebrity, she called you. Are you that, Mr Reynolds, a celebrity? And do you enjoy being one?'

Her questions came with a smile, but they made him uncomfortable. Underneath the pleasantry he detected a sardonic note. *Touché* again, he thought. A prickly lady this, no shrinking violet. Yet fragile where her mother is concerned, ill at ease. Again he felt a rush of sympathy. For the third time that day the memory of his father and their disastrous relationship came unexpectedly to mind – and his own equally inept way of handling it. Well, by hard experience he had learned at last to let go, but she was still young enough to hope for improvement, to look for a miracle in an older woman who would never learn to change. Suddenly the twenty-five years or so that separated them made him feel very old and the woman facing him seem absurdly young.

He put aside the temptation to tell her what he was thinking. He didn't want to stress the difference in their ages – suddenly it became distasteful, made him seem a cradle-snatcher. Although what he was snatching at, or what he was doing even thinking along these lines, for the life of him he couldn't explain.

Instead he reverted to safer topics, said gently, 'Writers are like other people. They prefer to do what they do best. Which is writing, I suppose. In my experience most of them act in a sensible fashion and leave the loud hurrahs to the general public while they get on with the work in hand.'

Perhaps in turn his reply caught her off balance. She smiled. The smile transformed her. As did her subsequent remarks. For, as if she had suddenly decided to let down her guard, she began to talk, easily and with growing confidence, as if, he thought, she's not been used to having anyone to talk to, or listen to, for a long time. Again this unexpected similarity between them struck him as she began to tell him about her teaching; she was a Modern Language instructor, she said, teaching French at a local college in St Austell. Her students, who came from nearby small towns and villages, were interesting, far better motivated than ones she'd previously encountered in bigger institutions. Not a well-paid job, he thought idly, not the sort to support extra luxuries. Then it must be the brutish husband who foots the bills.

The thought crossed his mind, slid away. The pain in his shoulder dimmed to a dull throb. It was a long while since he'd sat and listened to a woman and even in this room of jarring taste he felt the pleasure keenly. It was only when she looked at her watch and jumped up that he reminded himself the pleasure was forbidden, out of reach.

'I didn't know it was so late,' she said almost guiltily. 'I must fly. I promised mother I'd be back.'

She shot him a quick look. 'She'll be glad of company,' she said, with a wry smile that seemed to mock herself. 'As a private patient now she can be visited almost all the time.'

'Private patient?' Reynolds found himself repeating the expression stupidly.

She laughed. 'Oh, mother'll get her private room,' she

said, half mockingly, 'mother usually gets what she wants.'

Reluctantly Reynolds rose and followed her into the hall, senses coming back to full alert. He'd let himself be lulled too long – or had she deliberately done the lulling? He hadn't even managed to bring the conversation round to the jewelry box as he had intended.

'What about a lift?' he asked, snatching at a last chance. 'Or is your husband returning for you?'

She looked at him as if surprised, then laughed. He had the impression she hadn't laughed so freely in a long while. 'Mike? No, he won't be back,' she said. She looked hard at Reynolds as he hesitated on the threshold, the light catching on her cheek, revealing the bruise now and unexpectedly reminding him again of her mother.

'He won't be back,' she repeated, the derisory tone very clear. 'That's what we quarrelled about. As for being my husband – why ex-Inspector, what's gone wrong with our sleuthing today? I'm not married and don't want to be. That's the other thing Mike and I were quarrelling about.'

And with that double salvo she closed the door firmly in his face.

Caught out good and proper. Reynolds didn't know whether to be angry or amused. She's sharp, he thought as he went down the driveway, alert. She'd make a good police officer. But here's another twist I'd not thought of. We all assumed she was the married daughter, the one who shelled out cash when mummy needed something. So where the hell's that other daughter? And why, when mummy obviously needs her, isn't she here at mummy's side? And who's the rich husband?

By the time he had clambered back into the driver's seat

and gone through the hassle of starting off he was in a fine temper. Assumptions, assumptions, he told himself furiously. Mrs Sparks may have a whole slew of daughters for all I know; I just assumed there was one. And I still haven't persuaded this one to talk about that damned trinket box, let alone get a look at it! Just sat there like an idiot while she ran circles around me. Sloppy management, that's what it is, sloppy thinking, effect of old age, decrepitude . . . he saw a bleak future unfold. And then, more rationally, Derrymore ought to be on to this as soon as possible.

But when he returned home, he found another distraction that needed deflecting – his secretary, Miss Tenery, at her most fulsome. She'd been expecting him hours ago, she bleated, the chapter was finished but she hadn't liked to go home without having news of him. Her friend, Miss Seward, was waiting for her, they were supposed to go to the pictures tonight, one of the few times they were free to go out, but she wouldn't dream of leaving without making sure he was all right. And did he mind her rummaging through his clothes? She'd never packed a man's suitcase before (here she gave a nervous titter), she hoped he didn't resent her taking the liberty. And while waiting for him she'd made use of the opportunity to cook up something hot to eat, soup, she'd thought he could surely manage soup – her sad eyes suggested he was lucky to have that much, she and Miss Seward could starve for all he cared.

'Run along, Miss Tenery,' he said firmly, closing the door on her mixture of reproof and concern. He leaned against the wall wearily, then, making his way into his own living room, sagged down on the sofa, plunking his boots defiantly on the cushions, glad for once there was no one to nag. Under the sofa (hidden, he hoped, from Miss Tenery's prying eyes) was the whisky bottle he kept for emergencies like this. True, in the past there had been times when he'd kept it hidden for other reasons, but let's be thankful for small mercies, he thought – at least now I can have a drink without whisky getting the better of me. Although if ever a man deserved to get drunk, today might be the day. Run down by a hooligan; challenged by an old woman shrewder than is good for her; bested at my own game by a young one half my age, who seemed to take delight in mocking me, and who no doubt by now is gloating over her victory with her harpy of a mother! He took a hearty swig. And the best-looking young woman he'd seen in ages – Derrymore was right about that. But whether a father-murderer, or merely a suspect in a case which seemed destined to become more and more complicated, so far he hadn't made up his mind. As for his own misadventures, best not think of them, although they too remained a puzzle. He drank again – until the woman's mocking smile blended with that of the driver of the car, merged and faded . . .

In Mrs Sparks' house, her younger daughter went about the intricacies of locking up, carefully closing each internal door and making sure the windows were barred. Contrary to Reynolds' expectations, she wasn't thinking of him with mockery at all. Mostly she had put him to one side to deal with later. As indeed she had put aside another, even more important, personal matter – her quarrel with her would-be suitor Mike. That, too, must wait. What concerned her at the moment was carrying out her mother's orders, a rambling list of things to be done, or not done – and her own self-induced anxiety that she perform her duties exactly.

If her face wore a derisory look the derision was directed at herself, at her own lack of will. For if she knew that the quarrel with Mike was easily dismissed, on her side at least, other private problems couldn't be got rid of so easily. Chief among these was ex-Inspector Reynolds.

Her mother's warnings, and even Mike's more recent suggestions (sure though she was that they were melodramatic inventions, contrived to gain her attention), should have told her Reynolds was dangerous, should have given her every cause to steer clear of him. But she was honest enough to admit she was interested. Call it the attraction of an older man, the awareness of his strong personality, she thought, with a wry smile at her ambivalent feeling – surely I'm playing with fire in more senses than one. And how to reconcile that ambivalence? She shrugged. Wait and see, she advised herself. Perhaps the ex-inspector will himself 'clarify the situation'. And she laughed aloud at the euphemism.

It felt good to laugh. Otherwise there wasn't much cause for humour. Hadn't been for a long while, almost as long as she could remember. That too was something to put aside, to deal with at a later time, meaning never. Ten years, she thought, all mirth gone now, ten years since father died and everything changed at once, and has never been put right since. But that too didn't bear thinking on.

When she was certain that she had secured the house she went back into the sitting room and sat down on the chair in front of the glass table where the empty mugs had been left. She'd clear them away in a moment – mother would have a fit if she knew her daughter had invited a stranger indoors, especially someone as dangerous as ex-Inspector Reynolds. But sometimes it was only in these insignificant ways, small and unplanned, that she was ever able to defy her mother or exert what she had come to think of as her true personality.

Even Mike would never have dared come here as a mere admirer if mother had been at home; he'd always made up other excuses before, covering his intentions under the cloak of other, pressing business. Once more she blanked her thoughts down. It was only in her own little house that she felt free to be with anyone. And even there she lived under sufferance.

She blamed Mike for her present dilemma. She hadn't expected him and had been in such a dither that not only had she left the front door open but she'd actually let him see what she'd been doing. She pushed the mugs to one side and placed her mother's box in front of her, then, turning it over, let the contents trickle out. What a fool she'd been ever to look for it, let alone remove it from its hiding place and carry it about – none of which, she might add, were among mother's instructions!

But the most inept thing she'd done was to drop the whole contraption in front of the one man who could be counted on to notice everything it contained. Why else had the ex-inspector tried to help her except to get a closer look? She hoped in the confusion she hadn't left anything behind. She must go outside in a moment to double check; she didn't trust Reynolds not to come back later to search for himself.

Now her long, narrow hands moved quickly among the tangled jumble, sorting and counting. It behoved her to make sure all was arranged in order – although it defied imagination how she was to replace objects in a box she had never actually seen before and then had dropped before she'd had a chance to look inside! And mother had an elephantine memory at the best of times. When it came to her own possessions she'd know at once if they had been moved or 'meddled' with. She shrugged. That was a hurdle she'd have to cross when she came to it.

The gold gleamed dimly as she stirred the heaps. Her mother certainly had an obsession for glitter! Mrs Sparks' daughter smiled her derisory smile. Where on earth did mother acquire all this stuff? And why, when she's so nervous about intruders, does she keep it in a wooden box with a flimsy lock, the key still in it, in so obvious a place as under her bed? Might as well leave a note for a burglar telling him where to look.

Except perhaps here's a weakness, a chink in the facade. The thought leapt into her head unbidden. Perhaps, in this house of modern machinery and bolts and locks mother reverts to the old ways out of sentiment, in memory of what she once was, a simple fisherman's wife – in memory of what we all once were when we were a united family group.

That too was a thought to put aside. Although it was tempting, she didn't believe in it for a moment. Mother was never sentimental, didn't believe in sentiment any more than she did.

The piles were complete: bracelets, necklaces, brooches, rings. She replaced the first three groups in the box, laying them carefully on top of each other. Their beauty – and some were beautiful – made no impression on her, or no impression except the usual one (for the moment quickly dismissed along with all her other personal considerations) that here was a rich daughter's way of buying affection which she herself could never hope to match.

She was left with a pile of rings of assorted sizes and shapes. None seemed to have been kept in an individual container, probably all could be slotted among the other stuff at random; even mother couldn't remember the precise location of every individual ring.

She took up each one in turn, scrutinized it, turning it round and round to examine it. Some she dropped immediately back inside the box, others she kept to one side. And when she had discovered what she was looking for, when one last thorough search of the patio revealed nothing left behind, she replaced all the rings, closed the lid and stowed the box away where she had found it. After which, locking the front door, she left without a backward glance.

Later that same night, Mrs Sparks at last allowed herself to refrain from her play-acting. She gazed around the room, at the roses her visitor had brought, slightly battered it is true but now arranged in their appropriate vase, at the open window where the net curtains billowed gently, letting in the cooling breeze. All in all not too bad, she thought, smiling with satisfaction.

Cautiously she leaned over to the bedside table, withdrew her handbag and began to put her bracelets and rings inside. She drew each one off slowly, enjoying the weight and feel of it. She liked the look of gold; gold, like money, talked.

It was good that she was here alone, in her own room at last. No one to listen in when she talked of really important things, namely what was to happen, what should she do about returning to the house, should she move again – that thought took the smile away; she didn't want to move. And then there were other things that she didn't want to mention, that she would have to have out with her daughter – stupid girl, always blundering in where she isn't wanted. As for the others involved in future plans, here her face softened as she thought of them, surely they'd be more understanding. At least she hoped they would be, they ought to be . . . the possibility of misunderstanding brought the first hint of unease.

Her finery safely stowed away she began to prepare herself for sleep. No, she didn't need the night nurse hovering. The nurse'd done what she was told to, and that was that. And she certainly wasn't having the woman around when she got ready for the night. Even though for a moment it had been tempting to find out all the old Padstow gossip. But there, not even her nearest and dearest saw her without her war paint on; it was her one regret that she should have lain so exposed and well, naked, in all that dirt when there were so many people, so many men, about.

'Out you go,' she had said, and meant it.

The night nurse went, protesting. Stupid fool too, Mrs Sparks thought. Believing she hadn't been recognized. But I knew her at once. Great fat thing she's become, lumpish. Like her mum before her, common. I shan't say I know her, she decided, it isn't worth it. She stretched her own thin legs.

With practised skill she wiped away the remnants of the eye shadow, the lipstick, the powder and rouge, balling the used tissues and dropping them to the floor for the nurse to clear away later. Give her some real work for a change, she thought with a vicious dab, swanning about as if she's in charge, making herself important. I know where she came from and who she is, and she'll do what she's told if she knows what's good for her.

Tomorrow she herself would be clear about her future plans. It was clever, she thought, to insist on spending the night in the hospital to avoid any hasty decisions. She hoped her reasoning would be acceptable, it ought to be. She was always reasonable; it was one of her greatest assets.

Her face was clean now. She examined it anxiously in her hand mirror. At her age she admitted to shadows under the eyes, and creases, but not to lines; not, heaven forbid, to bruises. Her skin had always been her best feature. 'It's so soft,' Dick always used to say. In the old days, of course.

Thinking of her husband brought the anxiety back. She took off the wig and hung it on its stand. It wasn't the one she'd been wearing when she'd fallen into the pit. She shuddered as she thought of that one, all dirt-covered now and tangled. Her first request, the thing she'd expressly asked when she'd come to properly in the hospital, was for her daughter to bring the spare one from the house, and for once the stupid girl hadn't forgotten. But in other matters she wasn't to be trusted. That's what brains does for you, she thought, suddenly vicious, all book learning and no sense. And whatever the others said, she knew that for a truth, so they'd better listen.

Without a wig her short-cut grey hair gave her face a pinched look, narrow, old. She stared in the mirror and her frightened eyes stared back. Time is running out, she thought. Oh God, where have all the years gone?

Chapter 6

Despite his preoccupations, despite his shoulder, and probably thanks to the whisky, Reynolds slept like a log. He awoke abruptly to the sound of the telephone by his bed. Immediately awake, he reached for it, barked into it from habit, heard Derrymore say, 'She's dead.'

At once he thought of the young woman, the unmarried daughter. Thoughts whirled – another mine cave-in, a car crash on the road, some unimaginable accident. He was disproportionately relieved to hear Derrymore continue, in a voice still showing shock, 'Mrs Sparks. In hospital.'

Reynolds felt his pulse slow down to normal. Mrs Sparks was old, her life had run its course. Yet although he'd been suspicious of her he was surprised to find how much he admired her tenacity. She'd had a vitality about her, he thought, had rallied remarkably from her original fall. If he had thought about it he would have categorized her as the kind of woman who lives on well into her nineties, sprightly and active to the last. Before he could stop himself, the thought came into his head that at least in dying she had escaped the consequences of a murder charge – and was startled by his own cynicism.

Overreacting to this callousness, he said soothingly, 'It was to be expected at her age. Heart, I suppose?' and was shocked to hear Derrymore's response. 'Yes, heart if you can say it stopped deliberately. No, not from falling down a mine shaft. From being smothered, while asleep in bed.'

Reynolds sat bolt upright. 'You mean—'

Derrymore broke in almost exasperatedly, his voice unusually taut. 'Murdered,' he said. 'A right cock-up. The patients in hysterics and the hospital staff not much better.'

'How, when?' Reynolds heard the incredulity in his own voice.

'Middle of the night.' Derrymore was terse. 'The nurse on duty says she turned out the lights by ten. Says Mrs Sparks was sleeping peacefully when she last looked in, but admits she didn't actually go inside to check. Then, when early this morning she did, she found Mrs Sparks with her face covered by pillows.'

Reynolds was at a loss for words. In his career he'd seen many strange coincidences, but this seemed one of the strangest. Yet already his professional training was taking over. 'What's hospital security like?' he asked. 'How did anyone break in?' And was again surprised at Derrymore's bleak response.

'Don't think much of their security.' Derrymore sounded aggrieved. 'And no "break in" about it. A window was left open because of the heat. But no actual finger marks, no footprints, a real professional job.

'Against all hospital regulations, mind you, that open window,' he added, 'but there it is, an invitation.'

'A window.' Reynolds was thinking hard. 'An outside job. But for that matter it could be anyone, inside the hospital or out.'

When Derrymore didn't react he continued, 'I mean someone didn't have to climb in to kill her; they could have killed and then climbed out.'

'Could have.' Derrymore sounded grudging. After another pause he added, equally grudgingly, 'Anyway, as I said, I was real upset. What with all she's just been through, it doesn't seem fair.'

'Murder never is.'

Reynolds reached for a pad, kept by his bedside these days for writing ideas that might come to him in the night. Balancing it on one knee awkwardly, he poised the pencil. 'When did Mrs Sparks leave the general ward?' he asked. 'Where was her new room? Who visited her last evening?'

Derrymore gave a hollow laugh, again sounding uncomfortable. 'You'll never credit this,' he said at last, 'but she actually asked for, and got, the room you had. Kicked up such a row, the hospital staff said, they moved her lock, stock and barrel soon after we left. If you remember, it was a small room on the ground floor, at one end of a longish corridor.'

'Anyone in adjacent rooms?'

'No.' Derrymore's voice still sounded strained. 'It's on a corner, sandwiched between a bathroom and a storage cupboard. Opposite is another private room, occupied by a patient too far gone to have noticed anything. A perfect set up for a perfect crime. I mean, apart from what's going on outside, there's always people wandering about at night inside a hospital, bound to be, from high and mighty surgeons too important to be questioned down to lowly nurses and nurses' aides, some of them unable to speak English properly.'

He sounded querulous, unlike his usual self. Not surprising,

Reynolds thought, as Derrymore went on to explain, albeit in the same strained way, that the room in question faced a visitors' car park, normally shut after dark. But the parking area itself was unlit, unfenced and surrounded by a patch of woodland that stretched back to the moors. Anyone who wanted to, anyone with a grudge say, could have easy access.

On the other hand, as the car park was built on a hill, the lower windows on that side of the hospital were actually very high off the ground – not designed for easy climbing, in or out, which made it all the more remarkable that no one had heard a sound, apparently not even Mrs Sparks herself.

'All the single rooms are on that side of the building,' Derrymore grumbled, 'but that's what she said she wanted – privacy. As for visitors, she had only one, her daughter, who arrived about seven and left before nine. She spoke to the night nurse on the way out, so we've proof of that.'

Reynolds tapped his notes with the pencil. She'd said she was going back, he remembered, but not for how long. And there'd be no proof how far away she went after her visit, or if she returned. But he kept that thought to himself, said instead, 'Did you know there are other relatives, at least one other daughter . . .'

'Right.' Derrymore's voice was growing stiffer by the moment – as if he's a novice being grilled by a superior officer, Reynolds thought, what on earth's the matter with him?

'The hospital had the name of the first daughter we saw, Anna something or other,' Derrymore continued. There was the scratch of turning pages. 'Sometimes still goes by her maiden name of Sparks but her real name now is Anna Lewis. Divorced.'

So that's something about herself she kept hidden, Reynolds thought, something she didn't bother to tell me. He felt irked. There was no reason why she should confide in him, of course, and no reason why it mattered, her personal life was no business of his, but still – in spite of himself he was disappointed.

Derrymore was saying that apparently Anna Lewis, stroke, Anna Sparks, hadn't let her sister, the other still-married sister, know their mother was in hospital, hadn't told her anything, never even mentioned to anyone that there was a sister come to that. The hospital was rightly peeved, because it turned out this sister was the one who was left to pay the bill. But if there was some confusion about who was who, even Mrs Sparks hadn't bothered to sort it out.

It was at this point that Reynolds debated telling Derrymore what he'd learned about Anna Lewis/Sparks, then thought better of it. It could wait, especially since Derrymore apparently knew the most important facts already. And it wasn't the sort of information you blurted out. Besides, he argued with himself, Derrymore's upset. Finding out what I've been doing, behind his back as it were, isn't going to add to his peace of mind.

He waited for Derrymore to ask how he'd discovered there were two sisters, and when Derrymore didn't, asked Derrymore the same question.

'When the body was found about six this morning. We . . .'

Here Derrymore broke off. His voice grew muffled as if he had put his hand over the phone; presumably he was talking to someone else. After a while he turned back and continued, 'When we were called in, we went through Mrs Sparks' belongings.'

He emphasized the 'we', the professional 'we', Reynolds

65

thought, meaning presumably Head Office. He was about to ask who was in charge, what were they up to, when Derrymore hurried on, sounding more unhappy than ever. 'There was an address book in Mrs S.'s handbag. Funny thing, there was no entry at all for Anna, we got her number from the hospital. But there were pages full of listings, different addresses, different telephones, for the other, older, daughter. Seems she's moved about a lot.'

'What's her name?'

Again a reluctant silence, another rustle of paper. 'Shirley Farr, married to one Trevor. Presently domiciled in Bristol. We asked Anna who they were and she identified them. But when we rang they told us it was the first they'd heard. The whole thing came as a terrible surprise.'

'Any explanation why Anna hadn't contacted them earlier?' Reynolds asked, but he thought he knew one answer. Shirley Farr must obviously be the favourite daughter, why should Anna tell her anything?

'Don't know exactly.' Derrymore sounded anxious. 'And haven't had time to question Anna Sparks herself. Thought I'd let her settle down a bit before getting back to her.'

Here he seemed to hesitate a third time as if not knowing how to continue. In the past Derrymore had never hesitated like this. To keep the conversation flowing Reynolds asked what was Mr Farr's reaction, did it seem genuine, and was rewarded with a typical Derrymore observation.

'Hit the roof,' Derrymore said simply, 'kept on and on. Swore he hadn't even heard about the original mine collapse, or the subsequent discovery of the skeleton for that matter, although I know for a fact it was on the local news. Even pointed out none of their friends would have rung to tell them, thinking of course they must know and not wanting to seem nosey. Claimed his friends were sensitive to people's feelings. As for believing him, I can see why he'd be in a right old thrash. If my mam was in hospital I'd like to know at once, not hear it third or fourth hand. And if she was under suspicion of a murder, I'd prefer to be in touch with the law on her behalf, not have the law tell me in the meanwhile she'd been murdered herself. So yes, I'd say I'd be angry. When they come down today, as they've promised, I'd as soon keep out of their clutches. In any case, like I said, their not knowing is a real cock-up. Even Head Office picked up on it, came down like a ton of bricks.'

So I was right, Reynolds thought. Head Office's taken over and that's making him edgy. He felt the usual rush of empathy with Derrymore in his dealings with higher police authorities. A minor slip-up was the sort of mistake Head Office loved to get their hands on to make an underling crawl.

At the same time Reynolds felt a twinge of remorse. After all the mistake had been partly his fault. This admission was followed by another, equally annoying, that if Head Office found out he'd already been helping Derrymore, or been 'interfering' (the word they'd use) it would make matters worse. Once more on the point of telling Derrymore about his 'interview' (he supposed it would classify as that) with Anna Lewis/Sparks again he kept quiet, instead, his voice non-committal, asked if Trevor Farr had mentioned Anna.

'Cursed her up and down.' Derrymore was blunt. 'Said she's always trying to cut them out.'

That too tallied. But Reynolds kept his observation to

himself. 'Any other leads?' he asked.

'Well.' Derrymore brightened. 'There's the night nurse, Joyce Pengelly, who claims she knew Mrs Sparks in the "old days", meaning while the family still lived in Padstow. I get the impression she didn't like Mrs Sparks then and likes her even less now, "throwing her weight about" was the expression used. Hinted too there'd been arguments between husband and wife.'

He added slowly, 'But as I've not had a chance yet to question either daughter, there's not much other news. Except that the last person in the family to see Mrs Sparks alive was her daughter, Anna.'

The name dropped between them, like a stone into deep water, Reynolds thought, you can hear the reverberations. Now was the opportunity to tell what he knew. The moment lengthened, passed.

'Has Anna been told that the Farrs are coming down?'

'Probably. As I said, I've not spoken with her in detail but since then she may have talked with her sister herself.'

Here another burst of noise erupted in the background, died away to a faint hum as presumably once more Derrymore covered the telephone. When he spoke again his earlier stiff manner had returned. 'But if Anna's deliberately kept things secret, can't say I'd like to be in her shoes. Mr Farr let it be known he is a lawyer, a highly placed lawyer, mentioned it several times. The very hint of scandal was like a red rag to a bull.'

He started to say something else, fumbled for a moment, continued in a rush, 'Look, sir, things are difficult here. Head Office've set up an Incident Room in the hospital. Everything's happening at once. They've asked me to be part of the Inquiry Team so I'd better get on with the job.'

The idea of cooperation between Derrymore and Head Office took Reynolds by surprise – he'd presumed the opposite and again presumed wrong. And it certainly explained Derrymore's hesitations. Yet there was no reason why Head Office shouldn't liaise with a village constable who had himself discovered a murder, in fact normally they would. It was only because of Reynolds himself that there were any problems. He bit down the urge to ask, 'Is our old enemy in charge?' Derrymore had his career to think of, he didn't need to be identified with enmities that were of Reynolds' own making.

He suppressed a sigh, said instead, 'Who've they put on the case then?' and was agreeably pleased to hear names he didn't know, the senior officer presumably a newcomer since his day.

But Derrymore had something else to say. He spoke formally – Reynolds could imagine his standing to attention, heels close together, toes in line, regular-army style – but with his usual brand of honesty. 'I'm sorry you're housebound, sir. But perhaps it's better this way. With Head Office breathing down my neck I'll have to back off.'

Meaning you want me to back off too, Reynolds thought. The idea took him by surprise. 'Good luck then,' he said, equally awkwardly. His last words, 'And if you need me you know where I am,' were spoken to a blank as Derrymore hung up.

Disturbed out of all proportion, Reynolds banged the telephone down, snapped the notebook shut, cursing in several different languages, legacy of his soldiering days. News of another murder was the last thing he'd expected. Death, he thought, violent death again but fresh this time, with all its naked horror, not desiccated and hidden until even the horror seemed dried out. The image of Mrs Sparks, lying limp, all vitality pressed out of her, sickened him; what must have the effect been on the daughter? But gradually as his thoughts steadied he turned to his own position. And his feelings towards Head Office.

Actually it was only since coming to St Breddaford himself, several years ago now, that Reynolds had become an outsider to the police world he had once dominated. He had allowed this to happen deliberately (more than was usual in retirement, that is), the reason partly due to natural circumstances – after all he had left earlier than was normal, against his superiors' wishes, at what might have been termed the height of his career. But mainly it had as cause an unprecedented and ugly series of false rumours, innuendos, libellous gossip, which news of his retirement had sparked off. Matters had gone from bad to worse when the man responsible for these personal attacks had succeeded to Reynolds' own position – after having had an affair with Reynolds' wife. No wonder all my subsequent dealings with Head Office became discoloured, he thought, no wonder I'm disillusioned. And once my new career took off, no wonder the man who succeeded me was so consumed with envy that he deliberately cut me out, even to refusing my 'unofficial' help when I offered, and he needed, it.

But his anger now went deeper even than that and after a while he faced up to it. The truth was he had thought he and Derrymore were friends; if anything he would have called Derrymore his protégé. Of course he and Derrymore had never

worked together in any real professional sense. When, after
leaving the army, Reynolds had gone into the police, and
while he was carving out his career, the younger man was
probably still at school. They'd had no dealings with each
other when both were members of the force; it was merely
because they lived in the same village that they had met by
chance after Reynolds' retirement. But they had worked
together, 'non-professionally', and they had worked well.

Derrymore had fitted in easily with his ways, had been
deferential, if that was the word – at least had deferred to
Reynolds' superior knowledge and experience. Now it seemed
Derrymore was eager to take the initiative, was telling Reynolds
he would rather go his own way with a new set of allies, was
in fact dropping Reynolds as part of the 'team', a defection
which Derrymore's attempted sympathy accentuated –
'housebound', Reynolds thought irritably, makes me sound
like some Victorian parlourmaid suffering from some obscure
female complaint. The word 'ingratitude' came to mind until
he forced it down.

'Be honest,' he now lectured himself. 'It's only as a private
citizen that you've ever helped Derrymore with investigations;
in fact if anyone's the professional now, Derrymore is; you're
the amateur. And Derrymore's got his own way to make.
That's the law of the world. You can't blame Derrymore.'

But he did blame him. And he did feel aggrieved.

Putting these thoughts aside, stamping down the worse
thought of all – that rather than Derrymore's outgrowing him,
he himself had lost his touch – he tried to immerse himself in
the chapter which his stroll yesterday was supposed to have
clarified.

'The detective started down the cliff towards the sea below,' he wrote, then crossed the banal words out. The sentence was too bland for what he wanted to depict and his heart wasn't in his work. Who had really run him down, and why? Was it just for sport? If so, surely it wasn't someone local, more likely was one of the many visitors who crowded into the county during the summer months. And why should the driver's smile have so bothered him that even now, in the quiet of his own home, he could not put it out of his mind?

He could come to no satisfactory answer to these questions and now other pictures kept intruding upon his thoughts: the hectic vivacity of an old woman gallantly putting on a brave show, the self-mocking sarcasm of a young one, hiding vulnerability. Above all the spectre of murder cast its awesome shadow. And, of all places, in a hospital, a place of refuge – where a person had the right to feel safe, where a patient should expect protection and care, where the staff were dedicated to succour the feeble. Suddenly this unnecessary death seemed more of an outrage than ever.

Later that day, in his allotted corner of the Incident Room, facing the angry couple seated across the table from him, Derrymore was ready to admit he'd made a terrible mistake. By now it was mid-afternoon, overcast, dull, yesterday's heat giving way to threat of storm, a sudden change of weather common in the west of England – and in part the cause of a headache which he could sense growing behind his eyes.

The original uproar caused by the discovery of the murder had begun to die down, but the arrival of Mrs Sparks' son-in-law and daughter brought it all flooding back. Mind you, Derrymore now told himself, looking at Trevor Farr, a small

72

man with a squarish face like a bad-tempered terrier, even over the phone I knew he would be difficult. And the way he positively speeded through the hospital grounds, parking his great Mercedes with a squeal of brakes, bringing everyone to the window, all spelled trouble. To say nothing of how he got out of car, swinging his briefcase and locking the automatic doors before his wife emerged, causing a domestic wrangle while he fiddled with the keys.

Derrymore had assumed, wrongly (wrong again he thought glumly), that the daughter, if not her husband, would want first to see the dead woman, or at least pay their respects to her remains, kept in the hospital's mortuary pending forensic investigation. To his surprise the Farrs had headed straight for the Incident Room, set up hastily just inside the main entrance. There, to his even greater surprise, they'd asked for him by name, from the start giving the firm impression that, quite the contrary to his interviewing them, they were about to interview him.

His murmurs of condolence, perfectly genuine, had fallen on deaf ears. He was immediately inundated with questions, more and ever more aggressive questions, ending with the repeated query, 'Why was Mrs Sparks shoved into some out-of-the-way place? We could afford the best of rooms, the best of care.'

Patiently now he fielded off the aggression as best he could, saying only that, as far as could be ascertained, Mrs Sparks had received excellent nursing, that she had made a good recovery from her fall . . .

'She's dead, isn't she?'

Trevor Farr's voice rose. He knew the ins and outs of law,

he said, no one could pull the wool over his eyes. With what could only be called a sneer he thumped his lawyer's briefcase on the table top – and dropped his bombshell. 'I shall sue, of course.'

And having dropped it, he was ready to make a summing-up. He straightened his tie with the gesture of a man who knows how to convince a jury, the whiteness of his shirt contrasting with the sallowness of his skin.

'Dead, because someone made an error. Or rather, a series of conspicuous errors. To wit: first, the lack of judgement in moving Mrs Sparks to an isolated room; second, the lack of security in leaving her window wide open; third, the lack of supervision during the night while she was supposed to be sleeping; and fourth – to us the most distressing – the lack of concern for her closest relatives, who weren't even informed what was going on. If that's good care show me bad.'

He straightened his tie again, shot his cuffs so the links, gold, diamond-studded, flashed. Like many small men Derrymore had encountered, he used bluster to intimidate. 'As for the police, didn't bother to set someone to keep watch – never thought of that, I suppose.' Here he glared around the room, shaking back his fringe of frizzled grey hair, more than ever like a terrier warming up for a fight.

'And as a last straw, having stumbled on a bag of ancient bones, God knows how ancient, immediately cast suspicion on an old lady whose only mistake was falling by accident down a mine shaft.'

He paused for courtroom effect. 'Another slew of errors, constable,' he concluded, 'which someone's going to pay for. My wife's on the verge of breakdown.'

74

At this, the wife, Shirley Farr *née* Sparks, handkerchief conspicuously held to face, gave another sniff. Although she said little her sniff spoke volumes, as did her glance. Ferret-like, Derrymore thought, nasty if cornered. He made a mental note.

She sat beside her husband, a younger image of her mother, having the same artificially golden hair, and, beneath the cover of the handkerchief, the same darting eyes. But plump, twice her mother's size, stuffed into her clothes, Derrymore thought, like a Strasbourg goose. The realization that the hint of damages, of pay-outs, was causing the gleam in her eyes made him distrust her even more.

Derrymore had never encountered legal threats before and was at a complete loss. He too looked around him, but the other members of the Inquiry Team studiously avoided his mute appeal for help and the inspector in charge seemed to have chosen this inappropriate moment to be out of the room. The row of hunched backs and sudden concentration on work suggested only one thing – that the instinct for self-survival was well in control. If there were hints of malpractice, of criticism, of lawsuits, no one wanted part of it. Derrymore was the local policeman who had handled, or mishandled, the first part of the case, the part now under fire, let him handle intimidation as best he could on his own.

Derrymore may never have met legal threats before, but it wasn't his first encounter with what he had come to think of as a deliberate 'ganging up' by Head Office, the 'townies' versus local police constables, whom they dubbed 'country bumpkins'. It was an age-old quarrel, of course, given a new twist, but in this instance he had been lulled into a false sense of comradeship and was taken off guard. If anything, he'd expected the others to rally round him, to show all the support that he himself would have shown in similar circumstances. Suddenly he remembered the hints that Reynolds had dropped once, the warnings. The unfairness of the betrayal came over doubly strong.

Biting down a hot reply to Mr Farr, he repeated his words of sympathy, bracing himself to ask the questions that he himself wanted answered. Again Mr Farr was too quick for him.

Mr Farr must have noticed the reticence of the other members of the Inquiry Team, at least he made use of it. He stood up and swung to face them.

'That goes for all of you.' Trevor Farr's voice was suave now, in control, confident. 'The worst example of inept bungling I've ever had the misfortune to encounter.'

And with this last broadside he grabbed his briefcase and stamped off before anyone could stop him, his wife once more trailing after him. But not before she'd flashed another ferret glance in which a gleam of triumph showed.

So that was that, Derrymore thought. He sat back, hot and bothered, angry with himself, angry with his colleagues. Meanwhile, as if released by a spring from their self-imposed silence, the rest of the Inquiry Team immediately began to debate what they'd just heard, avidly arguing the pros and cons with each other. Their introspection jarred.

I'm a simple man, used to dealing with simple village crimes, he wanted to shout. All this yak, yak, yak drives me mad. If you want to know what I think – which I suppose you don't – it's simple too: I expected you to back me and you didn't. I hoped to get some information from the Farrs and I've failed. They haven't yet verified their story or explained their complicated family relationship – what do they know of the drowned father for example or the body in the mine? For that matter they haven't even volunteered where they were last night, or yesterday when Mrs Sparks fell in the pit. And because I've failed and because you didn't come to my help, if we summon them back – as you know we'll have to – ten to one they'll show up with their own lawyer who'll block all questioning. And not a word of grief from the bereaved pair, no time for that I suppose, all for greed, what they can get out of it.

He found that aspect of the Farrs most revolting, along with their conspicuous wealth.

Being mild-mannered he didn't say anything, merely listened as the other officers loudly expounded theories on what should be done to counteract Mr Farr's tactics – more loudly than was necessary, he thought, as if to compensate for their previous silence. His head began to ache more than ever. If Inspector Reynolds were here, he thought, he'd send us all, double quick, about our business – which isn't defending ourselves from shady legal threats but solving a murder to which as yet we've got no leads. Or rather, two murders, he amended, the death of a chief suspect in one doesn't mean the first is shelved. But ex-Inspector Reynolds isn't involved – and that's my fault.

The memory made him feel worse, as if he were teetering on the edge of a hole himself. In fact, looking back, he recognized that hardly had his talk with Reynolds come to its unsatisfying conclusion than he knew he'd expressed himself badly. That's the trouble with me, he thought, I blurt things out. And he could tell at once that Reynolds had been, well, surprised by his suggestion, surprised only half of it. But there, he told himself again, I can't always be dependent on him, it's not fair, especially now, what with the state he's in. And this is a chance for me, one I ought to take.

He hoped Reynolds would understand how he couldn't reverse what he'd said, not after the little hints that the Inquiry Team had dropped, the 'words to the wise' the inspector in charge had let slip to warn him. Well, he'd got the message clear enough. He was welcome; Reynolds wasn't. And if he wanted to keep on the side of the 'big boys in Head Office' (again an expression the inspector in charge had used) he'd better make sure Reynolds stayed at a distance, the wider the better. So what was a fellow to do after that, except what he'd done? And having done it, square his shoulders, ram his helmet on, stride forth, as it were, to do his part on his own.

More like to do battle, he thought now gloomily, with nurses, doctors, patients, public, all in full attack as the implication of a murder on the hospital premises hit home.

In fact the encounter with the Farrs wasn't much different from all the other interviews he struggled to make sense of, along with the other officers in the Incident Room. Hours of questioning, of double checking, of careful scrutiny (which he admitted freely to himself, he wouldn't have known how to handle without the previous example of ex-Inspector Reynolds) had brought no easy answers to a case which on the surface seemed more and more senseless – why choose Mrs Sparks as victim, for what reason?

Robbery wasn't a motive, not with her bag full of money and jewelry left intact. Nor, apparently, was dislike. Mrs Sparks might be disliked, but mere dislike isn't usually a cause for murder. And for that matter why kill someone who had just miraculously survived an earlier brush with death – unless out of madness, at random. There were no other clues, no other lines to follow – just the open window, the pile of pillows, as if insultingly obvious.

The hospital staff, as might be expected, were nervous, on their guard. They claimed they had no evidence, it was none of their business. Nor were the patients helpful – those fit enough to be told about the murder, or to be questioned about it. The cleaning staff, on the other hand, were full of theories, mostly wild and unsubstantiated, of which the killing of Mrs Sparks for revenge seemed most popular and had as origin a regular TV detective programme. The only piece of unbiased information came from a younger woman in the general ward where Mrs Sparks had first held court. She volunteered she'd heard a car start up about the time of possible death, but the car was later identified as belonging to a junior doctor, showing unusual concern for a patient by staying late. As for the night nurse who had known Mrs Sparks in the past, Joyce Pengelly, any hint of irregularity in her duty, any suggestion that she should have gone inside the room earlier to see to the patient, put her in such a state of panic she seemed an unlikely suspect for a greater crime.

Care of a dying man and unsubstantiated gossip don't give much basis for a murder charge. Meanwhile the Incident Room had been besieged by so many anxious relatives concerned about the conditions at the hospital that Derrymore felt more than ever that he was in the midst of a medieval siege rather than a police investigation.

79

The arrival of his last witness, the one he'd kept to last, Anna Lewis/Sparks was the final straw. Miss Sparks (as she preferred to be called) had been summoned to the hospital first thing, had arrived within the half hour, even before the police had finished their work with the body. Somehow she'd managed to squeeze her way into the room before he could stop her, had seen her mother, had witnessed herself the awful proof of death. Derrymore had felt sorry for her, doubly sorry that somehow he hadn't been able to keep her out. The look on her face alone would have convinced him of her innocence, if no other reason did.

Having given her the remainder of the day to attend to all the details surrounding sudden demise, and having, out of some surge of sympathy, allowed her to do her grieving in private, he'd asked permission to see her himself, and been, reluctantly, granted it.

Remembering her mood of the previous day, he was geared for hysterics, even for verbal violence, yet she was quite calm, certainly dry-eyed, only a tightening of the face, as if the skin had been drawn back round eyes and mouth, suggested emotion under control. And a look in her eyes that he couldn't fathom, either of relief that was kept well hidden, or, possibly, of grief too deep to express.

She was very pale, a paleness intensified by her dark hair. Contrasting her colouring and her reserve with Shirley Farr's extravagance, he thought surely they're not sisters. Just as yesterday he had wondered at her having the mother that she did. But my, pale or not, she was pretty. He sighed.

She sat down opposite him, her arms folded neatly on the top of the green baize-covered table that had been dragged out from some hospital games room. He glanced at her hands as they always do on television, but there was no twitching, no nervous opening and shutting of the fingers. As if she'd noticed his look she stretched them open, palms upward, as if to say, 'I've nothing to hide.'

He felt himself flush. His first question was more direct than he meant: why had she not informed her sister of her mother's accident and the subsequent police inquiry? He expected obvious excuses, that she wanted to spare her older sister worry, or that her mother had asked her not to, excuses that would be impossible to verify and yet might be perfectly plausible. Instead she said briefly, 'Why should I? They could wait.'

'Wait?' he repeated, puzzled.

Her answer was even more puzzling. 'Until I was ready.'

Baffled, stopping himself from asking, 'Ready for what?' he returned to her movements the previous evening: had she come back to the hospital at seven as she'd first said?

'Of course.' Her reply was curt. 'I told you so this morning. I also told you that I'd made a quick visit to mother's house to check all was in order. Then, after spending some time with her, and after chatting with the night nurse, who'll have the exact hour to the minute noted in a log somewhere I've no doubt, I went home.'

Her tone was dry, sarcastic he'd call it. No need to make him look a fool. Nettled, he asked about the night nurse, Nurse Pengelly. Nurse Pengelly used to live in her home village, did she know her? 'She left there a long time ago,' she retorted. 'And so did I. You know now exactly where I live. Well, that's where I stayed until your phone call this morning.

But I've no proof of it, if that's what you're after.'

To his next set of questions, about her mother's need for privacy – why had Mrs Sparks wanted to leave the ward, didn't her mother thrive on company – she was equally sarcastic, her replies to the effect that he himself had heard Mrs Sparks say she didn't like the public ward, and in any case her mother's change of mood was no concern of hers, she merely did what her mother wanted.

'Where was the money for a private room to come from?' His next question was equally blunt, as was her answer. 'Obviously I couldn't pay for it, not for luxuries like that. I live on a teacher's salary.'

'But your sister—?' he began, and, 'Oh, *she* could,' she broke in, 'Shirley's well off, she can afford anything.'

'Then wouldn't that have made it necessary to tell her?' Once more Derrymore felt he was floundering, a feeling enhanced by her reply, 'I've explained that.'

Another sarcastic look. 'When I was ready,' she said. 'You don't have to pay up on the spot you know; being in hospital's not like buying pints of beer over a counter top. The cash part could wait.'

Finally, asking if she had noticed the open window, he was rewarded with a flash of temper. Yes, she had noticed, she wasn't blind. In fact her mother had requested for it to remain open before she herself left; that's what she'd stopped to ask the nurse about, her mother had complained about the heat.

'Isn't that contrary to her usual practice?' Derrymore, proud of remembering the locked doors at the house, suddenly pounced. 'I thought she was nervous, kept everything shut up tight.' His pride was shattered as she turned on him.

'Ask one question so you can set a trap with another,' she said, 'my, haven't we rehearsed our techniques. Is that your usual method, constable? Or have you been taking lessons from your ex-inspector friend?'

And when, stupidly, he asked what ex-Inspector Reynolds had to do with it, 'Plenty,' she said. And so told him where Reynolds had gone after being dropped off at the car park. And gave her version of what he had done and how he had intervened between her and her boyfriend and what had been talked about afterwards. But never a word about the box she'd been carrying, nor what she had found in it. Even without that there was enough to keep Derrymore occupied.

Which was why, although he'd decided it wasn't fair to draw Reynolds into another case, and promised himself he would not trouble Reynolds any more, Derrymore found himself approaching the garden gate of Reynolds' cottage on his way home.

By now he too was angry. Angry and bewildered. It wasn't just that he was disappointed personally to find Anna Sparks had been married and had a current boyfriend – a girl that attractive was bound to be snatched up. Much more important was why Reynolds had made a fool of him.

Reynolds shouldn't have stolen a march on him, he thought, Reynolds should have told him immediately, should have shared information, out of duty if not friendship. But paramount in his mind was what he himself had said to Reynolds, about backing off.

He'd meant it partly in the kindest way possible, but not completely. He'd been thinking of himself too, that was for sure. Much good it had done him! Yet, even so, Reynolds could have understood his predicament. Or if he hadn't, it wasn't like Reynolds to be so petty as to want to pay him out.

He took off his helmet, ran a hand across his forehead. Another set of subtleties, another set of complications. Yet what did his mam always say? 'Never let the sun set on your wrath.' He suddenly wished that all people were like his mam, warm and comfortable and predictable. He was tired of subtlety, of sophisticated complication.

It was already late, past eight o'clock, and the rain that had been threatening all afternoon was streaming down, no soft evening tonight, with its long and languorous twilight, here was winter, cold and wet. Yet the scent of roses was very fresh as he opened the gate to Old Forge Cottage and a shower of white petals cascaded over his uniform. He brushed them off as he approached the door, noting as he did so that the house seemed empty. But where would Reynolds go in this sort of weather, with an arm in a sling and the car – he'd already spotted it – parked somewhat askew outside the garage at one side of the house. And he'd never known Reynolds go out at whim, certainly never to the village pub, recently re-opened; he wasn't a night-bird like lots of bachelors. But equally he never went to bed before midnight!

He rang the bell, but there was no answer. Damn, he thought. He peered in the sitting-room window, but the curtains were closed and he could see nothing, not even the flicker of television. Baffled, he withdrew, his headache dulled to a constant pressure as he made his way back through the village towards the house where he lived with his mother.

Anger was giving way to puzzlement, but was not yet completely gone. He didn't get angry easily, but when he did he was slow to cool down. Have it out with him tomorrow, he thought, as he went into his own home, where a hot supper and sympathy awaited him. As yet he felt no cause for alarm.

Nurse Joyce Pengelly also had gone home with a headache, earlier than Derrymore, but much later than was usual. She didn't live in Padstow these days. Like Mrs Sparks, her one-time neighbour, she had moved inland long ago with her mother, a few months before the Sparks themselves had moved. But as she sat in the bus with her packages about her (she always did some shopping when she came off duty, it took her mind off things) and stared unseeingly out of the window as the first raindrops splattered, it was about Padstow that she was thinking.

She was a big woman, heavy-breasted like her mother, tall. Being so large had always made her self-conscious (although with approaching middle age she didn't look so awkward). She liked things to be just so, never any change. And now, the whole day was already out of kilter. She should have been fast asleep hours ago, in the sort of dreamless sleep her pills produced, the house shut up close about her and the quiet wrapped round her like a security blanket.

She lived alone. Now that mother was gone she could please herself. And usually it pleased her best to sleep by day and work by night. She preferred it. She liked when the day nurses came on and relieved her, when she could escape to the hospital canteen and have a cup of tea and a good cooked breakfast without the bother of having to make it herself. Then, out to do her shopping, early in the morning when things like fruit and vegetables and bread were fresh, nothing stale, left-over, for her, she liked the best. A short bus-ride home – she didn't drive, didn't know how to – a short walk to her house, the opening of the front door usually coinciding with the arrival of the post, a pleasant little read if there were any letters or cards (she kept up a correspondence with lots of people, old friends, former patients, new acquaintances) another cup of tea, strong, and so to bed . . . while the rest of the world throbbed and buzzed and shook with its worries and woes.

Instead, like a fool, today after giving what she thought of as 'evidence', she'd stayed on to listen to the other nurses talk, to gossip with them, to find out what she could. With that the routine was broken.

But it had already been broken, and with it the harmony that she had striven so long to maintain. First and foremost, there was Mrs Sparks. Joyce had recognized the name at once when the news first broke on the telly, all that talk, she'd thought, about a stupid old bat falling down a mine shaft. But she hadn't made the connection, not really made it coherently, until she'd come on duty, earlier than she'd needed, and peered in the ward door (Mrs Sparks was still in the ward then). When she'd seen Mrs Sparks sitting up in bed and gabbing away just as she used to do – talk, talk, talk – her gold hair (false, they'd always known it was false) bobbing, it took one back, there was the truth, it was unsettling.

Joyce might have recognized Mrs Sparks and later on her two daughters, but they hadn't repaid the compliment by recognizing her! Thank goodness. And why should they? Joyce had been a young woman when they had all last met, older than the two daughters, older even than Shirley. Shirl might have known her, but she'd taken good care to keep out of the way when Shirl was about. In fact, after the first unpleasantness, all those questions, as if it were her fault (although the young constable who asked them was nice enough) it had been worth hanging on to watch Shirl and her husband arrive. She wouldn't have missed that for worlds.

Or at least I presume it was the husband, she thought, Trevor Farr, the one Mrs Sparks used to go on about although nobody in Padstow ever met him. And obvious now why, she'd thought, peering down from the little side window where she'd ensconced herself, not English for sure, a foreigner if ever she knew one, some Itie or Paki – that'd take a little bloom off the boast! Mrs Sparks wouldn't have wanted anyone to know her precious Shirl had married some immigrant.

As for Shirl herself, well, she'd recognize Shirl anywhere: the golden curls like her mother's, the plump self-satisfaction, the sly, underhand glance – Shirl's resemblance to her mother made your flesh creep. Never liked you when we were girls together, she thought, and like you even less now, decked out like some fairground tart, wife or not.

But back to Mrs S. The usual pomp and flutter as if she were still the queen, or at least queen in her own eyes. First the fuss about moving, followed by the fuss about the window, Anna Sparks giving orders in a hoity-toity voice.

I remember you when you were a grubby kid in dirty nappies, Joyce had wanted to say to Anna, so don't you put on airs with me.

But it was the contrast with her own mother in her last years that was the most galling, when mother had become so ill, growing thinner and thinner, wasting away. And while mother had to live off a state pension (plus the little Joyce herself could earn in between looking after her), while mother had to make do, starved of luxuries, there was Mrs Sparks preening herself, all decked out in gold like the Queen of Sheba. That jewelry for example, I wonder where it came from.

But of all the ironies, to be on night duty when Mrs S. moved to a private room, what a song and dance, 'My daughter'll pay for it,' as if her Shirl's little Paki owned the Bank of England. And if the rest of the hospital staff expressed surprise afterwards that Mrs Sparks had two daughters, why should she have told them otherwise? She didn't have to reveal all she knew, did she? She didn't have to set things straight.

Mrs Sparks' temper tantrums hadn't changed either. Mrs Sparks' tantrums had always been notorious; they'd made the cottage reverberate in the old days.

The word was her mother's choice. 'Mrs Sparks is having a tantrum again,' her mother used to say. She'd cover her ears with a shawl to block out the noise, but Joyce wasn't that punctilious. Ears pressed to the dividing wall, she had no compunction about listening in. Not many secrets they didn't share in the old days.

There, she'd brought her mother and Mrs Sparks together in her thoughts again, as she didn't mean to, just like when they lived in Padstow themselves, in the next-door cottage, and the vivacious and pretty Mrs Sparks wheedled or cajoled or nagged her way into the hearts of all she could lay her claws on.

Of course mother didn't put it that way then, and she didn't until much later, not until Joyce and she had made a new life together and were settled down comfortably, just the two of them. But her mother never forgot Mrs Sparks, and Joyce didn't either. And if mother forgave that was a different question, immaterial anyway because Joyce herself had never forgiven.

If there'd been any justice, she thought now, staring unseeingly as the bus lurched round the familiar corners, Mrs Sparks should have died miserably, years ago. At the time I'd have willingly murdered her myself.

Her stop was coming up and she wasn't ready. She felt panic rising. In fact she felt a bit queer, it must be the change in routine. Out of force of habit she gathered up her packages anyhow and shouldered her way to the door. Usually when she came home the bus was half empty, giving her plenty of leg room, and all this unaccustomed crowding made her nervous. 'Here, set me down,' she shouted to the driver, fear making her voice sharp, bringing the bus to such an abrupt stop she fell against someone.

What a muddle she'd made of it, she thought later, standing on the pavement, surrounded by her scattered belongings like some bag woman, looking round her as if not certain where she was. In the afternoon with the rain slanting down, even her own street looked different, somehow dream-changed. Her momentary confusion bothered her.

The last thing she wanted was to bring attention to herself and all that questioning had unleashed her old uncertainties. She felt the other passengers' eyes upon her as the bus pulled away from the kerb and her own eyes began to water with self-pity, but she couldn't stop.

Still in a watery haze she went up the garden path, unlocked the door, gathered up the post – circulars, the shopping catalogues she collected, her hobby. From force of habit she called, 'I'm back,' as if mother were still there to answer, as if mother were still alive.

While the kettle boiled she went upstairs and found the scrapbook, the pages numbered (mother always liked things neat), all the letters friends had written, the notes mother had made.

'Heard them at it,' the correspondent had written, another former neighbour, the handwriting large and ill-formed, but the information reliable. 'And so soon after Dick's death, you'd have thought out of decensy they'd stop.'

'Decensy' was misspelled, but no matter. What did matter now was what they had been talking about. But she hadn't mentioned it, not to the officers who had questioned her, not even to the young one with the accent she could understand, one of 'her lot' as she would have put it. When the police came again, as surely they would, would be the time to drop names and facts into the policeman's ears. That was what was called being helpful, she thought. And it would draw attention away from her.

Chapter 7

That same evening the sisters sat opposite each other in their mother's kitchen. As concession to the continuing rain the gas fire was on in the sitting room, but by mutual consent the women had left Trevor there to enjoy his usual evening telly. They themselves had withdrawn to what both might have thought more familiar surroundings – familiar in that the pine table and, behind it, the pine hutch, with its rows of plates and jugs, were relics from their childhood. In fact the last thing either would want to remember was their childhood home.

They did not speak. They seldom did nowadays, beyond the casual chitchat of strangers – unless their mother chivvied (or provoked) them into argument. Why should we talk? Anna thought. We detest each other. We have nothing in common except the same mother, and not really even that, since she loved one of us and hated the other.

There were things they should discuss; it was their duty to bring them into the open. But to do so was to reopen horror that neither wanted to think about. Only later would they come to it; it would keep.

Anna's failure to telephone her relatives hadn't been mentioned either, nor their anger at 'not having been informed'

– although these issues too hung uneasily in the shadows. I shan't bring the subject up, Anna thought. But although she swore to herself she wouldn't, she was afraid she would!

Usually when they met there was a quarrel, provoked by their mother. Over the years Anna had come to be labelled a troublemaker, against whom Shirley, too delicate for her own good, had to be protected. Now, without their mother to do the baiting or protecting, for the first time in their lives the two daughters faced each other on equal terms.

It was a strange situation. Neither knew how to react. At the last moment, as a kind of peace offering, Anna had made the tea and found the biscuits. She'd brought Trevor his tray and supplied another table for him to spread his papers on, after which she lit the fire, kneeling in front of it like a housemaid. These were the sort of chores she did automatically, like a robot she thought, again irritated at herself. Since a child she had been accustomed to defer to Shirley as the elder, the more important, and Shirley had accepted that deference as a matter of course. It had been only too easy to drop into the same habit with Shirley's husband, and equally easy for Trevor to accept it. Trevor loved subservience.

Now Anna saw that the waiting on her sister and brother-in-law (as indeed she had waited on her mother) had also become a kind of ritual, an atonement, which hitherto everyone took for granted, even herself. Atonement for what? she thought now, even more angrily. For being born, for living?

Leaving the sitting room she let the door bang behind her. Perhaps that'll make him look up, or even nod some thanks, she thought. From now on things will be very different. With mother gone there's no reason for me to pander to their wants.

92

I don't need them. Although they may need me.

She had to keep reminding herself of this because it was not easy to change the customs of a lifetime. Thirty years of submission, she thought, mutiny bottled down, waiting for the chance to break out into revolt. It was the possibility of revolt that preoccupied her at the moment; even her mother's murder, the possibility of her father's death, were lesser issues. Or rather they were so big she didn't know how to deal with them, so she blocked them out.

She looked at her sister. Shirley's hands were wrapped round the cup of tea in much the same way, she thought suddenly, as the ex-inspector had cradled a mug last evening. The memory was so vivid, so unexpectedly warm, she set her own cup down abruptly before the tremble of her fingers gave her away.

The cup slipped awkwardly and the tea splashed out. Shirley looked at her with a flash of irritation which gave her plump face more than ever a resemblance to their dead mother. But whereas Anna's face was still unstained, Shirley's eyes were red with weeping. How can you be so hard, Shirley's look said.

I could tell you, Anna thought, except I won't give you the satisfaction. Instead she said, 'They asked about the house always being locked, did they ask you?'

'No.' Shirley's face grew thin, her eyes narrowed. She stared at Anna intently. 'What did you tell them?' she burst out.

'Nothing that they couldn't find out by themselves.' Anna was succinct.

Shirley looked away. 'What a job,' she said then, meaning

presumably the clearing out of the house. She cast another glance around her, her eyes brightening. 'I always wanted this table,' she said, touching its surface possessively. 'It'll look well in my kitchen. Along with the blue plates.'

A thought struck her. 'Of course you must have something,' she added, as if in a burst of generosity, 'something to remember her by.'

Some little keepsake, Anna thought, some trinket. That's all I'm entitled to, any old knick-knack you don't want, a servant's portion. And if I protest, if I say I want my share, haven't I worked for it, doesn't running all her errands and doing all her chores, being at her beck and call at all hours, entitle me to a part of our legacy? – well, you'll say, how much are you entitled to? As if I never actually was part of you, as if I never lived under the same roof, as if this bloody house wasn't my home for a while after father died.

She too looked around the kitchen at the elaborate appliances: freezer, dishwasher, microwave, washing machine, dryer. Nothing was wanting, everything that money could buy. She thought, but here's the irony, you don't need any of this stuff, you've got it all already.

'What'll you do with it?' she asked, gesturing, just letting sarcasm show. 'Your own kitchen's already packed with everything you need.' Sell it all off I suppose, she thought. Certainly not let me have it. But I don't want the damn things anyway. You won't catch me haggling for them, like a dog snarling over bones. The expression made her wince. Bones she thought. Dear God, that's something else we've got to talk about.

Shirley folded away her handkerchief. She took a dainty sip

of tea. 'Oh,' she said, her eyes glinting under her eyebrows with the look that was ferret-like, 'we shan't sell. We plan to hold on to the house. Trev says we should keep it as a holiday home.'

'Keep it?'

Despite her resolve Anna's voice rose. 'You must be joking,' she cried. 'What on earth for? It's too dangerous.'

And, at her sister's second glance, 'On top of a tin mine!' she amended. 'Suppose there's another cave-in? I should think you'd want it shut up for good. Or knocked down.'

'Trev won't have that.' Shirley's voice was loud. 'He'll never let that happen.'

'What won't he let happen?'

Trevor Farr stood at the entrance to the kitchen, still formal in his city suit although he'd taken off his tie. In the evening light he looked more sallow than ever and, now he wasn't on display, he let his voice slip into a singsong accent. It accentuated his foreignness. 'He was brought up here in England.' Anna remembered how Shirley had argued with their mother before Shirley's impending marriage. 'He was at public school, then university.'

No matter that the 'public school' was a missionary nonentity abroad that passed by that name, no matter that the university was a do-it-yourself course at home after he arrived in England – at the time the claims had sounded impressive. And no matter that when I was old enough I won a scholarship, Anna thought, and my degree from Exeter was first class – none of that counted against his trumped-up credentials. A spasm of hatred, sheer and uninhibited, shook her whole body.

She didn't look at her brother-in-law. She'd never liked

him, nor he her. Now, at last, there was no one to keep her in check, no reason to hold dislike back; she owed him nothing.

Trevor Farr was repeating his question, adding as if on cue, 'Not squabbling about the family inheritance, are we? Because of course, as Anna knows, the house is ours. It's in our name, always was, because we bought it. And didn't Anna marry to escape from it? At least that's what she said. It's not our fault her marriage failed. But Anna's sensible. She wouldn't want something for nothing. She knows what's right.'

Suddenly he snarled, 'Right to make a decision not to let us know what was going on, for instance.'

'Perhaps she thought she was doing us a good turn.' As if waiting for the opportunity, Shirley pounced. When Shirley spoke in a friendly fashion, look out, Anna thought. Now Shirley glanced at her husband sideways, in her sly fashion. 'Said it gave us an alibi.'

'Alibi for what?' Trevor's voice sharpened, showing anger. When no one answered, he shook his head reprovingly. 'I don't need an alibi for a bag of bones that some bobby thinks he can identify,' he said, pontifically. 'Nor for my mother-in-law, God rest her, suffocated while she was asleep. Shirl and I were safe in Bristol, ask anyone.'

He took a step closer to the table where the two sisters were sitting. 'One thing I will say,' he added, with a little laugh that wasn't laughter, was menacing. 'Your family's careless. My late lamented father-in-law lost at sea; now his late lamented wife murdered. You two had better watch out you don't inherit the same unfortunate tendency.'

'Anna says the police have been asking about the house.' Shirley volunteered this information eagerly, steering her husband away from one nasty subject to another. She was successful. Again Trevor's face darkened. 'What did she tell them?'

'Nothing,' Shirley said. 'Or so she says. But they know now that she came here yesterday. After the accident. There was a box,' she added, with another of her ferret glints, 'mother's jewelry box. And there's been talk of a ring found with the skeleton. I went to look for the box just now, but even if there was a ring it isn't in the place where mother said it was.'

She didn't look at her sister, but she was well aware of the effect her words had. Meanwhile Trevor continued to stare at his sister-in-law, and Anna forced herself to pay him no attention. Let them talk, Anna thought; let them vent their spite. Then when it's over I can be free of them and all they stand for. She found her feet were actually making movements on the carpet as if wiping off the dust.

'I think,' Trevor said ominously, 'that Anna had better tell us all that she did and said yesterday. After all, as I understand it, it was her choice to act as spokesman, or spokesperson I think she'd call it, for the rest of us. In our absence mind you, and without telling us, unelected and unsolicited by us, out of some fancy notion she's cooked up on her own. Because I for one would like to know why she thought she had the right. Because the idea of an "alibi" is all bunkum and she knows it. And because of something else, which I tell you—'

What he was about to reveal was drowned by the sound of the phone in the hall. He stepped away from the door, closed it firmly and went to answer, leaving the sisters still sitting opposite each other. They heard him say, 'What,' followed by

'When' and 'Where', then a long silence as presumably he listened to explanations.

'Business,' Shirley said, with an important smile, 'always business.'

She went back to stroking the table top. 'You shouldn't rile him, Anna,' she said with one of her sharp glances, a 'big' sister giving the 'little' sister good advice. 'You really shouldn't. It makes things hard for us all. And mum wouldn't like it. You know how fond she is of him.'

She sniffed and corrected herself, 'Was. Was fond.'

There was a rustle as she felt for the handkerchief, another audible sniff. While Shirley once more broke out into loud and calculated sobs Anna sat dry-eyed. She was trying to listen to the conversation in the hall, or rather what snippets of it she could catch, and her face had drawn into its usual sardonic mask that hid her real feelings.

But later that night, when Shirl and Trevor had retired for the night, in the privacy of the spare bedroom which Anna had got ready for them, Shirley raged in whispers. Even though she knew that Anna, worn out by their hectoring, had stormed out of the house to return to her own, she was afraid of being overheard. She'd wanted Anna to go, of course – 'Couldn't sleep a wink with her under the same roof,' she hissed – but still she was afraid.

'Why didn't she let me know mum was in an accident? Why did she keep it from us? What does she know?' Over and over Shirl kept asking the same questions: what had Anna really told the police, and, most important for Shirley's peace of mind, what had their mother told her – had they come to some understanding?

'I knew I shouldn't have left her alone with mum.' Shirley's voice broke in a wail. 'Heaven knows what she may have wheedled out of her. And what will we say if the police ask us?'

She wiped her eyes. 'I wish we were back in Bristol, out of it,' she said.

'They won't dare ask us anything.' Trevor was complacent in blue silk pyjamas. 'I've put a stop to any of their little games. As for the bloody ring' – he made a vague gesture that was somehow all-encompassing – 'nothing we can do about it. It'll have to wait. Don't fuss so.'

'It's not the ring itself.' Shirley's voice had risen again. 'It's, you know, can I cope?'

'Yes, you can.' Trevor was all masculine firmness. 'Nothing's going to alter in essence, just in details.'

What the details were he didn't elaborate.

By early afternoon of that same day, inaction had driven Reynolds wild. He'd already rung Miss Tenery and asked her not to come. 'I've nothing new for you to work on,' he told her firmly, as her renewed offers of help came bleating over the telephone. 'No, I don't need anything; no, I'm fine.'

Remember next time to chose a secretary who doesn't live nearby, he told himself, and for God's sake get someone who's young and happily married with a score of kids. Somewhat ashamed of his bad temper he slammed the receiver down.

Finding the hospital sling too cumbersome he'd replaced it with one of his own making that enabled him to get into some clothes and not look too one-armed. The pain had dimmed into the background, he could live with it, but he still found bending or stretching difficult, making gardening impossible, and driving wasn't very appealing. The realization that the forecast bad weather might mean he'd be housebound for days depressed him utterly.

Succumbing to temptation, he searched for another notebook, old, battered, used for the solving of many crimes, more than he liked to remember. Turning to a fresh page he drew several columns. The first, labelled A and B, was for the two murders – unconnected at the moment, except that the chief suspect in the first was the victim in the second! By chance or deliberately? – that was something to think about.

In the adjoining column he wrote the word 'Motive', but for the moment he could think of none. What had Mrs Sparks been killed for? Why had Mr Sparks been killed? Presumably the Inquiry Team in their newly established Incident Room would be trying to find answers to the same questions, would be going through what evidence there was, trying to reach some conclusion. But if he knew Head Office, they'd instruct their Inquiry Team to concentrate on the new rather than the old murder. Solving a fresh crime would enhance their reputation, quick results were their speciality. In all likelihood the second crime would overshadow the first; real flesh as opposed to dry bones – the metaphor was horrible yet graphic.

And whatever evidence was collected would be of no use to him, he'd have no access to it, unless he could cajole Derrymore into sharing it and that he doubted. Derrymore had made his stand.

He tapped the notebook thoughtfully. I'm more used to

violent death than most, he thought, but Mrs Sparks' death baffles me.

What about suspects? He turned to his notes of the morning's conversation with Derrymore, cut so unfortunately short. There really weren't many new ones for this new murder; they were mainly the same family members and their entourage, including Anna Sparks and the Farrs from Bristol, as in the first case – minus the leading one, now dead herself.

Under the word 'Suspects' he wrote 'Trevor and Shirley Farr'. The Farrs were an unknown quantity to him but, according to Derrymore, 'had known nothing'. Yet if rumours were correct they had actually bought and furnished Mrs Sparks' house for her. They paid her frequent visits, were no strangers to St Breddaford. Bristol is close enough to Cornwall to get here in a hurry, he thought, although at times the traffic makes it seem at the other end of the world. They certainly could have driven down and back on Monday night, for example, no one the wiser. They need a stronger alibi than simply 'not being informed'. As a lawyer, Mr Farr should know ignorance is no excuse.

Next came the daughter, Anna Lewis/Sparks. (To his surprise he found his original distaste at her former marriage had disappeared; if anything divorce gave them some shared experience, perhaps some common sorrow; his original disappointment at her secrecy had given way to something approaching sympathy.) On the surface Anna had seemed devoted to her mother, or at least, he amended, devoted under protest. When away from Mrs Sparks she'd made no secret of her feelings. It was only in Mrs Sparks' presence, as it were, that she let herself be muted. Not as strange as it might seem,

101

he thought. It's usually the unwanted child who tries desperately to be wanted. He'd first-hand experience of similar family relationships.

Anna was the last known person to have seen her mother alive. She knew about the open window, she actually had asked for it to be left open. She could easily have left the hospital, gone round to the car park and climbed back in later. She had plenty of motives for a killing; if anyone had a grudge, a genuine grudge, Anna did.

He thought of Anna again as he'd last seen her, and it was the vulnerability that stuck in his mind, not the bitterness. She reminded him of a character in a Dickens novel, a starved waif staring in the window at a rich man's table, except it wasn't food she was looking for. And isn't love what we're all wanting, he thought, almost ashamed of his maudlin sentiment, and can't love turn as easily to hate when it's stretched too far – and can't hate twist and warp even the most normal mind?

He tapped the paper again. Somehow the images didn't fit. An Anna Sparks, he thought, who uses pillows to stifle her mother contrasts uneasily with the woman who permits her mother to abuse her verbally in front of others, who drops flowers when she's startled (even if she does so deliberately) and who is so clumsy she lets a wooden box fall and then scrabbles, child-like, on her knees to pick up the pieces. Although what she's doing with the jewel box is a separate issue, not yet resolved.

Despite his sympathy for Anna, if all the points against her were added up a case began to emerge. Reluctantly he underlined her name.

Apart from these, who else? The would-be suitor, Mike;

the night nurse, Pengelly; and failing them, no one else!

Mike first. Mike was someone he'd had the misfortune to meet, although the Inquiry Team hadn't, as far as he knew. Given the fact of Anna's first marriage, presumably Mike was a newcomer to the scene. But that would not at all eliminate him as a possible suspect for Mrs Sparks' murder and not altogether for Mr Sparks' – if indeed Mr Sparks had been murdered.

Mike was in his early thirties, about Anna's age, possibly a little older. When Mr Sparks died (of whatever cause) presumably Mike would have been old enough to have helped in a killing, even if he hadn't organized it. Reynolds himself had witnessed how free he was with his fists, and Anna had said he had a bad temper. He might well have some reason to dislike Mrs Sparks' hold on her daughter. Mike was a subject for more investigation. Again Reynolds underlined the name.

Nurse Pengelly was a complete nonentity at the moment, except that she had professed not to like Mrs Sparks. 'Not to like' sounds a weak foundation on which to build a murder case, but Reynolds had known weaker. And Nurse Pengelly had admitted leaving the window open, had admitted not going in to see her patient during the night. Nurse Pengelly too offered possibilities.

But if he eliminated these all-too-obvious suspects he was left with killings that were unrelated. And that was what had been lying at the back of his mind all morning, that was what he feared most.

He needed no reminding that random murder is the worst kind to solve – no clues, no motive, no reason, a killing perhaps ignited by nothing more than the sudden celebrity of the victim, giving the murderer some secret thrill. He himself had experience, again more than most, of psychopathic murder. He didn't relish finding it here in this little village whose complacency, whose innocence, was exactly why he'd chosen it as a place to live. St Breddaford'll lose all its tranquillity if it's true, he thought. The prospect of a random killer, a psychopath on the loose in the village, will set everyone on edge, destroy our calm, wreak havoc.

Getting up, he paced again, restlessly ill at ease, out of sorts with himself and with the world. These days there are so many unsavoury characters about, he thought, loitering in the High Street, getting drunk in pubs. Even in St Breddaford kids break windows, steal cars . . . That brought him up with a jolt. For the first time since his accident he let himself go over the previous day's events, his climb down the cliffs to the reef, his climb back, the sudden awareness of the speeding car.

His instinct not to speak of it had probably been correct. As he'd thought, some youth joy-riding had let things get out of hand. And yet, he wasn't sure. Or rather he was only sure that if he hadn't been quick, if he hadn't had luck on his side, he'd not be here now to think about it.

Two accidents in one day, he thought. That's what Derrymore first pointed out. Two accidents, unrelated, freakish, strangely resolved, having nothing in common except time and place.

Mrs Sparks' house is near the cliffs, he thought, suddenly interested. At the same time as she falls down a shaft I'm walking on those same cliffs and am run down by a speeding car . . . Coincidence, or mischance? What connection is there between these different things except that we both ended up as patients in the same hospital! The interest flickered and died.

He looked at his watch. Even if he could have managed the climb, already the tide would be coming in. Too late today to reach the reef, and the threatened rain and wind would ruin visibility. And with no low tide for another month or so, the only way to get out to the rocks would be by boat, not his favourite occupation. A childhood made hideous by his father's yachting obsession had long cured him of becoming an addict himself. Nevertheless the clarity of yesterday's sea, that amazing Mediterranean blue that takes visitors to Cornwall by surprise, kept coming into his mind, along with the equally startling luminescence of those floating birds.

Progressing from sea to boats, his thoughts, by natural transition, moved on to Richard Sparks, the unknown Mr Sparks who had been a fisherman and who had drowned. And who might, or might not, be buried in a mine shaft, however unlikely that seemed.

Having the remains identified isn't within my ability, he thought, although if I were in charge I'd put it as a first priority. And I've no right to make official inquiries. But there's nothing to stop me going to Padstow, along with hundreds of summer visitors, and taking a look for myself.

Once there, I can wander about, ask a few casual, off-the-cuff questions to satisfy my own curiosity. Material for a new book, I'll say if anyone objects, which they won't. (He'd learnt by now that people liked the idea of a local writer, a role he'd long ago decided gave him plenty of scope – as long as he was modest, didn't speak out of turn and kept his place, a tame attraction.)

The very idea made him feel better – a child let out of

school, he thought, or, more like, a child playing with forbidden fire.

The prospect of driving himself was daunting, although Padstow wasn't far, a few miles to the east. But a quick phone call, no sooner thought of than done, brought a taxi, and he was off to find out for himself what had happened to Richard Sparks and, incidentally, what the rest of the Sparks family had been up to before they left Padstow.

Padstow was a small fishing town on the north Cornish coast. In spite of the tourists it still kept the flavour of the past and unlike similar towns it still had its fleet of working boats. The crooked streets were crowded with holidaymakers, but that didn't diminish the charm of the stone-built cottages (some with their original slated walls), and the harbour was full of vessels, tied to a jetty, redolent of fish.

Saving the harbour for later Reynolds climbed slowly towards the church, up the narrow street with its raised footpath. Because he was unable, or rather unwilling, to contact official sources, the church had seemed an obvious place to start with, given Mrs Sparks' statement about her husband's religious bent. But although he searched the graveyard (large, its tombstones dating back many generations) and although he went inside the church (founded by St Petroc in the sixth century) he could find no reference to a Richard Sparks, deceased, nor indeed any evidence of any Sparks anywhere.

Turning out of the south gate with its ancient stone cross he went slowly down the back streets towards the harbour. A sudden shower sent him for shelter into one of the bustling cafés, then when it cleared he wandered on towards the stone jetty. I should have started here, he thought, when, within minutes it seemed, he found what he was looking for. I might have remembered that in a fishing village the quay is the hub of the universe.

Out in the estuary the water had taken on a greyish tinge, as if reflecting the gathering clouds, and white caps were showing. The tide was flooding under the gates to the inner harbour and already the wind was whistling along the quay that doubled as a car park. On one of the boats an elderly fisherman, impervious to the noise of the crowds and the threatening storm, was checking over his crab pots. He was old enough to have known Richard Sparks, or at least remember him.

The man was glad of the chance to stop work and listen to a stranger talk. When, gradually, Reynolds led the conversation round to accidents at sea he became garrulous. Padstow could be dangerous, did the gentleman know that, the Padstow Bar or sandspit at the mouth of the estuary notorious at low tide. 'Took three of our best men last year,' he said.

As for Richard Sparks – 'Know him,' he said. 'Used to work along of him, he moored his boat aside mine. Dreadful sad it was, he lived up there.' And he pointed a horny thumb at a cottage part-way up the hill.

'A local man, I suppose,' Reynolds said, sympathetically, and was rewarded with another confidence. 'Well now, in a manner of speaking you could say so,' the old man said. His dark Cornish eyes shone like wet sloes. 'His missus certainly was. But he came from up-country, northwards or thereabouts, a stranger. Not that I held it against 'un, he was a good worker, quiet. Didn't drink nor smoke mind you, so we didn't have much in common.'

'And how did he come to drown?'

Some late sense of caution must have come into the old man's head. 'And who would be asking?' The sparkle went from his eyes, his voice became suspicious. He let Reynolds ramble on about the joys and pains of authorship for some time before deciding it was safe to speak openly again.

'Well now,' he continued. 'I said I knew Dick well, and so I did. But only on the boat. Off it, he kept to hisself, a family man see, close. And his missus was a terror, had him under her thumb.'

He made a face, followed by a curious flapping gesture which he obviously expected Reynolds to understand. When he didn't, he hesitated for a second before interpreting. 'Fluttery like,' he said at last. 'Know what I mean.'

He leaned forward confidentially. 'Always atter something, never satisfied. Dick had some job to keep her happy; she had ambitions, see. Had children too, well she wanted him at home to keep them under his eye, stands to reason she didn't hold with him off fishing. But that's what he were, a fisherman.'

He paused to spit into the water, a well-directed aim past the crab pots.

Wanting to keep the story moving, Reynolds pressed on – how did Dick Sparks come to drown, was there any mystery attached to it?

Another long pause. 'Well, how Dick's death came about was a mystery to some people, but not to me,' the old man said. 'I've told you no lies when I say Dick weren't Padstow born but he knew all about Padstow waters. He wouldn't work on Sundays, see, the Lord's Day he said and I don't blame him. But when a month of storm and gales on weekdays cut work to ribbons, what was a man to do except take a boat out even on a Sunday when he shouldn't. Asking for trouble, didn't stand to reason.'

'That was how he was drowned?' Reynolds couldn't keep the incredulity out of his voice.

The old man eyed him up and down. 'I'll tell you something else,' he said in his lilting voice, with a touch of contempt just showing. ''Tis easy afterwards to say he did a foolish thing. But families have to eat, and men have to make a living. He thought he'd take a chance. Men've done so afore and got away with it. I've done it meself, many's the time, and afterwards swore it were the last.'

He spat again reflectively, about to embark on some personal reminiscence. 'So what happened exactly?' Reynolds held him on course.

'Don't remember.'

The old man was vague. Again he eyed Reynolds. 'You chaps who live inland,' he said, 'you city fellows, don't understand the sea. You come down here in your thousands, like they there.' He waved towards the crowds, beginning to hurry towards their cars as another downpour threatened. 'Think the sea's a thing to play in, to laugh at. If you lived with it, on it, like us sailors do, you'd have another think.'

Which is as close as he'll come to a rebuke, Reynolds thought, somewhat miffed that after all these years as a villager in his own right he was so easily identified as a city dweller by origin. But the old man spoke fairly. Who was he to judge why Richard Sparks had made an error of judgement? He was here to ascertain if he had made an error at all – or if he had been 'helped' into one by someone else.

'What time of day was it?' he asked, hoping to coax out

more information. He was rewarded with another pitying smile. 'We goes out when wind and tide run right, not at our choosing,' the old man said. 'But there, Dick shouldn't have gone alone, not atter dark, that was his first mistake.'

'What about the boat?'

Trying another tack Reynolds was rewarded with a third lecture. 'When Padstow Bar takes hold of 'ee,' the old man said, 'not much left. It's a strip of sand, see, but sand that moves. If the tide or wind catches someone near it, if the engine goes, not much a person can do but go with the drift until the waves turn the boat over.'

He made another of his curious gestures. This one Reynolds understood – the sudden flip of an upturned boat and the sea surging over it.

The old man leaned forward and reached for one of his pots. 'There,' he said, 'I've been a-talking too much. And if you wants a new story there's nothing new to this. We've lost men before, and since, as good men as you'd want to know, familiar with this coast since they was tackers, you can't take nothing fer granted with the sea.'

He shot Reynolds a last glance. 'And you do ask a lot of questions,' he said, 'fer a writing fellow.' And with that he turned his back to indicate the 'interview' was over.

Back on the main square, Reynolds agreed with him. It probably hadn't been wise to come openly like this. But he'd ascertained two important things. One, that although Richard Sparks had certainly been lost at sea no one had actually seen him drown; and two, his loss, although in natural circumstances, had not been altogether natural. The bad weather, the wrong tide and wind, even the night-time excursion on his own, were

110

unusual to say the least, could all be looked upon with suspicion. And three, yes there had been a third gleam of information – Richard Sparks had had trouble with his wife. Not altogether unsubstantiated, hadn't the nurse, what was her name, Nurse Pengelly suggested the same thing? Although weren't arguments between husband and wife common to all marriages? As he himself knew, to his cost.

By now it was drawing on to six o'clock and the rain seemed settled in for good. The crowds had thinned and there was a constant queue of traffic as cars tried to manoeuvre up the narrow roads. He'd turned to find a phone box to ring for the taxi again, when a car's horn startled him.

It sounded again, more loudly, and a voice shouted, 'Hi there.' The car, large, dark blue, relatively new, drew up beside him, blocking the road. A familiar voice said, 'I'm heading for St Breddaford, Inspector. You'll never get a taxi at this hour, I'll give you a lift.'

The last thing Reynolds wanted was to be indebted to Anna Sparks' former boyfriend, and Mike was the last person he'd accept a favour from. Remembering their former encounter, he reminded himself that the man if not dangerous was downright antagonistic. And how did Mike know that Reynolds didn't have his own car parked somewhere, unless he had guessed that Reynolds would still find driving difficult, or, more likely, had been watching since his arrival – not a pleasant thought.

On the other hand, here in a busy street, with the fellow actually smiling out of the rolled-down window (at least giving what passed for a smile, shark-like Reynolds thought), the temptation to accept was considerable. It would be a heaven-sent opportunity to find out more about him. And, incidentally, more about Anna Sparks herself. But still Reynolds hesitated. One didn't walk into the lion's den with one's eyes closed, or rather, he amended the metaphor, swim into the shark's mouth!

The hooting behind them increased. Someone shouted, 'Get a move on.' Making up his mind, although his sixth sense, his infamous sixth sense which so often kept him out of trouble, told him he was being stupid, Reynolds crossed behind the car, gave a thumbs-up sign to the impatient drivers behind him, and climbed into the passenger seat. 'Thanks,' he said. 'Much appreciated.'

He didn't at first do up the seat belt because of the sling, but when Mike accelerated up the road and he was jerked sideways he gritted his teeth and fastened it. A worse driver than Derrymore, Reynolds thought wryly, as the wheels squealed around the next bend – one of many as he was to find out soon enough. Why is it that for young men driving fast is an excuse for driving badly?

Neither he nor Mike said anything. Presumably negotiating the turns and twists in the road while avoiding running into cars ahead took all of Mike's attention; Reynolds meanwhile had an opportunity to study him surreptitiously. Mike was dressed in the same gear as the day before, blue jeans, thick jersey, standard fisherman's stuff. He glanced at the hands clenched around the steering wheel – a man who obviously did hard work for his living, nothing wrong in that. Probably a fisherman and probably works out of Padstow, that would establish the link with the Sparks family.

The smile had gone by now, Mike was staring in front of him, his mouth set. Handsome sort of fellow, Reynolds grudgingly admitted; looks typically West Country but by temperament is Mediterranean, mercurial to say the least. Moody. I'd better remember that. Still as good a way as any to kill two birds with one stone . . . if one pardoned the expression. He settled back and waited for the chance to begin.

When they reached the open road Mike speeded up, passing several cars in quick succession before another bend. Not the best of places for a traffic queue, Reynolds thought, as the younger man impatiently accelerated or braked and swore at the cars in front of him, and the windscreen wipers worked furiously at the lashing rain, blurring the view ahead. In spite of the seat belt, he himself was thrown forward, thrown back, jarring his shoulder mercilessly. He resisted the temptation to suggest they slowed down.

'What were you doing in Padstow?' The question shot out as once more the car hurtled forward. 'Talking to old Jeb there, he'll tell a yarn or two. Old village gossip.'

They swung wide round a corner. 'So don't be believing all he says. What were you asking him about, the Sparkses perhaps? Poking about again?'

Reynolds wasn't used to being questioned. Once more he resisted a temptation, this time to say, 'That's my business.' Either Anna's boyfriend was good at guessing, or had in fact been following Reynolds and had found out from the old man what they had been discussing. Neither mattered now, what mattered was salvaging something if he could. He said in his deceptively mild way, 'You know the Sparks family well I suppose. From their living in Padstow.'

'Never knew them then. I'm a Newlyn man.' Just as I thought, Reynolds told himself, his smugness at being right quickly obliterated as they overtook another car on a hill and swung back in the nick of time before an approaching lorry thundered down at them.

Then, without seemingly turning a hair, Mike added, 'And it's Anna I'm interested in. The rest can go to hell.'

'Since you seem so intent on sending us both there,' Reynolds countered, summoning up a smile, 'I'd like at least to know your full name. You know mine, I think.'

The driver gave another of his shark-like grins. 'A real joker,' he said. 'Anna said you were. Just call me Mike. And I warn you, if you're hanging around Anna there'll be trouble. Anna's my girl.'

Reynolds was torn between laughing and shouting 'Watch out' as the car veered widely around another bend. Whatever make it was it certainly had power. He looked curiously at the name on the dashboard. A hotted-up engine, he thought, I bet this car's got plenty in reserve. A thought struck him. He was suddenly in a narrow lane and a car was bearing down on him while its driver laughed – a dark-coloured car with a hotted-up engine . . .

A third time biting down the temptation to ask a leading question he said, 'You've heard about Mrs Sparks, I suppose.'

'What about her? Don't tell me the old bitch's fallen down another hole?'

'You don't like Mrs Sparks?' Reynolds was curious.

'Like isn't the word I'd use.' Mike was sharp. 'If you'd seen the way she treated Anna you wouldn't like her either. Miserable old sod. Ruined one marriage and won't allow another. And Anna, like a loony, just tags along doing what she's told. For an educated woman she's got no brains.'

If you speak like that about her to her face, Reynolds

thought, no wonder she won't marry you. He said, 'Mrs Sparks doesn't approve of you?'

'Not likely.' Mike accelerated hard. 'Not a fisherman for her daughter, although she was a fisherman's wife herself. But it's me she doesn't approve of mostly, me, myself, alone. I could be anyone, even an ex-inspector, I'd get the shove.'

He suddenly turned to face Reynolds, still driving fast. 'But if you've any ideas about making headway,' he said, scowling, 'I won't warn you again, there'll be trouble. And the same if I find you hanging round her house. Back off.'

Reynolds had had enough of threats. There was something about hearing the same expression that Derrymore had used that got his dander up. Resisting retorting, 'What gives you the right to threaten me? It's Anna's choice' (a thought that so surprised him that he blocked it down as both inappropriate and revealing), he said abruptly, 'Mrs Sparks is dead.'

He watched closely as Mike swung the car round a series of curves, but there was no change of expression, just a flicker of a ferocious scowl. 'Good job,' Mike was saying when Reynolds added, 'Murdered, in her bed.' Then the brakes slammed on so hard that the car came almost to a halt.

'Murdered,' Mike repeated, his dark eyes starting. If he's acting, he's doing a good job, Reynolds thought – an observation which was immediately cancelled out by Mike's next remark: 'You mean someone's rubbed the old bitch out at last. Well, she's had it coming to her. Other people beside me hated her enough.'

Convicted out of his own mouth, Reynolds thought. If I were still in the Force I would be warning him to watch what he said. And even if I'm not, he still should be warned he can't go round saying things like that. He said, his tone professional, 'It is a murder investigation, you know.'

'What the hell do you mean by that?' Mike's voice rose. 'Are you threatening me? Or are you telling me, ex-Inspector, that you're on an official visit here, making inquiries, I think it's called. Because if you are you can sod off fast. You've no call to question me.'

'Only if,' Reynolds said, 'you didn't happen to be in a country lane on the cliff top yesterday and ran me down in a fast car.'

It was a random shot; one he didn't mean to make until it came out. It electrified Mike. He gave another of his lowering looks and without a word rammed his foot down on the accelerator. Wincing as his shoulder hit the back of the seat, Reynolds was forced to watch as the car spun dangerously close to the hedge, rocketing back and forth from one side of the road to the other. Meanwhile through clenched teeth the driver was muttering, what exactly? Reynolds couldn't hear and wasn't exactly trying to. He was thinking the fool'll really kill us both and then, by God, how am I to stop him?

It wasn't the best of times to try reason, especially when with a savage curse Mike swung the wheel over hard, skidding off what was classified at least on a map as a 'main' road onto what was only too apparently a secondary one. They jolted over its narrow, rutted surface, the wheels bouncing, the engine revving. Smoke poured from the exhaust pipe. Out of the frying pan into the fire, Reynolds thought, avoid a head-on collision there, only to turn a somersault here. He was even less happy to hear Mike shout, 'Take me for a fool do you, see how you'll take this.'

Until then Reynolds hadn't regarded Mike's threats too seriously. Now he began to think he should. The road they had turned onto was one he didn't know. But it must lead towards the coast, never far away in this part of Cornwall, a lonely stretch of headland with a wild and rocky beach. For the first time too he noticed how the drops of rain still splattered on the windscreen. Not the place, he thought, for a temporarily one-armed man to be brought to against his wish, especially if the driver has already tried to run him down before.

He snatched a fast look around. The road was typically narrow, with the usual high hedges on either side, cut occasionally by gateways leading to fields. Soon the track would open out onto the headland proper, with its stretch of heather and gorse moors, and its high cliffs. Not much chance of anyone else being there now, no late hikers or beachers, not with the rain coming down hard and the wind getting up. He thought, with a sense of déjà vu, there's not much time.

Upon the thought came action. He braced himself, lurched with his sound shoulder against the steering wheel, at the same time bringing his head up hard against the driver's chin. There was a shout, cut short, a squeal of brakes. Momentarily out of control, the car slewed at an angle across the road, its front wheels hitting the hedge where jagged stones protruded from thick grass.

The car teetered; for a moment he thought it would turn over. Then it straightened, rocking gently on its wheels. There was no sound, and no obvious damage, at most a bent radiator or a burst tyre. As for himself, although his head buzzed and he was shaken, he was still in one piece.

Mike, however, hadn't fared so well. Blood was trickling

from a slight head cut and he was obviously dazed. Thank God, Reynolds thought, in no condition to make more trouble.

Checking that the cut, though bloody, wasn't serious, and that Mike, if not exactly unconscious, wasn't about to go far for a while, Reynolds eased himself out of the passenger side. Fortunately he could still open the door; the driver's side was blocked against the hedge.

By now the rain was really blinding, cutting visibility to yards, and within seconds he was soaked. Remembering yesterday's experience and not wanting to be caught again in a narrow lane, more than content to let the déjà vu relate to the ambience, not the event, Reynolds got away from the car as fast as possible, searching for the first gateway he could find. And, having found it, he opened the gate and at a slower trot started off across the field, heading obliquely towards the main road they'd left moments before.

It was heavy going through long grass. In patches where it had thinned water ran off the hard ground like a sluice. An adjoining cornfield, where he was caught in mud ankle thick, slowed him down more than he liked, but by then he was fairly sure he hadn't been followed. Angry now, at himself as much as at the whole incident, he cursed his own stupidity. But then, he tried to comfort himself, without taking risks sometimes you can't get anywhere. And where had he got to? Not far, he thought, as he negotiated a stone stile with difficulty, except that one of his suspects certainly had reason to hate Mrs Sparks – and had no inhibitions about admitting it. And who, by the by, might or might not have been the driver of the car that had run him down!

Working these things out kept him going until he came to

the edge of a third field, where a final hedge separated him from the main road and brought him to a standstill. Getting through the hedge wearing a sling proved as difficult as getting through with a dislocated shoulder, but he persevered, arriving on the road side with torn and muddy clothes, a throbbing arm and enough new scratches to make him look like a real vagabond.

The rain surprisingly had eased once more. He walked sedately along the verge to the next roadside garage, fortunately not far off. There he paused to make the phone call he should have made in Padstow. While waiting for the taxi to arrive, a slow business, he settled his conscience by dialling the nearest police station (not the one in St Breddaford) to report an accident, giving the location of the lane as best he could and the details of the car and so on, but not his name nor the name of the driver.

That was why Reynolds' house was empty when Derrymore rang the bell, and that was where Reynolds was, sitting by the road waiting for a taxi home.

As for Mike, when he finally pulled his wits together he didn't stop to be rescued by the police. Swearing mightily, he tried to wipe his face clean, in between restarting the engine and by alternately gunning and cutting it, rocking the car down from the bank. Not even bothering to inspect the damage, just glad that it didn't prevent his driving away, he reversed into the same gateway Reynolds had used and speeded back to the turn-off.

In spite of the knock to his head his thoughts were very clear, and very unpleasant. No one made him look a fool and got away with it. Even less make him look a fool in front of

Anna, as Reynolds was sure to do if given the chance.

Revenge was certainly in his mind as he came to the main road and hurtled along it. Only when he saw a phone box himself did he come to a screeching halt and, dabbing at his forehead, make a call.

Chapter 8

On that wet evening someone else was also worried. Isolda Tenery had discovered Reynolds' absence by the simple expedient of ringing his number every half hour or so, expecting to find him in and increasingly concerned when he didn't answer. The technical reason for her frequent calls was superficial, details concerning the typing – should certain passages be italicized, should certain headings be in capitals – none important, all invented on the spur of the moment. It was only her imagination that had built them into a major crisis.

Actually she was hurt. Twice now she had offered her personal help and twice been rejected. 'It's not as if he's a domestic man,' she confided to Janet Seward, another spinster lady who lived in St Breddaford and with whom she had developed a friendship, mainly because they were the same age and in the same (to her eyes) unfortunate single condition. A dialogue ensued in which both ladies laughed over Reynolds' culinary disasters, followed by more graphic examples of masculine ineptitude, an exercise which took some time but which did not in the end allay Isolda's fears.

'I made him soup,' Isolda said, reverting to her first complaint. 'You know the sort I always make, Jan, although of course there were no fresh veggies in the larder and he never uses the fridge. I had to take time off from work to buy something from the village shop.'

Here she had a moment's qualm. 'I don't mean he's stingy,' she hastened to explain. 'If I'd asked him for the money he'd pay up. But he doesn't think.'

'Men never do.' Janet Seward, speaking presumably from long experience, was firm. 'You can throw that idea away with your five pounds. But he might have said thank you. I don't like bad manners, and that's a fact.'

'Oh, he has beautiful manners, usually.' Isolda Tenery wanted no smear to tarnish her employer's reputation. 'But he wasn't himself. I could tell that straight away. He had a strained look about his eyes and a strained note to his voice. My heart went out to him.'

'Probably glad to get to bed. Or hit the bottle.' Again Miss Seward was firm. 'Wasn't there talk one time of his being on the booze?'

'Not that I've heard of.' Isolda, if nothing else, was discreet. 'But that's not the point. He certainly was under the weather last night and again this morning. He didn't want me to come in, although it's my usual day, just told me to get on with what I've still on hand. And I can't do that unless I talk it over with him.'

Once more she rehearsed the reasons for her phone calls. Added to which, Mr Reynolds wasn't one to be out at all hours, certainly not this late, look at the rain still lashing down. 'Something must have happened to him,' she cried. 'And there's no one else to . . . .'

She didn't like to finish the sentence. 'No one else to care,

122

except me.' Although true, she felt it sounded presumptuous.

'Oh, Issy, you worry too much.' Miss Seward, thwarted yesterday of a night out, was seeing this evening's promised get-together retreating. Her voice grew snappish. 'You're just exaggerating things, as usual. He'll be back soon enough.'

She snorted down the telephone. 'Let him get on with it,' was her final advice. 'He'll manage.'

'Without you,' she meant, and Isolda knew it, just as she knew Janet Seward was being spiteful, the use of 'Issy' was always a give-away. Jan could be so jealous sometimes, she thought, but then, she probably didn't mean to be. It was only Isolda's own sensitive nature that made her too aware of her friend's little failings.

And Isolda was sensitive. It was her heaviest cross, her sensitivity. Sometimes she even wondered if it were her name that made her different, as if by christening her Isolda, with its literary Celtic connotations, her parents had also endowed her at birth with all the trappings and burdens of legend. But Isolda was also practical. Somewhere she'd read the way to a man's heart was through his stomach and, although that was not an idea to confide to Janet Seward, at least it gave direction to her romantic yearnings. Going into her kitchen – painted buttercup yellow – she began to rattle determinedly among the saucepans.

When she had finished her preparations it was growing dark and the heavy rain had eased once more. Past ten o'clock and still no answer from Old Forge Cottage. No one had shown up there yet as far as she knew. Where could he have got to? She paced the floor of her tiny living room, stopping at every other step to arrange a book or straighten an already straight picture. She couldn't abide untidiness. As she walked, such tiny steps they really couldn't be likened to pacing, her thoughts went round in circles.

Suppose he's had a relapse, lying there in bed too ill to answer. Or suppose he's fallen down the stairs, slipped on a carpet, fainted from lack of food. All sorts of possibilities fed her imagination. She could stand the suspense no longer.

It was close to half-past ten, when, carrying a newly made bowl of soup, carefully covered, she came out of her house and locked the door. The surface of the lane was slick with wet and puddles had collected between the paving stones, but in anticipation of Reynolds' either being at home or returning while she was there she had put on her good shoes, not her wellies. She kept therefore to the side of the road where there was a grass edge, trotting along slowly and carefully so as not to spill the soup, nor get her shoes too muddy.

She was wearing a fawn mackintosh, the hood pulled well down over her face, but had tied a silk scarf under the hood, to be draped with becoming nonchalance round her shoulders when she took the raincoat off. She had a momentary vision of John Reynolds' opening the door and saying, 'Why, Isolda, my dear, how thoughtful.'

His eyes would flash – beautiful eyes he had, you could read his soul in them. And then he'd open the door wider and say, 'Do come in and share a bite with me.' Just as they might in the sort of films she liked, the old black and white films, with the old film stars who were ever so handsome and polite, and never let their lady friends down.

Lost thus in romantic yearning, she traversed the short distance between her house and Reynolds' in a golden mist, her own role a mixture of Florence Nightingale and Bette Davis. The soup, steaming gently in her mother's best Wedgwood bowl, was the ultimate excuse – and she had a key.

For her to use on 'her' days – the days she came to type in Reynolds' house or to collect pieces to be worked on at home – he'd given her a key to the front door, in case he was too engrossed to answer her knock, or in case he was absent – an increasingly frequent occurrence, she had noticed, over the past few months. (It was annoying, she had told Jan. 'He ought to be there to discuss things with me first. I can't type what's not written in.')

She didn't tell many people about the key, and she didn't tell Jan. She knew too well what Jan would say, or rather not say but suggest by the raising of her thin plucked eyebrows. It seemed somehow 'not nice' that a single lady should have a key to a gentleman's residence, even for business purposes. And in ordinary circumstances nothing would have prompted her to take advantage of what she saw as a 'trust'. ('I'd rather die than misuse it,' was her own way of putting it, a compliment to her fine-tuned fastidiousness.) But today, or rather tonight, she felt completely justified. The situation was extraordinary, one she was beginning to label 'life or death'. I'll just pop my head round the front door, she was thinking, and call out. Then if there's no answer I'll leave this in the kitchen with a note. But if he's there, I'll . . .

What she would have done was never finished. She opened the garden gate and smelled the scent of the roses, fresher than ever because of the rain. Something reared out of the darkness with such unexpected suddenness she couldn't scream. There was a dull thud, a ringing silence. Then nothing.

When Reynolds arrived back himself, some moments later, the lights from the taxi picked out the crumpled figure, the spilled soup, the fallen petals, splattered red. All at his garden gate like a tableau in a murder mystery, a set piece for him to find.

Later, it seemed hours later, after the victim had been lifted into the ambulance, after Derrymore, rooted out of bed, had made copious notes and the official photographer had taken all the pictures that he needed, after the village, roused by the noise and lights, had come streaming out to watch, Reynolds stood up wearily from where he'd been crouching by Miss Tenery's side. Now he watched the ambulance back down to the square and drive off, sirens blaring. Poor soul, he thought. He caught a glimpse of the shattered dish and a feeling of guilt came over him.

She was unconscious when they put her in the ambulance, but still alive, the thick silk scarf having dulled the force of the blow. Whether she would ever recover consciousness, whether she would live or die, with all her dreams and fancies locked inside her head, was another matter. The shards of china, the spilled dregs of soup, were the only proofs of her constancy.

Reynolds had found the attack weapon near the gate, a heavy stick, blood-marked, thrown randomly in the hedge. If there had been any fingerprints the wet would have washed them off, making identification impossible. Otherwise the mud showed no foot marks except Miss Tenery's own small ones, everything else had been deliberately trampled over. Apart from the stick, there were no clues. There seemed no reason, no sense – the signs pointed to another random assault. And yet Reynolds sensed another thought, too monstrous to contemplate, forming at the back of his mind.

Making himself focus on the immediate problem, he looked at Derrymore as the constable stood in the fine slanting drizzle, his large silhouette accentuated by the lights from his car. Speaking quietly, Reynolds said, 'You'd better get the village back indoors. Warn them to lock up and not go roaming about in the dark.'

He didn't have to say, 'There's a killer on the loose.' Derrymore knew it.

'Move along now.' Derrymore's time-honoured phrase was suitably ponderous. 'Come on now, let's all go home.'

He didn't have time to add the rest of the warning. A voice from the back of the crowd broke in. 'Too fond,' it said. 'I told her there'd be trouble, but she wouldn't listen.'

Jan Seward, cloaked and booted, pushed her way towards the front. It was her moment of triumph and she relished it. 'She'd still be alive,' she cried, 'if it hadn't been for him. If you're looking for a murderer, there he is!'

Her aristocratically long fingers flapped in Reynolds' direction. For a moment he was taken aback by the virulence of the attack, and its unexpectedness. Yet there was a touch of justification in what she said – hadn't he just had a flicker of recognition of it? He opened his mouth to respond, found he couldn't say anything.

It was Derrymore who rose to the occasion. 'Now, now,' he said, paternally severe, as if he were Miss Seward's age and she half his. 'You're upset. We can't have talk like that.'

'Why not?' she cried. 'Of course I'm upset when my dearest

Issy's been attacked by that brute, outside his very gate. Look at him. Ask how he got in such a state.'

As one, heads swivelled to follow her gaze; even those in the crowd who had begun to drift away turned back. And as Reynolds' dishevelled appearance, his torn clothes, his muddy shoes, came under close observation, as his scars and bruises, both old and new, revealed themselves in a new light, he felt himself falter. He fought down the impulse to argue, to say, 'I've been out and just come back, ask the taxi driver what we found.'

The taxi driver had long disappeared. Although helpful in the beginning, ringing the police, getting blankets from the house while Reynolds stayed with the victim, he'd been let go after he'd given his evidence. And whatever Reynolds said now would carry no weight, even silence would be misconstrued.

'You see,' Janet Seward's voice rose a notch higher. 'He doesn't deny it. Deny that she worked for him day and night, like a slave. Deny that he owed her money. Deny he took advantage of her and her love for him.'

The silence that followed seemed to stretch from one end of the village to the other. There was a collective sigh, like a cold wind. Damn the woman, Reynolds thought. Suddenly he was furious. He knew enough about village life to know how rumours grew, how they spread and multiplied, how they stuck. 'No smoke without fire.' She'll ruin me, he thought, and Miss Tenery too. The prospect of their names being linked by gossip for years to come depressed him utterly.

Perhaps Derrymore knew how he felt. He grasped Miss Seward's arm. 'That'll do,' he said. 'That's wicked talk. We all know who this gentleman is . . .'

'A policeman, like you.' Miss Seward gave one of her famous snorts. 'And like you, part of a cover-up. Gang together, what's new to that.'

She leaned forward, the edges of her cloak flapping. On the war path, she wasn't about to retreat. 'But Mr Reynolds doesn't dispute it, does he? He doesn't dare. And when poor Mrs Sparks was killed, where was he then?'

She paused for effect. 'In the same hospital,' she cried. 'They say he'd even occupied the same room. And when she fell down the mine shaft he wasn't far from her house either. It practically overlooks the cliffs he was supposed to be climbing on.'

She turned to the crowd. 'Who's to say he didn't get hurt from pushing her down the shaft?' she said.

Who indeed? Reynolds thought. You ought to have my job, you old harpy. You've just solved the case beautifully, except you've got the wrong bloke.

Leaving Derrymore to handle the crowd (in a moment they'll be baying for my blood, he thought), he turned and went up the path towards his house. It couldn't have seemed less inviting, although the door stood wide open and the path was flooded with light from the hall and living room. For a second he stood looking in as a stranger, at the well-known furniture and rugs, the familiar litter of papers and books. He noticed, as if for the first time, a vase of flowers, roses, their tracery of petals dimly white, probably Miss Tenery's touch . . . He felt another pang of regret.

The incident with Miss Seward could be put aside, hysterical self-gratification he called it, but he couldn't blank out Miss

129

Tenery. He'd known of course, in a vague, disconnected sort of way, of her obsession (he supposed that was the name); at least on one level he'd known it and had attempted in an equally vague way to ignore or at least defuse it. But now her obsession had put her in the path of attempted murder – Miss Seward was right about that at least – and all for nothing, all for some imaginary dream. Once again the other thought, the submerged thought, threatened to rise to the surface. He pushed it down.

Instead he made himself concentrate on an equally unwelcome memory, as his own unhappy marriage rose up with its mocking undertones, the marriage he believed buried, along with his ex-wife's carefully calculated infidelities. Surely there must be something between the two, he thought, some middle ground between sentimentalized fixation and acrimony. And the sudden recollection of that other evening with Anna Sparks and the calm he'd felt even in her mother's tasteless house, again took him by surprise.

'We're through here, sir, nothing more to do now until there's better light.'

Derrymore, at his most formal, stood at the gate. As he turned to leave, Reynolds felt himself start forward. 'Wait,' he wanted to shout, 'for God's sake man, don't stand there like an idiot. Come in. Sit down a bit. We've a lot to talk about.' But his shoulder was on fire, and he himself was tired and wet and hungry, to say nothing of having just being accused of various crimes in a public place, among them murder itself.

The moment passed; he said nothing. Whatever he had learned from his unofficial visits to Mrs Sparks' house and to Padstow would soon be known to the police, Derrymore

130

included. If not known already. And whatever had happened between him and Mike this evening was certainly private, not for open discussion.

Nevertheless too much had happened to keep Derrymore in the dark. And Reynolds himself had been too active, too 'interfering', for Derrymore not to find out sooner or later what he'd been doing, causing another rift in their relationship. And Derrymore should be warned of Mike's anger, however private the reason; and of his attempted attack on Reynolds today and his possible attack the day before. Although to do so would be to reveal Mike's jealousy – and Reynolds' interest in Anna.

Supposed interest, he corrected himself. But the words didn't go away. He had a vivid picture of Mike and him battling for Anna's attention while the whole village watched. Ye gods, he thought, as if I'm a regular Casanova, always chasing after women. He almost blushed. Since his wife had left him his life had been monk-chaste.

But to return to Derrymore, it was more than simply a rehashing of what he had learned about this case. On another level the misunderstanding was more involved. If he felt it wasn't completely his fault, that the relationship had soured because Derrymore had taken things too personally, on the other hand he hadn't exactly played fair with Derrymore. If pressed he would be the first to admit that if one of his colleagues had stolen a march on him as he'd done Derrymore, without a moment's qualm he'd have had that man disciplined.

Reynolds missed Derrymore's companionship. And what he'd done had not been done exactly to offend his former friend. Nevertheless, no matter how ridiculous the reason, there was a gulf between them that hadn't yet been bridged.

It was pride that wouldn't let Reynolds make the first move, and probably pride kept Derrymore as quiet. If the solving of two murders and a mugging were delayed because of the obstinacy of two men, well that wasn't something either could boast about.

Resignedly he watched Derrymore drive off, probably going to the hospital, he thought. And that's where I should be, if only to make sure a guard's in place. Because if this is a random killing and the killer finds out the poor soul's still alive who knows the lengths he'll go to to ensure she doesn't speak to identify him. Wearily he got in his own car and, again managing the controls with difficulty, drove out of the gates. As he passed, the headlights picked up the police tapes, fluttering wetly against the hedge, the broken dish, the remains of Miss Tenery's soup – beef and barley he had ascertained, one of his pet hates.

At the hospital he passed Derrymore outside the Incident Room. It was buzzing more than ever, on full alert. Reynolds nodded briefly, did not stop, went on down dim-lit corridors where patients moaned uneasily or shifted in restless sleep. The police've got all the gadgets known to man, he was thinking. Computers, telephones, infra-red detectors that can see underground, you name it. We still don't have the key to the human mind, how it works, what makes it tick, what sends it spinning off course to turn it into a monster. There we're still in the Middle Ages, thrown back to the realm of theory and supposition.

The room where Miss Tenery had been put was closely guarded. It was similar to the one he'd occupied, but on a higher floor. He was relieved to see a policeman outside in the corridor and, when he went in, a policewoman in the far corner of the room. A nurse bent over the bed, from which tubes and wires protruded. Going closer, Reynolds gazed at the bandaged head; the face underneath was motionless, the eyes closed.

Turning away, he saw Derrymore in the doorway. 'Just came to see how she's getting on,' Reynolds said awkwardly, and was rewarded with details of the doctor's report, a familiar litany.

'Fractured skull, bone fragments, blood clots.' Derrymore repeated the diagnosis woodenly. 'Only time will tell.'

'Time will tell.' Such an easy thing to say, Reynolds thought, three words that will decide Miss Tenery's fate. A broken skull caused by a piece of stick, wielded with a violence that was grotesquely out of proportion to the fragility of its target.

'Meanwhile we'll be keeping watch.' Derrymore was continuing in the same wooden way, this time using the professional 'we' to exclude Reynolds, in a tone police use to satisfy the general public. 'We hope she can give some information when she comes round. She may have noticed her attacker. He may be someone she knows.'

Or someone I know, Reynolds thought. The idea that he had been suppressing shouted out to him, the underlying cause of the guilt that had been haunting him since his return home to find Miss Tenery sprawled in an ungainly heap. *Someone I know.* Suppose after all Mike had not stayed meekly in his car to be found by the police. Suppose he had managed to drive off. And suppose he had come to St Breddaford looking for his rival. It wouldn't be difficult to find where Reynolds lived, anyone in the village could have pointed out the house; or he might have already known it, if Anna had told him where it was. Suppose it was Mike, an angry, jealous Mike, lurking by the gate, and in the dark mistaking Miss Tenery for Reynolds himself.

It's not far-fetched, he told himself, no more improbable than imagining Mike was also the driver of the first car. Even Anna called him violent. And in the dark a violent man can easily make a mistake. And if there exists even a remote possibility, then Derrymore must be told.

The telling wouldn't be easy, both place and time wrong, blurted out in a hospital corridor like a confessional box. He had enough sense left to know he still should keep back some of what he'd found out about Mike and the (presumed) reason for their quarrel. Nor did he mean to mention the first car incident – as he still was without a rational motive, he felt stupid to hark back to it.

He didn't get far with his explanation. In fact his awkward opening remarks actually overlapped with Derrymore's equally awkward ones – Derrymore's to the effect that Miss Seward had done the unthinkable, toddled off home and lodged a formal complaint with the police. The Incident Room was buzzing with the news – at least I was right about the buzz, Reynolds thought.

'Under the c-c-circumstances,' Derrymore was saying, stuttering with nervousness, 'it's mad of course, but they'll have to talk with her, and you, tomorrow, so perhaps we'd better leave it until then.'

Leave me dangling he means, Reynolds thought. He didn't know whether to laugh or cry. In a way he could appreciate

Derrymore's point. 'Under the circumstances' was a polite way of saying under accusation of murder himself! A mad claim perhaps, an hysterical claim by an hysterical woman, but nevertheless, if made, one to be acted on in correct fashion, even if not treated seriously. At the same time, another side to the whole incident now occurred to him, and it wasn't funny at all. There might be people, no, he corrected himself, there *would* be people, members of the Inquiry Team, who would latch on to such suggestions eagerly, leaping at the chance to make trouble. 'No smoke without fire.' Miss Seward's lit a bigger fire than she bargained for, he thought. Suddenly his position was not only ridiculous, it became charged with all kinds of pending unpleasantness that he didn't like the sound of.

Be serious for a moment, he cautioned himself. To counter one irresponsible charge with one sounding just as irresponsible, to drag out rubbish about attacks against yourself and denunciations about another man, reduces you to a child's level, crying, 'He done it, sir, not me.' And who's to believe your version of events any more than his?

This too was a prospect that hadn't occurred to him before, that his own statements might also be challenged – a novel situation, and again one Reynolds wasn't sure how to deal with. But if he looked at the facts dispassionately, as his training had made second nature, his own allegations were equally unsubstantiated and, to hostile ears, might sound as improbable.

He had no witnesses as far as he knew to the attack in the lane; Farmer Meneer had not seen or heard the car. The fact that Reynolds had never mentioned it until now could count against him. Even Derrymore couldn't back him there. Nor did he have proof of Mike's hostile intentions tonight. It would be his word against Mike's, one man against another, where his word would count no more than the other's, perhaps less, if prejudice played a part.

Mike would certainly deny any charges, might even, with some justification, instead charge Reynolds with assault – after all Reynolds had hit him, not the other way round! If I involve him I'll be back where I started, Reynolds thought, and look damn foolish into the bargain, lucky not to be booked myself on some stupid technicality. There're plenty who'd like to see me get my come-uppance and a few hours, days even, behind bars would be a nice little bonus as far as they're concerned. No matter that there's a taxi driver, to say nothing of a garage attendant and a boatman in Padstow, or an anonymous phone call to the Wadebridge Police, any way I look at it I see more hassle. And whatever I say will put a cramp into my style.

He glanced at Derrymore. Suddenly the gap between them, the gap between professional and amateur, stretched ever wider. He bit down an impulse to shout, 'Dear God, stop fooling around. Bring Mike in for questioning. Find a match for the bones in the mine shaft. Get hold of the wretched family, round all the suspects up; force some sense out of them.'

He didn't have the right, or the power, to say anything.

Damn it, Reynolds thought later as, unable to sleep, he sat and brooded, here's a right old mess. And doesn't it feel odd to be on the wrong side of the law? And, worse, isn't it frightening to be wrongly accused, an unenviable position

136

many honest men have found themselves in, by ill intent or bad luck?

The thought was chastening. In the meanwhile, what was he to do? Nothing, that's what, labelled a bloody interloper if he tried.

Well, suppose he was so labelled, he had nothing now to lose. Not that he wanted to pit himself against the authorities, not that he wanted to add to his problems with Derrymore, but still . . . He felt the familiar rush of adrenalin.

Here we go again, he thought, with a wry grimace. Reynolds versus the rest of the world. It's been that way in the past, I can live with it if I have to. But if I'm responsible, morally if not physically, for the attack on poor Miss Tenery, the least I can do is track down her assailant. Of course, without some official standing, his efforts unfortunately would be limited, he accepted that. It would be nice to have official backing, the sort Derrymore once had provided. As things now stood, his first task was to get off early before the Inquiry Team came bustling round. The prospect of being 'interviewed' by some pompous idiot was even more humiliating than facing the village agog with Jan Seward's claims.

As for his own list of priorities, apart from Mike, there were those characters he hitherto had classified as minor: Nurse Joyce Pengelly, familiar with the Sparks family from other times; Blewett the gardener who couldn't dig; and finally the Farrs from Bristol. He made notes beside each name. Again, without official backing the problem was how to approach them. Especially the Farrs. If they were as difficult as Derrymore had intimated Reynolds himself had best tread warily.

That left only Anna Sparks, the real conundrum. But whatever the reason, whether because Mike had warned him off and he didn't take kindly to warnings, or whether because he sensed some hidden secret, or whether for some other reason, such as personal attraction, he was determined to visit her again. And damned if I can justify my motives, he thought wryly, they sound dubious even to me.

At first light then, he began to telephone, calls delicately balanced between his former position and his present one. Mike himself was soon sorted; a quick call to the Padstow harbour master established his name as Tregonning, owner of the *Dead Beats*, lying at her usual moorings. And, in answer to Reynolds' insistence, Mike's boat hadn't gone out today. Nothing unusual in that, the harbour master explained, with the prevailing wind not many smaller boats would venture out until it dropped. Hopefully Mike's recovered from yesterday, Reynolds thought, certainly it can't have been too serious if he tracked me home to St Breddaford.

To his next questions the answers were more positive. The *Dead Beats* wasn't a deep-sea trawler, was a smaller vessel, used for local fishing, crabbing and such. So there was no likelihood of Mike trying to escape by sea. And when he didn't sleep on board, which he had got in the way of doing, no one knew why, Mike Tregonning lived by himself in a small cottage down a back lane, easily accessible on foot.

Baited, Reynolds thought, with some satisfaction as he put down the phone, baited and hooked, waiting to be caught.

The next call, to the hospital, was equally successful. He asked first after Miss Tenery ('No change') and then, by a series of devious queries, elicited the information he was really after. Nurse Pengelly came off duty at six, he was told, but it was usually mid-morning before she arrived home, where presumably she stayed, to sleep. No, her pattern seldom varied, and yes, although they shouldn't, here was her address, anything for an old friend. Pocketing the address – he didn't want to catch her at the hospital, better to steer clear of the hospital and the Inquiry Team, in fact better to get away from St Breddaford as soon as possible – Reynolds made a note to check on hospital security. Giving out addresses against regulations wasn't good news.

This left two other people he wanted to talk to, and who, perforce, were now allotted to the early-morning slot. He found Anna's home address by the simple expedient of looking in the telephone book. With luck he'd catch her there before she left for work. And that was all there was to it, he told himself sternly, a professional visit. Although another kind, non-professional, was equally tempting.

As for Mr Blewett, he had no telephone himself but his daughter did. A call to her, on the pretext of wanting some work done, and a countrywoman's voice told him where 'father was at' today, up bright with the dawn was dad, wet or shine, he always started at six.

Altogether a good morning's work, or, rather, a good night's work, Reynolds thought as, after a quick wash and shave, he went out into the fresh and windy day. He had almost forgotten his injury until he got into his car, then steering out of the narrow drive made him all too vividly aware of it. Watch yourself, old man, he warned, you're still not up to wrestling with a killer, or would-be killer, if it comes to that.

He passed the white-rose hedge, the fluttering ribbons, the

flattened grass verges where the marks of last night's attack were all too obvious. If anything could strengthen his resolve to go it alone, these reminders did. And once more, like some uneasy echo, the idea of challenge came to him, some personal contest in which he was involved against his will and knowledge. Although with whom and why, he had no idea.

Chapter 9

He found Mr Blewett, or rather Mr Blewett's van, loaded untidily with shovels and rakes, parked equally untidily outside the house where he was supposedly at work. In fact Mr Blewett was still inside the van, munching ham sandwiches and drinking the first of what would be many copious cups of tea, while listening to the weather forecast on the radio.

'Sun today,' he said, chewing. 'Makes a change. But too much wind. Bad for gardens, wind.'

And for going out in boats, Reynolds thought. Just as well. Not sure I want to be in one. But if it keeps Tregonning on shore, where I can get at him, so much the better.

'I've been looking for you,' he said to the old man. 'Your daughter told me where you'd be.'

Mr Blewett grunted. He was a small man, gnarled and ancient, like some gnome, his fingers knotted with arthritis and hardened with work. When Reynolds, with a catch of shame at his own duplicity, explained he wanted some bushes transplanted, deep-rooted, difficult, 'Nothing to it,' the gardener said cheerfully. He swallowed. 'Depends, mind you, what sort they is. Some don't take kindly to moving.' A nicety Reynolds appreciated.

Speaking of bushes in general led to bushes in particular, and by various twists and turns to the leylandii in Mrs Sparks' garden. Could they have caused the cave-in?

Mr Blewett swallowed his last morsel of sandwich, shook the dregs from his mug out of the window and wiped his fingers on his ragged blue jersey. 'Not likely,' he said. 'No problem when she put them in.'

'Herself?'

'Could have done.' Mr Blewett's eyes were knowing. 'I mean one day they wasn't there, then when I comed again, they was. Stands to reason someone did. But nothing to do with I.'

As if answering the obvious question, 'Why have a gardener and do the heavy work yourself?' 'She were like that,' he went on, 'bossy. One part of the garden to be tended, the rest let grow wild, and woe betide you if you stepped over the line. Don't do this, do that, watching every move. Wouldn't put it past her to have hired someone else behind my back.'

Mrs Sparks was obviously a favourite topic. As he warmed to it, his voice, gnarled like the rest of him, grew louder. 'Drove me wild there's a fact.'

'And never a hint of a mine underneath,' Reynolds marvelled, 'never mention of it.'

'Well, I wouldn't say that.' Mr Blewett wasn't ready to let the subject drop. 'I mean stands to reason there's mines everywhere along them cliffs. She were always on about them too. "Be careful, Blewett," she used to say, "don't dig too deep." Like she was some lady born. "My name's Mr Blewett to you, Mrs Sparks," I told her once, yes I did. "And if you want a proper garden leave it to me." But there, most people can't let well enough alone, interfering I calls it.'

He gave Reynolds a half glance as if gauging Reynolds' own reaction. And when, feeling more reprehensible than ever, Reynolds muttered that he liked a man to do a good day's work and had heard nothing but praise for Mr Blewett, 'Well, that's more like it,' Mr Blewett said approvingly. 'I prefers to work for people who know what they wants and trusts me to do it right fer 'em. And with your arm laid up as 'tis, there's not much interfering coming from you anyways.'

He guffawed. 'So when do you want me to come, and where?'

Reluctantly sacrificing a hedge that he was especially fond of, Reynolds gave dates and directions, and watched the old man shoulder his tools and trudge away. Not a bad life, he thought, watching the corded trouser legs swing with typical countryman's gait, not without its own charm and reward. Better at any rate than spending your days trying to catch people out, tricking them into admission of crime.

With a slight feeling of depression, which the two pieces of information he'd gleaned didn't mitigate, he climbed back into his car and set off for his next destination, driving fast, again glad to have a car that needed so little effort on his part. Before eight o'clock he was knocking at Anna Lewis's door, still in the same slightly depressed state, and with his own feelings more divided than ever.

He'd told himself he'd come early to catch her before she went to work and had prepared an excuse for not ringing her first, as would have been rational and as he was sure she would be quick to point out. The truth was he was confronted with a dilemma, one he hadn't met before, and one that he didn't know how to resolve. Certainly he'd have given anything, or almost anything, to be here with no ulterior motive, no false pretences, simply on a visit connected with his own private feelings – except that he wasn't sure what they were. The trouble is, he thought, I don't come empty-handed. Too much debris from the past, too much memory. And then there's age; what youth can shuffle off more easily, the older we become the harder it is to change!

There was no answer to his repeated knocking. He stepped back and looked up at the bedroom window. The house was small, the end one in a row of miners' cottages, unashamedly old-fashioned, their paintwork peeling, their gardens a cross between hen-runs and second-hand car yards, the cul-de-sac they stood on backing up to the edge of the mine (now disused).

Her choice surprised him. The village was in central Cornwall, as far from either coast as possible. Strange for a fisherman's daughter, he thought, brought up in a fishing port. Then, remembering her father's death, not if it's been deliberately chosen, to cut herself off deliberately from the sea. That's something I can understand.

He banged on the door again.

The neighbour's upstairs window clattered open and a man's head stuck out. 'She'm away,' the man said. 'Went off early to her mam's house. Her that was murdered.'

He was dressed in a shirt which presumably he'd slept in and he eyed Reynolds suspiciously. 'Who shall I say was calling?' he asked.

'At this hour,' he might have added, although by now, most working men would have been long out of bed.

'A friend.'

Reynolds heard the hesitation in his own voice as he withdrew in some discomfort. He heard the window bang shut behind him, knew he was being watched behind the grubby lace curtain, knew his appearance and way of talking, even his hesitation, would make their way around the neighbourhood, along with probable, and improbable, reasons for his being there. His reputation was growing, he thought. What would Miss Seward make of him now! Getting into his car and again thanking his stars for modern technology, he drove himself back the miles he'd come, through a landscape as grey and formless as the moon.

Here the sandhills of the clay mines towered overhead, at this time of day without colour except for a faint green sheen like mildew where their sides had been dusted with grass seed, a new scheme for hiding mine waste which had the look of failure – it took decades, if not centuries, for the mines to revert to the wild moorland from which they had been dredged. At the foot of these artificial hills, spreading far into the distance, vast pools of whitish grey mirrored the mistiness of the morning, the remains of the mine pits themselves, now filled with water. Not altogether eyesores, unlike most mining regions, he thought, rather strange and unsettling.

Glad to leave the clay region behind, pleased to see how quickly he could get from the middle of the county to the north coast at this time of day before the heavy traffic started, he still drove too fast. There might yet be time to catch Anna, although if she had returned to her mother's house possibly she was not intending to go off to work at all, thus demolishing one of his 'official' excuses for his own early appearance.

He should have thought that was where she'd be – and

presumably her sister and brother-in-law with her! If so the family encounter must have been more amicable than Derrymore had envisaged and he might have the chance to sum the Farrs up as well. He was certainly curious about them and as yet had not devised an easy way to engineer a meeting – unless, he thought, with another wry smile, I disguise myself as a travelling salesman or perhaps a Jehovah's Witness and go banging on doors in their neighbourhood in Bristol.

But if Anna and her relatives had come to terms, well, he thought, I won't even have the excuse of smoothing things over for her as I did when I came between her and Mike, although acting as defending hero twice isn't exactly a role I'm comfortable with. On second thoughts, he hoped the Farrs were gone. If he played his cards right Anna might be glad to see him on her own.

As he drove in through the gate, he was agreeably pleased to find she was actually in the garden. She looked up from retying some plants. She was in old jeans and shirt, her feet bare, her hair tied in a long plait down her back. Suddenly a day that had seemed destined to drag on for ever, that had in fact not started at all but had continued from the previous nightmarish evening, began to brighten.

She made no movement towards him, just stood there as he parked, with the twine and scissors in her hands, thigh-deep in a bush of white flowers that he hadn't noticed on his first visit and might have sprung up overnight for all he knew, with all the luxuriant growth of the French Riviera. Persephone among the lilies, he thought, and was startled by the aptness of his classical allusion.

She said nothing, watching detachedly as, with the

ungainliness he felt was becoming part of him, he hoisted himself out of the car. Then she said, 'I wondered when you'd show up.'

As an opening, her remark wasn't exactly welcoming, but neither was it completely hostile. He smiled, said merely that he was glad to find her, and wasn't she scared that the ground might give way again. 'Come and see for yourself,' she said, 'like you wanted to last time. But I need my shoes.'

She picked them up from the top of her straw bag, the one she'd tripped over in the hospital, slipped them on, then led the way forward. The ground around the pit was rough, bramble- and gorse-thicketed, although a recent path had been trampled down. Mr Blewett's right about this too, Reynolds thought, as they picked their way along, this part of the property hasn't been tended at all. If there were a mine-shaft opening it might never have been noticed, or, if it had been, it would be known only to a few.

Someone, the police probably, had made an attempt to barricade the pit off. Stakes tied with red bands lined the edge and a rope had been stretched between them, like some enclosure in a fair. As Derrymore had explained, there wasn't much to see, just a large slanting hole of fresh-fallen earth. Already a pond of water from last night's rain had collected in the bottom, destroying any lasting evidence.

'They're actually speaking of a swimming pool.' Anna, who had not approached the edge but hung back, sounded disgusted. 'Shirl and Trev.'

The way she said their names made him think of a music-hall act. 'All the digging's done already, Trev said,' she added, 'nothing to it. He's an eye for a bargain, has our Trev. Even if the whole garden collapses in the meantime.

'My sister and her husband,' she explained, in case Reynolds hadn't understood. 'You've just missed them. Left half an hour ago for Bristol. But they'll be back.

'The police have already had one go at them,' she went on, with her quick, intelligent glance. 'Or rather they had a go at the police. Trev was in rare form I hear, threatening lawsuits left, right and centre. Sorry you weren't there. Perhaps it wouldn't have been that easy then for him to put on his courtroom manner. He's used to intimidating jurors.'

She put her head on one side. 'I feel you don't intimidate easily,' she said. 'Or so Mike says.'

Once more he felt the quickness of her, never losing an opportunity, always on guard, the dark side of her complex personality.

'I've had a long drive,' he said, in his mild way. 'I went looking for you at your home. Your neighbour said you were here.'

'Next door?' She sounded surprised. 'Nothing usually stirs him before noon. He's on nightshift.'

Once more she regarded him, looking him up and down. Her eyes were very green in the sunlight; they seemed to shimmer – cat's eyes, he thought.

'So what's the rush?' she said. 'Or rather' – her voice mocked him, became more 'plummy' – 'to what should I attribute the honour of this visit at this early hour?'

He didn't answer. 'Isn't that what they always say?' she went on, giving her little laugh with the hint of sarcasm. 'Don't suspects always make that joke with officers about to arrest them?'

Reynolds refused to let her needle him.

'I've not come to do any arresting,' he said. 'I've come simply to say I'm sorry. About your mother's death.'

He was not prepared for the effect his words had. Suddenly her eyes clouded and tears coursed down her cheeks. She let them fall, wiping them off with the back of her hand like a child.

'I've not been able to cry before,' she said at last, as if in apology. 'Funny isn't it? After all mother and I've been through I couldn't mourn her at all. I think I was even glad she was dead. But not dead in that fashion,' she added after a while. 'Not while she was asleep, helpless. That's vile.'

He let her talk, the words flowing as freely now as the tears – therapeutic words, he thought, healing. 'I wish she and I had been able to come to some understanding, but we never could. Even when I was a child she held me at a distance.' She added in a bemused fashion, as if only now realizing what she was saying, 'It's strange, my father and I were always close. I was so much younger, you see, and my mother never wanted a last baby in any case. When my father died, Shirley was already married, who else was left to take the brunt of her unhappiness?'

He found what she was saying sad and familiar, again revealing her vulnerability. I know, he wanted to say, I've been that route myself. Except in my case it was my mother who died when I was born and my father who took her loss out on me.

'Of course,' she added, 'I ran away too. One does, you know, if one can. Not really running, and not very far. Exeter isn't far enough. And I came back.'

As if he had asked she added, 'After my marriage. I tried to make a go of that but I was too young, it didn't work. My ex-husband bought the house where I now live and when he went off he gave it to me, it was the least he could do I suppose. He knew how I hated living here.'

She made a gesture behind her. 'Hated it. And her. I think it was only when I was able to live on my own that I realized how strong that hatred was. But sometimes habit is stronger still. By then I was so used to doing what she wanted, and she so used to belittling me, neither of us knew how to stop.'

A long silence. She's told me more than I asked for, Reynolds thought, revealed more than she should have. He'd known that happen before, often with disastrous consequences. But in her case surely it would be different. Surely she'd confided in him out of trust. Or was she constructing an elaborate smokescreen to put him off the track? Damn it, he thought, suddenly angry with himself, can't I even think like a normal human being; do I always have to see too much?

After a while she added, as if in afterthought, 'Mother didn't approve of my marrying. "You're just a baby," she used to say, "you're trying to make him something he's not." But even babies grow up fast if they want to survive.'

There was a certain sadness to her voice that he found moving. She repeated the expression, mocking herself. 'So when my husband up and left,' she said, 'I'd been warned. And really I couldn't blame him. He didn't want to be married either; he certainly didn't relish being turned into the father figure I made him. And how do you like my character analysis, Mr Reynolds? I should be the writer, not you.'

She had stopped crying, had reverted to her usual prickly self. Don't, he wanted to tell her. He wanted to put his arms

150

around her. His vision of two young people, students, scarcely more than children, playing at marriage for the wrong reasons, disturbed him more than he wanted to admit.

Hush, he wanted to say. That part is over with. It's all right.

'You must be here for some reason,' she now said. 'Not just to hear me sound off on old sorrows. What's on your mind, Inspector? What clues are you looking for?'

He didn't contradict her, or correct her use of his former title. He said, 'The hunt for clues goes on until a case is solved. And in this one there're problems which aren't going to go away.'

'What problems?'

He looked at her quickly. But she wasn't joking; her forehead had creased into a frown, she looked genuinely puzzled.

'The murder of your mother, for one,' he said more sternly. 'The skeleton in the mine shaft for another. We need to identify the remains. Your father's missing ring would help establish who it is.'

When she didn't respond, he said, 'You were looking for the ring the first time I came.'

When once more she didn't reply: 'The box you dropped was your mother's jewel case.'

He had deliberately changed questions into statements. And when she turned on him, furious, her eyes snapping, again he was torn between sadness that she had let herself be caught, and pleasure that so common a ruse had worked.

She had let the scissors and twine drop and her hands were clenched. 'I knew you'd hold it against me,' she cried, accusingly. 'All right, I was looking for the ring. But if Mike hadn't started in at me I wouldn't have brought the bloody box outside.'

Ignoring the fact that inside or outside the house was irrelevant to what he wanted, Reynolds pressed on. 'We need to know if you found the ring or not. And then we need to know about Mike.'

'What about him?'

'He may have been the man who tried to run me down the day the shaft caved in,' he said, choosing the lesser of the charges first. 'He certainly had another go at me last night.'

'Rather you had a go at him,' she said. Again she looked him up and down, appraising him, arms wrapped as if defensively against her breasts. 'Don't see much wrong with you,' she pronounced, 'not compared with what you did to him.'

It was his turn to say nothing.

'A black eye,' she went on, almost with relish. 'A real shiner. And a great gash on his forehead. I'd say if you press charges against him he's every reason for pressing counter-charges against you.'

As I anticipated, Reynolds thought. Although, funnily, if he did at least he'd furnish proof of my alibi.

'Have you seen him then?' he asked.

'No,' she said. 'I told you before, we're through. But he rang. He rang here last night, full of it. I got the general picture without difficulty. And I shouldn't blame him if he took a slug at you back. He was only offering you a lift.'

Still loyal he thought. He suppressed the urge to ask, 'And what was he going to do when he got me alone on the headland?' Instead he said, 'When did he telephone? Who took the call?'

152

'Oh,' she said airily, 'I expect Trev did. Trev always answers. He likes to be seen "in control". His words.'

Her eyes widened. 'Why ask?'

'Because when I finally did get home,' he said, with a touch of her own brand of sarcasm, 'which I did first by trudging through the rain across several ploughed fields from the cliff top where he'd tried to dump me, I found my secretary had been attacked. With a stick. Outside my gate. Left for dead.'

He let that sink in.

'If she survives she may tell us who her attacker was,' he added. 'If she dies, that'll be another murder charge. Exact time and place are important. We're talking here about more than a mere slugging match.'

She had gone very pale. 'Mike wouldn't thrash out at anyone like that,' she said. 'He'd fight clean. And it was well after ten when he rang, I'm sure of that.'

She glanced at him to see his reaction, but he gave nothing away. Ten o'clock would fit, if Mike had come to soon after Reynolds had gone off, and had managed to drive away before the police got there (that too could be checked) then made the phone call en route back to Padstow. But equally it would give him time to make a stop and still drive fast on to St Breddaford, in the opposite direction. Miss Tenery had been attacked only a few moments before Reynolds himself arrived home, just after half-past ten. To put Mike in the clear his conversation over the phone needed to be long and protracted. About to ask how long Anna had spoken to him, he heard her add ingenuously, 'Trevor talked with him more than I did. Trevor would remember. Ask him. And what do you mean,

Mike almost ran you down the day before?'

Reynolds tapped his shoulder with his good hand. 'This,' he said quietly. 'After I climbed up to the farm lane someone going too fast in a damn great car near as damn it mowed me down. Not once. Twice. Not by accident, as I first imagined. If I hadn't got through the hedge into the field, and if a farmer hadn't been working there, I'd not be here now.'

For the first time since the incident he let himself think of it – and of the face with the jeering grin. Suddenly the idea of personal threat and challenge didn't sound so ridiculous. But all he said was, 'If anyone drives like a madman, Mike does.' And again let the thought sink in.

'But Mike didn't even know you existed then,' she protested. 'He'd no reason for quarrel with you then.'

He noted the 'then' in passing, put it aside for later. 'If not Mike, someone else,' he said. 'And that still doesn't explain his behaviour last night. Mike knew who I was last night. He certainly was angry enough to threaten me in his car. I got away the only way I could.'

He said softly, 'Perhaps he didn't tell you where he was going exactly, out to the headland, and what he planned when he got there?'

Again she was silent. He pressed his advantage home. 'He could have attacked my secretary later by mistake.'

'Not Mike.' Again she protested. 'I know he's got a violent temper. I'll even admit he's jealous. But he's no killer.'

She didn't say, 'Jealous of you,' but he knew that was what she meant. Again he let it pass.

'Someone's a killer,' Reynolds said. 'Someone in St Breddaford. Someone possibly with a grudge, against your mother and father. So you ought to do all you can to help.'

'But I'm sure the body can't be my father's,' she exclaimed. 'I've told you how he died. And how can I help the police? I know nothing.' She made what he took as a helpless gesture.

'Give the police the information they want,' he said. 'Even if they don't ask for it, tell what you know and suspect yourself. Give them the jewel box. Explain what you had it out for and what you found. You must have found something.'

As she still stared at him he repeated, 'Either you found what you were looking for, or you didn't. Surely I don't have to spell out the importance of the difference.

'Look,' he said, peremptorily, 'even if you implicate others, don't let that hinder you. Persuade your family to speak freely. Your sister, your brother-in-law – get them to cooperate, send in signed affidavits of where they were, what their movements were on the date in question.'

He hesitated. 'And if you can, before you're asked, offer to help with the identification of the first body.'

Briefly he told her what she'd have to do, and what would be involved.

She listened to him intently, giving the merest of shudders only when he spoke of the body in the mine shaft. When she raised no objections he thought he had convinced her, but after a moment or so she said, 'But all this is supposition, Inspector. As if only my own family is involved. That's ridiculous. Oh, I know I'm not fond of them, I've made no secret of that. But that doesn't mean I think they're murderers.'

The other side of loyalty, he thought ruefully, the down side. He was about to tell her that when she added, as if it had just come to her, 'And I don't think you're on the right track.

Children always turn against their parents and siblings always fight with each other; that doesn't mean we want to see each other dead.'

Standing there, knee-deep in flowers, she looked at him, the morning sun turning her hair to copper, her face stern, her arms spread wide. He thought he had never seen anyone so beautiful. For a moment he was reminded of some priestess of ancient times about to issue a prophecy. Desire struck through him like a dart.

'Mike's jealousy, if you want to call it that, is between him and me,' she said. 'You're wrong again if you think it has to do with you. But even if it did, I won't be responsible for blaming him, or others. Not until I'm sure myself where blame lies. You have to believe in people, you know, you have to trust everyone's not bad.'

There's plain speaking, he thought. But I know what lack of trust can do, he wanted to answer her, I know what real hate is. Once more he said nothing.

As if she had made a personal statement, she gave a sigh. 'As for identification,' she said even more softly, 'I can't help you there. And I'll tell you why. I called him my father, and so he is to me, and always will be. But he wasn't my biological father. We share no genes, no family traits, nothing of that sort at all.'

She looked at him with her wide-eyed stare. 'And that's the real reason why my mother hated me,' she said. 'I was a mistake, you see, an error on her part, an unwanted leftover from some sordid little interlude she wanted to enjoy and not have to pay for. Because as far as she was concerned, I shouldn't have existed at all.'

Her admission shook him more than he wanted. Ye gods, he thought, appalled, it never changes – the intricacies of other people's lives, the hidden miseries. He remembered his own assessment of Mrs Sparks as a woman who had once liked men. And he remembered the old man's hand fluttering yesterday, movements he hadn't understood and yet whose meaning he had somehow sensed. It was all of a piece – a flirtatious wife who goes off the tracks; a stern God-fearing husband, who doesn't smoke or drink, who stays at home to keep his children under his eye, and who not only supports his wife but cares for her bastard child as his own.

And the child herself made to suffer for the mother's mistake. Visit sin upon the children, he thought, with a double vengeance.

Anna suddenly shook herself, as if shaking off some burden. 'That's it,' she said, with a touch of finality, 'that's done with. I don't want to talk about it any more, and to be honest, *Mr* Reynolds, you really don't have the power to make me.'

Touché, he thought ruefully. Again he said nothing.

He looked at her. A smile had formed on her face, taking away the sting from her remark. 'So I have decided to put it on one side,' she said. 'On a glorious day like this I don't want to remember the past. If all I have left is this one day, I don't want to spoil it. Just for one day I want all to begin fresh and new.'

Her unexpected words so echoed his own previous mood that he might have spoken them himself. And the glance she gave him now was purest gold, the sort of glance, Reynolds thought afterwards, that would lure any man towards forgetfulness. So coming together seemed the most natural of

157

actions, so natural he never even knew who made the first move, she towards him, or he towards her. Their hands met and he felt the stir of her breath. For a first kiss, for a man with only one functional arm, it wasn't bad. As he released her, she said, 'Well, I wondered if we'd ever get round to that, didn't you?' and smiled again as if she knew her frankness would startle him. Well, he was startled, although not perhaps for the reasons she would imagine.

She was regarding him with her quizzical look. 'You're a strange sort of fellow, you know,' she said. 'Secretive. Bottled up. But when you look at me with those eyes I'm caught, like a rabbit by a hawk.'

She smiled. 'I don't know whether you really are on duty, or whether you're here on your own quest.' That's as close to accuracy, damn it, he thought, as if I'd spelled it out. 'But if the latter, I've a suggestion to make. It's time to relax. And I've a picnic waiting.' She gestured towards the terrace. 'As soon as I finish with these flowers I'm going out. Just to walk and enjoy the view of the sea. I miss it sometimes.'

She made another gesture, followed by a grimace at the leylandii hedge. 'Come on,' she said. 'Be tempted. We don't have to go far.'

Impossible, he thought, too much to do, too much depending on me. But instead of refusing as he knew he ought, he found himself glancing at his watch. Still an hour or two before Joyce Pengelly's arrival home. After that, Padstow and Mike Tregonning. Why shouldn't he be like other people and enjoy himself – even if the possibility existed that he was being tempted deliberately.

It didn't take much to let temptation win. She went first,

the haversack hitched on her back. 'No, I'll carry it,' she told him. 'Let someone do something for you for a change.' The track they took, out of a back gate and across a field where cows munched contentedly, roughly followed the direction of the road but kept well away from it, so that, when finally they came to another gate, he found to his surprise they were standing close to Meneer Farm, whose owner had so opportunely 'rescued' him two days previously.

He paused for a moment to admire the view, the sea today green, almost emerald, white-capped. No small boats out, he noted, and the rocks aswirl with foam. Turning back, he realized how close Mrs Sparks' house actually was to the cliffs. He'd failed to appreciate that before, coming to it as he had always done by car from the opposite direction.

They skirted round the farm, continued across another field, well away from the cliff here but heading for the promontory. 'No scrambling down rocks or jumping through hedges today,' she said with another smile, mocking him. 'For one thing I'm scared of heights.'

She laughed. It was good to laugh he thought, good to tease and be teased. He'd not known much of that in the past, certainly nothing of the easy talk into which they now slipped, without stress or awkwardness. He too felt a weight begin to lift, of responsibility and distrust.

She spoke about her student days after her father's death. She spoke too of her former husband, without regret or blame. But she talked most of her early life in Padstow, the place she obviously missed and longed to go back to, but couldn't. She said nothing more about her own birth, nothing of who her real father was. He found himself wondering about that too, in

159

a small community a scandal like that would be hard to hide. And yet, perhaps not. If the family were discreet, if the God-fearing father did his duty by his wife – and if, to make amends, he protected and sheltered the child, perhaps beyond his wife's wishes.

The path was well defined, the walking level, although in the open the wind was strong, bringing with it the distinctive smell of salt and sea. Another perfect morning, he thought, as they continued in the same companionable fashion until they reached the headland, where she paused to show him the cove on its far side.

It was the same one that he had been looking for on his earlier disastrous expedition, and he almost told her so, then for some reason didn't, mainly because he too didn't want to reintroduce the past. For the same reason he didn't ask her how she knew the place; he guessed she would have found it during those student holidays, when she came reluctantly back to her mother's new house, 'and hated it', before she made that hasty and ill-advised marriage to escape.

They picked their way carefully through knotted brambles and matted grass; he hadn't realized how overgrown the path would be. Again, without hesitation, she went in front, pushing aside the worst of the brambles and holding them to let him pass. It was quiet in the valley, warm, out of the wind. Linnets flitted through the bushes. Beneath the gorse was the faint gurgle of running water. When they came out into the open he could see how the cove had been formed, the stream widening into a small lagoon, lined with rushes, against which a beach had built up. Although the breakers surged against the shingle in a continuous roar, the sound of their quiet approach sent

mallards skyward in flight, along with blackheaded gulls that
screamed and circled in frightened swirls.

'Wonderful.'

Reynolds sat down on a strip of grass at the back of the
lagoon and pulled out the binoculars he always carried. While
she poured coffee and partitioned out food he ate
absentmindedly, scanning sky and rocks. It was with a start he
realized that the meal was finished and that she, having
repacked the rucksack, had gone off to wander along the
beach. He scrambled to his feet and followed her, to apologize.
'No need,' she said.

The tide had not gone out far today, not past the headland
he'd hoped to scramble round, and waves were breaking on
the rocks, then running towards the beach. Between her and
the open sea was a sand bar where the surf sent long eddies
with a swishing sound. Freshly uncovered, glittering in the
sun, the wet sand revealed a litter of stones and shells along
its edges, lying where the waves had tossed them.

She had been collecting shells. Her hands were covered
with sand and her feet again were bare. She threw back her
head. 'You may not believe this, Inspector Reynolds,' she
said, mocking him, mocking herself, 'but I'm used to taking
care of myself. And really, I'm not easily offended.'

Again he thought he'd never seen her so beautiful, nor so
vulnerable. Once more he drew her close and felt her body
yield beneath his, warm and young and pliant. And he thought
again that this was the way attraction should be, without
calculation or restraint – natural and uninhibited.

But afterwards, as they climbed back up the path, the load
of his self-imposed inquiry began to press upon him and his

depression returned. He wasn't a schoolboy playing truant, although for a moment she had made him think he was. And he wasn't living in a dream world, he had work to do.

Perhaps she felt his change of mood. Or perhaps, even, she felt the same way. She didn't say anything until they had come through the fields and were again standing in her mother's garden, then: 'I know what we've just had, Inspector, is called an interlude. But believe me when I say I won't hold it against you if you regret it.

'Oh, don't worry,' she added with a smile before he could mutter some unintelligible gallantry. 'You don't have to explain. I understand you better than you think. You see, one of the differences between us is that Peter, my ex-husband, and I parted as friends. I told you my marriage was bound to fail,' she went on, 'but there's no residue of bitterness. We even meet sometimes. I know he wishes me well.'

The statement rang out bravely, a challenge almost. If she had actually said, 'Not like you and your former wife,' she couldn't have been more accurate. Her words caught him on the raw, he didn't want to listen, although he felt the urgency of them. He didn't want to cope with any ex-husband, any more than he wanted to cope with an ex-suitor. 'Don't rush me,' he wanted to say. But he had the feeling, he couldn't explain why, that there was more to it than the personal implication. She's telling me too much again, he thought, telling me more than she ought, revealing her innermost feelings too soon, asking me to give mine back in turn. And I can't.

Hating himself, he heard his voice stiffen, become cold and impersonal, as he said, 'It's not just that, although it's part of it. I'm a stickler for work, that's all. And there's work to be done . . . I'm sorry.'

Sorry that I didn't know you before, he wanted to say, sorry that we've met too late, when I'm already disillusioned. Sorry I'm too old for you. He had the feeling that if he did she would counter, 'No more than I've been disillusioned, and you aren't old.' He wasn't ready to face those arguments yet.

Instead he sought refuge behind his professional image, although he knew it was cowardly to do so. 'I've other calls to make,' he told her as she said goodbye, standing by the side of the car while he eased off the brake. 'I'm still a police detective at heart.'

He looked at her so she would understand his meaning, and understand his warning. My type of loyalty, he thought, my old-fashioned, probably mistaken, adherence to what used to be called 'devotion to duty', loyalty to a concept rather than to people. But there it is, for better or worse that's what I'm like. And put like that, on those terms, suddenly it didn't seem so wrong.

For a moment then he thought he'd lost her. He waited for her to turn aside, with the scarcely concealed curl of lip that would brand him as a pontificating old fuddy-duddy. When she merely looked at him with a lift of her eyebrows, and a glance that showed she'd seen through his pretext and wasn't convinced, she left him without defence.

So as he drove away it wasn't devotion to duty, or even common sense, that came to his rescue. It was a feeling of euphoria such as he hadn't known since he was a youngster and had himself finally broken away from home – an awareness that if for a brief hour or two he had been able to forget the past and let her come under his guard then perhaps there was a chance for him after all. And a hope that the latent misery which still stalked him would finally be put to rest, an end to those years of living with a faithless wife, who revelled in her affairs the more to taunt him with her faithlessness. Perhaps for once he could believe in himself and others. If so, he thought, and here he did laugh at himself, then the gods of myth are still alive and are smiling in their heaven.

Chapter 10

By early afternoon (after a quick phone call to the hospital had established that Miss Tenery was still holding her own) Reynolds found himself knocking at a second woman's door. Another Casanova performance, he thought with a grin, hope Miss Seward doesn't spot me!

On the drive he'd had a chance to put some of his own thoughts in order, or rather to relegate them to the back of his mind to await attention. Now he was in full working trim, confidence high, ready for anything.

Joyce Pengelly also lived in a row house, in a small town so nondescript it could have been anywhere in England. Built at the turn of the last century for small-town businessmen, the neighbourhood reeked of respectability – a respectability too great for him to stand hammering indefinitely. He was about to turn away when he felt rather than saw the twitch of a bedroom curtain.

He knocked again, was rewarded with the tap of feet. There was a rattle and a sepulchral voice spoke through the letter box. 'What do you want?' it said.

He'd tried to conjure up various excuses for his being there, decided on the spur of the moment that truth was best.

'To find out about Mrs Sparks,' he said.

He thought he'd scared Miss Pengelly off, but after a second wait, while he was conscious of being peeped at from a downstairs window, he heard the bolts drawn. He caught a half-glimpse through the gap of a large woman (the sort once called buxom), broad shouldered, with large hands and small feet, her hair screwed half-heartedly into a bun – more, he thought, like a Victorian nurse expected to lug patients about under one arm than a modern sister in a modern cottage hospital.

Even without the hospital's hints he'd have guessed she'd been in bed. Although she was fully dressed, her clothes had the look of being dragged on and her eyes held that dull expression of someone still half-asleep. But in case he hadn't understood her position, 'I work at night,' Nurse Pengelly reminded him petulantly, when, having looked him over, she let him in.

She didn't ask for his credentials, seemed to take for granted that he was on police business, and since she was more intent on emphasizing how off-hand other professionals, especially the law, were to working nurses, and how nurses were so often misunderstood, sometimes not even granted professional status despite their many qualifications, he let her rattle on without trying to explain who he really was.

Still grumbling about how she wasn't one of those modern women who thought they could do everything – work, drive, keep home – she led him into the sitting room. It was, by the look and feel of it, seldom used – even on this summer day there was a smell of damp and the drawn curtains added a dreary air. The chairs were stacked with what he thought at first were newspapers but which she explained were magazines

– 'freebies', she said. She hurried to clear the piles off so they could both sit down, waving him off when he tried to help.

'Don't you dare touch them,' she scolded. 'With that shoulder you shouldn't be lifting anything.'

He caught a glimpse of what he was to think of as her caring quality, a characteristic fitting her nurse's image but conflicting with the impression he'd had from Derrymore. Gossip she might be, he thought, but not a shrew.

She seated herself in one flowing movement; despite her bulk she was unexpectedly quick. 'I collect them,' she told him, pointing at the magazines. 'You'd be surprised, Inspector Reynolds, the bargains you find. All kinds of gifts, prizes, free draws, competitions. I've won all sorts.'

She spoke animatedly now, and for a moment her expression lightened. And she brightened still more when, instead of asking how she knew his name, he expressed interest in her hobby. Before he could prevent her she had pulled open a cupboard to display her winnings, a collection of cheap brass and luridly coloured pottery, together with certificates of merit and commendation dating back over several years. Among them was the token of her greatest success, the tickets, bound in imitation leather, for a free trip to Brighton, which she explained she'd never taken because she hadn't had the time.

'It was right before mum died,' she added, 'and I'd just turned to night work to spend the days with her.'

The memory flattened her enthusiasm. She pushed the contents into the cupboard and resumed her place. 'So, Inspector Reynolds,' she said, 'at least you've had the sense to come and ask me what I know, which is more than the others have done.'

167

It was the second time she'd acknowledged she knew who he was. Her repetition of his name and former title surprised him. Probably in her job it made sense. Usually he was irritated by the habit of addressing strangers continually by name, like a nervous tick, either to emphasize the importance of the new relationship or, more likely, to prompt memory.

'Oh,' she said, as if he'd asked. 'I looked you up in the hospital records myself, after you left. We often get boys who damage their shoulders falling out of trees, but seldom grown men.'

She gave a laugh, almost a giggle, covering her face with her hands. For a large woman her laughter seemed out of place, delicate, unconvincing. He wondered what else she'd heard or found out about him.

'Well, it was a coincidence, wasn't it,' she said, reverting back to his stay in hospital. 'I mean you, Inspector Reynolds, being there and her, both at the same time.'

Her constant use of his name made the omission of Mrs Sparks' all the more obvious, but not once during the following conversation did either she or Reynolds refer to Mrs Sparks as anything other than 'she' or 'her'.

'You recognized her?' he asked.

'Of course. And even before you interviewed her we'd heard about the body in the mine shaft. We all knew something was going on. We aren't daft. And after you'd gone she talked a blue streak to her daughter, how it was a big mistake, how upset she was, how much she loved her husband, that sort of twaddle. The only person she ever loved was herself.'

This made interesting if second-hand evidence. 'You think she spoke loudly deliberately, to be heard?' he asked.

Joyce Pengelly bridled. 'Well, as I came on duty later, I wasn't actually there. So I didn't eavesdrop, if that's what you mean, and I don't suppose anyone else had to creep about with their ears flapping. You've heard her voice; she could screech loud enough when she wanted. As I learnt to my cost.'

He smiled to calm her ruffled feathers. 'You knew her well, I believe?'

'I've already told your nice young man that.'

Identifying Derrymore without difficulty, and finding himself rather flattered by the use of the 'your', he smiled again at himself but didn't contradict her as she added, 'Mind you, he went on something dreadful about the window being left open. But that was her wish. And Anna, the younger girl, could be bossy too. No question whose daughter she was, or who she was speaking for where mummy's wishes were concerned. I heard she bawled you out.'

She gave the same incongruous giggle. 'Real spitfire when called upon.'

Feeling a tinge of discomfort at this mention of Anna, Reynolds asked if Joyce Pengelly had recognized Anna, or if, conversely, Anna had recognized Joyce, and was rewarded by a shake of the head and pursed-up lips.

'Never let on if she did,' Joyce pronounced. 'Not even when she was ordering me about the evening before.' She hesitated. 'I mean before her mother was killed.'

'What did you make of that?'

She regarded him with her lips still pursed. 'Proper upsetting,' she said finally. 'I mean, she appeared fast asleep when I looked in. And people in private rooms, well, stands to reason they don't like being disturbed or kept to routine like

169

ordinary patients. So I didn't see any reason to make my presence known.'

A funny sort of reaction to murder, Reynolds thought, the understatement of the year! And a funny sort of excuse, although that may be part of genuine hospital practice. He made a mental note to check. Before he could ask another question Joyce went on, almost without drawing breath, 'And there was no call to disturb her, it wasn't as if she was taking medication, or her doctor had prescribed anything extra, or even told me to keep a special eye on her. She didn't need sleeping pills and she'd made such a good recovery from her fall she might as well have gone home. Bad luck she didn't. I mean, it was only out of swank, I'd say, that she insisted on staying overnight, to show she could afford it. Bragging how well off she was. Besides' – she leaned forward confidentially – 'I really didn't want to go and look at her snoring away, not when I think how my poor mum suffered because of her. I'd just as soon she suffered a bit herself for once. She deserved what she got.'

The third person to admit hatred of Mrs Sparks, he thought, almost flaunting it. Again he was tempted to issue a warning. Normally in murder cases he'd found people more circumspect about their real feelings after the victim's death; they didn't go about setting themselves up as suspects, revelling in it. Joyce here, Mike last evening, even Anna herself today – either he was dealing with a collective naivety he hadn't met before, or unexpected cunning! The problem was at the moment he didn't know which.

'What actually happened between her and your mother?' he asked. 'What did she do?'

170

He'd already come to a conclusion about that, probably the usual story, he thought. And in the light of Anna's revelation it had occurred to him that possibly Mr Pengelly had been the lover who'd made a play for Mrs S. and given her more than she'd bargained for. If so, a disaster, and in those days, at close quarters, asking for trouble. But apparently he was wrong.

As if sensing his preoccupation Joyce Pengelly said coldly, 'You think it was sex. That's all you policemen do think about, if you aren't up to it yourselves.'

For a moment he was confused, thinking she'd read his thoughts, or guessed what he'd been 'up to' himself earlier. It was only when she continued, in the same stern voice, that he realized she was still speaking of her mother's original quarrel with Mrs Sparks.

'It wasn't sex at all,' she said. 'It was sheer meanness. The walls between her cottage and ours were thick but her voice carried, well, she meant it to. "We need it, this cottage's too small for all of us, we could buy them out." Every day, nag, nag, nag. And if we met in the street outside, the same story. What did we need a three-bedroomed place for, when she was crammed into two. Drove mum mad.'

She laughed at his expression. 'Of course we didn't own our cottage,' she said, 'we only rented it. She meant to get rid of us all the same. Mind you, this was after Shirl was married, so there was one less anyway.'

How true this story was he had no way of telling. 'And that was the only reason for the quarrel, she wanted your cottage?'

He could hear the scepticism in his voice and perhaps she could as well. Again she bridled with offence. 'There was Malcolm,' she said.

About to ask, 'Who's Malcolm,' he stopped himself in time. He could tell she'd made an error; her eyes blinked rapidly and her hands, broad and red, twitched. Besides, he half guessed before she told him. Malcolm wasn't a usual name for any Cornish boy or man. If Richard Sparks was from the north, somewhere vaguely 'up country', presumably he'd named his son for some Scottish ancestor.

'They've surely told you about him?' Joyce Pengelly was saying in a voice that had become thin and sharp. Again her eyes blinked. 'We were friends, that's all it was, friends. Or so I thought, and if anyone says different they're lying. True, he was a bit younger, well, a couple of years or so, but I thought he liked my company. We used to walk along the cliffs and talk of an evening.'

A brother, he was thinking. No one's said a word about any brother to me, not even Anna. Anna never even mentioned him. Another thing she's kept hidden. He felt a stab.

'When she went behind our back to our landlord,' Joyce was continuing. She was sounding angry now. Here comes a genuine cause of hatred, Reynolds thought, bracing himself. 'Malcolm stuck up for her. Her husband was completely under her thumb, no one expected a peep out of him. But Malcolm took us by surprise.'

Reynolds had a sudden picture of Joyce as the young girl she must have been in those days. Big-breasted, heavy, probably not attractive to boys of her own age, she would have latched on to the younger Malcolm as to a lifeline. And it might not have been all one-sided. The young Malcolm might have appreciated her caring nature, the gift that would steer her towards nursing in the first place. His betrayal – she would call it that – would have devastated her, no matter what the cause.

But whatever it was, he thought, I'm pretty certain she hasn't told the half of it. But he had no way to put pressure on her to find the whole truth; that wasn't his function. He could merely accept and listen, and try to guess the rest. Only one thing was certain. Whatever the dispute between the two families, the effects had lasted for years.

'Not that it made any difference to mum and me,' she was continuing, defiant now, proud. 'When mum said let's leave before they throw us out, I couldn't wait.'

'What about your father?' he ventured and was treated with the same defiant pride, 'Oh, father had gone, years before; we had nothing to hold us. So we left. And do you know what?'

Once more she leaned forward, eyes glittering. 'After all that scheming, she suddenly decided it wasn't what she wanted at all. Our former cottage stood empty for ages afterwards, ask anyone. She cleared off instead. We needn't have gone, all that trouble for nothing.'

She took a breath. 'So you can see, when I heard she'd been murdered, I felt justice had been done.'

Another avowal of hatred, he thought, discouraged.

'And it wasn't all bad,' she was saying. 'I went into nursing, passed exams, made a success of my life.'

He could hear the satisfaction in her voice struggling with the venom. 'I bought this house, moved mum here. I know she was comfortable before she died. As for them, well, nothing went right. First Mr Sparks was drowned, then Malcolm cleared off, then she herself up and left and so did Anna. Got married did our little Anna, even though it didn't last long, and she was back in Cornwall – disgraced, I'd say.'

Again he heard the venom – an unmarried woman's envy, he thought. Or envy for a half-sister even, who somehow had done well for herself. But married so soon after Richard Sparks' death! Although Anna had intimated she was still at college, somehow the idea of her deprived of her father's love (even if he wasn't her father) and forced to go hunting for it among callow youths who were as young made him angry. The waste, he thought, the stupidity of it.

'That's a lot to happen to one family in a short space of time,' he said.

'What they deserve.' Her reply was inflexible.

To turn Nurse Pengelly away from her gloating, he asked if she remembered dates. A third time she bridled, as if he were challenging her memory.

'To the exact day,' she said, naming it. It was February 23rd, ten years previously, when Richard Sparks had drowned, in proof of which she drew out something from underneath the stack of magazines, a newspaper cutting, yellowing with age, giving the account. It tallied with the old Padstow seaman's story. On a raw February Sunday, in a Force-nine southeasterly gale, Richard Sparks had taken his boat out and capsized. The boat had been found later, smashed on the Rumps, a headland a few miles to the northwest. A terrible tragedy, the general verdict, not the night to be out at sea, alone. As for the body, it had never been recovered!

Just as Reynolds had feared. For if there was no body, no actual body rescued from the sea, the question still was open – what had really happened to Richard Sparks?

174

He handed back the clipping, noted how she folded it carefully and stowed it away, like a judge storing an exhibit of crucial importance.

'So when did the family leave Padstow?' he asked. 'And when did you?'

'Several months later, at the end of July.' Again she was specific. 'But we'd already gone by then.'

'And the son Malcolm?' (Who supported his mother against you, he thought – a likely story!) 'When did he leave, where did he go?'

She stared at him, her doll-like eyes round. 'After his father's death?' he prompted. 'After you'd gone?'

'I don't know, or care.' Her mouth shut up tight, a warning he'd better not ask any more questions, at least about that subject. He felt the sense of frustration which had been threatening all morning, the frustration of a non-professional who can't push his questions to the limit, who has to 'back off' (the expression Derrymore's made immortal, he thought) because he has no right to ask at all.

He tried another tack. 'If you knew there were two sisters, and a brother, why didn't you say so in the beginning?'

His question was sharp, but Joyce was prepared. Her eyes suddenly blinked, registering suspicion, but her answer was bland. 'Why should I? I told you I recognized Anna and Shirl. But we were never close . . .'

Cutting her off, he explained patiently that he wasn't interested in their actual relationship, or even in her recognition of the Sparkses, it was rather the muddle in the hospital – for example, there was a question which sister was to pay the bill. And the Farrs' anger at not being informed.

'That's odd,' she interrupted him. Again he noticed her animation. 'Said they didn't know?' she repeated eagerly. 'Well, I never.'

Once more she leaned forward confidentially. 'On the night in question, the night she died,' she said, again meaning Mrs Sparks, 'she asked for a telephone to be brought to her room. That's one of the perks, if you like, that a private patient pays for, and she was right annoyed that it wasn't hooked up permanently.'

This was news. 'What time was this?' he asked.

She considered. 'After Anna Sparks left.' She was definite about that. 'Before I settled her for the night.'

'Who did she talk to?'

'Wasn't my place to listen in,' she said, reverting to primness. 'Besides, she let me know she didn't want me hanging about. I just plugged the line in and went off again, then when she'd finished took it out. But surely you can find out who she was talking to? There can't be many people she'd bother to talk to at that hour.'

And, in case he didn't understand: 'I mean, there was only one person she had pages of numbers for.'

He had already remembered Derrymore's description of Mrs Sparks' phone book, the list of addresses and numbers for one daughter as opposed to none for the other. About to ask why Joyce had kept quiet about so important a piece of information, about to say the Farrs swore they'd heard nothing, he too kept quiet. If Joyce were making this up then she was making up trouble. If not, if there were some truth to it, the Farrs would have some explaining to do. And he had another clue that no one else had!

176

Several clues, he amended, as once more he got back into his car. He listed them.

He had proof of Richard Sparks' death but also proof that there was no body found. Obviously not, if it wasn't at the bottom of the sea, where Anna said it was, but in the mine shaft whose existence Mr Blewett had hinted was common knowledge. And Trevor Farr's claim 'not to have heard' had been challenged in such a way that it became ever more imperative to know what alibis he and his wife had.

He strained to remember what Mrs Sparks had actually said when Derrymore told her about the mine shaft. She had lied repeatedly about the mine shaft; had deliberately played the naive and stupid to put them off the scent; faced with the discovery of the ring she'd come up with a story which even at the time he'd felt invented. And Anna, the loyal daughter, had tried first to shut her up and then, when that failed, created a diversion . . . Hell and blast he thought, here we go again.

As for Malcolm Sparks, as far as he knew unknown to anyone in the Incident Room, here was another family member who reportedly had 'gone off' after some row. And if he had gone after his father's death, as Joyce Pengelly claimed, what had been the actual cause of the 'falling out'? A discrepancy here, he thought, which needs more investigation. And don't I wish I had the means. For if, again according to Joyce, on a previous occasion Malcolm sided with his mother there must have been a real turn-about. And that's what's really important. As always he was struck by the subterfuges people use to hide their own motives.

But had Malcolm actually 'disappeared'? Was he in fact

another suspect, perhaps the 'rich relative' whose car was frequently seen at his mother's house? He made a note to check on Malcolm's actual whereabouts as a priority.

But how authentic most of these new clues were, how real or invented – by a gardener with a grudge, or by a former neighbour who by her own admission had a slew of reasons for dislike – was impossible as yet to tell. And equally impossible at this stage to explain how to fit them together.

Back in the Incident Room, strangely enough Derrymore was coming to a similar conclusion. The frantic activity of yesterday, accelerated by last night's attack on Miss Tenery, had dropped now to a faint continual hum. Phones still rang, voices snapped, computers clicked and throbbed, but compared with the previous twenty-four hours the noise was bearable.

He sat in the confined space that had been allotted him as a makeshift office and from time to time stirred through his mass of notes to make it appear he was busy. What he was working on was secret, no one else was to know.

Outside the large dust-streaked window the tarmac was blurred as if with heat, against which the late afternoon shadows of the copse beyond danced in the wind. He deduced from the coats and jumpers people wore that the temperature was actually lower than it seemed. Trapped against the glass, a fly buzzed. He looked at it with sympathy. If he were in his own office now, on a normal day, he'd be putting on the kettle for a cup of tea before heading home.

He wished things were normal. The quicker they returned to normality the happier he'd be; he'd had a taste of the 'fast lane' in crime, and didn't like what he'd seen. In fact the more he saw of anything, the less he liked it – and there's the truth, he thought, and be damned to otherwise.

Take today, for example. Instead of concentrating on the three incidents that had shocked St Breddaford, he had devoted most of his waking hours to defending Mr Reynolds! Either defending him or trying to find him, he amended, by phone or by actual visits to his house, none successful. Like some will-o'-the-wisp, once more the ex-inspector seemed to have vanished.

Derrymore was sure he was on some business related to the three cases now in hand. But he couldn't convince Mr Reynolds' detractors of that, hence the secrecy.

Mr Reynolds' displeasure with the police force in which he'd once worked had been no secret, but until now Derrymore himself had never heard the full details. Now rumour and counter-rumour escalated through the Incident Room as various members of the Inquiry Team gave their version of the reasons for Reynolds' early retirement. These varied from claims of drunkenness to insinuations of gross misconduct with women, both of which Derrymore would have sworn blind were false. In fact the most heinous charge he himself could come up with, and, he thought, probably the most accurate, was that Reynolds had turned down an offer of promotion to write books.

Nothing to blame Mr Reynolds for there, Derrymore thought, embarrassed by the gossip, and nothing I want to hear or be party to in the rest. Except what he had already been told at the beginning: that the man who had taken over Reynolds' job was still the number-one inspector on the Force. And for some reason, never clear, still remained Reynolds' main enemy. Hence the warnings – choose which side you're on, love me, love my dog, if you want to get ahead. Do as I say and don't ask questions. Look out for number one. It was as simple as that.

To add to the difficulties, Reynolds might have disappeared but Miss Seward, alas, had not. Derrymore's hope that her accusations of the night before would be forgotten in the more sober light of day was unfortunately not realized. Earlier than he would have thought possible she had actually appeared in person to repeat her denunciation, embellished now with even more salacious suggestions – which were so patently invented they should have had the Inquiry Team in stitches, but didn't. Old-maid imagination, Derrymore fumed, old-maid longings. But no one paid him attention.

When an official visit to Old Forge Cottage proved it was empty, there was panic until Derrymore, sensibly, pointed out that the car had also gone. For a while the likelihood that Reynolds had driven off about his own affairs was accepted, until some bumptious little chap with an eye to promotion suggested that a suspect fleeing from the law might also use a car to make good an escape, thus bringing the whole ridiculous episode to boiling point again.

Derrymore balled up his notes and threw them into the waste-paper basket. Stupid to take a mad woman's ramblings even semi-seriously; stupid to insist on following laid-down procedures so punctiliously, as, God help us, someone actually was doing at this very moment, checking the registration of cars having left the Channel ports. But, most of all, stupid of Mr Reynolds to have cleared off without a word to anyone. He

180

was up to something, Derrymore was damn sure of that. And it wasn't a shopping expedition to the local supermarket, or some visit to the local library to exchange library books! And it damn well certainly wasn't on Brittany Ferries, heading for Spain.

Retrieving the screwed-up bits of paper, Derrymore studied his notes, put together as Reynolds had first shown him. Once more he made an effort to rearrange them. If he were Mr Reynolds and was faced with the problem of someone's whereabouts, what would he do first? Start with where he was last night, that's what he'd do, and then work backwards so as to go forwards again. So, where had Mr Reynolds been last night?

All Derrymore knew was that he'd come back by taxi just after half-past ten. Begin then with the taxi driver, the one who had brought Reynolds home and with him had found Miss Tenery. When Derrymore had spoken to the man last night and again this morning he was adamant that he'd picked up Reynolds at about ten-fifteen – from a garage along the main A30 road, miles away from anywhere, certainly miles away from St Breddaford.

The phone call to order the taxi had been made some twenty minutes earlier. The time and place had been verified by the garage attendant, who also confirmed that the call had been made from the adjacent phone box – he'd actually given Reynolds the taxi rank's number, watched him go into the box and then come out.

After which, as might be expected, Reynolds had waited for the taxi he'd just summoned. He'd sat outside under an awning to keep out of the drizzle; the garage attendant had him in plain view all the time, had once invited him to come in out of the wet, an offer Reynolds had refused, saying he was wet anyway and plastered with mud. But he hadn't explained how he'd got that way, and no one in the garage had asked. And no one had asked last night. No one had much thought about it until Miss Seward pointed it out.

Derrymore was suddenly excited. That's crucial, he thought, how did he get that way? Obviously it's nothing to do with the attack on poor Miss Tenery. In any case there's no way he could have attacked Miss Tenery, then somehow got back to the garage in the time involved. Any fool could work that out, and these others in the Inquiry Team could too if they'd stop playing games.

Derrymore's forehead was wrinkling with effort. He sweated in the sun and his eyes drooped. The buzz of the trapped fly became louder. Lack of sleep was beginning to take its toll – last night he'd hardly got back home after a dreadful day before being called out again. With a start his head snapped up.

Mr Reynolds may have taken his car today, but it had been there yesterday evening when, much earlier, Derrymore had gone to speak with him and found his house empty. So if Reynolds had been picked up at a garage miles away he must have had some means of transport to reach it! A taxi back suggested a taxi out . . .

Speaking softly so that his colleagues would not hear him, Derrymore began to ring the local taxi ranks.

The second inquiry brought him to his feet. Yes, of course they knew Mr Reynolds, the well-known writer, very nice gentleman too. And yes, of course yesterday they'd been happy to drive him where he wanted, happy and pleased. With his arm in a sling it was obviously difficult for him to get his own car out.

Hurry up, Derrymore was thinking as he nodded and agreed. For God's sake get to the point. Which was, yes, they could easily tell the time and the place, they'd check if Constable Derrymore would hold on.

Within seconds, hiding his excitement under a calm exterior, Derrymore was mumbling some excuse and was on his way to Padstow.

As his old banger rumbled and puffed along he wondered what he should do next. Why Padstow? And promptly answered himself – because that's where the Sparkses had lived. Mr Reynolds must have gone there to find out about them, and possibly something about Mr Sparks' death, Derrymore'd bet his next week's wages on it. But what Mr Reynolds had found out, and why it had taken him on yet another walk across muddy fields was still not clear, although presumably the two things were somehow linked.

In a small town like Padstow, even packed with visitors, a tall, distinguished man with a military stride and one arm in a sling would be noticed by someone. If Mr Reynolds had been there yesterday, ten to one someone would know where he'd gone afterwards. And where he'd gone now.

That's what Mr Reynolds calls a hunch, Derrymore thought happily. And the rightness of his hunch, when he drove into the crowded car park and spotted Reynolds' car, almost made him forget the quarrel between them, and his continuing irritation with Mr Reynolds' going his own way without telling him why and where.

Leaving his car in a no-parking place, one of the advantages of being on official business, dodging around a large group of Americans busy taking photographs (Texans, he assumed, from their accents and fancy headgear), Derrymore hurried along the quay to ask if anyone had seen the man he was looking for. And after he'd fended off the obvious questions back ('What's he up to then? What's he been doing of?'), asked a few more pertinent questions and had a few more impertinent answers back, he'd established that yes, the man had been here yesterday. And was here again today.

'He was after finding Mike,' an old man piped up. As if everyone should know who Mike was, or where Mike was to be found. Or what part he played in a police inquiry that seemed ever more prone to deviate onto side tracks.

It was only when Derrymore heard the second name, Tregonning, that he began to put two and two together. Of course, Mike Tregonning, the man Anna Sparks had mentioned as being in her mother's house when Mr Reynolds made his unsolicited call. And a name, it seemed to Derrymore, frowning, that had been on Mr Reynolds' own lips last night in the hospital when he himself had cut the older man off from saying anything.

'And where might Tregonning be?' he asked, and was somewhat chagrined to find his quarry was so close he could almost have touched him, aboard the *Dead Beats* moored opposite, against the quay.

Head down, helmet jammed on tight to keep it on (the wind was blowing something fierce today, squalls up the estuary setting flags and riggings twirling), avoiding the mooring lines and knowing he was being watched by several inquisitive eyes, he jumped on board just as the wheelhouse door burst open.

Chapter 11

After leaving Joyce Pengelly, Reynolds had driven to Padstow. The sun was still shining in bright streaks across the estuary, but the sea was rough. The north wind however didn't appear to be hampering trippers, happily engrossed in their holiday pursuits. Only a vendor, touting a local newspaper, disturbed their calm. A description of Miss Tenery's attack dominated the front page, along with a photograph, taken several years ago (presumably Miss Seward's choice). 'More like Miami every day,' Reynolds heard one visitor say. He bought the paper, tore off the page, and stuffed it in his pocket.

The commercial part of the quay was busy. The fishing fleet was coming in and several boats were chugging up the channel while others, already made fast to the jetty, were beginning to unload crates of fish, packed with ice. These were hoisted out of the hold, swung ashore and stacked into waiting vans. Men swabbed down the decks or chatted with each other, in a hurry now to get done and be off.

Among those lending the crews a hand was the old fisherman he'd talked to before. When Reynolds asked him where the *Dead Beats* was moored he was met with a silent stare that said, plain as words, 'I'm not speaking. I've already said too much.'

Reynolds felt frustration boil. It wasn't the first time. For years he'd been an investigating officer, now he was reduced to a plain busybody! Thrusting down the impulse to justify himself, he shouted loudly, 'I'm hunting for its owner, tough, looks like a boxer.'

'Ha.' The old man sniffed. 'Knew there'd be trouble. Always trouble when Mike's about.'

He turned away again, but one of his mates, less inhibited, pointed to a small boat, new, with a gaudy sign painted on its side.

There was no sign of activity, the boat seemed deserted, but when Reynolds came up to it he heard a dog bark.

'It lives on board.'

The old man had hobbled after him, having had a change of heart, Reynolds supposed, or perhaps just curious to see what was going on. 'Bad-tempered like its master,' he said. 'Watch yerself. Tregonning told me he'd kill me if I gabbed to you again.'

They were standing close to the boat's side, which was parallel to the harbour wall. Reynolds wished the old man miles away. He didn't want to be saddled with an onlooker who would, however unwittingly, hinder him. Heaven knew he had hindrances enough already. He cursed his injured shoulder. God, he thought, how I could do with two good arms right now.

'Okay,' he said. 'Thanks.'

The dog barked again and he hesitated. The boat rocked gently at its berth. The deck was dry, the ropes were coiled, the crab pots were stacked neatly in place. Surprising, Reynolds thought, then decided not; probably in his good moments Mike made an efficient seaman.

There was a wheelhouse at the front end of the ship (the prow, he reminded himself) but its door was closed and the window panes had been darkened with what looked like blankets. Behind the door, the dog's barking increased. Mike can't be in there, Reynolds was thinking, even he couldn't stand that din, when the door banged open and Tregonning looked out.

His face was flushed and angry, his dark hair on end, the white plaster on his forehead in stark contrast with the colour of his eye, blackish blue and purple. With one hand he held the door, with the other a Rottweiler's collar. The dog barked again, tried to rush forward, was throttled back.

Blinded by the sun Mike Tregonning blinked for a moment, then focused. 'You,' he said thickly and unnecessarily, then, 'Get off my boat.'

Before Reynolds could say anything the old man leaned forward, pulling on the mooring rope. 'Isn't on it yet,' he cried, with a note of triumph, 'and don't you let that dog go or I'll have the police on you. And what've you been doing to yourself, I wonder.'

Yanking the dog backwards and kicking the door behind it Mike came full out into the sun. 'Clear off, you old bugger,' he shouted in the aggressive tone he'd used to Reynolds, 'or I'll ram you head first in your own crab pots. As for you' – he pointed at Reynolds – 'if you're here harassing me again, under pretext of the law, I'll make so much trouble you'll be sorry.'

'He's no policeman,' the old man piped up, 'he's a writer fellow. Told me so yesterday.'

'Could tell you the moon was made of cheese, you'd believe it.'

Funnily enough after this exchange Mike's rage slackened, a shadow of a grin crossed his features. 'Well,' he said to Reynolds, 'whatever you are, if you've something to say, no point in shouting it across the great divide. Step aboard. The dog's fine with friends.'

And, as Reynolds still hesitated, 'For God's sake, I'm not likely to bash you like you did me, not with old Granny Gossip here listening in. Beside my head aches fit to burst, thanks to you. Why the hell did you go for me?' he added almost plaintively. 'I didn't mean anything. And Anna swears there's nothing between you and her.'

Reynolds heard these last words, but they didn't register; he willed them not to register as he swung himself on the boat. It was just Mike's way of expressing himself, nothing more.

The boat rocked again as he moved, then steadied. The inside of the wheelhouse was dark until Mike ripped down the blankets. A small functional space was revealed, containing only a battered bench, a bait bucket stinking to high heaven, some cans of what looked like petrol and a screw of dirty rags and bits of string. Somehow it seemed familiar, as did the smell of fish and grease and oil, which Reynolds recognized at once, dredged up from God knew what childhood recollection. He felt faintly sick.

Mike sank back on the bench, where he lay with his legs up. There was no place for Reynolds to sit, so he remained standing. Meanwhile the dog had gone to lie tranquilly enough at Mike's feet, but it never took its eyes off the intruder. One gesture from its master and it'll be at my throat, Reynolds thought.

Mike moved his head, and groaned. 'Where'd you learn that trick?' he said touching the plaster gingerly. 'You a Commando or what? Keep away from me on a dark night, that's all I ask.'

'It's about a dark night I'm here.'

Reynolds moved so his back was against the door. He kept his voice smooth but his pulse raced. He said in the same even voice, 'About something that happened last night after we left each other.'

'And what in hell does that mean?'

Mike had closed his eyes, but his hand was still resting on the dog's collar; occasionally he moved it to pull on the dog's ears. 'I had enough after you'd gone,' he volunteered. 'Tottered off to bed. Should have stayed there.'

A truculence was creeping back into his voice. 'And if the wind weren't up,' he added, 'reckon you'd owe me for a lost day's work as well. Instead had to spend most of the time asleep here, ask anyone.'

He indicated the makeshift curtains. Careful, Reynolds warned himself.

Still speaking in a level tone he said, 'Well, the wind's been up all week, except for Monday. Can't blame me for that. However at the moment I'm not speaking about the weather. Did you stop to make a phone call?'

Then, as Mike's eyes snapped open and the dog, as if given some secret signal, arched its back, 'I'm not interested in who you spoke to, not yet at least.'

'Then what are you on about.'

'This,' said Reynolds.

He felt in his pocket and produced the front page he'd torn off, flipped it open to show the headline and Miss Tenery's photograph.

'Attempted murder,' he said, watching Mike and his guard dog closely, 'with a piece of wood.'

Mike began to say, 'Nothing to do with me,' when Reynolds added, 'Outside my house.

'At my very door,' he went on, 'in the dark and wet. Left for dead.'

Mike's face changed. 'You've got to be joking,' he cried. 'What would I attack an old woman for? Someone I've never seen in my life,' he continued, rallying well from his initial surprise. 'I told you I went home. All right, I did make a phone call on the way, what's that to you?'

'Nothing,' Reynolds said. 'Except if after that phone call you went on to St Breddaford. Which you told me in the beginning was where you were heading for.'

'Shouldn't have believed me.' Mike sounded sulky. 'Only said I was going your way to get you into the car. And I certainly didn't go there after you smashed it. That's something else you owe me, the damage to my car. Who's to cough up for that, I wonder? And . . .'

'You could have driven to St Breddaford and found my house,' Reynolds interrupted. 'The way you drive you had time to spare.'

When Mike didn't reply immediately: 'Time to hit her instead of me. From behind, a real coward's blow. Time to finish what you tried to start when you had me in your car.

Except you got the wrong person.'

He threw these accusations out quickly, aware that if he waited for a better opportunity he wouldn't have the chance to make them at all. The dog had pricked its ears, a low rumble was coming from the back of its throat; any moment now, at Mike's command, it would launch itself.

But Mike still hesitated. 'Christ,' he said, almost admiringly, 'you've got balls. But Anna said you had. Anna told me all about you.'

He threw back his head and laughed, although the effort made him wince. 'Anna said you had a vivid imagination for a policeman fellow. All right, imagine this. I admit she's the one I made the phone call to, asking her to join me, a little love and comfort for my injuries. Why not, she's my girl. And didn't she show she was, yesterday, and again this morning, my word, didn't she just prove it. Not to put too fine a point, mister, I spent the night with her. And there's my alibi.'

Once more Reynolds willed himself not to listen. But the words wouldn't go away. Last night, this morning, in her little mine-worker's cottage probably, then away at dawn, Mike to sleep his excesses off here; she back to her mother's house and garden – no wonder the next-door neighbour stared when I turned up, Reynolds thought. The picture of Anna standing in a bed of flowers suddenly darkened, as if a shutter had been closed. He forced the thought away.

He looked at the figure lounging there in front of him. Mike's lying, he told himself; he must be lying. A moment ago he admitted he wasn't in shape for anything, now he's boasting of a night of passion! It takes a strong man to attempt murder and then go off calmly with a girlfriend, as if nothing had happened. Mike's only trying to provoke me. The argument sounded convincing, but it didn't convince.

Mike's a handsome devil for all that, he found he was thinking, dark-haired, dark-visaged, buccaneer material. The kind of man a young woman who's had a failure of a first husband would be attracted by. But two can play his sort of game.

Speaking even more quickly, because he wasn't sure now how long he had, and because he was equally unsure how to deal with the personal implication of what he was saying, certain only that once the conversation ceased things would erupt quickly and nastily, he said, 'My interest in the Sparks family in general is purely professional. I told you before, we're talking murder here. Two murders in fact and now an attempted one. And possibly an earlier attack on me. By a speeding car in a farm lane.

'These aren't inventions, they're facts,' he continued. 'But my interest in Anna is more than professional, and if she welcomes it, that's for her to decide. And so I told her this morning when we were out together. While you were snoozing, we spent the morning profitably,' he added softly, salt into the wound. 'And if you don't believe me, ask her yourself.'

And if that doesn't bring the house down, I'm a loser anyway, he thought, with a touch of satire directed at himself, like a man who grasps a nettle tightly in the hope its sting will disappear.

He wasn't wrong. With an oath Mike jumped up and took a step towards him. Freed of restraint, the dog crouched and sprang. Reynolds ducked instinctively, using his good arm to ward it off and protect his injured shoulder; as he went down the door behind him crashed open and Derrymore came tumbling into a tangle of man and dog.

For several moments, chaos. The boat rocked violently, the deck heaved. Mike and Derrymore straddled Reynolds' prone body like two gladiators, tussling with each other, while the dog, kicked out of the way, whimpered in a corner. Then Derrymore managed to haul Mike off, half choking him in a wrestlers' grip – a furious Derrymore, his helmet gone, his tunic ripped open. Reynolds, sure his shoulder was permanently damaged, sat on the wheelhouse floor, trying unsuccessfully to ignore the pain that threatened to engulf him.

'You listen to me,' he heard Derrymore say, panting. 'Enough is enough. I'm booking you for interfering with an officer of the law, so don't give me any of your lip.'

He heard a roar of outrage from Tregonning, another scuffle. The boat rocked violently, there was a slithering sound followed by an almighty splash. He hauled himself upright and limped to the door. Derrymore and Tregonning were coming up to the surface, spluttering and gasping, while 'Granny Gossip', convulsed with laughter, was hobbling to throw them a lifeline. It didn't help that, roused by the noise, several other people in the vicinity were hurrying to the spot, joined by a stream of curious spectators, a real afternoon diversion. He leaned back and groaned. So much for discreet detection, he thought – caught red-handed before I've detected anything.

When he looked again the two men had pulled themselves up on the slipway. They stood there dripping, like a pair of drowned rats, although if anything Tregonning appeared to have had the worse of the encounter. Once more Derrymore intoned the terms of arrest while a subdued Tregonning, his cut head and black eye pitifully obvious, let himself be handcuffed and led away, presumably to Derrymore's car.

After a short interlude he heard Derrymore return, ducking his head and then standing large and awkward in the doorway, still oozing water. He heard Derrymore ask if he was all right, and his own voice, strangely numb, reply, 'Carry on, constable. You've done me a good turn.'

Derrymore hesitated. 'About the arrest . . .' he began. As if he were looking to Reynolds to make a decision.

Reynolds wasn't sure this was the best moment for Derrymore to appear, not given the situation between them. Nor, to be frank, what good could come of arresting Tregonning on a flimsy charge. He started to say, 'Knock some sense into, or out of, him,' when a thought struck him. He'd been frustrated enough by the lack of proper 'official' back-up, why not use it now it had been offered although it came gratuitously, as it were, and without Derrymore's intention or approval.

'Oh, book him,' he said. 'Squeeze any info out you can; for starters, find out what he knows about the attack on Miss Tenery. And what his movements were all week come to that. And, incidentally, what specifically he was up to last evening – before we parted company.'

He forced a grin. 'If nothing else, that'll confirm my whereabouts. And get your Incident Room off my back.'

He was somewhat mollified to hear Derrymore say stiffly, 'Don't think that's really necessary, sir,' when there was another scuffle at the door. Old Jeb, now permanently labelled 'Granny Gossip', was peering in, his sunken eyes bright with malice.

'Told you he was nasty,' the old man cackled. 'Him and his dog. But I'll tell you some'at else.'

He jerked his thumb. 'Ask where he gets the cash for that fast car of his'n. Never does much crabbing that I see. Too fond of women, up at all hours. And when he does go out, always complaining, as if it's the crabs' fault they don't swim up to the surface and shake their clippers, begging to be caught.'

He cackled again, and spat. 'Like all young 'uns these days,' he spluttered, 'wants it on a platter. Wants everything for nothing, afraid of hard work, afraid of getting his feet wet. Now we old fellows are a tougher breed. And so I told him' – he pointed at Reynolds – 'yesterday. Told him straight, I did. Not all of us are like Dick Sparks, I said, but these modern inshore men, well that's what they calls themselves, they're inshore all right, scared silly by a puff of breeze. Not one of 'em willing to stir, you mark my words, until the sea's flat as a pancake.'

There, he's done it, Reynolds thought. Let all sorts of cats out of bags, to say nothing of dogs. Probably deliberately. Most gossips are dangerous, damned out of their own mouths.

He looked at Derrymore. The constable's face had shuttered down. Soaked to the skin, his tunic smeared with green seaweed, he still looked every inch a policeman – who knew very well which of the two men before him had been interfering.

Suddenly Reynolds felt weary, dead weary. There was too much happening here for Derrymore to take in and no time to explain it all. And there was equally too much for himself to think about – and his shoulder prevented him from thinking.

Derrymore still didn't move, still stood there dripping water on the deck. He was rubbing a sodden handkerchief solemnly across his face, waiting.

197

'Tell you what,' Reynolds said at last. 'You go ahead. After you've gone I'll take care of here.'

Find out what I can, he meant, and hoped Derrymore understood. 'Then I'll trot back to St Breddaford. Can we talk? The usual place. I'll wait for you.'

He met Derrymore's gaze squarely. Derrymore would know he meant the scruffy little café in the centre of the village, where in the past they had frequently come together. And Derrymore should know it was a fair offer, a peace offering. If you'll meet me half way, he thought.

Derrymore still hesitated. 'It's about the dog,' he finally blurted out, half formally, half apologetically. 'Must have got hurt in the scuffle. I've tied it to the railing but it needs seeing to. Tregonning's going on about it dreadful. That's why I came back. Says it protects his gear better than any locks or bolts. Says there's all sorts about these days, mucking about with other people's boats.'

Here, for the first time, his face creased into a tentative grin. 'So would someone lock up for him. The key's in his jacket somewhere abouts.'

Granny Gossip, who had been straining to follow what was being said, now piped up with, 'Damn dog, I'd drown it.' A suggestion that the other two ignored.

'I'll cope with the dog and boat. I've got my car. You bring Tregonning in as trophy instead of me.'

Reynolds again smiled, and watched Derrymore leave with what he hoped was a glimmer of appreciation. But when he had seen Derrymore and his prisoner bump along the quayside in the police car, and he was left with the dog and Granny Gossip, he wasn't sure that he had made a right decision.

Especially since the old man now shrugged his shoulders as if to say, 'Your funeral.' The only bright spark left was imagining how one mad driver would enjoy an enforced ride as passenger in another mad driver's car – an image quickly suppressed.

Suddenly he had an idea. It came out of the blue, he couldn't really take the credit for thinking it up. Beckoning to the old man, who was about to shuffle off, he said, 'Tell you what. Let me know when Tregonning takes his boat out next.'

The old man looked even more suspicious. 'And how'd I do that?' he asked. He came closer. 'And what's in it fer me?'

'Nice little tenner,' Reynolds said, fishing in his wallet, 'and another when you ring me. Here's my number.' He tore off a corner of the page of newspaper, printed the number in large, careful figures, restrained himself from asking, 'You know how to use a phone?' and was satisfied to see the old man pocket both note and paper before scuttling away.

Find out what Mike's up to, he thought, before he does it. And a few hours' detention may break him, if they ask the right questions. Because, although I don't know how he's mixed up in this business, he certainly had something to do with poor Miss Tenery. If he didn't know about Mrs S.'s death until I told him, he as sure as hell did about her.

Left alone now, he had the perfect opportunity to search Mike's boat, a prospect that had been in his mind all afternoon. He wanted to make full use of it, although unfortunately his shoulder limited his ability. Each move was wrenchingly difficult at first, but gradually, as the pain subsided, he began to probe around.

He knew he had no right to make a search, and was well aware that if Mike or the Inquiry Team found out they'd throw

199

the book at him. Offering to take care of the dog had given him a genuine excuse; no one, least of all Tregonning, could blame him if, he improvised, he hunted for its food, its water, its leash. If at the same time he spotted something out of place, that couldn't be called 'searching without a warrant', it would be just good luck.

He wasn't sure exactly what he was looking for, but high on the list was Mike's clothing. Mike was dressed today in his usual fisherman's gear, but if he'd been the one to hit Miss Tenery the clothes he'd worn yesterday were bound to be stained. She'd lost a lot of blood. Tregonning might have hidden garments somewhere on the boat, if of course he hadn't chucked them overboard already.

On the open deck the dog was lying on its side. It scarcely raised its head when Reynolds finally moved out slowly. But after making a tentative attempt to shift some of the crab pots he soon gave up. He couldn't search them all, couldn't even move them with one hand, and unfortunately the dog was tied close to the engine casing, which probably had some sort of lower deck beneath it. A quick look convinced him that climbing down into the hold, with or without dog, was not feasible. Disappointed, he turned to the less obvious places in the wheelhouse, the nooks and crannies where smaller personal items could be stored in the forepeak (he clawed that name out too, from some forgotten trauma of his father's yachting days).

He found Mike's flask and the remnants of what looked like a shop-bought pasty, a couple of magazines (rock music), some tins of dog food and a tin opener (which he pocketed) and a photograph, torn, of Anna. He replaced this last item thoughtfully. Apart from these, nothing at all.

That left the dog. Opening the dog-food tin took more ingenuity than he'd expected, but eventually he managed; then, locking the wheelhouse door with the key he'd found in Tregonning's jacket, and holding the tin tentatively in front of him, he approached the animal.

The Rottweiler lay in the same position. It paid scant attention when Reynolds placed the food within easy reach. Then, with obvious difficulty, it rolled over on its back, legs in the air – a sign of submission, Reynolds thought, or a trick it's been taught.

After a moment or two the dog rolled over again. Its yellow eyes gazed at Reynolds plaintively. It wants to be petted, Reynolds thought and, good Lord, it wants me to do the petting.

Close to he could see the cut in its flank where it must have come into contact with some sharp object. The wound still ran red, would need seeing to. More gingerly than ever he made himself lean down, put his good hand out to stroke the fine short hairs, feeling the powerful muscles ripple along the back.

The dog stretched; if it had been a cat it would have purred; stiffly it rose to its feet, yawned and licked Reynolds' hand. It ignored the food but stood trembling a little as the blood seeped to the deck.

Good Lord, Reynolds thought again, somewhat taken aback, Mike said you were all right with friends, and for what it's worth that's what we've become. You and me, old fellow, in the wars together, mates.

He fumbled with the rope, untied it, and led the dog calmly off the boat. It followed him readily, limping a little. He repressed the thought again that they both looked like wounded soldiers.

He hoped that the dog's reputation would keep trespassers away, although to be honest he wondered. Bark worse than its bite, he thought, like all creatures not all bad. Still in a thoughtful mood, he returned to his car, bundled the dog into the back seat, drove off to the nearest vet's (which he found by the simple expedient of asking the first person he saw walking a dog, a dachshund on a lead).

At the vet's he left the Rottweiler to be looked after, along with the boat key, paying for an overnight stay – the least he could do, he felt. Then he drove on. What he was looking for now was a phone box and when he found it he went inside and dialled Mrs Sparks' house.

No answer. He fumbled through the phone book, found the name A. Sparks, rang that number instead.

The phone rang and rang. I seem to spend my time these days on the bloody line, he was thinking. Then he heard the receiver being lifted at the other end. A voice, Anna's voice, said, 'Who is it?'

For a moment he couldn't bring himself to reply. All the accusations, the suspicions, he wanted to hurl at her rose and choked him with their familiarity. As if he hadn't lived with accusation and suspicion all his married life, as if he hadn't had enough of lies and subterfuges to last for ever.

When his voice was under control, he said neutrally, 'I thought you ought to know Mike's been taken into custody.'

At her gasp – he didn't know whether of astonishment or dismay – he continued, 'Whether he stays there, we'll have to wait and see.'

What he wanted to shout at her was, 'And whether it's true you slept with him while conning me.'

But he couldn't ask. He couldn't put it to her straight. He didn't want to hear her lies. He was afraid of the truth.

'What do you mean, wait and see?' Anna was saying. She spoke rapidly; he could hear her breathing. 'What has happened, Inspector, what's he been accused of, what's he done?'

He said, in a voice that years of practice had honed to cold precision, 'He lost his temper. Yes, unfortunate, you could say that. As for who with, I suppose with me, except, also unfortunately, there was a police officer present.'

'Why would he do that?' He could hear the anxiety in her voice. 'What did you quarrel about?'

Again he banked down the wish to shout, 'You tell me. What do most men quarrel about? If it isn't money, it's women. So which shall it be?'

'He's nothing to do with the murders,' she was continuing, even more anxiously. 'I told you he gets mad.'

'Yes, you did,' he acknowledged gravely. 'And he's denied any part in the murder of your mother. Or your father. On the other hand, since he's also claimed no knowledge of the attack on me, or the attack on my secretary, I'm not so sure he's telling the truth. I—'

She broke in even more quickly, he could hear the tension now. 'My father's murder. So you're sure it was my father's remains in the mine shaft; you're telling me there's proof?'

He hadn't expected her to pick up on that so soon. Suddenly he was angry. 'No, you tell me,' he said. 'You want proof, you've got it, in your mother's jewel box.'

When she didn't say anything: 'You haven't shown the box

203

to anyone, although I asked you to. You haven't revealed what you found the day I caught you looking for it.'

The statements came out like bullets. 'You've withheld clues, tampered with evidence. That makes you suspect.'

He didn't know what made him push her like that, as if he really had the right to interrogate. He felt a qualm, more than a qualm, almost an affront, when she ignored him to reply gamely, challenging him in turn, 'That still doesn't implicate Mike Tregonning; he's not involved.'

When she added, 'I told you I've no call to give evidence against Mike, and I won't,' he was torn between wanting to give a satirical round of applause for her continuing devotion and begging her to come clean. For underneath the stout-heartedness he caught a whiff of fear.

He hardened himself. That's not what Mike says, he told himself. And at the moment the only evidence you could give is to verify where he was last night, what time you and he met and what time he left you. Because if he were with you then he certainly wasn't trying to murder Miss Tenery. But I'm not sure I'm ready to hear those things yet.

Beyond his personal involvement another part of him was still functioning on a business-like level. He wanted to ask her why she insisted on Mike's innocence, what lay behind her conviction. Eliminate Mike, he was thinking, and there're not many suspects left, except you yourself. Or your sister and brother-in-law.

It was then he remembered the other piece of information he wanted to question her about, the other thing she'd kept so cleverly hidden.

'What's become of your brother Malcolm?' he said, and

was instantly aware of the silence as she searched for an answer. When she did reply he was taken aback.

'He's in Australia,' she said, 'Adelaide, to be exact. In fact I have a letter from him, postmarked a fortnight or so ago.'

He heard the bitter sarcasm as she continued, 'Want me to read it aloud? I've got it here, in my bag, it'd be no trouble.'

There was a rustle. He imagined her delving into that straw bag which she kept packed with so much clutter. Before he could stop her, she started reading, domestic trivia about house and children.

'You're sure he wrote it?' he broke in. 'You've never seen him since he left England?' And why carry a letter with you, he wondered – sisters, half-sisters at that, aren't usually that sentimental – except perhaps to have it at hand if unwelcome questions are raised about his whereabouts.

'You don't fly back from Australia every weekend,' she retorted, 'and you can look at the letter yourself if you want. Real evidence for once.'

He ignored the sarcasm. A letter dated two weeks ago – but it could have been posted for Malcolm. He could have left long before, or never been there at all. And it doesn't take that long to fly back from Australia nowadays – twenty-four, or thirty-six hours, he'd have to check. But Malcolm was supposed to have left Cornwall after his father's death. If he had, he wouldn't know about the new house. Therefore he couldn't have put his father's body in the shaft. And to have arrived back now to murder his mother would have taken major management, to say nothing of major timing. Come to that, if he wanted to murder her, why wait until she was safe (presumably safe) in hospital? Why not kill her at home?

There, he'd have better opportunity, ten years of it. So much here that needs to be checked, he thought, and no hope of checking on my own. Once more the familiar frustration seized him.

He knew somehow he still wasn't seeing things in the right perspective. There was something else he hadn't grasped yet, something that lay tantalizingly out of reach. Without meaning to, he snapped, 'Are you alone? You said your sister and brother-in-law were coming back.'

When she explained they'd been delayed until the next day: 'What's their excuse this time?' he asked. 'Did they give one? Are you sure they still aren't hanging around somewhere without your knowledge?'

She said slowly, 'It sounds as if you think the murderer is one of us. Or even is after us. Which is it, Inspector? You ought to tell me which.'

She added, even more urgently, 'You owe me that.'

He said nothing. But to himself he said, 'I owe you nothing.' And it seemed to him afterwards that he might have actually spoken the words aloud, he seemed to hear their echo so loudly inside his own head.

She had begun to say something else, something about what's the matter, what's happening, asking, he supposed, what had happened to change his attitude towards her – as if she couldn't guess.

Even more coldly, he said, 'I think you haven't realized there's still a murderer at large. And your family is especially vulnerable.'

He heard her give a little laugh that was half sob, half laugh – putting a brave face to it, he thought, playing the gallant little lady. He hardened his heart as she said, 'You and my brother-in-law. He said the same thing, the other day.'

When he didn't react she added slowly, as if reciting something she'd learned by heart, 'I thought I'd explained. Remember what I said this morning? You have to trust people, you can't go through life believing everyone is bad. So you're wrong, Inspector,' she repeated, speaking quickly but firmly, 'if you think any of us, our parent's children, are involved. And you're making an even greater mistake if you imagine we would betray each other. And if you try to break that trust, you'll only cause disaster.'

She had no call to remind him, he was already remembering what she'd said before and how she'd looked when she'd said it – a prophetess he'd thought her then, and so she seemed now, warning him instead of his warning her, issuing her own type of defiance, like some classical goddess. And even as he thought this his anger was passing, to be replaced by nostalgia, sharp and sweet.

He had nothing more to say. Nor apparently did she. She put the receiver down, and for a moment he stood looking at the silent phone. Then he too hung up and walked away. It seemed to him afterwards that was one of the hardest things he'd ever done.

In her little cottage, Anna Sparks also stood looking at the phone, hoping perhaps it would ring again. When it didn't, she continued with what she had been doing before, sorting through her belongings and arranging her books in piles. Upstairs on the bed her suitcase was open. When she had finished here she would go up there and pack, and then it would be done and finished with.

She probably shouldn't be bothering with the books, but although small her library (she thought of it as that) was precious, a collection made over several years and in its way significant to someone with her taste and interests. If she didn't put it in some kind of order, no one else would.

The same went for her other belongings – the pictures and china, the clutter that she surrounded herself with – she didn't want strangers poking around her things.

Of course she had nothing of value, monetary value, but each piece had some memory or experience connected with it that made it treasured. And in that perhaps she was her mother's daughter, a collector, in a funny sort of way. Except now there really was no time to be bothering about collections or memories. The fear that she had been hiding all day swept over her in waves.

Thrusting it down, she continued with her sorting, logical and precise. That was the only way she could keep on functioning. Get through tonight she thought, tomorrow's another day.

It was warm in the little room, close. From time to time she pushed her hair back. The smell of the cream she'd put on her sunburn smelled sweet on her skin, as sweet as the lilies she'd picked in her mother's garden. It's such a pity, she thought, I could be happy here. I was happy this morning.

There was no time for regret either.

Moving quickly but deftly she began to wrap the objects in blue tissue paper, carefully stacking the pieces in a cardboard box. Funny, she thought, one's little life reduced to the size of a package, just as one's body is reduced to coffin size.

A line of scripture from her childhood rolled through her head, about bringing nothing into this world and taking nothing out. She shook herself to get rid of morbid fancy. No time either for that.

It was when she was starting on the second box that she heard the tap on the door. For a moment she froze. The tap came again, a voice said her name. Grimacing, she rose from her knees and went to answer. She opened the door, said, 'What a surprise, come in.' Even though she knew she had no way of hiding what she was doing. And no way of explaining it. Except by doing what she was most afraid of.

In their home in Bristol the Farrs too were packing. But for a different reason. They knew that when they returned to Cornwall it would be for a long stay. The idea didn't please Shirley, her mouth was set into a pout as she picked out her dresses and crammed them into bags. I left Cornwall because I didn't like it, she thought, banging the lid shut, the last thing I want is to be stuck down there again, no end in sight, just because Trev says so. Trev isn't always right.

She thought of her house here in the city, with its smart gabled front and its gravel drive and its iron gates with the carved stone lions on top of the gateposts. The lions were positioned with lifted front paws balanced on a ball – very swish! Everyone who visited mentioned them. She thought too of the cinemas, the restaurants where she liked to meet friends for lunch, the big department stores where she spent many happy hours. And she contrasted all of these things with a winter Padstow, when the mist settled for days and the cold seemed to bite into your bones and the few shops were closed at dusk and the streets were empty. Might as well be buried alive, she thought.

However for the moment she didn't mention her misgivings to Trevor, she didn't dare. She knew what he'd say. And it was true he wouldn't settle happily there either. 'I'm used to a warmer climate,' he always said whenever he went to Cornwall, as if Cornwall wasn't known as the Riviera of England, as if it wasn't warm enough to grow palm trees and such. But Trev was like that, obstinate. And 'It's the only thing to do,' he'd say if she insisted, as if that explained everything.

In the course of his many business enterprises he'd made her move many times. She should be used to moving. And once her mother's house would have seemed a palace, after what they had been used to. Not any more. After ten years of luxury, giving up all this came harder than ever. And seemed so unfair.

She pursed her lips. Her eyes narrowed. It wasn't her fault that everything had gone wrong, so why should she be made to suffer. If the worst came to the worst, she told herself, then it's everyone for himself, and the devil take the hindmost. And Trev better remember that. And with that thought to comfort her she finished her packing.

Chapter 12

Driving back towards St Breddaford was a painful business, in more senses than one, but by the time Reynolds reached it he'd recovered sufficiently to forget both physical and emotional difficulties and concentrate solely on the meeting with Derrymore.

He'd suggested they talk, but 'talk' needs translation he thought later – when he had installed himself in the café that incongruously graced (or disgraced, depending on the point of view) St Breddaford's green – how about 'explaining myself' or 'coming clean'?

And although his body craved the comfort of home (another sign of age, he thought glumly), he felt that a meeting in Old Forge Cottage would give him an unfair advantage. Neutral ground was better and the café was certainly that – seedy enough for the unbosoming he had in mind. It was too grubby to be popular with an older or more prosperous generation (who deplored its existence); in summer months, when it stayed open late, it was patronized mainly by a younger clientèle who ordered eggs and chips or pizzas of dubious origin. He pulled a wry expression.

At this time of day however it was never busy and Reynolds

had the place to himself. Telling the waitress (young, plump, what he would have called 'slatternly') that he would wait, he had time to study the artificial plants, the stained plastic table covering and the thumbmarked menu and take stock of himself. A painful experience. You're no better than the others, he berated himself, you've made a right old mess, nursing petty grievances, letting personal feelings get the better of you. For all your vaunted intuition you're still not much further forward. And you still owe Derrymore an explanation.

Derrymore – once more correctly stiff, in a dry uniform – finally appeared, muttering, 'Sorry to have butted in this afternoon.'

'Jesus,' Reynolds said, 'if you hadn't, I'd be dog meat.' He suddenly laughed. 'God,' he spluttered, 'if anyone's intruded I have. But when the ten-day wonder of Mike's arrest evaporates, it might help to have some other leads. Apart from Jan Seward's I mean. So let me tell you what I've got, if that's of use to you.'

He was laughing, but his tone was dry. There was a pause. 'Well,' said Derrymore slowly, but not without humour, 'it would help if you'd explain what you've been up to. There's a lot needs clearing up.'

He didn't say, 'To start with, fooling around with Mike Tregonning,' but he must have thought it.

'’Fess up, you mean.'

Again Reynolds felt the laughter forced out of him. But Derrymore didn't use expressions like 'explain' or 'been up to' without good reason. And his original stiffness hinted at some underlying grievance.

'Right,' Reynolds said, although he saw tricky moments

ahead. They were still the only customers. The waitress had served them their dubious-looking beefburgers and stale chips and gone to chat with the cook, by the sound of it her current boyfriend. Outside the sun shone in a sky that seemed never to have known a rain cloud, and although the windows were open the room felt airless in spite of the continuing wind. There was a smell of slightly rancid oil and, behind a partition, the sound of laughter. It was not exactly a convivial environment, yet not unpleasant either. Reynolds felt a momentary qualm. It was bad enough to be caught out in deception, but to have to answer for it . . . He shifted his position on the hard wooden seat, willing his shoulder to settle down.

'Now then,' he said. He pushed his own plate, largely untouched, to one end of the table. 'For the moment let's put hold to this afternoon – I mean why I was on Tregonning's boat. I'll come to that later. Except to say thanks for your help. I'm sorry it ended in a ducking, but rather you than me. I don't like water.' Which, for the time being, was the closest he could come to apology.

Without more preamble he told Derrymore all that he had learned in the last two days. He began with the details of his 'encounter' with the car on the cliffs the Monday morning, and his meeting with Anna and Mike Tregonning afterwards (this at least partly known to Derrymore). Next came his first visit to Padstow and his second encounter with Tregonning, followed by his return to Old Forge Cottage to find Miss Tenery's body. Today came his most recent 'interviews' with Mr Blewett and Nurse Pengelly, and their statements; finally he explained in detail his return to Padstow and his third encounter with Tregonning – all in all a considerable amount, most of it new. But he still did not mention the time spent with Anna Sparks this morning, or the real reason for his quarrel with Tregonning. Nor did he speak of his most recent conversation with Anna. He found these matters too complicated; he'd deal with them later.

'You've been busy!'

Derrymore's observation was matter of fact but terse. Reynolds was abashed. Derrymore's the last person in the world to be ironic, he thought, yet he's every right.

The recounting took considerable time. It was well into early evening when in turn Derrymore related all that he'd learned. In several instances the Team had come to similar conclusions – for example, they'd latched on to Mr Sparks' reported drowning and were already inquiring about the wrecked boat (although how they hoped to salvage it after all these years, Derrymore didn't know). They had also learned of Malcolm Sparks, but had dismissed him as being too far away to be involved. And they still had made no positive identification of the body in the mine shaft – Pathology were being slow and there were no dental records (not surprising, Reynolds thought, men of Richard Sparks' age didn't care about teeth).

At the end of this mutual exchange of information Reynolds leaned back. 'So what have we got between us? Not a lot. We know for fact that Mr Sparks was a fisherman believed drowned at sea, whose body was never found. If the remains can be identified officially, that immediately throws us back to our original third scenario.'

'You mean he's somehow been murdered and buried in the

mine shaft?' Derrymore nodded to himself. 'And presumably by someone who knew the family well. Or by some member of that family.'

'As for them, what do we have?' Reynolds continued. 'Two sisters who don't like each other; a fat cat of a lawyer who thinks he can make money out of the situation but who may not have a leg to stand on if Mrs Sparks actually telephoned him as Nurse Pengelly suspects. That's something to check out, by the by – the hospital should be able to furnish a list of out-going calls. And are there any plans to interview Farr when he returns? What about his and his wife's alibis?'

Assured that the Inquiry Team had certainly checked and double checked those, and that there was no doubt that the Farrs were where they said they'd been at the time of the second murder, that is in their home in Bristol, he wasn't surprised to hear Derrymore add, somewhat relievedly, that next time the Inquiry Team proposed to put someone 'experienced' (their expression) on to Trevor Farr. A relief to Derrymore perhaps, Reynolds thought, but nevertheless an unnecessary and insulting downgrading, which the constable, with his customary good nature, fortunately seemed not to resent.

Continuing with his own litany of ideas, Reynolds went on, 'And there's a new addition to the Sparks family, a son, Malcolm, who sloped off soon after his father's death. Said to be living in Australia. Hasn't been talked to, or seen, since, as far as I know, although Anna Sparks says she's just had a letter from him. Outside of them we're left with Mike Tregonning and his bad temper, Nurse Joyce Pengelly and her list of grievances, and Mr Blewett, gardener, who thinks that

Mrs S. and her family knew about the mine shaft from the start.'

He paused to look at Derrymore. He'd slipped Anna's name in, almost casually, although it cost him some effort. And thought he'd got away with it until Derrymore said, 'Anna Sparks' boyfriend is Tregonning. Who takes two, perhaps three cracks at you.'

He didn't ask the obvious question of why, sat fiddling with his teaspoon. Reynolds drew his breath. 'Well,' he said at last. 'I can't vouch for the first time in the farm lane, but it's my impression he certainly meant to dump me on the headland last night. Because he thought I was involved with Anna Sparks.'

It came out more easily than he had imagined. 'That couldn't have been the reason for the first attack, as obviously I hadn't met Anna then. But I'll grant that last night, and this afternoon, what prompted his actions was probably suspected and unsubstantiated jealousy.'

He looked at Derrymore – a hard, straight look. And that's as much as I'm prepared to say on that subject now, his look said; like it or not, the rest is restricted material. And if there were other things he didn't mention, such as Anna's search for her father's ring, it was because these were issues he still felt he could handle better himself, in a low-key fashion; even now he hoped to get Anna Sparks to accept responsibility for what he was more sure than ever she must know about.

To his relief Derrymore made no comment. Reynolds took another breath. 'As for the incident in the farm lane,' he added with a ghost of a twinkle, 'Tregonning's an erratic driver, as perhaps you noticed. And he drives a fast car, the only two

216

clues linking him with it. But I can vouch that he was in the neighbourhood later in the day, he and his vehicle.'

He thought for a moment. 'On the other hand, I've already considered that perhaps the driver was only having a bit of fun for the heck of it, at my expense. Or might simply have been going too fast in a narrow lane.'

He gave a rueful smile. 'In fact I'm still in two minds about what actually did happen on Monday morning, that's why I've never spoken of it. Felt a right fool, to tell the truth. And yet . . .'

Faced with the idea of mentioning that fixed grin, that aura of personal animosity, he decided to keep these observations to himself for the moment. They served no purpose as far as he could tell, and certainly weren't based on facts.

He leaned back. And there you have it, he thought, another round of explanations which may also serve as apology.

Again Derrymore said nothing.

'Now because Tregonning always denied so vehemently that he'd knocked me down,' Reynolds went on after a while, reverting back to the main topic, 'I began to have my doubts.'

He took another breath. 'It's been my experience,' he explained, 'that people react to accusations of lesser crimes mainly to turn attention from greater ones. To be honest I've racked my brains to see why mowing down a casual hiker should be considered "greater" or "lesser" than hitting a middle-aged woman on the head, and come to no logical conclusion. But I'm pretty sure Tregonning attacked Miss Tenery because of, and instead of, me. And I hoped, under pressure, someone in authority might pry that admission out of him.'

'Well, he's booked for obstruction of the law only,' Derrymore said. 'As far as I can tell he's somewhat disgruntled

217

by the charge, repents "losing his cool", his phrase, but isn't overly concerned at being accused of anything worse. We did try to squeeze him as you suggested, but nothing doing. Except of course he furnished your alibi.'

Derrymore's tone was noncommittal. Not convinced I'm on the right track, Reynolds thought, still uptight.

He said, with another smile, 'Anyway, my affairs aren't important. I'll sort them out later. What is important is getting on with the main events in hand. That is, if identification of the first body can be completed – surely you can get hold of some early records from whatever northern parts Mr Sparks originally sprang from – we should concentrate on Mrs Sparks' murder. Has it ever been ascertained for sure how the murderer gained access to her room?'

Assured that the consensus of opinion was that the window was the only means of entry and exit: 'Are there any extra details available about the runaway son? Because according to Miss Pengelly he was hand in glove with his mother.'

He repeated Joyce Pengelly's story about her courting days in Padstow. 'Not that she mightn't be lying,' he added. 'She sounds like a trouble-maker.'

'Or in other words, provides us with another red herring.' Derrymore looked at the floor. 'There seem to be a lot of red herrings in this case,' he said. 'I don't like them, and that's a fact. There's nothing holding anything together.'

'Except, for various reasons, no one liked Mrs Sparks.' It was Reynolds' turn to look down. 'Certainly several people have indicated they wouldn't mind she was dead.'

'Including her own daughter,' Derrymore said. 'And I don't mean the married daughter or her husband, for all that they're scum. They've no cause to kill her. As you've said, they were firm favourites.'

He played with his spoon again, scratching it along the plastic cloth. 'As I see it,' he said, 'according to your own description, the younger sister, Anna, never felt secure, had to fight for attention, was constantly put down – well, you saw for yourself how her mother treated her. She admits she hates her mother. So suppose one day she's had enough?'

'But suppose the other sister, Shirley, has a nervous crisis too,' Reynolds countered. 'Oh, I know she always has her own way, is the firm favourite, yet she still toadies up to her mother, still gives her everything she wants. So I ask myself, why?'

Derrymore looked at him. He explained: 'I mean why buy favouritism if you're already favourite? It doesn't make sense. To begin with it's a waste of effort, an expensive waste. And from your description of him, I don't imagine Mr Farr throws money around.'

'Something to that.' Derrymore mulled over the idea.

'Of course you've met them, I haven't, but favouritism is more complex than you'd think,' Reynolds continued, off on a pet theory. 'Mothers, or fathers for that matter, often favour one child over another. When that favouritism spills over into gross imbalance one child is loved and wanted, another is neglected, mistreated, abused. Yet it's been proved over and over again that often the favourite child feels as unloved as the unwanted one, sometimes is even more insecure.'

'Why?'

Derrymore sounded sceptical. But Derrymore, an only son, the loved only son of a sensible if doting mother, was himself sensible and well balanced. He wouldn't know, Reynolds thought, about the crippling insecurity children in a biased environment suffer; it's never happened to him.

'Perhaps the favoured child feels guilty,' he said sombrely. 'Perhaps he wants to make sense out of a senseless situation. Perhaps he's aware of the injustice and thinks it'll happen to him next. Whatever the reason, favouritism can destroy both loved and unloved children to the same extent. The courts are full of cases resulting from that basic tragedy.'

And lives can be ruined by it, he thought, and don't I know it.

'Of course there's usually a host of excuses,' he went on, 'why the unfavoured child is neglected: an unwanted pregnancy, a difficult birth, even a clash of personality, you name it. Take Anna Sparks for example.'

Again he'd slipped her name in. 'Anna is much younger than her siblings. I gather she's what could be called the result of an indiscretion, resented by her mother, accepted by her non-father and made much of.'

He looked at Derrymore. 'Anyway, if you're on the bottom you haven't anything. But if you're the one on top, and have got it all, you have all the more to lose.'

'Then that would make Shirley Farr a prime suspect.' Derrymore tapped with the spoon a third time. 'She's certainly a right old schemer in my opinion. But to go back to Anna, Anna would have everything to win if she killed her mother. Especially if you say she's illegitimate.'

He looked at Reynolds thoughtfully. 'With mother gone the struggle's over.'

'Only if she decides she doesn't want what she's been

wanting all her life,' Reynolds said. 'A worm turning with a vengeance.'

Seeing Derrymore's bemused expression he added, 'Suppose all your life you've coveted a certain house; then one day you decide if you can't have it you'll burn it down. Problem solved. But because you've destroyed it, you also can no longer have the thing you wanted.'

'What my mam would call cutting off your nose to spite your face.' Derrymore's own face lightened. 'I can't see Anna Sparks being that sort of person. But I can Shirley Farr. I'm worried about the Farrs – suppose Mr Farr does sue.'

He brought this out spontaneously. For a moment he looked worried, older. Reynolds felt the familiar sympathy.

'Not worth a moment's thought,' he said. He gave an encouraging grin. 'Just track down that phone call. He won't stand a chance.

'Not worth a moment's thought,' he repeated. 'Not much is, you know, constable, except misunderstanding between good friends.'

A third attempt at apology he thought, can't do much more than that.

When Derrymore didn't respond, perhaps not understanding the allusion, stalemate, Reynolds thought, can't go butting against a brick wall for ever. That's the end of my efforts at good will.

He stretched his legs, prepared to get up. 'Well, there it is,' he said more coldly. 'I don't promise I won't interfere again. Like it or not, I've gone so deep into this case I can't let it go even if you paid me. You'll have to take it or leave it, because that's the way I am. I can't change.'

He didn't know what to say when Derrymore's face brightened into its familiar grin. 'I know that, sir,' Derrymore said soothingly, 'so don't you think twice about it.'

Which was about as close as he'll come to apology himself, Reynolds thought. But he was wrong. For suddenly the younger man burst out as if he had been winding himself up, 'Well, there it is, never meant anything by it myself, you see. And it was all a big send-up anyway, my being on the blasted Inquiry Team. Not a thing I really cared about, like, and nothing in it for me. And I felt some bad about the consequences to you, sir, except that with you out of action and all, it didn't seem fair to pull you in.'

He had flushed furiously but his gaze too was level. With some difficulty Reynolds understood him to mean that he genuinely had been concerned for Reynolds' own well being – and that his honeymoon with the Inquiry Team was already over. 'Not that I say they aren't a capable lot,' Derrymore hastened to add. 'I mean they're solid, all in all, and I'm proud to be a member of the Force. But I don't go with not sticking together when there're difficulties, and I don't like setting man against man, if you get my drift. And I don't like nasty gossip, never did.'

Which was both an apology and in its own way a statement of loyalty.

'Anyway, I should have known better.' Back on more familiar ground, Derrymore allowed himself a grin. 'Even one-handed you'd be up to as many tricks as a barrel-load of monkeys. I said so to my mam.'

'And she said, "Up to no good."'

Reynolds was laughing in turn.

'No,' Derrymore said bluntly. 'She said you were a lonely fellow needing a good meal under your belt. So I was to bring you home one night and she'd fix you up.

'Not that you mightn't regret it,' he added. He patted his considerable girth. 'So you remember that. And now, if it's all the same to you, sir, if you feel up to it, that is,' Derrymore continued, treading more carefully now, 'you shouldn't take so many risks until your shoulder heals, but we've a campaign to plan.'

And the 'we' he meant now was not the professional one!

As if glad that explanation was over, as if relieved of embarrassment, Derrymore harked back to Tregonning. If Reynolds had no objections, and in light of Reynolds' previous observations, he'd be glad to have another go himself at finding what made Tregonning tick.

'Lost my temper with him myself,' he admitted. 'These days I'm always snapping at something. Never used to.'

That's stress, Reynolds thought. Happens to us all, old son. 'You're welcome to him,' he said aloud, 'him and his dog.'

Mention of the dog brought him up with a jerk. Damn, he thought. He explained how he'd left the Rottweiler at the vet's. Would Derrymore let Tregonning know where it was?

'Might collect it myself,' Derrymore said thoughtfully. 'Fond of dogs. They don't have to be bad-tempered you know, they're not made that way. It's usually their masters' fault. And after that, if you don't object, I'll have a chance to nose around the boat myself. Like you said, might be something in the hold.'

Since he had easy access to the hospital from the Incident Room he also offered to check Nurse Pengelly's claims about its regulations, including her strange statement about 'not disturbing private patients'. Finally he mentioned the young woman who'd heard the car start up – again he offered to track her down, along with Mr Blewett, whose story needed confirmation.

'Great.' Reynolds was pleased these leads were being given priority. 'And I'll tackle Nurse Pengelly as soon as she gets home from her stint in the hospital, probe a little deeper. And if you feel reluctant about making a search for Malcolm Sparks (Derrymore had said he didn't think he had the clout), I'll undertake it myself. But I'm not sanguine about my chances of coming up with anything – that kind of information's difficult except through official channels.'

By mutual agreement, they left the Farrs to the mercy of the Inquiry Team, who by now would have had time to think up ways of dealing with Trevor Farr, if proof of the presumed phone call didn't materialize.

'There's just one last thing,' Reynolds said as they were preparing to call an end. 'I've been wondering how to get out to the reef again.'

He didn't know why he brought the subject up. It sounded odd after his last remarks that he didn't like water and preferred to put that whole episode aside. He caught Derrymore's look of surprise, but persisted.

'Do you have any charts of that area, navigation charts showing rocks and shoals, that sort of thing?' he asked. 'And do you know anyone with a boat?

'Not sure what I expect to find,' he added in apology. 'And

no point in trying yet, they say the wind's got to drop. And no way down the cliffs until the next spring tide, a month or so off.'

'Well,' said Derrymore dubiously, 'I'll have a think. Several of my mates are always messing about with boats, and I do a bit myself, fishing at weekends. I'll see what I can find.

'So that's it, sir,' he added. 'All accounted for. Except Anna Sparks.'

After the first mention, Reynolds had spoken little about her, had attempted to keep any talk about her to a low level. Where it should be kept, he reminded himself, a very low level, kaput. He was somewhat disconcerted, therefore, to hear Derrymore say as he left, with his shy grin, 'But if it's all the same to you, perhaps you'll tackle her.'

He gave a wink that could only be called matey. 'You can probably think up an excuse, seeing you're on friendly terms like.'

Cheeky sod, Reynolds thought. He muttered something noncommittal and watched Derrymore stride away. It was only later that it occurred to him that if, in spite of all his care, he'd made his interest so obvious, he really must be losing his grip – an observation that didn't make for cheerful reflection.

But it wasn't Anna Sparks or even the murders that occupied his thoughts as he strolled home by way of the stream that ran along the village green and gave St Breddaford its name. Although late it was still bright, the long twilight of midsummer, and rooks were cawing from the old beech trees in the churchyard. Tonight they were in competition with the church ringers, who were at their weekly practice, and the bell chimes came swinging out from the little twisted steeple that topped the twelfth-century church. Several pub-goers were lounging on the grass in front of the Fox and Goose, and on an impulse he turned in to join them.

They made room for him readily and continued chatting about various events – the local cricket scores, the bankruptcy of another business – until someone mentioned the murders. Then they were well away with theories of their own, with worried complaints about the safety of their womenfolk and the lack of clues. No one said anything to him directly, they were too polite for that, but they obviously hoped he would have news. And no one said anything about Miss Seward. Thank goodness for small mercies, he thought – although it would be the womenfolk who would most likely chew over that tasty titbit for years.

He told them what he could to reassure them, then sat nursing his tepid beer, not his favourite tipple, while the light faded and night came on. Just an ordinary Cornish village, he thought, where everyone knows everyone's business, and where, in times of trouble, they close ranks against outsiders, a village with its own share of small everyday problems, not really equipped to deal with large-scale crime. And when at closing time everybody got up, shook themselves, plodded homeward across the green, he reflected that there was no need for fast cars in this dense little community, no need for large-scale histrionics. Everything simple and quiet. Derrymore's right. He's a village policeman and this is where he belongs, in a country village. Thank God for that.

He came to his gate, opened it, twenty-four hours since he had last come home to horror. Tonight all was serene. He fumbled for the keys, switched on the lights, watched the late news on TV – war and famine and riot in far-distant parts of the world. And went to bed, as he had done more times than he could count since coming here to live. All was as it should be. Without the need of whisky he fell asleep. But not for long.

Chapter 13

He woke with a start, for a moment not recognizing his own bedroom with its rows of books, its carefully chosen landscapes and garden pictures, its scatter of shirts and boots and other masculine gear. A bachelor room, no feminine frills.

The moonlight was pouring through the window and at first he thought its large brightness had awakened him. But it was the dream, a nightmare in which a dog and its owner ran along a beach – just two shapes running in the sunlight. At the water's edge the dog lay down while its owner waded, fully clothed, into the sea and began to swim. The waves curled lazily but there was a current. He could see its line of foam, and as the figure swam towards it he wanted to shout, 'Turn back.' Because the swimmer wasn't Mike Tregonning after all, it was Anna Sparks. And although he tried to shout no words came, and although he tried to wave his arms he could make no movement; he was trapped immobile on the shore, the surf surging round his feet, the dog lying looking anxiously out to sea, the vast expanse of water suddenly empty.

The dream made him sweat. There'd be no more rest tonight. He looked at his watch – barely three o'clock. Within an hour or so the new day would have dawned. He threw back the covers and padded downstairs, where he switched on the lights. While he waited for the kettle to boil he made a phone call.

This call was protracted, and not without its own brand of intrigue. But he knew his old acquaintance would be up and about, he scarcely ever slept. He and Fred – a cover name – shared memories going back many years to their army days, when they had worked together in hush-hush operations. He hadn't used Fred's services for a long time, but Fred was still in business, and owed him a favour.

Reynolds didn't like calling in favours; both in his professional and private life he'd found it was always better to be owed than paid, and certainly bad policy all round to be on the owing side oneself. But he had no other way to find out what he was looking for, and no time to get the information legally.

When he'd explained all that he wanted, adding one last wild card for good measure (and been ticked off good and proper for even thinking of getting any of it – a breaking of the rules, as he knew very well), the voice on the other end of the line relented enough to ask how he was and to commiserate over his 'shabby treatment' when he left the Force.

'There were plenty of us rooting for you,' was the final and not-unkindly pronouncement. 'Don't you forget it. I'll find out what I can. Actually' – there was the ghost of a chuckle – 'things have changed a lot since our army days. Thanks to electronics, computer link-ups, inter-country networks, we're all part of one big happy pool of knowledge, free for the dipping. So some of what you're asking's as easy as picking plums. I'll be back sooner than you think. But' – here the voice deepened mysteriously – 'if the authorities get wind of what you're up to, then you're on your own. And don't ring me again, too risky. I'll be in touch.'

Typical self-protection tactics, Reynolds thought, common to all agencies these days, can't blame them. He hung up uneasily, recalling those shared experiences, so many years ago, when they had both been young, enthusiastic, certain what they were doing was for the good of queen and country, when taking risks had been natural and no one thought of cover-ups. And when getting information had to be struggled, fought for, didn't come so easily at the push of buttons.

The dream also still haunted him. Ignoring the clamouring demand of his book (at sleepless moments like these normally he worked on his current manuscript), he carried his other files into the kitchen. Sipping a pre-morning coffee, he began to riffle through the notes he'd made after returning from hospital on Monday, mainly abandoned since Derrymore'd told him of Mrs Sparks' murder. So much had happened in the past two days he hadn't had time to keep them up to date. And as he had been an outsider, an onlooker, they hadn't been really relevant. Yet in previous cases often his best theories developed from close study of his records; he was famous for that. And Derrymore's observation this evening about too many false clues had stuck, as had his own subsequent remark that nothing held together except hatred of Mrs Sparks.

He settled down to think. He had more or less come to the conclusion that hatred was the prime motive, but now, as he considered carefully, he wasn't so sure. In other murders he'd worked on, hatred was often a leading cause -- hatred or love, the two sides of the same coin. This case seemed different. For one thing it was too simple an answer. And there had been too many too obvious protestations of hate; they cancelled each other out. Then too he sensed there were many other strands, nebulous for the moment, floating out of reach. Just because he hadn't pinned them down didn't mean they didn't exist. Or that eventually he wouldn't unravel them.

He turned to the page where he'd written down the names of the first two victims. Now he added Miss Tenery's and, half defiantly, his own. Four separate incidents, two of which ended in killings, two in which somehow death had been avoided.

The killings of Mr and Mrs Sparks were years apart. He needed to think about that too. Ten years is a long while in human experience, a long while for revenge, or whatever motive connected them, to lie dormant. For a moment he thought briefly of the man by whom Mrs Sparks was supposed to have had the child Anna (and who he suspected might be Nurse Pengelly's father, who himself 'had gone off') and for that moment anticipation grew, then faded. Improbable, he thought, dismissing the idea; the 'child' by now is a grown-up young woman. Too much time has passed. But something out there links them. What?

He was convinced that these two murders were somehow connected. He was equally sure that the attack on himself was an isolated event. Miss Tenery, on the other hand, had suffered a brutal and vicious assault because of, and instead of, him. Here something struck him that he had only noticed vaguely before. He had assumed, without much to go on (he'd had no opportunity, of course, to examine the evidence in the first or second killings), that the murders of Mr and Mrs Sparks had been by the same person. Now it occurred to him that if the body in the mine shaft was that of Richard Sparks (which of course had not yet been proved) there was an audacity about the manner of his killing, an almost flaunting boldness, which suggested a similarity to the way in which Mrs Sparks had been killed. Not so much in the actual method but in the style, if he could use that word about murder. Whoever had the nerve to arrange a faked boat wreck had the same mentality as the person who had climbed into a hospital room and smothered a sleeping patient, under the nose, as it were, of authority. Suddenly he saw that the same kind of brazen audacity (again he wasn't sure of the expression, he didn't want to exaggerate) was apparent in the attack on him in the farm lane, in mid-day, in the open, with a farmer at work on the other side of the hedge. No wonder he'd felt that he was in the presence of a maliciously dominating personality, no wonder he had sensed the personal challenge made explicit by that grinning face.

He tapped thoughtfully with his pencil. Who of the suspects was capable of such deviousness? Not Tregonning, rough and ready, lashing out with fists and sticks. He was virtually sure that Tregonning had attacked Miss Tenery, yet Tregonning had denied it, and when Reynolds had shown him the newspaper article today he had seemed genuinely upset. True, he'd recovered quickly enough, but acting didn't seem in character either; the one thing Tregonning never did was hide his feelings or his anger.

He ran over the names of the other suspects. Who among them possessed the characteristics he was looking for? What about the Farrs? They were an unknown quantity (to him) and, according to Derrymore, had watertight alibis for Mrs Sparks' murder. Yet watertight alibis are often found to be full of leaks, and obviously Trevor Farr had shown dangerous, and devious, qualities when he was questioned. As for Anna Sparks, he wasn't sure how to fit her in or, now, how far to trust her, but of all the people he'd had contact with she certainly was the most complex. Then there was Joyce Pengelly, large enough to have had no difficulty in suffocating Mrs Sparks, and possessing the means and motive to do so. However hadn't she made a point of saying she didn't drive?

That left only the wild card – Malcolm Sparks, the half-brother who might or might not have gone to Australia and whom Fred said he could easily track down. But until there was some information about him, Malcolm Sparks was only a name.

His lists were getting him nowhere; he might as well be a child, playing with bricks, making castles to be knocked down because he wasn't building them properly. Angrily he put the notes aside. Hunt for a common link, he told himself, think.

He remembered Derrymore's words when Mrs Sparks had been killed – 'Doesn't seem fair' – and his own, 'Murder never is.' But suppose it wasn't just the uncovering of Mr Sparks' grave that was 'unfortunate' for Mrs Sparks, he now admonished himself. Suppose it was something more important, common to all three incidents, something no one so far has thought of.

He began to pace to and fro, his steps keeping in time with his thoughts. Mrs Sparks is not killed because unwittingly she reveals her husband's grave, although that may well be part of it. Rather, she threatens something else, something bigger than a mere murder, the reason *why* her husband was killed.

She may not have gone along with the killing, of course, she may have been forced into acceptance, but she has had to live with the consequences, underfoot as it were. He winced at his unintentional pun. We know she settles down in a posh new house, even though a short while before she's been happily trying to oust her next-door neighbours. Suddenly she's loaded with gold and jewels – where does the money come from for those, assuming they aren't all gifts from a loving daughter and son-in-law? A pay-off, a kickback, a bribe to remain silent?

The idea seemed outlandish. And yet he'd known more outlandish things. So all goes along swimmingly until one day she falls down a mine shaft. Then, boom, the killer's cover is blown. And, as Derrymore said from the beginning, whoever arranged such a complicated murder must have had a damn important reason, even more important if it means he has to kill Mrs Sparks as well. The same reason in fact that will cause him to try to kill me.

He felt the hairs rise on the back of his neck as they always did when he was about to make a discovery. If what he was beginning to suspect was so, then it made Miss Seward's accusations look like child's play. For although the fall down a mine shaft had threatened the murderer, so had something he himself had done, or was supposed to have done . . . in which case, quite the reverse of what he'd come to think, the incident on the cliffs must be of major importance and that sense of challenge, of mutual challenge, should be taken seriously.

I'm walking along a farm lane, he thought. I climb down the cliffs, go out to a reef because I see some birds and when they fly away I come back. And as I do someone runs me down, the same person who will kill Mrs Sparks later that same evening.

So what happened on my cliff climb to cause such a reaction? What did I do, or see? Again he paced. Once more in his mind's eye he saw the goat-like trails, felt the hot sun, saw himself stop by the gorse bush whose scent was so intensified by the heat he could almost smell it now. He stood there for a while, looking out to sea, down at the translucent water where patches of weed made great purple shadows on the sandy bottom, and the flock of white sea birds bobbed up and down.

He was startled from his reverie by the ring of the telephone, one of those outside interventions which could be called luck, but which he himself preferred to think of as calculated chance.

Fred's voice, chortling almost with triumph, came over the line. Reynolds could picture his grin as he said, 'Told you I'd be quick. It's a communications world we live in nowadays, old buddy, nothing hidden for long, nothing we can't pry out.'

He didn't have the answer to Reynolds' main request; as he went on to explain, more seriously now, that would take a little more investigation, involving as it did another country's records. But the wild-card request, the last-moment request Reynolds had tagged on more for Derrymore's benefit than his own, had been a piece of cake. And if Trevor Farr hadn't made such a spectacle of himself, Reynolds thought, as he now listened to what Fred had discovered, if Trevor Farr hadn't threatened a lawsuit (which, even if he'd won, would have raked him in nothing more than pennies for his piggy bank), I'd never have asked Fred to track him down.

As the list of Fred's discoveries about Trevor Farr grew, as the number of Trevor's little peccadillos was revealed, including forged credentials, backstreet scams, shady deals in various locations, always suggested, nothing ever proved, Reynolds

236

realized the sort of man he was dealing with. But when Fred mentioned suspected drug dealing, he knew he had struck gold.

He knew it even more when, after Fred had hung up, promising to 'get back to you, tomorrow at the latest', a second phone call filled in the remaining gap.

The voice was one he didn't recognize at first, bellowing in the way non-phone users imagine is essential, asking Reynolds if 'he'd looked outside this morning?'

'Wind's gone,' the voice continued, shouting even louder as if Reynolds had disappeared into an adjoining room. 'And he'm gone too. Told you he would.'

Without difficulty identifying Granny Gossip as the speaker and the 'he' as Mike Tregonning, Reynolds heard the old man add, 'Took his dog with him, so up to no good I shouldn't wonder. I told you he'd stay put until the calm. And you owe me a tenner.'

I owe you double that, Reynolds thought, excitement suddenly mounting, ye gods, you don't know how much I owe you. For if I'm right at last, and I think I am, you've just given me the last clue. And if Tregonning's after what I think he is, it's something I saw, or was supposed to have seen, floating in the water below the reef. A something worth retrieving as soon as possible, a something worth killing for. And the only thing I know, these days, that's worth that much is drugs.

All his previous suspicions of Tregonning came to a boil, along with those suggestions dropped by Granny Gossip about where did he get his money and why did he sleep on board with a dog for protection. Why indeed! And why his belligerence spilled over so readily at the very sight of Reynolds

– nothing to do with jealousy, all part of this new unsuspected facet of his life.

Tregonning supposedly had been scared off after Mrs Sparks' fall revealed the first murder (I bet that's what he wanted 'out of', he thought, enlightened, of course it had nothing to do with marriage). Subsequently bad weather had kept him on shore. But, if Reynolds were right, why now, after murder and attack had brought the police out in force, did he change his mind and go out today? It didn't make sense – unless he were retrieving the cache for himself.

If I were in Tregonning's shoes, he thought, I'd not hang around to become the next victim; better to cut and run, taking the stuff with me. In which case it's no good waiting for him on shore, hoping to catch him there. Padstow won't see him again.

The thought was sobering. But it made it even more imperative either to beat Tregonning to the spot or at least to catch him hauling the stuff on board.

All thoughts of his and Derrymore's previous plans put aside, what was he to do? The obvious step, to present his ideas to the Inquiry Team and get them to act, was barred. They'd never accept his theories – 'Guesswork,' they'd say, 'where's your evidence?' More time wasted while he argued and Tregonning got away with whatever evidence there was. So how to present proof, if he didn't go and get it in person, catching Tregonning in the act.

The idea, once implanted, couldn't be shaken off. Not an ideal solution, he admitted; he knew well enough how dangerous Tregonning could be if cornered. But if this latest hunch was right and Tregonning was making a run for it, there might not be another chance. He didn't mean to forfeit it.

He'd need a boat, and he'd already asked Derrymore to get hold of one. Apart from that he'd need a witness – Derrymore again, of course – if he had the right to ask Derrymore to come, that is. But Derrymore was a good man to have at one's side in case of trouble. Moreover, if he did catch Tregonning, with Derrymore as witness, he'd have the opportunity to talk Tregonning round and get out of him the information needed to solve the rest of the case. For all his bluster and bravado, Tregonning wasn't a real leader; he'd never have the patience or ability to organize on this scale. And for what it was worth, there was something likeable about the man. I can't believe him capable of cold-blooded murder, he thought, but he may know who the real murderer is, and be persuaded into revealing the identity in return for indemnity and protection. Plea bargaining in fact. I can't see Tregonning taking readily to a prison sentence. All of which make the reasons for trying to catch him myself even more valid.

But there was one other reason. And as he hastily pulled on his clothes he let himself face and accept it. It was his conviction about the nature of the killer and that nagging sense of challenge he'd been aware of from the start. Until now he'd been floundering in the dark; at last he had a chance to accept the challenge on equal terms, and issue one of his own. If he's the man I think he is, he thought, after all the effort he's made to protect himself and his organization, thwarting him will be a crushing blow to his ego, one he won't recover from.

The confrontation was personal, of course. It was one he'd met before – the master criminal versus the master detective.

But somehow here it was intensified – at stake, not just the solving or non-solving of a crime but their own conflicting personalities. And who that unknown man was who could laugh as he gunned his car to run Reynolds down still not revealed.

If at the back of his mind was the equally unprofessional thought that here was an opportunity to vindicate himself with the Inquiry Team, prove to them and their backers in Head Office that he hadn't lost his skill, well, that was only human.

But time was wasting. Snatching up his coat, stuffing a survey map of the region in his pocket, he was out of the house and down the path to find Derrymore before the thought of that boat and the water between them and the reef got the better of him.

Following his release, Mike Tregonning had made his way back home as best he could, by bus, stopping only to pick up his dog (which the sodding constable who'd arrested him had explained he himself hadn't time to fetch). Once in Padstow he went straight to the quay, to spend the rest of the day, and the following night, on his boat – which he'd found locked and still in order, thank God for that.

He felt safe on the *Dead Beats*. Or rather he felt safe because of the dog. There was no way anyone could approach the boat without the dog hearing them; and if anyone did, they'd still have it to deal with, if he loosed it on them. Finally, if the worst came to the worst, he might be able to get away by sea, a better escape route than by land.

The dog seemed fine, frisking around as it always did. He paid it no attention. He didn't want it as a pet now, although in the past he had. Now it was as a guard dog that it was important to him.

Leaning against the wheelhouse door was a new double-pronged boat hook he'd bought when he'd reached Padstow. As an additional precaution he'd re-covered the windows of the wheelhouse with the same heavy blankets. Stocked up with supplies, with the little quayside shops and kiosks open, he was well taken care of, and his boat was comfortable, more comfortable than the poky little set of rooms he called home, down an even pokier side alley. But all that would change. Just be patient, he told himself, no more squalor, live high off the hog.

From time to time he peered from behind the curtains. But throughout the day, when the crowds served as extra protection ('emmets' he called them, swarming like ants), and the long night, when he'd slept fitfully, no one had disturbed him. He might be exaggerating the danger, he thought, but there was no point in taking risks.

His anger over his original arrest had now been replaced by real anxiety. For one thing he shouldn't have let himself be goaded so easily into anger; he shouldn't have made a scene. But being picked up like that was humiliating, to say nothing of being kicked out like a piece of left-over rubbish. As if the police had hoped to pin something on him, as if they had been searching for a way to accuse him of a greater crime. Accuse away, he'd thought, you'll find nothing. But now he couldn't be sure; it would be too easy to denounce him, if someone wanted to.

Sometimes he felt like cursing the man he held responsible for his troubles, the interfering ex-inspector whose poking around had focused too much attention where there shouldn't have been any. Yet Tregonning didn't exactly dislike Reynolds, had a sneaking respect for him. He wasn't like a lot of those city slickers, waltzing down into the country, aping country squires. The vet had told him who'd brought the dog in, who'd paid the bill, that made you feel kinder. Besides, Reynolds was tough; knew what's what. Knew too much unfortunately, Tregonning thought, frowning. Anna was right about that too.

At times he'd even toyed with the idea of confronting Reynolds – well, it was tempting. Wasn't there a word for it, turning king's, or was it queen's, evidence? Now, he wasn't so certain. And he still wasn't clear what had happened between him and Anna.

Every time he thought about Anna his anguish grew. 'Bad temper'll be your downfall,' Anna had told him. 'Keep a low profile.' Easy to say. Anger hid so many other feelings; you could shelter behind anger, take your emotions out in anger. Like the situation facing me now, he thought. If you don't wind yourself up you're a goner; you'll be sunk, hook, line and sinker. You have to keep up a brave front. But not much point in telling Anna anything. Anna always knew best.

Anna might have warned me, he thought bitterly, all right for her to talk me down as if she's the schoolroom teacher and I'm the class idiot. His resentment grew. He was only a common fisherman, not clever enough to have worked out what was staring her in the face. He wasn't rich enough, or smart enough, or worth enough for Anna to pay attention.

Well, perhaps one day he would be rich enough. If he played his cards right. Then they'd see, then she'd act differently. And if she didn't, well, he'd done everything he could to make her see reason. How could you deal with that sort of woman, he thought – obstinate, strong-willed, her own worst enemy.

Here his face crumpled in genuine regret. He allowed himself to caress the dog, trying to block out the hurt. If she'd done what he'd first suggested, if she'd listened, they might have got away with it, despite the odds. She'd been stubborn about that too. Said things like, 'What's the use,' or 'There's no need,' contradictory things that showed her confusion. By refusing to accept the truth she had made things even more difficult for him and for herself.

The morning mist was clearing, soon the sun would break out, illuminating the quay and estuary beyond. Undoing the door and looking around cautiously, he stepped out on deck to smell and taste the wind. I could make a run for it, he was calculating. Been trapped on shore too long. Bloody English climate. For a moment, he had a dream of Caribbean beaches, palm trees and sand and sun.

This morning he was in luck, no doubt about it. In the night the wind had shifted, was slackening. For a moment he hesitated. Then he thought, she destroyed what I felt for her, it's too late to turn the clock back.

At about the same time Derrymore was sitting in the police station in St Breddaford, relieved to be there on his own. Tunic undone, bootlaces loosened, he was supposed to be catching up on village matters (his excuse), but was in fact going over in his mind the happenings of the past few days.

The station was typically rural, used to petty transgressions, where offenders tended to be dismissed with what Derrymore called a ticking-off. The outer office was small and shabby; its walls needed painting and its furnishings were battered hand-me-downs from grander quarters. Derrymore felt at home there as he'd never done in the modern, if temporary, splendour of the Incident Room.

All in all he never remembered days so frantic. Death piled on death, he thought, like rotten apples – and was horrified by his own comparison. But that was the way he felt. And life in St Breddaford didn't stop just because he was off on other more immediate business – as if there could be anything more immediate than keeping your home village in line. Well, murder is important, he didn't deny it, but so was living. And a village police office doesn't run itself.

At least it was a great relief to know that he and Mr Reynolds were on good terms again. That thought cheered him up no end. Yet there were still some things he didn't understand, and perhaps shouldn't, especially about Anna Sparks.

He thought of his closing remark to Reynolds last night and was abashed at how crass it sounded. He'd meant it for a joke. Even if he himself had come to dislike Anna Sparks – too sarcastic for his taste, too smart for her own good – and although Mr Reynolds had been generous at explaining later, still he sensed there was more than met the eye. And if in fact Reynolds and Miss Sparks were attracted to each other, after all the years that Reynolds had lived alone, if something went wrong it would be, well, tragic.

Tragedy wasn't part of his usual vocabulary. It made him embarrassed, as if he were in church. And, barring an odd girlfriend or two from the village, so far he himself had steered clear of female entanglements. He sensed that if the ex-inspector became involved with a woman his feelings would run deep. Yet you'd never know it. Trust Mr Reynolds to keep his thoughts under control, no emotional upheaval about Mr Reynolds, no embarrassing personal detail.

Of course in most other ways he himself couldn't really keep up with the ex-inspector, never knew in fact where Mr Reynolds' ideas would land them. Sometimes he felt his real purpose was to keep the other's feet on the ground. Although he didn't mind. Better than sitting round on your backside, carping at your companions. And if that was what 'experience' meant, glad he was a novice!

And see how things had turned out for the best. Take today for example. Here he was all ready to do what he liked most and what the ex-inspector was so good at, working together, fitting evidence into place, creating a picture out of what, to the uninitiated, were just scattered bits of jigsaw.

It was while he was mentally patting himself on the back for having come to the right decision – that is, telling the Inquiry Team thanks very much but his own village beat needed him more than they did, that he became aware someone was outside the office. As he started up, the door opened. As if on cue Mr Reynolds appeared – his usual self, unflappable, but obviously in a hurry.

'The wind's dropped,' was his first cryptic pronouncement. His second, 'About that boat.'

Chapter 14

'That boat I asked about,' Reynolds repeated. 'I need it. And I need you. If you'll come, of course.'

The younger man took the questions in his stride, as if expecting them. 'The boat's at Silver Sand Bay,' he said, 'laid up behind the beach. It has to be dragged down to the water. I've already got the keys. And if you need me, here I am.'

'Good chap.'

Reynolds knew he sounded unusually hearty. He added, partly apologetically, 'It may be dangerous, certainly messy, so if you can, ditch your uniform. And you realize you're talking to a total landlubber here, not fond of water and unable to distinguish a ship's front end from rear.'

And that's the understatement of the year he was thinking, when he saw Derrymore's eyes brighten. But all the younger man said aloud was, 'Then you'll need me more than ever. And if it helps, the front end's sharp.'

Reynolds felt a wave of relief wash over him. He'd always known he could count on Derrymore. The constable stripped off his jacket, donned a jersey kept in a locker and checked the weather with the local coastguards. Then at Reynolds' request he rang the Incident Room telling them to hang on to the

Farrs, using whatever reason they came up with, but for God's sake don't let Shirl and Trev go, because this time they're hot.

While this was going on, Reynolds stood just outside the door, looking about him. By now it was close to nine o'clock. In St Breddaford the main street was stirring. Shops were opening. A woman came out with a loaf; another began to water the hanging baskets of flowers. The air was warm and heavy, smelling of fresh baked bread. Village life at its most peaceful and unsuspecting, Reynolds thought. Probably half the people here don't even know what drug running means, probably they equate medicines with drugs. Yet if drug running goes unchecked they or their children will be as exposed to infection as any slum kids.

And one of their own involved! That'll be a shock, he thought – a Cornishman like Tregonning, abusing his own knowledge of things Cornish to bring disgrace among them. And I, a comparative newcomer, once more the bearer of bad news, the unlucky talisman. Although, come to that, Cornwall's the very place for drug running – those miles of inlets and isolated beaches, those hidden coves, a drug runners' heaven.

His first excited reaction now became tempered with more sober thoughts, foremost among them what his own slowness of perception had set loose. True, whenever he solved a case, he was always amazed that the solution hadn't occurred to him earlier – but this was one he should have recognized from the beginning.

It wasn't as if he hadn't had dealings with drug users and dealers in the past; he'd worked with Narcotics, was no stranger to the methods drug pedlars used and the consequences of their traffic, knew that drug dealing was the fastest-growing crime in the world, the most dangerous, and the most lucrative. No modern law official could function without being aware of all these facts.

And the bigger the incentive, he thought, the greater the determination to protect it. After all these years in operation, a large and well-organized gang (as this one must be by now) won't be dealing in peanuts! It may even be their most important run; it wouldn't surprise me that it was the haul of a lifetime. No wonder Mrs Sparks had to be got rid of, no wonder I was a risk to be eliminated as soon as possible. But ten years of deception, of living an outwardly normal life, ten years of hiding and scheming and planning to that end – it's enough to make one give up on human nature.

But that's beside the point, he thought. If I'd still been on active service, if I were still a real professional, not playing at being one, I'd not have let this peaceful seclusion blinker my perceptions; I might have become suspicious sooner. It was an unpleasant thought.

But later, when by common consent they took his car because it was faster, gradually self-defence came to the rescue. My dealings with the trade were all inland, city rings, slum operations, Reynolds told himself. I never dealt directly with shipping or coastguards; I never saw a haul retrieved from the water. And for that matter I doubt if many officials have actually seen the stuff *in situ* as it were or stumbled upon its hiding place by accident. Suddenly this aspect of his discovery struck him forcibly, an opportunity to record how the drop was made and retrieved, a unique opportunity, about to be lost if they didn't get a move on.

By then he had driven several miles, lost in his musings. He came to with a start, to hear Derrymore asking, somewhat plaintively, not looking at Reynolds directly but keeping his gaze out of the windows as the hedgerows flashed past, 'So if the weather's settled, and the Farrs are taken care of, what's in it for us, sir? What's it all about?'

Pulling himself together, forcing himself to slow down and speaking with exaggerated care, Reynolds found himself outlining what he thought he'd discovered, in between explaining who Fred was and what Fred had told him in answer to the wild-card question. (Although he didn't mention why he'd asked it. No point in telling Derrymore it was in his interest, no point in belabouring the younger man's vulnerability.)

'And then,' he went on, 'just as Fred's information suggested a possible line on what was involved, Granny Gossip's phone call confirmed other suspicions I had. God knows, I'd juggled with hundreds.'

Although I never understood them until now, he thought. He was still driving fast, too fast, but Tregonning was ahead of them, he'd had too good a start.

'But how did you guess it was drugs?' Derrymore persisted, his own excitement, still under control, just showing. 'I mean, what first gave you the idea?'

'It was just a vague hunch.' Reynolds' answer was truthful. 'To be frank, I should have thought of it earlier – I mean before Fred gave me a lead. And when you consider it, Trevor Farr always sounded shady. Remember you pointed out how many entries there were for him in Mrs Sparks' address book. He must have had to move constantly to cover himself – even

Fred called him a chameleon. And probably Farr's very shiftiness attracted Fred's attention and put him on his track. But for all that, I think we'll find out Trev's not clever enough to mastermind the sort of operation we're envisaging here, although his criminal activities might seem to give him an edge. Farr's too self-important to lurk in the background, and the very inconsistency of his crimes smacks of small time. We're looking for concentrated cunning allied with ruthless determination.

'What about Tregonning?'

Reynolds shook his head. 'For what it's worth,' he said, 'I think Tregonning's involvement is small time too, probably as a carrier – the picker-up, not the main organizer.'

'But you were on to him from the start.'

Well,' Reynolds said more diffidently, 'there were always clues.' He concentrated on his driving for a moment before continuing. 'Besides Granny Gossip's hints. For one thing, it's just come to me, but if you look back at the conversations Tregonning and I had, there's one subject common to all of them – apart from mention of Anna Sparks that is – the car that ran me down in the farm lane.'

Derrymore nodded. 'You never would make much of that,' he said, almost reprovingly.

'It's the one thing that seemed to make Tregonning angry,' Reynolds went on, 'and the one thing I couldn't understand. Why was knocking me down a greater crime than trying to kill an old woman? Well, if it wasn't the knocking of me down that mattered (although for the longest time I thought it was) then there had to be another reason. So I began to wonder what I had been doing – or they thought I'd seen.

'Like Mrs Sparks,' he added, 'I was thought to know too much. Although in my case that wasn't so. As you remember, I never actually did see what it was, just climbed out onto the reef to look for it.'

Once more he considered for a moment. 'You know,' he said, 'I remember now when I was coming back I saw glass winking in the sunlight. A window, I thought at the time. I'll bet you anything it was someone's binoculars, watching me as I was looking out to sea. And I'm certain it wasn't Tregonning.'

He didn't add, 'Whoever it was, he was determined to get me. Just as now I'm determined to get him.' Instead he continued, 'I'm sure Tregonning couldn't fetch the stuff when he was meant to, on Monday, because of the mine cave-in and its aftermath. He'd have nowhere to land it for one thing, or stow it, if the house was used. After that the weather was wrong.'

He thought for a moment. 'And I'll bet you, too, when he told Anna Sparks he wanted to be "out" of drug running it was because he'd just learnt from her that the police had shown up to interview her mother with the very man who was supposed to have spotted the haul in the water.'

Each mention of Anna came seemingly effortlessly. In time, he thought, there will be no need for effort, it will all fade. And it won't even matter whether she was attracted by, or only pretended to make a play for, the same man, and perhaps didn't know which.

'I also guess,' he went on, 'that Tregonning's after the stuff today for himself. It's the only thing that makes sense. But he hasn't yet been tempted into cold-blooded murder and, now I come to think of it, that's another good reason for trying to

252

stop him before a further slide into crime. But certainly something's happened since Monday to make him change his mind back to wanting to be "in" rather than "out". And I suspect it's the prospect of feathering his own nest, rather than sitting around waiting to be targeted as the next victim.'

That too was a sobering thought.

'So, after all, the real motive for both the killings,' Reynolds summed up, 'wasn't hate. It was greed. Cold and calculated greed.'

And the sort of mentality, he added to himself, that delights in showing off its cleverness, flaunts it. And again didn't know what made him so sure.

Derrymore's reply was unusually thoughtful. He stared out of the window again. 'You know,' he said, almost shyly, 'when I was in the army, I saw what drugs could do to a man. Not just the physical effect but the moral. I mean the graft, the money grubbing, the sleaze. I can see how someone would kill for it.'

Suddenly he was angry. 'To think I interviewed Trevor Farr,' he shouted, 'listened to his twaddle, worried about it. Mind you, I knew it was money he was after. But not in that filthy way.'

Reynolds had seldom seen Derrymore lose his temper. His niceness (or naivety, if it could be called that) was one of the things about him that Reynolds found especially endearing. It made up for what Reynolds sometimes thought of as his own world-weariness.

'So our plan is to get there before Tregonning, and pick the evidence up.' Recovering his composure, Derrymore sat more upright. 'Or catch him in the act of removing it.'

'Right. Following which, in either case, we shouldn't have a problem presenting our solution to the boffins in the Incident Room.'

'But what if Tregonning won't cooperate?'

A fair question, Reynolds thought, the weak point. It brought him back to the underlying reasons for going out to the reef without asking the Inquiry Team for help – to say nothing of personal vendetta, and the ignoble wish for personal triumph! In any case, persuading Tregonning to hand the evidence over might sound very well in abstraction, reality was another matter.

Seized again with a fit of anxiety, he found himself re-emphasizing his earlier warnings. 'We should expect trouble. We know he's capable of violence. He may be armed, we're not . . .'

'Violence is as violence does,' Derrymore said cheerfully. He didn't exactly flex his muscles, but Reynolds could see he was remembering his previous satisfying encounter at Padstow. True, in his off hours Derrymore was a wrestler, a Cornish champion; he was probably more than capable of handling Tregonning on his own – provided Tregonning didn't pull a gun.

But it was too late for regrets; they couldn't turn back now. Reynolds had made a choice; it was his responsibility, he'd have to deal with the consequences.

Fortunately Derrymore's next questions were more practical – how long a start had Tregonning had, how far were they behind? 'He's further to go than we have,' he said with quiet satisfaction, 'west from Padstow. Silver Sand Bay's much closer. With luck we'll get there first and lie in wait.'

If my hunch's right, Reynolds thought – if he hasn't already got the stuff and is heading in the opposite direction. I've never had anything to do with drug running at sea, he wanted to explain again to the younger man; this is new to me. And if you actually persuade me into a boat, without having to drag me, that'll be new too. But that's a problem we'll deal with later.

Silver Sand Bay, where Derrymore's friend kept his boat, was a good name for the stretch of dunes which widened at low tide into a long flat beach and today was only half covered by a lazy sea, looking as if it didn't even know what a wave was. Behind the beach a car park took up most of a field, at this hour almost deserted although soon it would be crowded with cars and people.

At one end of the field, close to a gap in the dunes, was a strip of grass where several boats of various shapes and sizes were parked, next to a wooden hut where owners kept their gear. Derrymore had the key ready, opened the hut and fumbled around inside, eventually emerging with an outboard motor, a couple of life jackets and a case of what looked like charts.

While Derrymore lugged the engine down through the gap Reynolds flipped the chart case open. It was stuffed with miscellaneous papers but contained only one chart, that of Falmouth harbour, of no use whatsoever. His apprehension grew.

Derrymore was coming back, and pointing to the boat with a cheerful expression. To Reynolds' dismay it was the smallest one, what he would have called a heavy rubber dinghy, black and orange, chained to a log. Ye gods, Reynolds almost said aloud, just my luck, a kiddy's wading pool.

The dinghy was heavier than it looked and at least they

wouldn't have to row. After a protracted struggle, during which Derrymore did most of the carrying, they got it through the gap down to the beach. There the going was easier, the rubber slid over the wet sand, and a couple of surfers, seeing Reynolds' predicament, came to help.

The tide was going out, but there was virtually no surf; the sea was as calm as the first day Reynolds had seen it from the cliffs. That cheered him up, although the surfers were clearly not so pleased. 'Perfect before,' was their grumble – perfect for you perhaps, Reynolds thought, this is more my style.

Getting into the boat proved difficult, as indeed did the simple task of removing shoes and socks. Finally giving up, he waded through the shallows until the dinghy was well afloat, then, without the humiliation of further assistance, managed the scramble over the side, while Derrymore, obviously competent, busied himself with the engine.

Putting on the life jacket defeated Reynolds. In the end he threw it down beside him, trying not to look at the water as the dinghy bobbed up and down before drifting sideways to the beach. After a while he heard with relief the sound of the engine catch. 'Cast off,' Derrymore shouted, with a fine nautical flourish, and they chugged away, leaving the disgruntled surfers behind.

As they left the shelter of the beach, the dinghy's engine picked up speed; the rubber sides, barely inches above the surface, bounced and lurched. Derrymore sat in the stern, hand on the tiller, hair blowing, head back, happy as a lark, Reynolds thought morosely. In the well of the dinghy, the first too-well-remembered wave of nausea hit.

He settled back, trying to ignore the rising sound of wind

and sea. In answer to Derrymore's question – 'Where to, sir?' – he answered abruptly, 'The reef where I went the first time. If we can find it.' He felt in his back pocket for his map but there was no way to make sense of it from this angle, everything looked the same.

Derrymore didn't reply. Turning his head gingerly, Reynolds saw now that out in the bay, away from the shelter of the beach, white tips of waves were showing. 'Nothing to worry about,' Derrymore said soothingly, as if he'd guessed what Reynolds was thinking. 'Just a tad of breeze.'

The dinghy bounced again and the spray rose as the engine revved. Derrymore laughed, said, 'When you were in the army, sir, did you see much action in landing craft?'

Reynolds shook his head, muttering that his fighting days had more to do with sand than sea, desert sand at that. 'Beauties, these boats,' Derrymore enthused, patting the dinghy's side affectionately. 'Just the ticket. Virtually unsinkable, even if they do flip over.' Which wasn't exactly encouraging.

Derrymore pushed the tiller hard, veering now to the left. 'The awful thing about night patrols at sea though, was you came to like them,' he said. 'I did at any rate. Pitting your wits against enemy and water, a great adventure. You never thought you might be killed.

'I suppose you never thought about it, being killed I mean,' he added unexpectedly, 'until you were. And then it was too late.'

Again he pushed the tiller, holding the course steady, bracing himself against a wave that hit the prow with a thud. 'And I suppose murder hunting's rather like it,' he said, 'all the excitement of the chase, then hard reality.'

And after that he was silent.

By now they had come out into what was surely the open sea, and as far as Reynolds could judge Derrymore was heading west down the coast towards that little strip of reef that was big enough and sharp enough to rip the bottom out of any rubber boat, landing craft or not. But the wind, or breeze, as Derrymore insisted on calling it, didn't increase, and although the dinghy continued to be buffeted by the swell, the boat itself seemed to have settled better and was making good headway. Nice little engine, Reynolds found himself thinking. And Derrymore still seems to be enjoying himself, an even better sign.

Out in the bay the sun was very bright, the sea a brilliant blue. Closer to land, the water looked darker, more forbidding. Stacks and pinnacles, the twisted cruel shapes of the northern rocky shoreline, rose out of a grey surface. Thank God there's no surf, Reynolds thought, as they edged closer to the cliffs that began to rear up ahead of them, tall and forbidding.

Looking at them from this perspective Reynolds was surprised how high they were. As they came under their shadow the wind died altogether, and he began to feel better. Together he and Derrymore studied Reynolds' map, trying to pinpoint the exact place where he'd climbed down. And found it, by virtue of the little crabber that was puttering westwards slightly ahead.

'There he is,' Derrymore cried. 'Hard abeam.'

Reynolds swore savagely to himself. All the while his secret hope had been to arrive at the reef first, avoiding real confrontation with Tregonning, or at least, if there were one,

258

arranging it on his terms. For a moment he even considered aborting the journey, turning back empty-handed. More like running with tail between legs to the Inquiry Team and letting them get on with it, he thought, when, the second time to his relief, he saw Derrymore grin happily.

'He may be ahead of us,' Derrymore shouted above the roar of the engine, 'but he'll take us straight to where we want to go. All we've got to do is follow in his wake.'

It sounded simple. And if Tregonning had spotted them he made no sign of turning away or even trying to go faster, kept his same easy speed. Once or twice he even stopped. 'Making a pretence of picking up crab pots,' Reynolds said, watching through binoculars. 'In case someone else is looking. But he must have seen us, can't be otherwise.' Like the waves out to sea, his hopes rose and fell. Perhaps, with luck, their mission wouldn't be so foolhardy after all; they might be successful despite his misgivings.

It was past twelve when they were near enough to recognize the headland, the point that Reynolds had originally been making for, with the little cove that Anna had shown him tucked away on its far side. If Reynolds was right Tregonning would stop before he came to it.

He felt a certain triumph as the *Dead Beats* now turned and headed directly towards shore, presumably making for a group of isolated rocks that stuck out like a row of teeth above the waterline. There it paused, the engine stopped. Rocking a little with the swell, the boat disappeared slowly among the rocks.

As they closed the gap he spotted the track he'd used, a faint line wavering between the gorse he remembered. And as

259

they glided, almost without movement, round the edge of the reef, they no longer needed anything to point out the way. Mike Tregonning was leaning over the side of the *Dead Beats*, hauling at ropes that were green with weed, so intent on his work he never even saw them, perhaps never heard them until their own dinghy came nudging alongside.

Then he started up, the dog beside him, the decks wet and dripping, the loosely coiled ropes baited with what looked like hooks but were in fact bottles, a line of stoppered glass bottles that sparkled in the sun. Tied to each bottle by a long piece of string was a white package, squarish in shape, solid, wrapped in folds of waterproof oilskin.

The water gurgled by, the same Atlantic swell. The fronds of brown seaweed rose and fell. Beneath them, for a second, Reynolds caught a glimpse of the mussel beds he'd clambered over, well under the surface now, and the narrow channel separating the reef from the bottom of the cliff, several hundred feet away.

It was clear enough today to look through the water. He spotted more bottles, to his surprise not floating on top as he would have thought, but somehow anchored below by the weight of the packages resting on the sea bed. A line of floating bottles just below the surface, what he'd seen from the cliff top earlier in the week, presumably what had attracted the birds to the spot in the first instance . . . He remembered the strange brightness of their plumage, lit up by the reflected light from the glass underneath.

'Clever, isn't it,' Tregonning said. 'Simple. Keeps everything tucked out of sight. Although how you saw it, must have been a fluke I suppose, some damn trick of the sun. Bet you didn't know what it was when you came hunting for it, did you, although my God you set a cat among the pigeons, didn't you just.'

He didn't sound particularly upset to see them. He bent down and continued to haul on the ropes until, presumably, he'd retrieved the whole consignment. Then he stood back and looked at them, hands on hips, head on one side. More and more like a pirate, Reynolds thought inconsequently, all he needs is a red head scarf and brass earrings.

'Nice little catch,' Tregonning was saying, almost smugly. 'And so you thought you'd share it. Saw you following me a while back. Heard you for that matter in your contraption here.'

He shrugged. 'Now what?' he said. 'Supposed to go shares are we? Kept quiet did you, all this while, just to get your cut? Think I'll go to all this trouble to make you a partner for nothing?'

Reynolds didn't reply. Tregonning looked from him to Derrymore. 'Brought your own pet hit man,' he said with a hint of a snarl. 'Looking for another excuse to arrest me, hoping to stick me with something real? Think again.'

Once more neither Reynolds nor Derrymore said anything. But Reynolds willed the other to look at him, and when he did, stared him down.

There was a pause. Then Mike said slowly, 'All right, damn it, I admit it's my job to collect it. And yes, I was supposed to have got it on Monday if Mrs Sparks hadn't fallen down the shaft. But I had nothing to do with any of the murders, and you can't pin them on me. Not the attack on you, not the attack on Mrs Sparks. Not the man in the shaft.'

'But you know who did.'

Reynolds was watching Tregonning closely, and by now Derrymore had edged round beside him. He felt better with Derrymore's solid bulk nearby. It evened the odds. He said, 'You know who's behind it all.'

He caught the involuntary flutter of Mike's eyes, a hit. But Mike didn't bend.

'Haven't a clue,' he said almost matter-of-factly, 'no more than you have. I'm at the bottom of the chain, no one confides in me.'

He added, 'And you can't press charges for non-cooperation in a criminal act. Because, as I keep telling you, I wasn't involved.'

Suddenly Reynolds' anger boiled over. 'And what do you call this?' he bellowed. 'Fishing for tiddlers?'

He made himself calm down. In the war of nerves between them Tregonning would win if he lost his temper. Trying another tack, 'Who put this stuff here?' Reynolds asked, almost conversationally. 'Where did it come from?'

His question was unexpectedly mild after his outburst, so mild you might have thought he didn't care whether Tregonning answered or not. Again Reynolds sensed the flicker of the other's eyes. There was another silence during which the two men continued to stare at each other. Then Mike picked up a rope and began coiling it, while the dog, as if sensing that this was to be a lengthy business, settled down in its usual position, head on paws.

'Spain, where else,' Tregonning said. He threw the words over his shoulder as he worked, offhandedly. 'Before that, somewhere in North Africa – who knows or cares? And who brings it up from Spain? Could be anyone, I suppose. They collect it from one of those southern ports, then carry it on in plastic bags, tucked in fish crates, nailed to the hull, stuffed in the mast, you name it, they know how to run it through. Easy as sucking eggs. Mind you,' he added, 'I speak from hearsay; I've explained I wasn't part of that. I'm a crabber, see, and a crabber keeps pots among the rocks, right? No one suspects him if that's where he goes.'

'And how did you get it to them after it came ashore? There must have been one last drop?'

When Tregonning didn't answer, 'Somewhere nearby,' Reynolds improvised for him. 'Mrs Sparks' house perhaps. Or' – comprehension dawned – 'in the same mine shaft that collapsed. A perfect hiding place.'

'Thought it was perfect.' Tregonning was sulky. 'Wasn't bad though, just a short piece of tunnel close to the hedge, overgrown with bushes. Probably been used by smugglers for centuries. You know the house was a coastguard cottage once, a nice little change. Could have knocked me down with a feather when they said the mine'd collapsed. But when they told me what else'd been left in it . . .' He gave a whistle.

'And who took the stuff after you left it there?' Patiently Reynolds persisted; he might have been leaning over a back fence passing the time of day. 'Who's responsible for handing it on?'

Tregonning shrugged. 'My duties ended when I'd brought it on shore,' he said. 'I made a phone call or two at an appointed time to let them know my part was done, then, if all was clear, a night or so after, I brought it along in the back of my car and stowed it where I've just told you. After that, who knows. All I wanted then was my wages; the rest was up to them. And don't ask again who they are, because I'm not speaking. I don't have to do your job for you.'

'What brought you into the trade in the first place?' Reynolds' question was even more mild. 'What's more, why did you want to be "out of it"?'

When Tregonning didn't reply, 'Was it because you too saw the game was up? Or was it' – here Reynolds' voice dropped, came out as a whisper – 'that you guessed Mrs Sparks would pay for . . . her stupidity, shall we call it? And you didn't want to be part of the same price?'

This time the response was marked. Tregonning's face darkened. He picked up a crab pot and held it with both hands as if he wanted to pry it apart.

'I'll tell you how I got into the trade,' Tregonning said at last, ignoring the other questions. 'What's the use of fishing?'

He sounded bitter, and yet he spoke more rationally than he had ever done, presumably his way of truth as he saw it. 'My father was a fisherman before me, I told you, down at Newlyn. We've been fishermen for generations, no harm in that for all that in her later days Mrs Sparks thought fishing beneath her. Anyway when my father sold his boat I was heartbroken. I cut off on my own, came to Padstow, thought I'd earn a living.'

He brooded, his handsome face, with its eye still discoloured and the half-healed scar almost hidden beneath his hair, grave. 'Dreams,' he said softly, 'young men's dreams, no point to them. To begin with there's precious little fish left. Either polluted, or so many bloody restrictions, just as soon stay at home.'

He seemed to muse again for a moment. 'Mind you, I've

always said I was a small man myself, an inshore fisherman, but even there you can see how the way lies. Every year less crabs, and less time to get them.'

'So you thought you'd make a packet while you had the chance,' Reynolds finished for him. 'Didn't they pay you well enough? But if you decided to stay on for one last pick-up there must be a reason. So tell us why?'

He was relieved when Tregonning laughed. He nudged the packages with his feet. 'Reckon this says it all,' he said. 'Know what it's worth on the open market? Well, I thought to myself, why take all that risk just to line someone else's pocket – especially if in the end they don't treat you right. Course they always left the little details like when and how to get it, to me. Had to – they know nothing about this coastline. So it was easy to say, wait for the weather, wait for the wind, they had to take that on trust. But, this time, the longer I waited the more I thought I'd be a fool not to get something out of it. And you're a fool too, not to have thought of it yourself.'

Reynolds accepted the insult. After all it was no more than he'd said to himself. 'Trevor Farr wasn't the man you made the phone calls to, was he?' he asked. 'Shirley Sparks' husband—'

'That little creep,' Tregonning broke in. 'Thinks he's the cat's whiskers, but he couldn't pee in a bottle. Whatever he tells you, he's just a go-between. Like me.'

It was beginning to be clear the 'interview' was fast drawing to an end. Although Reynolds had already amassed a good deal of information, now came the more essential, and more tricky, bit – persuading Tregonning to cooperate with the law, turn over the evidence and give himself up. But first there was one last essential question that had to be answered. He braced himself.

Tregonning himself was getting restless, fiddling with the ropes and glancing over his shoulder towards the open sea. 'And what about the rest of the family, the daughters, the brother?' Reynolds came to it more abruptly than he meant. 'Shirley and Anna Sparks, how much do they know?'

Again, when Tregonning said nothing: 'To my mind they must know something; it's their house. So if they've been using you, why don't you use them. Cooperate with us, we'll see you clear.'

There was a momentary hush. Beside him, Derrymore (who had been listening quietly to this exchange) strained forward, as if expecting a vital bit of evidence to be produced from air, or from some secret pocket.

All Reynolds' concentration was on Tregonning, willing him to respond, willing him not to notice the importance of this question, willing him to react as he wanted him to. When Tregonning answered, in a voice that was a cross between triumph and dejection, for a moment he thought he'd won.

'As for Anna, I'll say this much,' Tregonning said. 'Don't expect her help. Anna's like the rest of us – blinkered when it suits her interests best, trusting, too trusting, won't think ill of anyone.'

Reynolds seemed to hear her voice echoing those same thoughts, even as Tregonning added, 'As for me, enough is enough. Why should I give up what I've got. You can't match it, can you? And a bird in the hand is worth two in a bush. So I'm off.'

Confidence was coming back into his voice. A touch of his

former truculence reappeared. 'But I've got to be quick. The tide's on the turn.'

With a movement that was too fast to describe he snatched up a curved boat hook. He lashed out with its spike, ripping through the dinghy's sides. The *Dead Beats* rocked violently, one edge dipped, the water swirled. Beneath the larger boat's prow the dinghy lurched sideways as the rubber tore. Within seconds it was reduced to a flabby black and orange mass as the water flooded in, sending the red life jackets bobbing away.

'Look out,' Derrymore cried. Reynolds saw him leap for the crabber's tether and hang on determinedly. There was a flurry of foam, a swirl. He himself was being sucked under, the seaweed wrapped around his legs, the water not so much cold as salt, stinging eyes and throat. Then he was thrashing on the surface, his one good arm flailing, the sun in his eyes, and Derrymore shouting, 'Swim.'

He tried to answer, felt himself go under again, felt the depths beneath him, treacle thick. He was suffocating, drowning, sinking like stone. Yet when a dark shape came nudging up to him under water instinctively he recoiled as from a shark.

It seemed to push him from beneath. His head broke the surface again, he gulped for air. Beside him the Rottweiler nudged against him again, its head under his chin. He caught a glimpse of red and white, snatched at it with one hand, a life jacket. Resting his face on it, panting, he let his legs trail towards a sea bed that still threatened to suck him down.

Making a superhuman effort to conquer the fear that robbed him of movement, he turned slowly to hunt for Derrymore and failed to find him. Then, seeing he was drifting back towards the reef within reach of Tregonning's hook, he began the laborious paddle towards shore, aware that Tregonning was howling at him and the dog, unable to come after him because of the rocks.

The distance seemed endless. Land was miles away, not yards; he'd never reach it. Working with his feet and gripping the life jacket with one hand so tightly that afterwards he thought they'd have to cut it loose he forced himself on. The dog swam beside him, sometimes seeming to look at him with its strange yellow eyes, sometimes actually circling with an anxious far-away expression.

Now each time he raised his head to snatch a look the cliffs were closer, so close that eventually he could almost believe in their existence. Then his feet were touching bottom, a rock probably, for the next moment as he thrashed to stand up he was under water again. Still clutching the life jacket he flailed forward, crashed into more rocks with his knees, was pulled backward by the swell, then thrown none too gently on a shingle patch between two large boulders. He was lying on the shore, sprawled out like flotsam, spewing out the water he'd swallowed and gasping like a landed fish.

After a while he rolled over and sat up. Through blurred eyes he could make out the distant outline of Tregonning's boat and as he watched a figure, Tregonning presumably, leaned over the side and hauled something out of the water. He heard the dog yelp as it was dropped on deck. Then the engine roared into life, the boat backed off, turned in one final swirl and began to throb out to sea. And with it went their evidence.

He almost cried out in frustration. Along the coast were a hundred inlets that would hide Tregonning and his boat, where he could find easy shelter and lie up for as long as he wanted and where neither dealers nor police would find him . . . Suddenly he thought, my God, where's Derrymore?

He scrambled to his feet, shouted the name, panicked, thought *he's gone*. He had a moment's horror imagining telling Derrymore's mother he'd drowned her son for real this time. Then he heard a sound of splashing, a dark head cut across his line of vision, materialized. Derrymore came thrashing onto shore, a fine display of Australian crawl. Minus his friend's dinghy and motor, minus all his possessions, but with a grin a mile wide.

'Well done, sir,' he puffed, as if Reynolds had just swum the Channel. He followed Reynolds' look at the vanishing crabber, said soothingly again, 'We'll catch him,' and then, 'At least he left some evidence behind.'

From behind his back he flourished his trophy, one of the bottles with the string and white package still attached.

'Managed to cut it off,' he said modestly, when Reynolds had finished lavishing praise. 'Reached over the side and grabbed his knife. Mind you,' he added, 'couldn't have done it if the dog had been on board. When it jumped over it distracted Tregonning, and while he turned his back I took the chance.'

Derrymore was breathing heavily but contentedly. 'Would have got on board too,' he continued after a moment, 'if Tregonning hadn't turned round too soon, and seen me before I got a proper hold.'

Matter-of-factly he showed the back of his hand, where the boat hook had sliced down to the bone, a white line that welled out red as he flexed it. 'Nothing that a stitch won't hold,' he went on, fishing a dirty rag out of his heavy serge trouser pocket. 'A pair of old wounded soldiers, aren't we just.'

He laughed, then more seriously said, 'Thought you were a goner sir, there's a truth.'

Suddenly he flashed round at Reynolds. 'You said you didn't like water,' he said, 'but I never took you seriously. Without that dog I don't know what would have become of you. Never seen the like, and that's the truth.'

Old wounded soldiers, Reynolds thought, reminded suddenly of what he'd said to the dog itself. Now there's real gratitude, he thought. I wonder if it knew how I was feeling. He got up slowly although his legs flapped like paper.

'Can't swim,' he said, and suddenly this confession too wasn't as bad as he'd imagined. 'Hated the sea from childhood. We're not all like you, old son, salt in your blood.'

'Don't know about that,' Derrymore said, reverting to his practical self. 'And don't know what my mate'll say about his boat. Or his engine for that matter. That's what really sunk us,' he added virtuously, 'the weight of the motor. If we had the time I'd try and pull her up.'

Dissuaded from this, with the promise they'd either come back or Reynolds himself would foot the bill for a replacement, he sat beside the ex-inspector on the shingle, two swimmers sunning themselves on shore after a cooling dip. And after a while, when they'd got their breath back, they began the long trek up the cliff.

Chapter 15

The climb was hard. Reynolds had lost a shoe and Derrymore's boots, which he'd tied together and stowed under the seat in sailor fashion, were at the bottom of the sea, along with the rest of their gear. And they only had one hand apiece! The more laborious task, though, lay ahead – putting together what they'd found and confronting the Inquiry Team with their first piece of hard evidence.

Cadging a lift back from the cliffs, and, via a quick stop in St Breddaford to change, submitting to an unpleasant little interlude of bandaging and rebandaging by a clutch of clacking nurses (which Derrymore appeared to enjoy, much to Reynolds' irritation), they made their entrance in the Incident Room – to be met by a barrage of hostile questions. Uncontrolled frenzy. Piranhas feeding, Reynolds thought. Which turned to genuine excitement when Derrymore produced his package.

Suddenly Derrymore was the hero of the hour. Prudently Reynolds kept in the background while the constable told the story – a truncated version which he and Derrymore had concocted on the way back, to protect not only Reynolds but also Fred. And, to a larger extent, to protect Derrymore. No one now knew better how impossible it was to run with both sides at once.

Good for you, Reynolds thought, listening to the younger man's restrained account, you've come of age. He admired the way Derrymore skimmed over the first part – that is how they knew where to find the cache – and concentrated on the more important details of how the haul was transported, stored and retrieved. There were still obvious gaps, the main ones being how the drugs came up from Spain and how they were distributed when once on land. The answers to those and other questions presumably lay not only with Tregonning but with others involved in the enterprise.

Meanwhile, somewhere not many miles away, the prime suspect on his small crabbing boat, with an illegal fortune on board, had gone into hiding, although if the weather forecast was correct he might yet be forced out – the north Cornish coast was notorious for its lack of shelter in storms.

Drug running, most probably heroin (that was yet to be determined), gave a new perspective to the investigation. The Inquiry Team wasn't geared for drugs. That wasn't their territory; the Narcotics Section handled drugs. And Reynolds had remained on good terms with the Narcotics Section – some of his best cases had been connected with them.

A flurry of phone calls erupted: messages to coastguards, a scramble of a helicopter, the ordering of police barricades on the main roads out of Cornwall. Tregonning might know where to hide his boat but it looked unlikely that he'd get far with its contents. As for Narcotics, they didn't care who'd actually done the finding. Certain it was a significant breakthrough, the tip of an iceberg, they sent congratulations.

Apart from that the other main topic was who else was involved. Interest immediately focused on Trevor Farr and his wife. Trevor Farr had been held, against his wish of course, on the pretext of routine questioning about his mother-in-law's death (had she seemed worried or despondent?) while his alibis for the Monday evening were checked and re-checked, and were found impossible to fault.

Having proved to his satisfaction that he was where he'd said he'd been, in his own house minding his own business, Trevor had relented sufficiently to answer questions with more willingness than had been expected, and the interview by and large had gone well. It was only on seeing Derrymore that his manner changed, more than ever making him resemble an outraged terrier, hackles raised.

'What's this?' he cried, affronted. 'I hold this man responsible for Mrs Sparks' demise. You're only adding insult to injury to let him question me,' and so forth, until Derrymore produced the white package.

He placed it slowly and deliberately on the table top. The effect was dramatic. Suddenly the little lawyer faltered; he felt for a chair and half sat, half collapsed into it. The Inquiry Team equally fell silent.

It was a moment to savour. And after he had enjoyed it Derrymore took control. 'Now,' he said, his round face stern, 'I'll tell you where and how we found this beauty and perhaps you'll tell us the rest. There're lots of blanks needing filling in.'

Faced with the charge of drug dealing, confronted with a list of his various shady doings, his various aliases, his various underworld activities, Mr Farr's bluster collapsed like a pricked

273

balloon. But he still knew nothing.

'I'm only the family solicitor,' he whined. 'Merely Mrs Sparks' lawyer, doing what I was told. And you've checked my whereabouts in Bristol. You know that's where I'm based.'

By this he meant he gave 'legal advice' on illegal matters, an inconsistency in which apparently, with a singular lack of humour, he seemed to see nothing ludicrous. Too easy to lay blame on a dead woman, Reynolds thought, listening in the background, she can't answer back.

Rallying, Trevor protested. About those other accusations – there were no convictions, there was no previous record. And the evidence was biased anyway, based on false and lying testimony. There was nothing concrete, nothing proved, it was all hearsay . . . As ever, looking out for number one, Reynolds thought, sneaky. He'll wriggle clear yet if he can. They're wasting time.

The constable glanced at the Inquiry Team, a reminder of how they'd reacted when Trevor Farr had been on the offensive. 'You've lived like a king on ill-gotten gains,' he pointed out. 'You and Tregonning. To my thinking that's complicity.' Which for a village policeman, a mere constable, was harsh speaking. Silently, Reynolds applauded.

'Added to which,' Derrymore continued, 'there're murders to solve.'

His stare now at the Inquiry Team was an open challenge. 'Plus an attack on a hiker in a farm lane.'

Again Trevor Farr began to babble. He'd cooperate willingly if he could. But what did he know about murder? When his mother-in-law died he wasn't even in Cornwall. In fact he wasn't here most of the time. If Mrs Sparks' house was a rendezvous, how was he to know it? And so on. More clever marshalling of excuses, Reynolds thought, exchanging a disgusted look with Derrymore.

When Shirley was brought in to join her husband at first their stories ran in tandem. Like Trevor, Shirley Farr claimed innocence. She went a step further. Why were they all so serious? she asked. Wasn't drug running the latest version of smuggling, and weren't all Cornish men smugglers at heart? It was only when she heard Trevor insist her family had drawn him into their affairs, rather than vice versa, that a rift appeared.

The breach was sudden and vicious. She turned on her husband with a snap that made graphic Derrymore's earlier observation that she was like a ferret. It wasn't pleasant, Reynolds thought, still keeping in the background, to hear wife and husband spar so openly. But then he never ceased to be amazed at the lengths humans go to, the lies and semi-lies they weave, to protect themselves.

Shirl certainly went beyond the bounds of dignity. Contrary to what her husband claimed, she insisted that drug dealing was Trevor's game. Even before the family had left Padstow, he'd been the one to persuade them into it. Of course in the beginning it was only meant as a one-off chance, then it gradually escalated. Again Reynolds exchanged glances with Derrymore.

Shirl didn't quite say but implied that Trev had courted her to use her family. Only after she and Trev had married had she found out what he was up to, the earliest runs arising, she thought, because of his foreign connections. Yes, he still had family overseas.

'Shut up, Shirl,' Trev snarled.

But she was not to be stopped, went on to confirm Tregonning's story about the use of the old mine workings. Yes, they'd moved closer to St Breddaford because of them. And the house's location. Perfect. And yes, they all knew the shaft was there. She and Anna had planted the leylandii hedge themselves, not to block the sea view out but to hide what was in the garden.

At mention of Anna's name her nose sharpened. Again her eyes took on what Derrymore had called her ferret look. 'If you're looking for the real culprit,' she cried, 'find Anna. Force her to talk, then your problem's solved.'

Useless for Trevor to try to hush her, Shirley was in full flow. Anna was deep, complicated, riddled with jealousy and hatred, who knew what schemes fermented in her brain. All that book learning wasn't healthy. And when their mother was in hospital, what had she done with their mother's jewelry box? 'Gone,' she said, 'vanished, I've looked everywhere. Anna always coveted it.'

This was a new development; something to question Anna Sparks about. Reynolds made a note, while Derrymore, giving up on that line of questioning, next asked about her father. Would Richard Sparks have known, or approved, of these early ventures? If not, was that perhaps why he had been killed?

Here Shirley dug her toes in. She began to hedge, veering between laying blame on her husband and Anna. 'If anyone had a reason to kill him, Anna did,' she finally cried. 'Imagine, she claimed he wasn't her real father. Broke mum's heart that did.'

At this point she looked round her craftily, as if the thought had just struck her. 'Perhaps she killed my mother too,' she said. 'It's no news she hated her.'

When Malcolm's name was mentioned she grew even more cagey. What part, if any, she was asked, had Malcolm played? Was he also involved?

'Oh,' she said, her face lightening, as if she'd thought of an excuse. 'Anna and Malcolm were hand in glove. Went to pieces Anna did, when he left. But Malcolm had visions of grandeur too. Malcolm was like Anna. Wanted to better himself.'

Ambition seems to be a family weakness, Reynolds thought, still listening. But if anyone had visions of grandeur it wasn't Anna. He noted that none of Shirley's answers came out straight – they were devious, self-serving. Once more he was struck, as he always was, by the way different people react under pressure.

Finally, asked if there were some higher authority, some outside connection to which they all answered, Shirley grew indignant. 'Nobody told my mum what to do,' she said. She seemed to miss the point that if there were a chain of command Mrs Sparks' part might be viewed more leniently.

A litany of deception, Reynolds thought. Hard to distinguish lie from truth. But already she's sowing seeds of suspicion, especially about her sister, or half-sister (she seems to throw doubt even on that).

He himself didn't know what to think. Shirley's evidence brought all his own doubts flooding back. He'd once wanted to protect Anna from suspicion. It would be too easy now, out of vindictiveness, or revenge, to accuse her indiscriminately of major involvement, an equally unfair distortion. Yet if Shirley's testimony achieved anything it certainly cleared away any illusions he had left.

On one thing alone did husband and wife agree. Although both were grilled for hours – even the Inquiry Team relenting to let Reynolds have a go at them, he being an old hand at breaking resistance down – the Farrs, like Tregonning before them, steadfastly denied any knowledge of the actual murders.

'Do we look like murderers?' Trevor Farr pleaded. And at that moment, with his grey hair matted, and his eyes frantic, with shirt collar wilting and sweat marks beneath his armpits, he certainly didn't. Nor did he resemble the dapper lawyer who had threatened lawsuit. Stalemate.

At the close of the day then, the Inquiry Team still had made only little progress. Except for the possible motive, and the evidence of it, they had no other clues.

But they had gained one advantage, although this was never openly admitted. Like Topsy of the story-book fame it just 'grow'd' and was accepted – Reynolds' interest in the case was no longer challenged and his help, if not exactly asked for, was tolerated, under pretext that his services were needed by the Narcotics Section. In other words he was given a free hand, as long as no one formally recognized what he was doing – which, he told himself, was what should have happened from the start, if people had been sensible.

'Farr's enough legal training to see the danger he and his wife are in,' Reynolds said later when he and Derrymore conferred. 'But he's still afraid to admit to anything. My guess is there's probably a network, and although this may be only a small branch, it will have its hierarchy. The Farrs may know who is actually in charge, but they're not going to talk. Given what's happened I can see why. On the other hand I can't exactly envisage Trev and Shirl climbing in and out of windows or dirtying themselves with mud.'

He and Derrymore had come back to the café again by mutual agreement, and were sitting wearily at their corner table.

'Of course,' Reynolds added hastily, 'I know these are only assumptions, not proven facts. We still need more evidence to prove them. And with Tregonning out of the picture, and the Farrs in custody, our list of suspects is dwindling fast.'

'So what do we do now?' A tired Derrymore looked at Reynolds.

Reynolds stretched his legs painfully; like Derrymore's, they were cut from the rocks and shale, his feet a mass of blisters worse than any he'd experienced even as a raw army recruit. His shoulder felt twisted into an especially tortured knot. He didn't want to think about the cases at the moment, he didn't want to have to work out evidence, or worry about putting theory and fact together. Still, while there was work it had to be done.

'There's Anna Sparks,' he said.

Thankful that no change in his voice showed, he went on, 'What do you make of Shirley Farr's testimony?'

He hoped Derrymore would laugh it off, but to his relief, or despair, Derrymore didn't. 'I'm not sure,' Derrymore said. 'I'd like to say it's no more than I'd expect of Shirley Farr . . .'

'But?'

'Well.' Derrymore looked uncomfortable. 'I know there were things between you and Anna,' he said tactfully, 'and that's none of my business, but Shirley Farr's suggested she

279

knows a lot more than perhaps we thought. So we ought to find out the truth if we can.'

Fairly put. Derrymore was always fair. Fair but honest. Reynolds looked at him affectionately.

'All right,' he said aloud. 'I have something to tell you, an error of judgement, an indiscretion. Although it may have righted itself by now, through no help from me, I may add.'

His look was straight. 'I went to visit Anna on Wednesday morning. We spent a long time together. I daresay if I'd had the chance I'd have spent the night. But she didn't invite me. And I didn't invite myself. Because Tregonning told me she'd spent the previous night with him.'

Unlike other admissions, the unburdening of this wasn't easy, didn't finish once he'd confessed, would last a long time.

'As to the truth of Tregonning's claim,' he went on, 'at this point it doesn't matter. What does matter is if we should take Shirley Farr seriously.'

He took a breath. 'I saw Anna with that damned trinket box,' he said, 'the first time that I met her.' And so revealed the final part.

Finished, he looked at Derrymore, hoping he'd understand.

And Derrymore rose to the occasion, as he always did.

'I think,' said Derrymore, 'we should visit Anna Sparks without delay. Get things tidied up once and for all.'

He stifled a yawn. 'And if it's the same with you, sir, I'll tag along to see fair play.' Which again was an honest way of looking at a problem. And helped Reynolds more than the younger man perhaps knew.

Once more Reynolds didn't try to contact Anna first by

280

phone. He didn't want to scare her off. But more than that, he didn't want to talk with her alone. Acknowledging this took more effort than he liked, cowardice on his part too, he accepted that, but he wouldn't, or couldn't, go back to what he'd felt before. The sort of entrapment he'd known with his former wife had left too deep a mark. Even seeing Anna would be difficult; having Derrymore to act as go-between, the detached observer, the police witness, was a godsend. He knew he could rely on Derrymore.

The journey, in Derrymore's car this time, seemed endless as they drove in silence across the moors towards the clay tips which dominated the landscape behind St Austell. Reaching the village, while Reynolds went down the road, alone, Derrymore parked the car out of sight (although we could have left it here, he thought, it doesn't look so out of place; Derrymore could have bought it from Anna Sparks' neighbour).

The end house looked like the others, slumbering quietly in the late afternoon sun. Reluctant to disturb its owner right away, Reynolds wandered round the side and looked across to where a small red car was parked on a tarmac square that took up half the back garden. Its doors and windows were locked, its college parking sticker conspicuous on the windshield.

Seeing it, he felt absurdly relieved. She's here then, he thought, hasn't gone off anywhere, hasn't gone into hiding herself as he had half expected after Shirley had put so many suspicions into his head.

A rotting hoarding at the rear of the garden shut off access to the disused clay works. He was surprised to see how close the workings were to the cottages – in places the sand hills spilled almost against the fence. The accompanying pool of water, where the mine pit had been, stretched behind like a miniature sea, like a strange holiday resort with cottages for beach huts and white mud for a beach. Even with the sun full out, as today, the water still reflected a cloudy blue and along the edges, between beds of rushes, sticky white clay deposits clung in deep patches. Typical clay-mining terrain he thought, anything less like Padstow I can't imagine. Yet with the sand in the background and the vast expanse of cloudy water there was a strange similarity. Suddenly, for no reason, he thought of his nightmare and repressed a shiver.

He stayed leaning against the fence for a while, arranging his own thoughts in order, all the things that either he or Derrymore must ask to try at last to get to the bottom of what Anna must know. When Derrymore joined him, he nodded to the younger man; both went up the path to the door. Once again Reynolds hammered on it, and stood back to let Derrymore speak first. Once again no one answered.

'She's got to be here.'

Reynolds was looking at his watch – it was close to seven o'clock now – when Derrymore pushed on the door. It swung open. They were looking into a small sitting room, neat, dominated by a large poster of a fishing harbour, under which several shelves of books were arranged. Derrymore went from there into the kitchen, and then, two at a time, up the stairs – typically narrow, old country stairs that no modern planner would pass.

Reynolds meanwhile stood looking at the books – for some reason it seemed very important that he remember their titles. Many were in French – Modern Languages, he thought, that's her subject. They were arranged in rows, not very neatly – one or two were upside down and several were out of order. Scraps of blue tissue protruded from some of the shelves; they reminded him of the paper sometimes used to pack oranges and other fruit. Caught in one of the books, tucked in sideways, was a photograph, blurred, of an older man, tall, with what looked like a thatch of greying hair and a wide smile, standing by a harbour wall Reynolds didn't recognize. The man looked familiar. Of course, Reynolds thought, her father. He put the photograph back, turned as Derrymore clattered down the stairs.

'She's not in.' Derrymore looked puzzled. 'Bed not slept in last night. Or' – he looked at Reynolds and awkwardly changed what he was going to say – 'slept in and made up again as if in a hurry. Anyway, nothing out of order, even her handbag's gone.'

'But her car's here.' Reynolds was suddenly tense. Ignoring Derrymore, he took up the phone, tried to ring her mother's house, forgot the number and dialled Enquiries instead. The phone rang and rang until Derrymore took the receiver from him.

'No one at home,' Derrymore said reprovingly as Reynolds swore. 'Remember, the Farrs are still with the Inquiry Team. I expect a friend drove her to work this morning, and she's stayed late to catch up. They say teachers these days are overloaded,' he added, 'like the police.'

Reynolds didn't answer. Derrymore's prosaic reassurance didn't satisfy him. He was remembering yesterday when she was in the garden. 'On a glorious day like this I don't want to remember the past.' He thought of her bare feet and the picnic

283

she'd prepared and her sand-covered hands, and felt absurdly anxious.

'You're probably right,' he forced himself to say, not believing it. 'But I'm surprised she left the door unfastened.'

Derrymore was saying with a laugh that she wasn't like her mother, and Reynolds was putting the phone back on its stand when both men at the same time caught sight of something that cancelled out the laugh. Tucked in behind the stand, or rather stuffed in behind it, was the straw bag both recognized. Careful not to destroy finger marks, they removed it and tipped out the contents. Wallet, credit cards, money were stuffed in haphazardly. Along with the crumpled envelope from which Anna'd read aloud her half-brother's letter the previous evening.

Her keys were in the bag too, keys of house and car. While Derrymore hastily dialled the Incident Room, Reynolds went into the kitchen. Nothing out of place either, the back door firmly bolted and in an adjoining bathroom the window locked, its blind neatly down. He went outside again, squinting into the sun. Without touching, he examined the front door. There were no marks on it, no sign of forced entry, nothing.

'They'll get on to it right away.' Derrymore joined him on the front step, looking pale. He wetted his lips nervously. 'Perhaps she's gone—' he started to say. But Reynolds was looking beyond him towards the broken fence, where even as Derrymore turned a man came running towards them.

It was the man from next door, the neighbour 'who slept to noon'. He had a leash in one hand and a pair of dogs, whippets, raced beside him, hindering his getting through the gap. In his other hand he held what looked like a jersey, a blue woollen jersey, streaked with white.

Faster than he thought he could move Reynolds ran to meet him, a scrawny little fellow who barely came to his chin, caught him up with his one good hand and held him like a whippet might hold a rabbit, shaking him. He heard from a distance his own voice crying, 'What've you done with her?' while the dogs snapped and snarled around his ankles and Derrymore tried to loosen his grip.

Then his vision cleared. The little man had collapsed on the doorstep, fingers to his throat, was gasping something out about it being his day off, and having to take his whippets for a run. 'Always get some'at,' he was saying, beginning to get his breath back, 'rabbits and such. Like a run they do, my dogs.'

But Reynolds barely heard the rest, how walking along the far crest of the hill, where sand was giving way again to rough scrub dotted with rabbit holes, he'd spotted something strange beside the water among the rushes. By now Reynolds himself was through the gap in the fence and was running towards the water's edge, Derrymore at his heels.

Reynolds supposed it could be called running, in clay so sticky he didn't seem to move at all, as if he were trying to wade through glue. When they got there, they stood looking at the heap of clothes, women's clothes, the shoes carefully placed beside them. And a line of footprints that led from them to the water. One line out, none back.

On top of the clothes, anchored by the jeans, was a piece of paper. Derrymore picked it up and read. A hastily printed one word message – 'Sorry'.

Throughout the rest of the evening, while ambulances, police cars, police officers, photographers and forensic experts cluttered the little road and dodged each other in the little house, while neighbours stood in frightened clusters, clinging to each other, while the man with the whippets was interviewed and questioned and doubly interrogated, until even Reynolds couldn't get another word from him, Reynolds himself remained in tight control. Where emotion could not reach, discipline took over, that, and the routine of a lifetime.

Through all the comings and goings, the fuss and confusion, a scrap of doggerel verse persisted, a child's song: ''Twas on a Monday morning when I beheld my darling, she looked so neat and charming in every high degree, she looked so neat and nimble oh, a-washing of her linen oh . . .'

On Monday, he thought, Mrs Sparks fell in the shaft and I went down the cliffs. On Tuesday, Mrs Sparks was dead and Mike Tregonning tried to kill me and Miss Tenery. On Wednesday – what happened on Wednesday? She should have been ironing or starching or folding of her clothes, but was in fact playing, taking time off from work and enticing me to play with her. And what about Thursday, and Friday, and Saturday and Sunday when she should have been wearing of those same damn clothes, and going to church or whatever damn thing they did in those days? When she could have been my darling and stole my heart away – if I'd let her. Not dead in some stagnant clay pit, drowned, because she chose it, because she'd had enough of men and couldn't bear one more failure.

Tests showed no evidence of any fingerprints except her own, not on door or bag or car. Not on clothes or paper. Only on the jersey, those of the finder, who insisted he'd picked it up and brought it back as proof.

'So they'd believe me,' he kept insisting – the 'they' apparently being the rest of the cottage inhabitants who didn't approve of his dogs or hunting any more than they did his slovenly habits. As for anywhere else Anna Sparks might be, neither college nor relatives (the Farrs once more facing a situation they 'knew nothing about') had any suggestions. And where else could she be but beneath the water that mercifully still hid her remains?

While the others, careful at least not to disturb him, went their own way, Reynolds concentrated on the pitiful bits of clothing, looked for clues in grass or sand or mud, searched for the other presence who had taken such pains to make her death, or disappearance, appear self-inflicted. Nowhere could he find anything. And the more he looked, the more he strained for something that wasn't there, the more he became aware of the irritation of the Team that he wouldn't accept what everyone else took for granted. If he'd learned anything from long and bitter experience, taking things for granted isn't the way murders are solved.

The same lack of evidence was apparent indoors. Nothing out of place or extraordinary. Except for the few upside-down books, the blue tissue paper, and on top of her wardrobe a suitcase with a pair of shoes inside, the house seemed untouched. Yet he couldn't be sure. He sensed some lack of harmony, which the milling about of so many other people nullified. And nowhere was there any sign of her mother's jewelry box, although he made a special search for it. Either she hadn't taken it or had hidden it somewhere else. This lack of clues, contrasting with what there was – the note, the untouched house, the clothes neatly folded, the line of footprints

– nearly drove him wild. He knew it was contrived – the deviousness, the complicated and intricate method, were a familiar signature – deliberately arranged by someone she knew and to whom she had opened the door, trustingly.

In the midst of this long, protracted search, Shirley Farr dropped her own bombshell. 'Anna's not dead,' she cried. 'It's one of her tricks. She's gone off with Tregonning and pulled the wool over your eyes.'

She was told that Tregonning was on his boat alone, in hiding. 'Stands to reason she's waiting for him somewhere else then,' Shirley insisted. 'I won't believe she's dead until I see the body.' And it wasn't love that made her so convinced.

Of course there was no body. Although it was probable it might rise to the surface later of its own accord, discussion was already under way about the possibility of using divers to find her. And with a body one could determine if she had killed herself, or been killed.

'Leave her be,' Reynolds thought, suddenly sickened by the whole procedure. The image of her caked with clay, hair, eyes, mouth plastered with it like a solid shroud, rose before him with such horrid clarity that it smothered the memory of her on the beach, alive, hair blowing, face smiling. If only I had acted sooner, he thought, numb with regret, if only I had taken some of the things she said seriously. '*If all I have left is this one day* . . .' she'd said.

He came to himself to hear Derrymore say, 'Shall we go, sir?'

Derrymore was standing beside him, his shoulders hunched in an unfamiliar stoop, a sign of embarrassment. 'And about leaving, sir,' he went on, still not looking at Reynolds, his eyes downcast, but his very bearing full of sympathy. 'I've had a thought. I took the opportunity to ring my mam and she's expecting us. If you can bear it, that is, if you don't mind. Nothing fancy,' he hastened on, as if guessing Reynolds might imagine the invitation came out of charity, or worse, pity. 'But better than those frozen fast foods you're so fond of.'

'Nothing special,' he repeated, treading even more diffidently when Reynolds didn't at first reply. 'Casual like.' And at Reynolds' shake of the head (which hid what he was really thinking – a lifeline, which, if I accept, has nothing to do with gratitude or ingratitude, goes far beyond those), 'We don't have to be long about it. And then tomorrow, well, if you'd like, we've still a murderer to find.'

Chapter 16

Derrymore's cottage was as Reynolds had imagined – small, comfortable and homely. And Derrymore's mother fitted it; she was neat, rosy-cheeked with cooking and, like her son, sharp-tongued on matters she felt strongly about. Which she soon proceeded to demonstrate, without preamble, making it very clear that she, and the village in general, wouldn't put up with such goings on as had plagued them the last few days.

'Drowning my Derry twice,' she said, beginning with the one closest to her heart, 'ruining his best uniform, and cutting his arm to shreds. You ought to be ashamed of yourself, there's a fact.'

Here she rattled dishes energetically, while Derrymore, blushing scarlet, tried to hush her and she brushed him aside. 'As for Miss Tenery, she's a lost soul, although her family's lived here for ages. We know all about her and her prissy ways. But that rattle-headed friend of hers ought to know better, sheer hysterics if you ask me, nothing what a good bucket of cold water wouldn't cure.'

Again she rattled dishes. 'Now about Mrs Sparks, she's been a good customer at the village shop, roast meat twice a week and pays cash on the spot. And even if I don't hold with oldsters decking themselves up to look like spring chicken, isn't proper in my opinion and she never looked good in that yellow wig, still there's no call to kill her or her daughter. My dear,' she said quietly, and suddenly her eyes had filled with tears. 'I'm so sorry.'

A moment's awkwardness followed. What has Derrymore been telling her? Reynolds wondered. But he was too tired to care. Especially when, recovering, Mrs Derrymore went on bravely, 'So if that fancy upcountry team from across the Tamar River can't manage' – here her voice had revived to show local distrust of things 'non-Cornish' – 'then you and my Derry'd better take charge and get a move on. Because we won't feel safe in our beds at night until you do.'

A spiel, the end of which left her more red-faced than ever but whose final words Reynolds took as flattery of the most genuine kind, until she added shrewdly, 'Except don't you go tipping him in the water again.'

After which, irrepressible, she shooed them like children into her dining room.

They talked of nothing that mattered – local news, light, none of it important. He could keep quiet or not as he chose and no one would make judgements. Her meal was typical Cornish, straightforward and simple, cooked in traditional fashion, no rich sauces, no commercial vegetables, good butcher meat, and everything else home-grown. And she was right, it was what he needed, Reynolds thought, as he and Derrymore sat on afterwards in the cosy little room, with a fire that even on a warm night seemed to brighten the surroundings, with the sound of her washing up in the scullery to the strains of old-time dance music.

By then he too had recovered, to pick up threads, to listen to Derrymore's stories of war exploits, to add a few of his own. But gradually, without his being aware of it, the music faded, as did Derrymore's voice, tactfully avoiding all mention of Anna, speaking now of other fishing trips, of other expeditions at sea. Reynolds' cuts and bruises subsided, he felt his head nod forward, snap back. Sleep, the one thing he'd not expected, stole over him.

Which is why he ended the night on Derrymore's sofa, too short for him, covered with Derrymore's mam's best blankets, a sleep so deep there was no place for nightmares or regrets or brooding.

Awake next morning to apologies and another home-cooked meal, a gargantuan breakfast which Derrymore seemed to have no trouble in digesting, he felt back in his own skin, ready to pick up the pieces and start again. Until a second urgent dispatch reached him.

It came by special messenger, reaching him through that mysterious inter-village network of communication which enabled every St Breddaford member to know exactly where his neighbour was and what he was doing at any given time, the information suppressed unless, or until, there was some advantage in releasing it. Somewhat sheepishly then, the delivery man came knocking on Derrymore's door, pulled out a package addressed clearly to Reynolds, of Old Forge Cottage, and without the raising of an eyebrow the thing was signed for and handed over. Makes Fred's own methods look small potatoes, Reynolds thought, recognizing Fred's work. He grinned. Fred should take a closer look at how English village life is run. But the amusement didn't last long.

Fred had been quick. That was certainly true. And thorough. Although he'd always been thorough, that's why he and Reynolds had worked so well together. But now information that in former times would have taken days was available in hours. Again he imagined Fred's delight. The message was written in Fred's distinctive cramped hand, as if he felt safer if no one could read what he wrote. But when Reynolds finally deciphered it, it was short and decisive.

'No trace of a Malcolm Sparks. No application for a British passport, likewise none for an Australian visa. No leads, not even tax or medical records. Gone to earth. The fellow you're after has changed his name. Or he's dead.'

He'd added as if in afterthought, 'Won't tell you how much this non-information costs you, but you owe me a bottle of whisky, Glenfiddich.'

'And you shall have it.'

Reynolds was grim. He crumpled up the paper and threw it savagely aside.

'Bang goes our last lead.' Derrymore looked rueful. 'That's a bummer, sir,' he burst out. 'I had him pegged for sure.'

I had him pegged too, Reynolds thought. That's thrown me for a loser. So much for damn theory, stick to fact.

Derrymore hovered, as much as a young man of his size could be said to hover. 'So what next?' he asked anxiously.

'Start again,' Reynolds said as wearily. 'Scrap everything and go through the whole damn routine.'

He managed a smile. 'That's the way it is, old son,' he said. 'Sometimes repetitious. Boring even. Can't expect a breakthrough every day.'

But don't expect a downer either, he thought. This case has

had more downs than ups as far as I'm concerned. He stooped for the paper, smoothed it out and turned it over. As he began to write, his own thoughts cleared. When you've faced the worst, he told himself, then there's nothing worse to face – a truism he'd learned the hard way, as had Fred, in an Arab prison. And if you start with nothing, then there's all the more to gain.

As he wrote, confidence started to flow. He was there to help an Inquiry Team solve three murders. And, equally, Derrymore was there to help him. And if he'd learnt anything this past week it was that solving murders on one's own, without official backing, was not only time-consuming and frustrating but could too easily degenerate into personal vendetta, unprofessional behaviour and downright illegality!

'We'll still take for granted the three murders are by the same person, he said, writing as he spoke. 'Tregonning must answer for Miss Tenery, but the others are connected. All originate from the same motives – the discovery of the body in the mine shaft and my supposed discovery of the heroin. Although, again, how they thought I'd use this information I haven't yet worked out. Except, since I obviously didn't report it, they may have believed I'd try to get it for myself, as Tregonning did. And because Malcolm was never in Australia, that doesn't make him less a prime suspect . . .

'Unless' – here his pen stopped writing of its own accord – 'unless he really is missing. Which would mean a major disaster to all our theories.'

Quickly he went over in his own mind the other suspects in the case: Tregonning, never a strong contender, except for the attack on Miss Tenery; Mr and Mrs Farr, with alibis for Mrs

Sparks' death and, as Derrymore had pointed out, in custody when Anna Sparks disappeared; and Anna Sparks herself (to his relief he found he could think of her coolly and rationally now). None of them was strong enough to stand in place of Malcolm. But if Malcolm wasn't the prime suspect, here was another problem, having nothing to do with the solving of these murders. It concerned Malcolm himself. Where was he?

He noticed Derrymore was staring at him and realized he had broken off his summing up midway. He straightened his shoulder. Despite the battering of yesterday it felt better, the ache had subsided into the constant throb that he associated with healing and he could almost flex his hand freely again. And Derrymore at least was functioning; between them they'd manage.

'We've several priorities,' he told the expectant Derrymore, 'but the first is to get Pathology to divert attention away from Richard Sparks and focus on his son. At least find out if the bones are of a young male. Because I've a hunch where Malcolm Sparks has gone.'

He saw Derrymore's eyes widen in understanding. 'A hunch, if you can bear it,' he repeated, 'not a happy one, that we'll find Malcolm Sparks where we thought his father was. Put there for the same reason.'

He heard Derrymore catch his breath. 'And put there by the same person who committed the other murders, an unknown someone we haven't considered before, a real outside contender that we've got to start from the beginning to find.'

He reflected for a moment. 'Someone we *do* know something about,' he contradicted himself. He felt excitement grow. 'By

God, several things. To begin with, he's connected to the family in some way, known to them in the past at least and still familiar enough for Anna to let him into her house. Come to that he may have been the person Mrs Sparks was supposed to have telephoned from hospital. Probably was. Someone must have told him what had happened, if Tregonning wasn't on that sort of intimate level and Farr didn't dare.'

He thought about that too for a moment, about Mrs Sparks' presumed phone call. If Nurse Joyce Pengelly was right it may have been that in the end which killed her.

After a while: 'And we know he's ruthless,' he went on, 'a killer when it suits him, to punish or to hide evidence. And if he's into drugs in a big way, which I think we can assume, he'll do anything to hang on to this shipment. Once he hears how Tregonning tried to trick him – and may have succeeded – he'll be doubly dangerous. Tregonning's only hope is that we find him before he finds Tregonning.'

And with a sudden sense of foreboding he added to himself, 'Whoever he is he won't let go, he'll fight back. A man who thinks he can outsmart the world doesn't take defeat lying down, will hunt for revenge.'

All this while he was watching Derrymore, testing his reaction. And was pleased when Derrymore, as if in tune with his own thoughts, also straightened up and nodded.

'Right,' Derrymore said. 'I'll get on to Pathology first thing. But what a terrible thought if it is Malcolm Sparks. And all the while poor Richard Sparks where they said he was, at the bottom of the sea.'

He added, almost with a touch of wonder, 'And of the three original scenarios the one that now seems most likely is the one we agreed was impossible! And the final red herring is Mr Sparks' wedding ring.'

'Red herring perhaps,' Reynolds said. 'Or error. We'll wait and see.' And, despite Derrymore's questioning, refused to be drawn further along that line.

'As for Mrs Sparks' – after a while Derrymore returned to his own analysis – 'all along I've had difficulty reconciling her part in the first murder, or Anna Sparks' for that matter. But I'll tell you one thing. It was hard enough to accept the body as the father's; it seems worse somehow if it's the son or brother.'

It was Reynolds' turn to nod. Positively Freudian if not Oedipal, he thought, and was struck by the aptness of the classical allusion.

'About Mrs Sparks' own murder,' he went on. 'I'd like to check a few things. I presume of course the room's been occupied since, and much of the evidence – bedding, pillows etc. – has been cleared away. It's the window I'm interested in.'

He elaborated: 'I remember you pointed out that there was apparently no noise, although the window was used. I mean, there was no sign of struggle, Mrs S. died without waking. So how did someone climb in without rousing her?

'At the same time,' he continued, 'I still want to talk to the patient who claimed to have heard a car. And both Joyce Pengelly and Anna Sparks' neighbour need revisiting.

'If you agree, constable,' he added, the time-honoured ritual. But he wasn't smiling. Suppose Derrymore doesn't agree, he was thinking. I need him to give bite to the interviews, but does he need me?

He was especially pleased when Derrymore, as if answering that question, said, 'Lead on, sir. This time it's my turn to stay in the background.'

They started with the hospital, partly because they wanted to check on Miss Tenery. In a day full of disaster here at least was good news. Miss Tenery had regained fitful consciousness, but her memory was blurred. It might be weeks before she recovered enough to be interviewed, and most likely she would never regain memory of the night in question.

Following a visit to her room, where they could see little change, but stood at a respectful distance while the nurse on duty explained the improvement, they managed a quick survey of the room where Mrs Sparks had been murdered, mainly to satisfy Reynolds' curiosity. He himself had been in it so briefly he didn't remember much about it except the curtains which had shielded out the light. Crossing now to the window he drew them and looked down at the car park, which was already beginning to fill as morning visitors arrived.

As Derrymore had originally explained, although the room was on the bottom floor the height above the outside ground level was considerable, the car park being built on a slant. If someone tried to climb up from the outside he'd have a real scramble. So Reynolds' early question still remained unanswered: why hadn't the sleeping patient been wakened by the noise?

Who would know most about sleeping patients? He said nothing, but he made a note.

Next on the list, by dint of Derrymore's managing to get hold of the name and address while his hand was being dressed, they made a quick detour to see the young woman who'd

299

heard a car in the night. It was only by chance they took her next in order, partly because she lived in St Breddaford and was close by, partly because when Reynolds was in full pursuit, as now he was, he was always thorough. He was wary of loose ends when it came to witnesses. If she were an observant girl she might have noticed other things.

However, getting her to speak at all proved tricky. She was not willing to be interviewed again, she said – or rather her mother, bossy and old-fashionedly protective, said – apparently, as Derrymore eventually coaxed out, because she felt her daughter's original testimony had been treated in an off-hand fashion.

'Didn't even get back to thank Marlene,' the mother complained, her voice taut with indignation. 'Told her it wasn't important. As far as I can tell she was the only one with any information. And why did they say it wasn't important? It might have been, look at the news, whatever next.'

Apparently she was referring to the find Reynolds and Derrymore had made, which was already causing a stir, as Reynolds had foreseen. The disappearance of Anna Sparks as yet seemed less important, but then that was because the murders and the find presumably had not been linked.

Eventually, by dogged determination, they got the girl to talk, mainly because Derrymore occupied the mother in the background while Reynolds exercised his skill on the young woman.

Marlene was a slight fair girl, with a sickly complexion and a fretful twist to her mouth, startling red against the pale skin. Although she was on the mend from a minor knee operation, her recovery seemed slow, or perhaps her mother liked keeping her an invalid. Reynolds had spotted a certain proprietary air as the older woman bustled round the sofa where Marlene reclined, leg still propped up.

When he asked the girl about the night in question – well, to be honest, begged her to answer, telling her how important her statement was, they couldn't do without it – my, he thought, surprised, didn't she let her hair down!

She confirmed that when the police had left Mrs Sparks and her daughter had talked loudly about the discovery of the body, Mrs Sparks in particular raging at the daughter something dreadful for letting on about the father. ('An awful mother,' she said with a sidelong glance at which her own mother positively beamed.)

She also admitted to hearing not one but two cars!

Before yesterday's events they'd have thought she was exaggerating, now it seemed like a bonus. As it was, under their close interrogation she stuck to her story, a car about four in the morning, but another earlier, closer to midnight. One that snarled!

Patient questioning elicited that by 'snarl' she meant a loud and powerful engine; that whereas the four o'clock car sort of 'rattled' (a typical GP's car, Reynolds thought, no speed or whoomph), the midnight one had sounded quite different, like a racing car. And, although the car park was on the other side of the building, she had been able to distinguish the difference since both had gone down the drive.

As to why she hadn't said so earlier, why she'd not explained about the two cars instead of one, she'd opened her eyes wide and tossed her hair. What with the confusion and her own medical problems, she said, she'd simply forgotten. And no one had asked. Which goes to show, Reynolds thought, that even witnesses expect some recognition. Only natural. But still he was uncertain.

'What do you think?' he asked Derrymore when they left. 'Marlene may have come up with a tale after the event to put herself in the limelight.' And was glad to hear Derrymore say, 'I don't think she's looking for attention; her mum gives her plenty. And she wasn't that keen to talk in the beginning.'

'So, another fast car. Who else do we know with one?'

'Well,' Derrymore said, settling down to what Reynolds knew he liked best, what he called a 're-hash' and what Reynolds thought of as 'letting ideas flow'. 'There's Mr Farr's Mercedes, and Tregonning's souped-up Ford. Oh, yes, there were always rumours of Mrs Sparks' relatives having posh cars, but that may have been referring to Trevor Farr's.'

'Wasn't there talk of one being seen the morning she fell in the shaft?' Reynolds said suddenly. And at Derrymore's nod: 'But that wasn't Farr's car, we know now he was in Bristol. And by no stretch of imagination can Anna Sparks' car be called posh. So whose was it, then?'

He thought for a moment. 'You know,' he said quietly, 'I think we'll tackle Nurse Pengelly next, to hell with her routines. If she led me on before it must have been for a purpose. And there's no one who knows more about the family than she does.'

What they were to find out was beyond their imaginings.

It was early for Joyce to be home from the hospital, but when they saw her tripping down the road, laden with parcels, they realized she had been shopping. She didn't seem unduly disturbed by the car parked outside her gate. 'I recognize you,' she said to Reynolds, bending her head to peer in at them, 'and I recognize you, Mr Derrymore.'

As he clambered out of the car, 'Goodness me,' she cooed, patting his bandaged hand, 'I heard you'd been in the wars. I wondered when you'd be along to see me, constable. I missed you.'

'And I've heard what you'd be up to,' she said, after the shopping had been carried indoors, and put away, and she was insisting on making them both a cup of tea to 'wash down' one of the many fancy cakes she seemed to have bought.

'The news was full of it,' she went on, almost gleefully. 'I told the girls at the hospital there was more than meets the eye. There was always something fishy about our Trev, I said. I'm sure he killed his mother-in-law, aren't I right?'

She leaned forward expectantly and seemed genuinely disappointed when they explained that whatever else he was accused of, murder of Mrs Sparks wasn't one of the charges. But they also noted she didn't mention Anna Sparks.

'Now, Miss Pengelly,' Reynolds started gently. 'When I first came I believe you told me several dates. Can you give us them again?'

This she did willingly, almost triumphantly, the list of dates and events that he guessed were ingrained in her memory.

After which it was time to get down to business. 'What really made Malcolm leave?' he asked, starting with where he knew she was most vulnerable. 'Did you know he'd gone? And when you couldn't reconcile his going with what you felt, did he become part of the general hatred you had for all of them?'

303

He sensed that familiar flicker of fear. 'Why all these questions?' she cried.

His answer, made in his most affable manner – 'Because it's come to our attention he may not have left at all' – had a dramatic result.

She heaved herself up and with her quick flittery walk, like an abnormally large wagtail, went over to the chair where she'd found the article about Mr Sparks. She drew out something from the bottom of the heap, a scrapbook, full of newspaper cuttings, postcards and old letters – all dealing with the Sparks family and their vicissitudes, all labelled and carefully pasted in order. A policeman's treasure trove, Reynolds thought, as he and Derrymore examined the brittle pages.

'Mum made it.' Joyce preened herself. 'It kept her busy.'

I'll say, Reynolds thought. He had the sudden vision of an elderly invalid filling her time making a family album about people to whom she wasn't remotely related. For what purpose – merely to occupy herself, or to keep for some future occasion not yet established? Whatever the reason, here was the model for Joyce Pengelly's own magpie hoardings; he even wondered briefly if she herself were the actual compiler and used her mother as subterfuge, then decided not to press the issue. If it became relevant it wouldn't be difficult to ascertain the real author, for one thing the labelling was consistent, the writing distinctive, large and ill-formed. Besides, most of the letters and cards were addressed to the mother; he felt a touch of respect for such calculated malice.

Some of the letters were rambling, the sort friends write; others were specific; he caught a description of Mrs Sparks after her husband's death – how she'd wept aloud that since his body hadn't been found she had nothing to remember him by. It seemed somehow pathetic now to think that the widow's grief might have been genuine – in that at least she'd been maligned. But not a word then about a ring.

The arrangement of the scrapbook followed the same order of events that Joyce Pengelly had originally described, with two exceptions. Stuffed in at random was a section devoted entirely to Malcolm – a postcard from him, a list of his favourite books, a note about some bird he'd seen – Malcolm was a naturalist, he gathered. There was nothing to suggest Malcolm had been anything other than what Joyce had claimed, a friend. And yet, why treasure these odd scraps – as Anna Sparks had kept Malcolm's letter – unless they had some use, or, in this case, value, way above the obvious one?

Also in this section was a batch of correspondence that dealt with Malcolm's disappearance. Reynolds guessed that that wasn't the mother's work, was all Joyce Pengelly's doing. 'Heard them at it,' someone had written, 'thought you'd like to know. And so soon after Dick's death . . .'

By all accounts there'd been a family quarrel before Malcolm left, although no one seemed to pinpoint the cause. One night Malcolm had stormed out of the cottage, been seen wandering on the shore, throwing stones into the water. After which he'd never been seen again, had presumably come back at daybreak to pack his things and take his leave . . . a second quarrel then, other than the one that she'd reported. Reynolds felt the familiar shiver of discovery.

The second random set of papers related to Anna Sparks. These seemed to have been ripped out of context rather than not properly filed, again he guessed Joyce's handiwork. Anna had gone off to college that autumn, and had married in the same year. There was a passage from a local paper describing the wedding and giving the bridegroom's name as Peter Lewis, and a vague photograph of Anna in her wedding dress, with a tall man beside her. He identified the man as Anna's father, whose photograph he'd seen in Anna's bookcase. But that couldn't be right as Richard Sparks was already dead!

Reynolds hadn't realized her marriage had come so soon after her father's death and Malcolm's disappearance. Of course she'd admitted it was to 'escape', and other people, including her sister, had verified that, but she certainly hadn't wasted time. And from the start she had been serious about wanting a father figure. Presumably then the husband must have been someone she'd known before she went away, she couldn't have met and married someone new within a couple of months. Therefore he was unlikely to be the college student, the young and callow youth, that Reynolds had always imagined.

'Who's that?' he asked Joyce, pointing to the photograph, and was surprised and annoyed at himself when she answered, 'The groom of course, who else?'

He took the clipping out and studied the picture closely. The man was tall and broad-shouldered – not exactly your typical weedy youngster, Reynolds told himself. And the smile that somehow seems familiar, and which I'd identified with Anna's, now has no connection. Thoughtfully, he placed the photograph at one side.

'What do you want that for?' Joyce Pengelly was sounding querulous. 'Silly piece of nonsense, Anna's wedding, just to show she was as good as her sister. One of Trev's acquaintances, they told me, but rich as the devil. Wonder what she had to give out to catch him?

'Not that it matters,' she added with a knowing shake of her head. 'Dead, they say a suicide. Well, none of them was very stable, and she'd a lot to answer for.'

At last she'd mentioned the missing woman. A cold elegy, Reynolds thought, a cruel one. Under the chatter he caught a glimpse of the same deeply hidden venom that had marred Joyce Pengelly's previous testimony. But if her dislike of Anna was as intense as her dislike of Mrs Sparks, there had to be some reason – other than the losing of a house that, by her own admission, Joyce and her mother were glad to leave.

He banged the scrapbook shut – a family album created by a dead woman who wasn't even related and revealed, willingly, almost triumphantly, to a police investigation by her daughter, apparently blissfully unaware of the suspicions it aroused.

'What was the real quarrel between your two families?' he barked. And when she didn't answer: 'It wasn't what you suggested last time, was it? Not about Malcolm's mother wanting your house. Nor about his siding with his mother. You made that up.'

Again no answer. 'I rather think,' he went on slowly, 'it had to do with your father's daughter. Wasn't Anna Sparks your father's child?'

Joyce Pengelly was crying now, fat tears rolling down her cheeks. There was something grotesque about those tears, as if a large floppy doll had suddenly come alive.

'They did want the house,' she hiccuped, 'that part's true. And, all right, I admit it, they kept the baby when they shouldn't have. The way Dick Sparks doted on it made you sick. Mind you, I didn't know about it myself until mum was dying, all I knew then was that something was wrong.'

She blew her nose loudly. 'When my father left – well, he had to leave if she didn't, and it killed him, he died within the year – you can imagine what it was like for my mum. I was not much more than a child myself, she was left alone to manage as best she could. So when they started on about a bigger house, my mum was glad to go. But all those years, seeing her husband's daughter brought up by her husband's mistress, it took a saint not to want some sort of compensation for the ruin they'd caused. Yet my mum never complained once, never would.'

With some difficulty distinguishing between the different 'she's' (for once again Joyce Pengelly could not bring herself to mention Mrs Sparks by name), Reynolds continued more softly, 'And as you grew up you liked Malcolm Sparks didn't you, and thought he returned your liking, shall we call it that, until he went off. Without explanation, without a goodbye, in fact without a word.'

Joyce Pengelly wiped her eyes, and stared in front of her. 'What I couldn't stand,' she said simply, 'was that they made a fool of me. All of them to greater or lesser degrees, Malcolm included. Malcolm didn't have to act friendly just because she told him to. Just to keep things on an even keel, he said, but not until I asked him, and at the time I didn't know what he meant. Yes, I thought he owed me more than silence.'

She sat quietly for a moment while Reynolds thought of Anna Sparks. After a while, Joyce continued, 'As for Dick Sparks, he didn't have to go along with his wife, hide her shame because he was afraid of her. He could have spoken up for us, that'd have been right. And those girls, making good marriages and all, climbing the ladder of success, it wasn't fair, was it, that we had to lose it all?'

Reynolds remembered Derrymore's outburst, and his own reply. He stifled a sigh. Life as well as death isn't fair, he wanted to say, there's no justice in this world.

'So when she showed up in hospital' – the sympathy in his voice was genuine – 'it was like one of your "freebies", wasn't it? Your chance to make up for all your mother's sufferings, no need for you to show your mum's restraint. Didn't you say she deserved her end?'

Once more she nodded, listening intently. 'So what did you do,' he asked her, 'to make sure justice was done?'

Joyce Pengelly's eyes had filled again at the sympathy; she wiped them with the back of her hand, a great lumbering child of a woman, grieving for lost loves and lost hopes. She gazed at Reynolds with open mouth. He felt a qualm.

'Oh,' she said, suddenly practical, 'it wasn't very strong. Just enough to knock the stuffing out and make her sick. When she woke, that is,' she said, virtue triumphant. 'I thought, let her wallow in her own vomit for once.'

As if, in her practicality, she didn't even notice the importance of what she said.

'But she didn't wake.'

Reynolds didn't have to say this aloud, but his look at Derrymore said it. Derrymore, who had been sitting quietly in his usual way, feet together, helmet on lap, stood up. 'I think, Miss Pengelly,' he began solemnly, 'you'd better come along with me. Because if what you've said is true, then we have to take it seriously.'

She looked at him as if she thought he was joking. 'It wasn't strong,' she repeated. 'A child's dose. It didn't kill her . . .'

'But it probably enabled someone else to do so,' Derrymore said. He put his unbandaged hand on her arm. 'So, if you will come along quietly, we need a statement down at the Incident Room.'

It wasn't until the police car arrived and she'd been led to it that she began to scream. Reynolds could hear the screams for a long time.

He sat on in her stuffy sitting room, surrounded by the memorabilia from the past, and thought of many things.

When Derrymore came back he looked grey, and kept wiping his forehead as if the room had suddenly become too hot. He didn't say anything, just sat down heavily, with his hands between his knees. Reynolds felt sorry for him. It's a rotten role to play, he thought, brought along to listen to confessions, the confessions themselves cajoled out of people without their knowing how – almost as bad as having to do the cajoling. There's something to be said for comparing police work to the Inquisition; I've always understood they were masters at getting suspects to damn themselves.

He was still holding the newspaper cutting of Anna's wedding. He put it down and stood up briskly. 'Now for our last port of call,' he said, indicating the picture. 'A little matter of wrong identification I want to clarify. In fact' – here he did hesitate – 'as far as wrong identification is concerned, the whole case from the start has been riddled with it.'

'You mean the body in the mine shaft?' Derrymore's face lightened.

310

'I mean,' said Reynolds tersely, 'the identification of everyone, Anna Sparks most of all. The wrong identification as the married daughter, and the wrong identification of the husband. I've always had her married to the wrong man.'

He didn't expand on that remark until they had once more driven up to the row of cottages. The red car was no longer parked in the back, having been removed for forensic tests, but the house was in the same state as they'd seen it only two days before. Reynolds, standing in the doorway and looking in, could imagine Anna might appear at any moment and say, 'I've been expecting you.'

The Inquiry Team had been thorough; he couldn't fault them in that. There wasn't anything they'd overlooked. But the main room still didn't look right, although of course he'd never seen it before the day Anna had disappeared. Now, looking at it freshly and calmly, without all the fuss and bustle of police investigation, he was struck again by the lack of harmony he'd originally sensed.

It wasn't that books had been pulled out and replaced or even that cupboards and drawers had all been emptied and searched. 'Did they move these pictures?' he asked Derrymore suddenly. 'I don't remember their touching them. Or that vase – did it always stand in that position?'

'I don't know.' Derrymore looked carefully. 'I suppose they might have been checked for fingerprints and such, then put back. I'll find out.'

'Good.' Reynolds spoke absentmindedly. He himself had gone to the bookcase and, after a hunt, drew out the photograph to compare with the newspaper clipping. No doubt about it, it was the same man, the former husband with whom Anna

311

Sparks/Lewis had remained on such good terms that he'd given her this house when they parted.

In the background he heard Derrymore talking to the Incident Room, speaking quickly, and nodding as they answered. Quietly, not to disturb him, he got up and went out, stepping across the low wall that divided Anna's front garden from the next-door neighbour's, the man who slept until noon and who should still be sleeping.

There was a longish wait. By the time the neighbour had got up and pulled on trousers and socks, Derrymore had joined Reynolds on the front doorstep. He'd just finished telling Reynolds what the Team had done or not done, when the man opened the door and, seeing Reynolds, retreated rapidly.

'Told what I know,' he shouted through the gap. 'Don't have more to tell.'

'I've come about something else,' Reynolds said, one foot out to stop the door being closed completely. 'About what visitors you've seen next door, and what cars they drove.'

The man stared at him. 'Come on.' Reynolds was impatient. 'Your garden's stuffed with bits from every make known to man. Don't tell me you don't know the difference between a Volvo and a Ferrari.'

'Seen your car,' the man spat out, suddenly angry. 'Seen it the other day. Great big automatic job. And seen you knocking at her door one morning before she vanished. But didn't tell about it.'

Reynolds didn't comment. If he felt Derrymore's gaze turn to him he paid no attention. 'What about the night before?' he asked, 'any strangers, any strange cars?'

'No.' The answer was sullen. 'Kept asking me that, if there had been, I'd have telled.'

There was a yelping behind him, a scuffle. His dogs trying to get out. About to turn away, Reynolds said suddenly, 'Those dogs of yours, whippets, I hear they're champions.'

The man's thin face softened. And as Derrymore here interposed some remark about the County Fair and the winning breeds, and weren't whippets preferable to greyhounds given their speed and temperament, the two were soon deep in discussion as if they were both dog breeders. And if Derrymore was genuinely knowledgeable, his interest paid dividends.

As they finally took their leave: 'There was a fellow who comed sometimes,' the whippets' owner shouted after them. 'I didn't see him that night but he was there often enough.'

They waited expectantly. 'Her former husband,' he said. 'At least she called him that. Had a damn great car. Blue. Could hear its snarl a mile off.'

Chapter 17

They sat in the car outside the house looking at each other. 'She'd have let him in.' As ever Derrymore was practical.

'Of course there'd have been no struggle. Unless,' he paused a moment, 'she'd become suspicious. I mean during these past few days, if she didn't know from the beginning, that is.'

For once Reynolds didn't pick up on Derrymore's observations right away. Peter Lewis, he was thinking, the ex-husband whom I dismissed as a nonentity. He thought too of the harbour in the photograph, a foreign harbour with its expensive backdrop, a rich man's playground where men 'who knew nothing about the sea' (Tregonning's description) moored their yachts and hired other men to sail them. I categorized Tregonning in that role when I first met him, Reynolds thought, and was mistaken. This time there's no mistake.

He remembered the way Anna's ex-husband posed, leaning towards the sun, tanned and confident, the harbour (wherever it was, they'd find it) one Lewis knew well and would return to at will, whenever he wanted. It was the smile he should have remembered, the smile that was so familiar. Idly for a moment he even wondered how the photograph had come to be left behind. Perhaps Anna had never told him she had it. Or he had missed it in the search through her things.

That was one point he was certain of – someone, now identified as Peter Lewis, had searched her house at some point before the police got there. Even before Derrymore confirmed (as he just had) that the Inquiry Team had not moved those certain objects he'd noted, he had sensed the disturbance.

He had no proof of course; he based his observation on instinct, what he called common sense, from the way the articles in question had been placed, or rather misplaced, in positions he knew Anna herself would never have chosen – although as yet he had no idea what these aberrations signified. Now the careless positioning of the books, the scraps of blue tissue paper, even that suitcase with one pair of shoes cried out for explanation.

And as he sat and thought other clues, unnoticed before, revealed themselves. If Peter Lewis had access to Anna Sparks' home, had been a frequent visitor to the home he'd given her (and was that a pay-off too, like Mrs Sparks' gold gewgaws?), equally he could have been welcomed by Mrs Sparks, might have had a key to her house, might have become privy to all her secrets. For one, if he had married into the family soon after her husband's death, wouldn't he have heard the story of the ring, how it was always left behind when Richard went to sea; wouldn't he perhaps have been shown it, or at least known where it was kept? And wouldn't he have a key to enable him to open locked doors to look for the ring when he needed it, and to remove the whole box later as it suited him?

Once more he felt the familiar tingle of discovery. If this were true, then of all the wild scenarios he and Derrymore had

316

concocted that first afternoon, the one they had dismissed as most improbable was the one that had actually happened – Mrs Sparks had fallen down the shaft; someone, again identified now as Peter Lewis, had unlocked her front door, gone upstairs, drawn out her wooden box from under her bed, coldly and methodically gone through the contents to find her husband's ring, then as coldly come outside again, climbed down into the pit and placed the ring among the dead man's bones – without one attempt to rescue or revive her, probably without even bothering to look. And then, after one quick check through his binoculars, had driven off in his 'posh' car – to run Reynolds himself down!

But what part had Anna played in all of this? Had she known, or guessed? Harking back to Derrymore's original remark, Reynolds pointed out, in his most disinterested voice, that if she had suspected her former husband, as surely she must have done at some point, Lewis would have no option except to get rid of her. In which case, he argued, Lewis could have murdered her whenever he wanted, at the same time as her mother perhaps if he really mistrusted her. So why did he wait? Why did he feel he had to make her murder look like suicide, if indeed she had been murdered and not just 'disappeared' as Shirley suggested? It didn't seem like him to want to conceal the results of his actions, although the elaborate cover-up would be typical.

But if, on the other hand, Anna had had no suspicions of her former husband then she had presented no danger and he had spared her up to now. And if he now felt threatened for whatever reason, possibly not having anything to do with her at all but somehow connected with his original purpose –

which, they must not forget, was the safe retrieval of that haul of drugs – then Anna might still be alive, because he still had some use for her. In which case she must be found, because the use wouldn't be for her good.

Once more he didn't like his line of reasoning. And when he had explained all this to Derrymore, he added, 'She may be alive in any case, because her knowing or not knowing may be irrelevant. If so, her disappearance has been arranged for only one purpose – to provide her former husband with a scapegoat if he needs one later. Meaning,' he said more soberly, 'she's held as hostage, although she herself may not yet realize it.'

As the implications of this hit home, he continued, in a voice which hid his real feelings, 'I may have misjudged everything else but I know that whoever this killer is, Peter Lewis or not, he's lethal. And he's not yet caught. For that matter he may not even stay around for us to do the catching. He'll already have contacts, safe places, bolt holes in or out of England. This type of criminal always does.'

He heard Derrymore say, 'Then the Inquiry Team'll have to track him down. Although whether they can make the charges stick is another matter.'

There are so many charges, Reynolds thought. A clever man may be able to balance them against each other, manipulate them. If Anna's ex-husband is half the man I think he is he'll run circles round our Inquiry Team, just as he's run circles around us.

Both he and Derrymore were silent for a while, working out the complexities.

'Of course, there's another possibility.' After a while Reynolds continued unemotionally – he might have been

318

speaking of someone he'd never met. 'If, from the start, Anna was an accomplice, as we originally thought, if her marriage, for example, was arranged as part of the general cover-up, she herself may now be reaping the reward of complicity—'

'That really makes us look like idiots!' Derrymore broke in angrily. 'And the disappearance is a fake, like Shirley Farr suggested.'

Reynolds stirred uneasily. Put bluntly like that the words stung, even more than Tregonning's claims of sexual deception, even more than his own sense of sexual betrayal. Because, if it were true, she'd had the last laugh after all, conning all of them.

Nevertheless, personal discomfort apart, there was no reason to feel confident that danger was over. I've dealt before with men obsessed with success, he thought, they're never easy to handle. He remembered his earlier assessment, that the man, whoever he was, wouldn't give up readily, and wouldn't forgive. And he remembered too the fear he inspired in his presumed associates. Most of all, he remembered the driver of the car in the lane, and his jeering grin.

He came out of his musings, to hear Derrymore ask, 'Shall we put a search warrant out for him, sir?' and his own reply, 'Not yet.' Snapped out so quickly it took even him by surprise.

Quickly he explained his misgivings to the younger man, adding that he felt the Inquiry Team wouldn't be able to cope. 'They have to answer to Head Office,' he reminded his companion. 'And we know Head Office prefers the heavy-handed approach. We'll have to find some way of restraining them first.'

He didn't explain what he meant by 'first', but to his relief

Derrymore understood. What was more, he caught on to the other idea that Reynolds was hinting at.

'Seems a pity, doesn't it,' Derrymore said, thoughtful now in turn, 'to be so close to success and not to make it on our own?'

Pressed as to what he was suggesting, he admitted that he wasn't happy about having the Inquiry Team take all the credit for the final denouement; that 'foreign', upcountry lot even his mother had been contemptuous of didn't deserve the honour. More than that, he confessed to a burning desire to get even with the man who'd wasted so much of their time and effort. And who, as far as Derrymore was concerned, was the monster responsible for all the killings.

'Look at him,' he said, indicating the photograph that Reynolds had shown him. 'Needs a sure touch to reel in a man like him.'

The sort of touch we've got, he intimated, the sort of operation you and I were trained for.

Emboldened by Reynolds' silence, he hurried on, speaking more quickly than usual. 'When I was in the army there was one device that never failed. Find some lure that an enemy couldn't resist, you had him hooked. If only we had a lure now . . .'

'We do.' Reynolds kept his voice low, but his excitement was matching Derrymore's. 'The haul on Tregonning's boat.'

Quickly he explained. 'According to yesterday's newspapers the Inquiry Team has located a drug drop and the search is still on for the drugs themselves. As far as Lewis and the general public know they haven't been found. True enough. But suppose we let out now that they have been picked up, and thus the whole operation's over.'

He looked at Derrymore. 'Finished with, done for,' he said. 'What did Narcotics call it? The "catch of the decade", the one they're always dreaming of. Well now, suppose we elaborate upon this little lie in such a way as to suggest I'm behind the recovery. We know he won't take kindly to failure. And if anything'll goad him into action, my name should.'

Again he eyed Derrymore. 'It's me he recognizes,' he continued. 'It's me he's already tried to kill for threatening his enterprise. Revenge is sweet. Ten to one if he thinks he's lost, he'll try again. He'll need something, or someone, to vent his anger on.'

'Live bait.' Derrymore looked worried. 'It might work,' he conceded, 'if certain precautions are taken.'

He looked at Reynolds and his mouth shut up tight, just like his mam's. He means if he's part of the exercise, Reynolds thought – but why not? Better him than anyone else I know. And he won't give up until I agree.

So when Derrymore, all efficiency, asked, 'How do we bypass the Incident Room?' he began to laugh.

'Easy,' he said. 'Hoist by their own petard.'

He laughed again. 'Remember we're part of Narcotics now,' he said. 'We've been palmed off on them. So all we have to do is get them to back us, and we're home and dry. And believe me, they're so anxious for success, they'll follow my lead.'

'Our lead.' Derrymore stressed the 'our' defiantly, a defiance which again Reynolds let pass.

All of which explains why, without further preamble, and with the minimum of fuss, the Narcotics Section came swarming down to St Breddaford, bypassing Head Office and its Inquiry Team, to assist an ex-inspector and his country colleague in setting up a trap, using the ex-inspector himself as decoy.

Grudgingly, told that Narcotics expected 'a major breakthrough', the Inquiry Team were obliged to give way. As they concentrated on more routine work, namely the identification of Malcolm Sparks' body, and the hunt for Tregonning's boat (threatened bad weather not having yet materialized), the Narcotics Section set up their own command post in Derrymore's house, much to his mother's delight (although she would have died rather than admit it). There phone lines were rigged so that messages could be recorded and traced if calls were made to Reynolds' number; the task of identifying Peter Lewis and associates, if any, was put into motion – the sort of information that Fred had originally supplied and which now was collected with full official sanction. As a final touch, an anti-terrorist squad was brought in and deployed around the village, lying in wait for the trap to be sprung. Within hours of these new developments the media was permitted to broadcast full details of Reynolds' "discovery".

Information about the new prime suspect soon poured in, a mixed and disappointing flow. Like Trevor Farr in earlier days, Peter Lewis seemed to have no fixed abode or profession, being variously listed in various cities as an export-import trader, a wine merchant and an antique dealer – all occupations notorious for sheltering illegal activities. Moreover his home addresses showed he lived in places that did not exist, such as long-abandoned post-office box numbers and recently closed bed-and-breakfast establishments. Even the swank rooms he'd favoured more frequently these days, in large and expensive hotels here and abroad, proved impossible to check and gave no leads. Nor did the Farrs, once more grilled about their relationship to him, add any more information, except to reiterate that Anna had married him out of pique, and had only herself to blame when the marriage failed.

All these activities were a bitter pill for the Inquiry Team to swallow, but actually the term 'bitter pill' applied to Reynolds as much as to them, although they wouldn't have appreciated his dilemma. To begin with, in letting his name be put forward so openly he was breaking every rule he and Fred had lived by – keeping a low profile had always spelled survival. More than that, in his personal life, Reynolds had chosen to settle in St Breddaford not only because of its much appreciated peace and quiet, but also because he had enjoyed anonymity there. Fame, as he'd once pointed out, had no charms for him, either as a police detective or a writer; he cringed at publicity. If anything, the fulsome praise would be as hard to live down as Miss Seward's accusations of womanizing. In short, his own cover had been blown and his new notoriety was as distasteful to him as it probably would be to his neighbours, a situation he feared he would bitterly regret, if he lived to regret anything, that is.

He had plenty of time to mull over these and other related problems as he sat in his quiet house, waiting. Apparently alone, certainly unarmed, for two consecutive days and nights he conspicuously occupied his favourite place in his sitting room, feet up on sofa, windows open, lights on, acting out the role of unsuspecting victim – what Derrymore, more graphically, had called live bait.

True, Derrymore kept watch in an adjoining room and, in judicially concealed positions about the garden and house, members of that anti-terrorist squad were on guard, with strict instructions to remain under cover until the bait had been swallowed – an euphemism Reynolds himself preferred not to dwell on.

In his wartime experience Reynolds had had plenty of practice at ambush. But ambushing someone is quite different from allowing oneself to be ambushed. The closest he could get to it was the way he'd once seen a goat tethered at a forest edge to attract a tiger, again not a pleasant comparison. Yet in the scale of things he was not unduly alarmed. Or, rather, his senses were so on the alert he had no time for fear. If he still sensed that personal vendetta, first glimpsed from a speeding car, if he had no illusions that he was, in truth, a decoy (which a high-velocity rifle, or a fire bomb, or any of a score of other modern weapons could scarcely fail to miss) he also banked on the assumption that his enemy would try to make contact before killing him.

He based this assumption on his knowledge of human nature. It had occurred to him that if for him the real battleground was one of will, of personalities, his opponent must feel the same way. To strike indiscriminately, from a distance, anonymously, would lack subtlety. The struggle which had started, what now seemed a lifetime away, in a narrow lane, one man on foot, unsuspecting, the other in a powerful car, laughing as he gunned the motor, was now intensified. Since the original offence was more than doubled, and since Reynolds, the apparent loser, was now revealed victorious, surely Lewis wouldn't resist one last actual confrontation before he got revenge? Otherwise, how would Reynolds ever know who had struck him down, or why?

The waiting to see if he were right was long and seemed longer, yet the first day and night passed, and then the second day, without incident. The information that had been leaked so carefully through the first afternoon, becoming headline news by nine o'clock, was now worn thin by repetition. The familiar official impatience with his methods was beginning to resurface; there were barbed comments from Head Office, and the Incident Room was said to be in open rebellion. Although Narcotics were used to waiting and as yet paid no attention, Reynolds knew time was running out.

He listened dispassionately to the news, then forced himself to return to his manuscript. Once more he began the familiar struggle to retrieve his main character from pending catastrophe – this time out to sea in a small boat . . .

A rustle in the bushes made him look up. By now the grey of twilight had given place to darkness, and yet it was not completely dark; there were stars, although no moon, and the lights from his living room cast pale gold streaks across the pale square of grass. From time to time he caught the tantalizing scent of roses. The back of his neck tingled, he felt a shiver of tension. Willing himself not to turn his head, not to look, he began studiously to correct what he had written, again forcing himself to deal with fiction rather than reality. It was only when he heard the voice speak that the final solution, again the one he hadn't let himself think of, revealed itself in all its potential for disaster – and for death.

'So, ex-Inspector,' a voice said, 'for once you aren't expecting me.'

The voice was the usual mocking one, you'd have to know it well to detect the undertone of fear. There was an ethereal quality about it too, a lack of fixed location – a microphone, he guessed, that made it seem to come from several directions at once. Fighting down the instinct to jump up, keeping his reactions slow and his hands clearly visible, doing or saying nothing threatening although every sense was straining to locate where she was, 'Who the hell's that?' he asked, pretending astonishment. And for God's sake keep down he silently told the other watchers, hold your positions until I give the word.

Her reply, in her old teasing way – 'Don't say you don't recognize me' – at least answered one other question: she was here in person, her voice hadn't been pre-recorded. Christ, he thought, feeling the sweat break out, here's vengeance with a twist. She can't be alone. Still making no sudden or awkward move, savagely he swore at himself. He'd been afraid Peter Lewis might make use of her, but not as deliberately as this.

He hadn't expected her; and neither had the surveillance squad. Christ, he prayed again, struggling for calm, don't let them move too soon. And don't make a mistake when you do, take him out first. For if she were here, so then was Lewis. He was as certain of that as of himself. He sensed the presence, the presence he had felt in the lane, that he had felt in her house. He steadied himself. Her involvement made springing the trap more difficult, but not impossible. And, for a start, Lewis must be kept occupied, the talk must go on in such a way that Lewis's attention would be drawn.

He tried to summon up all the skills the years had honed, to use all the resources that experience had given. 'You mean all those clues were wrong?' he asked, allowing just the right amount of bewilderment to show, addressing her as if she were alone, using her as intermediary to reach Lewis, yet somehow not letting Lewis know. 'Then you certainly had us fooled. What made you do it?'

There was a pause. He felt the indecision palpable. Yet, if he were right, Lewis wouldn't resist the temptation to gloat. And the more he talked the more the unseen listeners would collect as evidence. When she replied finally, again he felt the sweat.

'Oh,' she said, in her airy fashion, 'there was nothing for me here.' The words came slowly, he almost felt the gun prodded against his own ribs. 'It was finished with. The decision to leave was easy, and so were the arrangements. If you misinterpreted them, that's your fault.'

'And your mother's death? Was that arranged as easily?'

Again a pause. 'That was different,' she said. 'She deserved to die. But if you had been in the room instead of her, as you should have been, that would have been even more deserved.'

Of course, he thought, light dawning. I never thought of that. But *she* knew I had left the hospital, so that clears her of that charge at any rate. And proves, if I need proof, that, although the voice is hers, the answers aren't.

It was his turn to be silent. He heard her say softly, 'Always questions, ex-Inspector. Too many questions, too much curiosity. Don't you know when to leave well alone? Or is it a lack of confidence that makes you always want to be right?'

His answer was conversational, equally cool. 'Killing your mother must have been easy; and I suppose "killing" you was child's play. But murder of your brother, Malcolm, that was complicated. When did you learn about that?'

It was a chance, a calculated risk. It worked too well. He heard a scuffle, a cry cut short. 'What does he mean?' He felt rather than saw her figure caught for a moment in a streak of light, then lost again in the shadows. He felt rather than saw the other figure beside her, gun pressed against her spine. Of course, he thought without surprise, the hostage if things go wrong. And if they go right, then two for the price of one.

Still keeping his voice calm, Reynolds said, 'Who the hell's out there?' and heard the hiss of anger before the answer came, prodded out from Anna. He caught the pain and fear clearly now. 'Why, my ex-husband. I told you we were close.'

'That close,' he said challengingly, 'that close that he could arrange to make you look like dead. That he could make you go along with all he did. That he could sling your dead brother in a mine shaft and pretend he was still alive.'

Once more he sensed rather than heard the cry of disbelief and the sound of struggle, but he did actually hear the gun go off, twice, and did actually feel the flash of pain as he hurled himself sideways to the floor in awkward parody of his usual agility. Then he was on his feet, hurtling through the doorway into the garden. He was leaning over Anna, feeling for her pulse, blood spurting from his arm, and her own blood welling in a pool on the paving stones.

Her eyes opened. He bent to hear her. 'Always questions,' she whispered. 'Nothing on trust.' Then he was dragged back and Derrymore charged past, followed by a group of others, guns at the ready. There were shouts, lights blazing, more shouts.

'You won't catch him,' the whisper went on, a thread of sound. 'No one will. I told him it was useless, though; you're on the wrong track, I said. Bringing me here won't trouble Reynolds. Reynolds owes me nothing, it's all for nothing. Wasn't I right?'

Again he felt for her pulse, her hand in his. 'So at least he got that wrong,' she said. He thought she smiled. 'The final satisfaction he saved me for. As for the rest, don't worry, Inspector. I can look after myself.'

Long after they had taken her away, after doctors and ambulances and police had come and gone he heard the words.

329

Chapter 18

It was several months later that Reynolds and Derrymore sat in Reynolds' living room, on a warm September morning with the garden looking its autumn best, the roses replaced by seasonal chrysanthemums and the terrace carpeted faintly by the first scattering of leaves. Between them on the coffee table lay Reynolds' finished manuscript, which his long but relatively uncomplicated convalescence had enabled him to finish – another potential bestseller his new secretary claimed, a jovial young woman who lived in the next village and whose only fault was constant optimism, a failing that life with a farmer husband and three energetic sons made a necessity. (Miss Tenery, having finally recovered, had gracefully bowed out of work 'for the present' thus giving Reynolds the opportunity he'd been looking for.)

But it wasn't the new book that the two men were speaking about. 'Well, here it is,' said Derrymore, recently promoted and still accepting congratulations modestly. He pointed to the police report compiled by Narcotics with his and Reynolds' help. 'All tidied up. Even to Pathology's positive identification of Malcolm Sparks' body in the mine shaft, thanks to you. And, of course, Nurse Pengelly's testimony. At least she had the satisfaction of knowing he didn't go off without saying goodbye. Although the quarrel with his mother and other relatives wasn't over her but over his refusal to continue in what Shirley Farr still persists in calling "the family business", as if they were into greengrocery or hats!'

He laughed, then sobered. The report made difficult reading, based as part of it was on Anna Sparks' last statement before her death in hospital.

'I'll leave it with you,' he went on hastily. 'But I did want to tell you something personally. The news has just come through today that we've finally tracked down Lewis, although how he managed to slip through our fingers on that night I'll never understand. And guess how they caught him?'

Not waiting for Reynolds' answer he went on, 'Through identification of the photograph. You were right about that too, sir, some little harbour in some minor South American country which, luckily for us, gives us extradition rights. Suave sort of fellow, Lewis, they say, smooth-talking; oozing charm, until they told him how he'd been caught. Then he went berserk. Could hardly hold him. "The third mistake," he's supposed to have shouted, then shut up like a clam. Won't speak again until he's brought to trial, and God knows when that'll be. At least he's out of action in the meanwhile. But what did he mean, three mistakes? Any ideas about that, sir?'

When Reynolds didn't reply: 'Forgetting the photograph must be one, and presumably the choice of refuge another. But what's the third?'

Reynolds stirred himself. He welcomed the report as much as anyone. He liked things finished and done with, and this case presented more than its share of problems. Strange, from the beginning he'd anticipated complication, but not pain. Anything to do with Lewis, recalling as it must Lewis's association with Anna, was calculated to open old wounds.

'Lewis did make a third mistake,' he said after a while. 'Although I didn't spot it until later.' Too late to be useful, he thought. 'In the chronological timetable however it was actually the first – putting Mr Sparks' ring in the mine shaft among Malcolm's bones.'

As Derrymore started to protest: 'Oh yes, I grant it was clever, heartless, typical of his other crimes. And I grant he was desperate to turn attention away from whose body it was. But he was too clever by half. By making the skeleton look as if it were Richard Sparks' he created unnecessary complications. He actually concentrated our attention on the Sparks family instead of diverting it. He'd have done better leaving well alone.'

Derrymore digested this idea slowly. 'Then whatever made him do it?' he asked.

'I don't really know,' Reynolds said, 'and I suspect he doesn't either. Panic probably. Don't forget, this run was crucial for him; he was desperate for things to go smoothly. And he may have thought DNA testing would link the body definitely with the Sparkses anyway, and if there was any suspicion that Malcolm was the victim, he'd lose his hold over the rest of the family. I gather, by the by, that the other members really didn't know Malcolm had been murdered? Like Anna Sparks they all accepted that he was in Australia, and the letters supposedly written by him and sent to her, I presume by Peter Lewis, were accepted as such, without question?'

333

Derrymore nodded, shifting uncomfortably at this mention of Anna. It's all right, Reynolds wanted to assure him, that part's done with. You can't mourn death twice; grief doesn't come so hard a second time. I know that much of this report deals with Anna's last testimony before she died but I can read it and read about her with regret only. And if he wasn't sure he believed in these platitudes, that too was something else he'd have to live with.

'There's one other thing.' Emboldened by Reynolds' attitude, Derrymore asked a question that had puzzled Reynolds also: how had Lewis, and for that matter Trevor Farr, been able to ingratiate themselves so easily with the Sparks family?

'They were vulnerable.'

In this brief sentence, Reynolds tried to sum up his own more intricate conclusions, albeit he was still not sure his arguments were completely sound. 'Think of it,' he invited Derrymore. 'They lose the father, a God-fearing man, honest, hardworking, whose influence on his children must have been considerable. If he'd remained alive I'm sure even Mrs Sparks wouldn't have dared get involved with the two other men. Malcolm, on the other hand, was young and idealistic. According to Shirley Farr, his first involvement with Trevor Farr was to land illegal immigrants on an isolated beach – probably some of Trevor's "foreign" or Pakistani relations. Malcolm may not have seen this as a breaking of the law, probably viewed it as a mission for human rights, appealing to what Joyce Pengelly called his good nature. Unfortunately for him, it gave Farr and Lewis a hold over him. However, when he refused to turn from helping people to running drugs, possibly threatened to inform the authorities, he had to be got

334

rid of. That left the women on their own.'

Again he paused to clarify his thoughts. 'Shirley has already made what her mother thinks of as a "good" marriage,' he said, 'certainly up-market from her own. Shirley is easy enough to manipulate. She wants loot. She's dominated by her husband. And to my way of thinking she's a bit dense. Shirley's no problem. As for Mrs Sparks, we know Mrs Sparks is attracted by wealth and influence. Peter Lewis, Trevor Farr's "wealthy" friend, gains immediate favour – although it soon must have become clear that, if there're any favours about, Lewis is going to be the one doing all the granting. When Lewis proposes that Mrs Sparks help him in his drug running she may have been flattered. She certainly tries to persuade Malcolm to go along with the idea; tries to oust the Pengellys from the house next door to give Lewis more scope; then, when Malcolm leaves (as she thinks), readily goes along with the suggestion of moving to a bigger, fancy house, further along the coast, more suited to the expanding trade Lewis now has in mind. My guess is that flattery, as much as money, originally bought Mrs Sparks. And she'd have liked the idea of being in partnership with such an influential and charming man. Remember, of all the family she was the only one who had direct access to him, as her telephone call to him from hospital showed. (I gather the phone call was in fact to him, so Trevor Farr and his wife were right when they said she hadn't informed them.) And, I may be wrong, but as women's physical attractiveness diminishes, their hold on men weakens; then, if they're strong characters, they turn instinctively to intrigue and manipulation instead. Lewis may have played on that side of her character.'

(And that observation may be prejudiced by my own experience, he thought wryly, but I don't have to admit that.)

He tapped the report thoughtfully. 'That leaves only Anna Sparks,' he went on. 'I don't know what this says yet, but my guess is that the young Anna was also flattered by the older Lewis's attention. She missed her father, who had always been her protector; she missed her half-brother. And even if, as soon became apparent, the marriage was one of convenience, at least it made her half-sister and mother take notice of her. Mrs Sparks and Shirley might have been delighted when the marriage broke down, but for a while there Anna queened it over them. And afterwards Lewis made sure she was well enough provided for to be independent of them.'

'And the attraction may have not been all one-sided,' he added to himself. 'My guess is that for looks and charm Anna Sparks gave her mother a run for her money.'

'But that still doesn't explain what Lewis, and, for that matter, Farr, got out of it,' Derrymore persisted. 'And for good measure, why, having married the younger sister, presumably to cement his hold, Lewis divorced Anna so soon, and apparently on such generous terms?'

'One thing we can be sure of.' Reynolds' rejoinder was measured. 'Lewis didn't do something for nothing. I think he knew when he was on to a good thing. He needed that sea link somehow; it was vital to his plans. The Sparks family gave it to him. Even when Malcolm dug in his heels he could rely on the Farrs and Mrs Sparks. He may even have tolerated Tregonning's infatuation with his ex-wife for the same reason, Tregonning presumably having taken Malcolm's place in the over-all game plan.' (And for the same reason tolerated Anna's liking of Tregonning, he thought, but again felt no obligation to say so aloud.)

What he did say however came to the crux of his own argument. 'Myself, I think Lewis kept on good terms with his ex-wife, not out of sympathy or pity for the young and naïve girl she was then. I think all along he had at the back of his mind that one day he might have to use her to extricate himself from difficulties she didn't understand but would be too loyal to refuse to help him with. And, God forgive him, that is what in the end he did. And that's something else I hope the courts will really make him pay for when his case is brought to trial.'

With that salvo he fell silent, leaving Derrymore to take his leave, awkwardly hemming and hawing before promising to come again soon so they could plan a real fishing expedition, from dry land – the end of a jetty to be precise – where Reynolds need have nothing to do with the actual sea.

When he had gone, Reynolds steeled himself to pick up the report and turn the pages. He passed quickly over the testimony of the others, the factual reports of Pathology and Forensic, the formal identification of the drug and its probable worth, and came to Anna's part.

It was brief, a dying woman's attempt to set things to rights as she thought best. All through her statement were woven the twin threads of her original ignorance of events, and her refusal to believe the worst of anyone, even of her mother and sister who had caused her such unhappiness.

To the end she insisted her husband's deception had not been all self-serving. If he had used her so had she used him – as Reynolds had deduced, to find the affection that she lacked, to make her own place in the world. When her marriage

337

foundered she'd borne no ill-will. If now she saw that Peter Lewis had bought her with gifts, just as he bought her mother and half-sister, if her pay-off included her cottage and her college education, she still refused to accept they made any difference to her feelings or attitude. Shirley and Trevor Farr had finally admitted they knew what silence was expected from them; even in death, Anna never knew.

To sum up: Anna Sparks hadn't known what was hidden in the mine shaft, although she knew the shaft was there; she hadn't known what it was used for, although she had suspicions of Tregonning and thought perhaps he was trying a little smuggling on the side, smuggling for her meaning vaguely some eighteenth-century brandy running. She hadn't suspected her former husband of her mother's death, although certain happenings had obviously caused her concern, the story of the ring for one – and, of course, the police suspicions that the body was her father's.

On the other hand, she half knew of but refused to pry into her ex-husband's business matters. When he told her he was in the export-import line she believed him. If she wondered at Trevor Farr's familiarity with his affairs, or Tregonning's for that matter, or there were hints of problems, she persuaded herself that these must relate to things like customs duties – perhaps he wanted to avoid paying them. Until a friend (she meant Tregonning, although she didn't name him) put fear into her head she had no idea what he was talking of and refused to accept his hints of danger to herself as well as others.

But Tregonning's warnings had this much effect. Starting with her mother and the scene in the hospital when she had felt obliged to cover her mother's mistake, moving on to her search for her father's ring, which of course she never found, she had begun to suspect something was amiss. She wasn't stupid. But she wanted no part in what her suspicions suggested, no part in revealing those suspicions to the police. On that she was adamant. She was no informer. Seeing no alternative (and I gave her none, Reynolds thought, I harried her), she had decided to move away – driven out like her brother before her.

It was in that mood, half determined, half fearful, that Lewis found her that Wednesday night, the same mood Reynolds himself had noted earlier (although she made no mention of that).

Lewis's story that evening had been calculated to rouse all her feelings of loyalty. Telling her that he had got into trouble with the law, unwittingly, that his business (that ubiquitous export-import business) was about to be confiscated, finally suggesting that other family members and friends would be implicated, he persuaded her to leave with him – because he needed 'someone to talk to'.

She had not known of Lewis's subsequent movements – his arrangement of her belongings, the leaving of her clothes and note. He had taken her to the house he was staying at, in the country near Newquay, rented she thought for a week or so: she hadn't even known he was in Cornwall, he came and went irregularly. Then, later that night, he had left her for a while, he said to have an impromptu meeting with his accountants. Although Newquay itself is a large holiday centre, the house was isolated, there was no telephone, no television; when he returned early next morning they didn't go out. It was only after the news broke that Tregonning and his boat had been discovered by ex-Inspector Reynolds that Lewis finally revealed himself in his true guise. By which time it was too late for her to do anything else than what he forced upon her.

She said nothing about Tregonning's claims about the nature of their relationship, said nothing more about her personal life, added nothing to her final words to Reynolds in his garden. She expressed no regret at having taken part in what she must have known would end in a killing; even if she were an unwilling participant she showed no sense of responsibility. In the end her statement, although explaining many of those loose ends Reynolds had wanted tied, left him more dissatisfied than ever – until he realized that her silence also left him unmarked, officially, by any involvement with her. And if that were her last gift to him, it was more than he deserved.

When the report was written Lewis was still at large, so several pages were occupied with details of how he had made good his escape, the numbers of his pursuers and the confusion following the shooting of his ex-wife being blamed, as was his superior knowledge of the village and its back alleyways and passages. Dire predictions were also made as to where he had gone, a certain African country a hot favourite, and details were suggested of how probably he had stashed away enough cash to last several lifetimes, and how by now plastic surgery would have changed his appearance – all fortunately cancelled by news of his capture in South America.

The rest of the report outlined what had actually happened on the Monday morning, as told by Shirley Farr (so much for her and her husband's pretences). If Mrs Sparks hadn't telephoned them someone else had, the best guess being Peter

Lewis himself. Lewis (whom she still wouldn't name, such was her fear) had come into Cornwall the day before, she said, in anticipation of the landing of the drugs. He was actually in Mrs Sparks' house when the shaft collapsed, and as Reynolds had finally recognized, his was the car seen parked in the drive. When he realized the attention the collapse of the shaft would cause, to say nothing of what it had uncovered, he had immediately planted Richard Sparks' ring as a diversion – a tactic which Shirley Farr seemed to think was proof of his quick thinking, making her strangely insensitive to the fact that while he was thus occupied her mother was lying helpless at the bottom of the shaft.

The rest – the attack on Reynolds in the lane after Lewis had spotted him, Mrs Sparks' confusion in hospital, Anna Sparks' attempts to cover for her – now all fell into place as had previously been surmised. What was new was Shirley's claim that her mother hadn't been the intended victim in the hospital, substantiating what Anna had hinted at.

Lewis had gone there to track Reynolds down. Balked of success earlier and mistakenly believing that Reynolds was still a patient, he had found out the room where Reynolds had been put on first arrival, had climbed in the window and, in the semi-darkness, had murdered the wrong person. Not until he had pounced and smothered did he realize that the figure lying in drugged sleep was that of his mother-in-law. 'At night, you know, she looked, well, different,' Shirley had said, wiping her eyes and referring delicately to her mother's wigless state. And whether Lewis felt any remorse for his mistake no one ventured an opinion. He had simply climbed out again, and driven off in his car, which 'snarled', as Marlene had testified.

341

The attack on Miss Tenery, however, hadn't been planned or intended. Lewis was said to have been furious about that. It was all Tregonning's fault, Shirley was sure of that. And it too was a mistake, otherwise why Miss Tenery? She was nothing. All of which, if true, gave point to why Tregonning changed his mind and went after the haul himself. Having incurred Lewis's displeasure, what had he to lose?

Like Lewis, Mike Tregonning had managed to get away, but unlike Lewis he was not yet found. As the days went by neither he nor his boat were seen; there was no wreckage, not even after an unexpected storm blew out of the west with such severe winds and violent waves as to make survival doubtful. And even if he had run for shelter to a real harbour (of which there are few in that part of the north Cornish coast) they were all being carefully watched. As it was equally doubtful that he had gone to sea in a boat that he himself admitted was not made for distance, the mystery of Tregonning's whereabouts was never explained. But as the drugs never appeared on the market (and they were, as Reynolds had suspected, of the highest quality, the 'haul of a lifetime'), for lack of any concrete evidence Reynolds preferred to think that Tregonning had somehow escaped after his boat had sunk. He liked to imagine Tregonning and his dog swimming to shore, there to sit out the worst of the storm before scaling the cliffs and making a getaway. And if it was only in imagination that he could show his gratitude to Tregonning's dog, that was the way it was.

As far then as was possible in this imperfect world, the case was finished. The main suspect was apprehended and never found what he was really looking for; the Farrs and Nurse Pengelly had their just deserts. Marlene was gratified to see her testimony vindicated; Granny Gossip basked in glory; and the next-door neighbour and his dogs were praised for their cooperation.

Derrymore, quite rightly, was complimented for his part in the business, and Reynolds, perhaps less rightly, was allowed to forget his, thus teaching him another lesson of village life – that sticking up for one's own against outside interference is only just and proper.

The only person left unaccounted for in this list of successes was the gardener, Mr Blewett. And on this September Monday, when the weather couldn't have been finer if it tried, it seemed fitting that the garden gate should creak open, and an old man should come swinging down the path, his thick corded velvet trousers labouring stiffly, his back bowed with pick and spade.

He put his tools down and leaned on the spade, the good triangular-shaped Cornish one. His eyes twinkled as he looked at Reynolds. 'Seems you'm still in the wars,' he said, taking in Reynolds' newly healed gunshot wound, which had replaced the damaged shoulder. He nodded to himself with satisfaction and picked up his spade. 'Now about that hedge you wanted moving,' he said. 'Just tell me where 'tis at, and I'll have it out in a jiffy. Nothing I likes better than a bit of digging.'